Praise for Jean Marie Ward's and Teri Smith's
With Nine You Get Vanyr

With Nine You Get Vanyr is a great fantasy. ~ *Harriet Klausner*

"The plot is thought-provoking, the characters are in the midst of coming-of-age identity crises, and the immortals are seriously hot. What more could a reader request?" ~ *Euro Reviews*

"Full of intricate details, many twists and turns and so much sexual tension between the main characters, this reviewer almost thought her computer was going to combust!" ~ *Love Romances & More*

"The complexities of modern women suddenly thrust into a fantasy world were explored in a very realistic way. The world seemed very full and well developed. I can only hope that Ms. Ward will craft more tales set in this world." ~ *Two Lips Reviews*

"…*With Nine You Get Vanyr* is a long, delightful read. You will need several bowls of popcorn and a gallon or two of your favorite beverage." ~ *Romance Reviews Today*

"Ms. Smith has left a legacy that Ms. Ward will hopefully continue." ~ *Coffee Time Romance*

With Nine You Get Vanyr

Jean Marie Ward and Teri Smith

A Samhain Publishing, Ltd. publication.

Samhain Publishing, Ltd.
2932 Ross Clark Circle, #384
Dothan, AL 36301
www.samhainpublishing.com

With Nine You Get Vanyr
Copyright © 2006 by Jean Marie Ward & Teri Smith
Print ISBN: 1-59998-360-5
Digital ISBN: 1-59998-166-1

Editing by Jess Bimberg
Cover by Anne Cain

First Samhain Publishing, Ltd. electronic publication: November 2006
First Samhain Publishing, Ltd. print publication: February 2007

Dedication

To our husbands, the heroes of our lives. And to our beta readers (you know who you are) for reading this story and helping us make it *much, much more.*

Chapter One

The skinny, bald guy's fur boots and matching fur condom weren't that unusual by the standards of Atlanta's Dragon*Con. What pushed the costume right into the ozone, however, was the chainsaw attached to the guy's left wrist like a weird prosthetic hand. What kind of caveman had a chainsaw for a hand?

"Thea, you're dripping."

Thea Gardner jerked the Styrofoam cup away from her lips. Drops of iced tea splattered the convention programs and glossy gaming fliers spread across the table where she sat with her friend.

"Liz," she whispered as she shook the papers dry, "check out the chainsaw guy who just walked into the lobby."

Liz glanced over her shoulder in the direction of the freestanding bank of elevators dominating the Hyatt's lobby. In front of the elevators, a pair of escalators and a carpeted staircase connected the lobby with the auditoriums and meeting rooms of the lower levels. Unfortunately, at that moment, a double line of white-armored Stormtroopers blocked Liz's view.

Thea sighed with disappointment. From their table in front of the coffee shop, you could see from one end of the lobby to the other—except when the crowd got in the way. By the time the parade of Stormtroopers passed, the guy with the chainsaw would be halfway down the escalator.

Luckily for Liz, there were too many people, costumed and not, between chainsaw guy and the stairs. Chainsaw guy obviously thought so too. With a fearsome yell, he brandished the saw over his head and pulled the cord dangling from the gearbox covering his left hand. Stormtroopers scattered like white rats at the sound of the lab assistant's bell. Liz gasped as the saw growled to life.

Only it didn't. The lethal looking teeth of the saw remained stationary over its owner's head while the "engine"—probably a disguised tape recorder—roared like a motorcycle going from zero to eighty in ten seconds flat.

A smattering of applause from a few of the other coffee shop patrons greeted chainsaw guy's special effect. He bowed and melted into a welter of Hobbits the size of professional football players. The Stormtroopers, their helmets probably hiding more than a few red faces, reformed their ranks and marched into the bar. With a sheepish expression in her own slate blue eyes, Liz leaned back in her chair.

"Gotcha," Thea said. "And the rest of us too. By the way, how many of these fantasy conventions did you say you'd been to, Ms. Been There, Done That, Got the Henna Tat? Any idea who or what he was supposed to be?"

"In order—not enough, nope, and I don't plan on asking anyone either." Laughter bubbled under Liz's words. "Damn, I needed that. I need this."

Liz flung her arms wide, as if to encompass the entire lobby. In typical Liz fashion, her grand gesture didn't cause so much as a ripple in the streams of humanity swirling around their table. If Thea had tried anything similar, the best she could've hoped for would've been multiple charges of aggravated assault. That was only the tip of the iceberg as far as their differences were concerned.

Liz Devereaux was a slender, high-level civil servant with expensively styled, titian-colored hair and an equally expensive wardrobe to match. Thea, even though a year younger, looked ten years older. A marriage gone horrifyingly wrong and a spate of bad health had left Thea overweight and careworn. Her graying blonde hair had been cut by a discount salon and her clothing was retail—and aging retail at that.

Yet for all their differences, in so many ways they were alike. Thea needed Dragon*Con too. She thanked the stars she'd agreed when Liz suggested the nine members of their Internet fan group meet at the Labor Day convention. The con was worth every hard-earned nickel of Thea's savings.

Coming to Dragon*Con was like coming home. Only home had never featured hordes of science fiction and fantasy fans dressed as their obsession du jour, or wandering medieval singers doing their best to be heard over the boisterous crowd. The fact the minstrels were failing miserably seemed to bother neither the singers nor the crowd.

It was a shame real life couldn't be like this. Small as it was, a hotel room shared with a friend felt a thousand times more welcoming than the arctic emptiness of Thea's efficiency apartment. The number and variety of costumed fans gave the illusion of a universe of limitless possibilities.

I don't want to go back.

Like the note of a pitch perfect Tibetan singing bowl, the thought circled through Thea's mind. She didn't want to go back to her cheerless apartment and dead-end job. She didn't want to go back to her *life*. She wanted to go forward instead of back. Most of all, she didn't want to slide into the darkness at the end of it all without something to mark her passage through the light.

"Earth to Thea. You okay?"

Liz's chin rested on her laced fingers. Her somber gaze gave the impression she could see the dark thoughts inside Thea's brain. It was a good act, but the translucent quality of Liz's pallor and the slight puffiness around Liz's eyes told a different story.

Thea knew stress when she saw it. "I'm fine. But you aren't. Come on, Liz. Talk to me."

"It's nothing, really—or nothing new. I can't seem to handle the crap at work like I used to."

"What happened?"

Liz shook her head. "Nothing. Same old same old."

Thea raised an eyebrow and waited.

"No. Really. If Johnnie's death didn't take me down, those turkeys at the State Department don't stand a chance. It's just…" Liz gazed toward the bar. Thea had the oddest feeling Liz wasn't seeing the Stormtroopers playing cards or the werewolf with silver-tipped fur drinking his Bloody Mary through a straw.

"I wish I could make a difference."

Liz's wistful remark was so close to what Thea had been thinking, the short hairs on the nape of Thea's neck stood straight up. The skin on her arms prickled as if the air had become charged with electricity.

Liz didn't appear to notice. She stared straight at the werewolf. The werewolf cocked his masked head in her direction. When Liz didn't react, he shrugged and turned to a pair of Eowyn look-alikes to his left.

"I wish I could too," Thea said.

Liz patted Thea's arm. "It's funny, people think because I work in Washington I can actually do good. They think I've got some kind of power over the system, that I can make the world a better place. But I can't. No matter how hard I try, I can't seem to make things any better. Hell, it's a good day when I can keep things from getting any worse."

"How do you think I feel? I'm so low on the corporate totem pole, I can't get my human resources person to answer my calls—even when I'm standing right in front of her desk with my cell phone in my hand. Damn straight I want to make a difference. But I have about as much chance of changing the world as one of those giant Hobbits has of ever finding their way to the Shire."

"Oh, I don't know," Liz mused. In the blink of an eye, her expression shifted from melancholy to mischievous. "Who's to say they aren't in the Shire right now? Look at it this way, if somebody looks like a Hobbit and talks like a Hobbit and acts like a Hobbit—and his friends are all doing the same thing—doesn't that mean they *are* Hobbits for the duration? In which case… Oh, shit."

Liz pushed her chair away from the table. She pointed to the left of the elevators. "The little old lady in the blue caftan—I think she's in trouble."

It took Thea a moment to spot the old woman. The crowd, several hundred strong, surged like a restless sea around the elevators. Its breakers spilled out toward the escalators. The old lady couldn't have been much more than five feet tall. One wrinkled hand clutched a silver-headed cane. Her silvery-gray hair was caught up in a neat bun. The old lady frowned at the hordes around her.

Thea could understand why Liz thought the old woman was in trouble. People in the lobby were packed body to body. A dark angel's faux wings flapped against a Gondorian knight who was backed against a Teletubby dressed in satanic black.

The angel whirled around and slapped the knight. The knight staggered into a Vulcan, who howled and grabbed his foot. The Vulcan fell into the Teletubby. The Teletubby swung at the angel. A KISS-booted Darth Vader look-a-like wandered into the pentacle-topped Teletubby's right hook. Darth toppled like a redwood, felling nearby con-goers like so many psychedelic mushrooms. The old lady smiled and trotted forward. Thea's eyes widened.

"Liz." She caught her friend's arm. "Wait."

Liz tried to pull away. "Thea, let me go. I need to help that old lady."

Thea held fast to Liz's arm. "Liz, look again. I don't think she needs our help."

"Of course she needs…oh."

The domino effect of Darth's fall spread through the lobby, opening a path from the elevators to the escalators. The old woman strolled through the chaos as if she were walking through daisies instead of an impending riot. A trail of sapphire light followed the old woman through the lobby.

Thea let go of her friend's arm. Liz rubbed her eyes. "You know, we might want to call it a night soon. My eyes are playing tricks on me."

Thea dragged her gaze away from the old woman. "Mine too. Everything is coated in blue."

Liz frowned. "Did you say blue? That is too weird."

"Hello there, dears! Would you mind if I sit with you for a minute?"

Both Thea and Liz jumped. The old woman stood by their table.

"Excuse me?" Thea stammered. "I don't believe…"

The old woman smiled. "Of course you don't," she said. "But you will."

A Stormtrooper materialized next to the old woman and proffered her a chair. "Why thank you," the old woman cooed. "You're too kind." The Stormtrooper helped the old woman sit and arrange her cane to her satisfaction. He saluted and wandered away.

Thea gaped at the old woman. Why did she feel like she'd fallen down a rabbit hole? What the heck had that cryptic "But you will" been all about? But she would *what?*

"Thea's not used to conventions," Liz said. "Of course you can sit at our table for as long as you like."

"Thank you, dearie," the old woman said. "It's so crowded a body hardly has room to breathe, much less think."

Thea hoped the old woman wouldn't want to sit for too long. Thea wanted to get to bed. That freaky moment with Liz must've been the first stage of a migraine. Now Thea was seeing blue auras—especially around the little old lady, who seemed to be dripping with iridescent blue light.

A deep-toned *bong* resonated through the lobby. Thea shook her head and pulled at one ear. Now she was hearing bells—bells nobody else seemed to hear. The crowd flowing around their table displayed no visible reaction to the ringing. Was the sound all inside her head? Maybe she was coming down with something?

"Marvelous!" the old woman crowed. "Let me introduce myself. I'm Madame Reyah."

Thea choked on an ice chip. Did the old lady actually believe she was a character in a TV show?

Liz, evil wench that she was, obligingly pounded Thea's back. "Like the mother goddess on the television show, *Domain?*" Liz asked between thwacks.

11

The old woman beamed. "The one and only. Are you *Domain* fans too?"

Thea didn't trust herself to speak. She set down her iced tea. In contrast, Liz appeared to have no problems making polite conversation with geriatric delusionals. "Are we ever! It's the best fantasy television show in years. Between your sons, the Vanyr…"

"Madame Reyah" grinned from ear to ear. The theme music from *Jaws* started playing in Thea's brain. Thea had no idea why. The little old lady's dentures didn't look all that pointy.

"…and the guys you've selected as your Chosen champions, *Domain's* got more gorgeous young immortals than the first three seasons of *Highlander* put together. You've got magic and adventure and stories that don't rehash *The Lord of the Rings* every other week. And did I mention great looking guys?" Both Liz and Reyah laughed.

"You did, dear," Reyah said, "and I'll have you know I'm very proud of them myself."

Liz took a sip of tea. "What made you decide to attend Dragon*Con, your…" Liz's voice trailed away.

Thea hoped the pause didn't mean Liz was going to fumble the conversational ball. The hairs on the back of Thea's neck were still standing at attention, and her weirdness meter had gone off the charts.

"You know, that's something they never addressed in the show." Liz spoke as if she occupied multiple realities every day of the week. "What *is* the proper honorific for the mother goddess of a planet?"

Oh! The old lady was role-playing, and Liz was playing along with her. Well, duh. Thea got it now.

This must be what Liz had been talking about earlier with regards to the Hobbits. It was more than putting on a costume. As Thea could attest after only a few hours at the con, a lot of the fans tried to live the role they were playing. Liz was humoring the old lady by acting as if her Reyah fantasy was real. It was a variation of what the live action role-playing gamers did. Thea could deal with that.

"How about 'Your Divinity'?" Thea suggested.

Madame Reyah tittered. Thea had never truly heard anyone titter before, but that was the only way to describe the sound coming out of the old bird's mouth. Reyah's spangly blue aura tittered too—even though according to everything Thea had ever read on the subject, colors didn't have sounds. It was fascinating as hell, but Thea was beginning to think she needed to get back to her room five minutes ago.

"How clever you are!" Madame Reyah caroled. "I'll have to remember that when I get back home." She tittered again. "However, I don't go in for that kind of formality *here*. 'Madame Reyah' is fine."

Liz winked at Thea.

"You must come visit me. I've got a booth over at the Marriott, in the exhibit hall, right between Eric Bernard and Michael Ryan," Reyah said. "Eric plays the Lord of my Keep, and Michael plays my son Deryk. He's a lovely boy."

"Who, Michael or Deryk?" Liz purred. Thea stifled a groan. At this rate, they'd be here all night.

"Why both of them, of course," Reyah replied.

"Give me Michael, any old day," Thea said. "Deryk is too extreme."

"You don't like Deryk?" Reyah asked.

Thea took a deep breath and faced down the irrational panic Reyah's question inspired. What was it about this old lady that had her so spooked?

"No. With all due respect, Your—Madame Reyah, Deryk's an evil, murdering sorcerer who slaps people around. What woman in her right mind would like that?"

"Oh bother," Reyah grumbled. "Has he been naughty again? I'll have to put a stop to that. It gives people entirely the wrong idea."

"I'm partial to Roarke myself," Liz said.

"Roarke!" Reyah squawked. She sounded genuinely outraged. "He can't hold a candle to Deryk."

"Only if you like blonds," Thea countered. "Some of us like them tall, dark and—"

Reyah sniffed as if anticipating the h-word.

"Wounded," Thea finished with a small grin of triumph.

"Bah," Reyah answered. "Deryk is twice the man Roarke is."

"Twice the scoundrel," Thea replied with some heat. "At least Roarke isn't trying to take over Seshmeel like Deryk is."

"Yeah, but he's given the producers a great reason to set most of next season in Seshmeel," Liz said. "Studio shots are always good for the budget."

Reyah's cane clattered to the floor. "What did you say about Seshmeel?"

Chapter Two

Across the universe, on the planet known as the Goddess Reyah's Domain

Salentia, the capital city and busiest port of the kingdom of Seshmeel, hid her age well. In fact, she buried it. It was one of the things Roarke liked best about the place, especially on nights like this.

Late winter moonlight silvered the facades of the seafaring associations, guilds and businesses along Dock Street. Burnished by the faint mists wafting off the nearby river and the buttery glow of wizard lights, the cobbled street gleamed like a ribbon of pearls.

But an alley stinks like an alley no matter how much moonlight you throw at it, Roarke reflected as he massaged the chill from his gloved hands. The alley behind the Wayward Bard tavern at the corner of Dock Street and Poole Lane was no exception. From the pungent aroma of the slop buckets outside the kitchen door, today's bill of fare had consisted of cabbage, cabbage and…cabbage, none of it particularly fresh. Adding to the bouquet was the unmistakable stench of putrefying rodent and the even less savory odors from the storm sewer running down the center of the alley.

Roarke wished the local scavengers could've disposed of the animal before he arrived. But he had to admit there was something terribly fitting about sharing his vigil with a dead rat. With a little luck, tonight he'd send the biggest two-legged rat in all of Reyah's Domain straight to hell.

Again.

Roarke pushed the thought aside. He didn't want to queer his luck.

Some might argue standing in a stinking alley with nothing for company but evil thoughts and a three-foot length of serrated volcanic glass was hardly a suitable occupation for the immortal son of a goddess. Roarke's lips twitched as he triple-tested

14

the obsidian blade's draw from its padded scabbard. In fact, he could imagine his mother expressing Her opinion on the subject in exactly those terms.

Not that it mattered. Roarke had stopped caring about Reyah's opinion over a thousand years ago when She allowed Her pet executioner to strip him of the magical power that was his birthright as a Vanyr mage. A thousand years later the loss still burned physically, in odd places and times, like the phantom pain of an amputated limb.

Roarke more or less accepted he would never approach the thaumaturgic strength of the rat bastard occupying the corner room on the third floor of the Wayward Bard. Roarke's magic was barely sufficient to mask his presence in a dark alley in the middle of the night. But he liked to think those who underestimated him did so at their peril.

The unknown person who'd slipped a sealed note under the door of his lodging seven days ago hadn't underestimated him. Printed on the paper in carefully anonymous block letters was a list of fourteen names and a date. The twenty-ninth day of Crowsmun.

Roarke had recognized the name of a Seshmeel nobleman with an interest in the shipping guilds. The quartermaster general of Seshmeel's army was also on the list. Both men were distant cousins of Seshmeel's teenaged Queen Isabeau. Although the relationship wasn't terribly close, both were still in direct line to the throne.

Roarke couldn't think of any reason why someone would send a list of Seshmeelan aristocrats to a Tambaran merchant trading for mountain kava beans in the middle of nowhere. Despite the fact it was his favorite mortal disguise, Roarke could count on two hands the number of people who would recognize the sun-browned, bearded Tambaran, Captain Nikitin Usatov, as the Vanyr demigod Roarke. He couldn't afford to ignore a message from any of them, no matter how cryptic. He hastily secured his business interests and Ported to Salentia within the day.

As Captain Usatov, he discussed a shipping venture with the nobleman and three others on the list. A shave, a haircut and a change of clothes later, Captain Usatov disappeared. It was Vanyr Roarke who arrived at the royal palace bearing the gift of a rare magical text for his old friend Lady Gwynian, the immortal Chosen wizard assigned to protect the royal family of Seshmeel.

Together, Gwyn and Roarke arranged seemingly casual meetings with the remaining people on the list. To Roarke's disgust, every single one of them carried the mark of blood magic on their hands—though the fools lacked the heart and magical training to perceive it.

15

Worse yet, Roarke recognized the specific reek of snake, iron and malediction marking them. It belonged to his brother Deryk, the rotten apple of their mother's eye.

"They plan to assassinate the queen!" Gwyn paced back and forth in her snug, book-lined sitting room. "They're stupid enough and conceited enough to think Deryk would reward them for it too! I wonder which one of them is crazy enough to think he's going to be king.

"I should've seen this coming," she growled. The resonant magical force of her anger set her collection of porcelain teacups rattling in their saucers. "About a month ago, eight children disappeared from the workhouses on Ragpickers Row. Everyone thought they ran away. It never occurred to me Deryk might have taken them. He hadn't appeared at court, and there hadn't been any trouble. I had no reason to think he was here. Stupid... Stupid! Goddess help them, he killed those children to power his spells against the queen."

Roarke studied the pattern in the thick Tambaran carpet beneath his feet. There was no point in contradicting, even to comfort her, when he knew Gwyn's suspicions were right. The children were dead.

He would've known if Deryk had secreted them anywhere in the city. Roarke could detect the metallic taste of Deryk's magic from fifty zakkans away. It was like a hole in his gut that grew wider the closer he got to the source of the poison.

Roarke had made a discreet tour of the docks in the guise of Captain Usatov. He'd found seven of Deryk's haunts, old and new. He'd identified all the seafarers and tradesmen who'd come into his brother's sordid orbit. But there had been no children in the mix and no trace of any magically shielded prisons.

Roarke rubbed the bridge of his nose. Where in Kalin's Seven Hells was Reyah when Her people needed Her? Reyah didn't always view the deaths of Domain's mortals in the same light as the mortals themselves. But She was obsessed with the political and social stability of Domain's Eight Lands. The first hint of a threat to one of the major dynasties usually caused Reyah to dispatch the Old One—Jagger, Her oldest living son and personal executioner—to deal with the instigators. Seshmeel was the brightest jewel in Her temporal crown. But as far as Roarke knew, the Old One didn't have a clue about Deryk's activities in Salentia. What was Reyah waiting for? Was She even aware of how bad things were?

"We can't do anything about the children now," Roarke said to himself as much as to Gwyn. "The important thing is, with this information, we can stop Deryk— maybe for good. We can trace the magic he attaches to his people back to its source.

That's the one evidence·even Reyah can't deny, no matter how much She wants to protect him."

"How are we going to stop him from getting away after the plot fails?" Gwyn demanded. "What's to stop him from Porting out of Salentia and killing his henchmen from a distance? You can't trace a spell from a pile of ash."

"Simple. We keep them alive, and we don't let Deryk get away."

Gwyn seared him with a glare. "And how do you propose to do that? Only Vanyr magic can bind a Vanyr. With all due respect, *Vanyr* Roarke, you don't have enough power to bind your boot laces."

Roarke gazed at Gwyn's motherly, pink-cheeked face and sturdy body. With her large hands and muscled arms, she looked like a prosperous baker's wife, more than capable of hefting hundred-weight sacks of flour and wrestling bread loaves into submission. Goddess help the spell that tried to defy her.

"You're right. *I* don't," Roarke agreed. "But *you* do."

"But, but..." Gwyn sputtered.

"Your lack of faith wounds me deeply." Roarke opened the book he'd brought to a previously marked passage. He handed it to Gwyn. "This is a formula for fusing the spells of a mortal and Chosen wizard. The same principles should apply to Vanyr and Chosen magic."

"That would allow us to combine our different powers in the spell itself without trying to link our magic at the source. It could work," Gwyn muttered, squinting at the crabbed text.

"It'll work. Plus, I've got a few other ideas I'd like to try."

She shot Roarke a crooked grin. "The things I do for Seshmeel. Show me what you have in mind."

The next day, Gwyn arranged for the conspirators to be shadowed non-magically so as not to arouse Deryk's suspicions. Roarke started scanning the palace to ensure Deryk didn't plant something nasty in the building or bespell any of its inhabitants.

Roarke passed word of the plot to two of his warrior brothers, Hawke and Conlan. Their mother's Natal Day—the first day of Reyasmun—fell two days after the twenty-ninth of Crowsmun. Deryk wouldn't be surprised to see Hawke, Conlan or even Roarke celebrating the holiday with a weeklong binge in Salentia.

Roarke had expected it would prove a lot more difficult to bring the Chosen Lord of Reyah's Keep, Alfred DuMarc, into the counterplot. Alfred was Reyah's

Justiciar as well as her paramount commander. His presence at the arrest and questioning of the conspirators would go a long way to prevent the charges from being dismissed on a technicality. Unfortunately, custom demanded Alfred be present at the Keep's Natal Day celebrations.

Then luck smiled on Seshmeel's young queen in the kind of backward fashion that amused Roarke no end. A trade dispute with the Protectorate of Hiawat escalated into a small but vicious diplomatic crisis that required Alfred to arbitrate, in person, between Isabeau and the Hiawati ambassador.

It was all falling into place—if the scope of the undertaking didn't fell Roarke first. Roarke and Gwyn had less than six days to weave two inherently incompatible magics into a net large enough, strong enough and flexible enough to meet the most likely contingencies. There was no way to predict what course Deryk's plot would take, and they couldn't put any of his henchmen to the question without giving the game away. At the same time, Roarke had to keep up the pretense of roistering with Conlan and Hawke, two tavern hounds who never believed in doing anything—carousing most especially—by half.

In one sense, the thinness of Roarke's magic worked to their advantage. The spell anchors he sank into the physical fabric of the palace and the area surrounding Deryk's rooms at the Wayward Bard were as insubstantial as thistle seed. He prayed they would be as tenacious.

Roarke wished he could do more. He wished he could destroy his brother completely. Destroying Deryk wouldn't bring back to life the hundreds of thousands of people Deryk had killed over the course of three millennia. It wouldn't absolve Roarke of the crimes he had committed so many centuries ago as Deryk's lieutenant and shield brother. But it would spare untold future generations from being slaughtered at Deryk's malicious whims. The peace that would bring Roarke would almost, almost compensate for the loss of his magic.

Then again, perhaps not. Roarke couldn't repress his bone deep envy as he watched—and felt—Gwyn's potent wizardry transmute the cobwebs of his magic into sorcerous steel, with energy to spare.

Nevertheless, true to his nature, Roarke worried every step of the way. He reasoned whoever had sent him the list had compiled it from observation. But Deryk would never be seen in public with his real candidate for the throne of Seshmeel. It was a given Deryk's game would go deeper, but how much deeper? Was the list itself part of the plot?

18

Roarke decided to trust his instincts. To keep worrying about every "what-if" was an invitation to madness. If the list was a ploy, there was little Roarke could do except warn the others about the possibility. Fortunately, the plot seemed to be playing out as he and Gwyn speculated it would.

But one worry wouldn't go away—the jury-rigged net itself. Seen through the prism of Roarke's magical senses, it resembled a haphazard spider web which would almost require the flies to blunder in. Not that there was any help for it. There wasn't enough time to craft a more aesthetic trap or even to find a better way of attaching Gwyn's magic to Deryk than by Roarke's presence at Deryk's command post—the Wayward Bard.

Which was why Roarke was spending the twenty-ninth night of Crowsmun in the alley behind the tavern. Drawing his thin Spell of Shadows tighter around him, Roarke hoped he would be the spider in this particular web, not the fly.

Through the spells connecting him to the palace, Roarke felt a magical object crafted by Deryk cross the threshold of Queen Isabeau's chambers. An instant later Roarke identified the item as the vessel for a privacy spell. There was no other hint of Deryk's magic beyond the taint that attached itself to Deryk's talisman and its bearer.

Good, Roarke thought. *The bastard's being careful.* Deryk must have planned to kill the queen by mundane methods. Alfred and the queen's guards were more than capable of dealing with physical threats.

Other, more subtle tugs on the commingled strands of Vanyr and Chosen magic alerted Roarke that Deryk was casting a spell in one of the upper rooms of the tavern. Roarke had known his brother would want the pleasure of watching his assassins work. The characteristic rhythms of the scrying spell Deryk favored shivered across the threads of Roarke's and Gwyn's net. A nasty smile spread across Roarke's face.

Gotcha!

Gwyn's magic swarmed up the red enchantment binding Deryk to the talisman in Queen Isabeau's rooms. Thorns of power sank into Deryk like fishhooks. Roarke held his breath. With any luck, Deryk would be paralyzed, magically and physically. They needed to immobilize Deryk until he could be turned over to Jagger. Afterwards, Deryk would wish he wasn't immortal and could die for real. Roarke was looking forward to that part.

Sudden agony crushed Roarke's hands. He gagged, hunching over his hands as if to protect them from the unseen force splintering the bones beneath his skin. *Shit! The bastard is using pain to defeat the spell.* Bound to the spell, Roarke suffered the full effect of every measure Deryk took to break it. But the essential difference between Vanyr and

Chosen meant the pain stopped with Roarke. Gwyn wouldn't be affected by Deryk's desperate attempt to escape.

What's the bloody fool trying to do, Roarke howled inside his head, *beat his hands against the binding magic? That's insane.*

Roarke panted to keep from screaming. His steaming breath glimmered blue-green in the darkness. *Perfect,* he snarled to himself, *now I'm bleeding magic.* Clamping his lips together, he lurched further away from the bronze glow of the tavern's kitchen windows.

Through the fog of pain, Roarke's magical senses registered the pops of displaced air signaling the opening of several Portals on the streets surrounding the tavern. The smoke and salt tang of Gwyn's sorcery drifted across his magical senses. That meant she was in position beneath the portico of the Seamasters Guild Hall across the street from the tavern.

The steel blue signature of the Chosen captain of Isabeau's guards flared to life at the far end of the alley. A troop of palace guard took up defensive positions around the Chosen officer. A second troop Ported into position on Poole Lane about a half a block north of the alley. Roarke knew the obsidian blade he carried was invisible to Deryk. But the etheric smell of the soldiers' well-oiled armor and freshly sharpened swords would strike Deryk's magical senses like hammers.

If he could move, Deryk would try to make a break for it. They were counting on that to reduce the chances of collateral damage. He wouldn't want to confront Gwyn or the others gathered around the tavern. He was too careful to allow himself to be implicated in the plot against the queen that easily. Like any rat, he'd be looking for the escape path of least resistance—the "empty" alley where he couldn't see any foes.

Gwyn summoned her power.

All of Deryk's pain, blood, fury and fear seemed to explode inside Roarke's head. The spell line to Deryk snapped. And so did Roarke. The bastard had figured out a way to kill himself. Since Roarke was bound to him through the spell, he killed Roarke too.

Roarke knew he was dead. His disembodied consciousness looked down on Salentia as if from a great height. He found himself bewitched by the embroidery of lights—occult and ordinary—glittering over the patchwork of bricks and mortar, wood, glass and stone making up the fabric of the city. It was beautiful—except for an awful welter of muddy red and blue-green smoke roiling around a steeply gabled building near the docks. *The Wayward Bard.* The name came to Roarke in the jangle of broken crystal.

Deryk must have broken his scrying bowl.

The thought aroused a distant feeling of pleasure. Breaking Deryk's evil toys seemed somehow very important. The image of one particular toy flashed across Roarke's mind, the gold-scaled, ruby-eyed snake torque Deryk always wore around his neck—the symbol of his allegiance to the Serpent's Path, the rites of blood magic.

Fortunately, being immortal meant never having to stay dead. Unfortunately, coming back to life this time meant being plunged into the poisonous cloud of warring magics. The red belonged to Deryk. Where did the blue mess come from? It couldn't be Gwyn's, and it was far too big to belong to him.

Roarke scratched the back of his head with a hand that felt no more than mildly cramped. *Ah, the healing powers of a Vanyr*, he thought as he returned to his senses in the stinking cold alley. Roarke staggered to his feet. How long had he been dead? A minute? Five? Had he awoken too late and let his brother escape?

A whizzing sound came from the vicinity of the Wayward Bard's kitchen door. A shadow Roarke didn't recall from earlier loomed between the door and window. Before Roarke could puzzle out what was making the noise, the pure, blue-violet light of Gwyn's magic billowed like a giant sail over the tavern and the other buildings on the block. The magic settled into every angle of the rooftops, sinking through shingles and tar. The gritty chalk of plaster walls ground against the grain of the studs and murmured to the nails buried into the heart of the wood. Each separate atomy promised, *No Vanyr magic will escape our notice.*

Which meant no safe Porting from the inn for the rat bastard. Another escape hatch closed.

Gwyn's magic sluiced down the tavern walls, illuminating a lone drunk propping the back wall of the tavern with his forehead. The man cursed under his breath. Piss streamed between his widespread legs. The drunk might have been relieved but Roarke wasn't. On the contrary, the drunk's presence added a whole new worry to the million riding on Roarke's shoulders. He had to chase off the drunk before Deryk tried to escape.

Roarke hissed, "Get out of here!"

"Hsssh yourself," the drunk muttered to the wall. "M'got better things t' do."

Roarke looked around for something to throw. If the offal on his side of the alley had been solid enough to toss, he wouldn't have hesitated. But Roarke couldn't see anything with enough substance to chase away the drunk without attracting unwanted attention. Roarke couldn't risk anyone in the tavern alerting Deryk. The whole point of the snare was to herd Deryk into the alley where Roarke could take him down.

Powerful as she was magically, Gwyn was no match for Deryk physically. If he cut her and drew blood, he would absorb enough of her essence to bind her. Gwyn possessed the Chosen gifts of perfect healing and the ability to survive wounds that would kill an ordinary mortal. But Deryk's binding would eat away her life force like a cancer. Eventually he would succeed in killing her and taking her magic for his own. Only a Vanyr could face Deryk and live, and since his warrior brothers were helping Alfred at the palace, Roarke was the only Vanyr around.

Knocking the drunk out would probably be easier than chasing him away. But either course meant luring him away from the door.

Needs must. Roarke peeled the glove from his left hand. The supple leather slipped over his skin with a soft whisper of protest. Roarke twisted the glove around itself. He threw it with just the right amount of snap. The knotted leather struck the drunk behind the ear.

"Huhn?" The drunk pushed away from the wall. "Who's there?"

From inside the kitchen, Roarke heard a muffled bleat of surprise. A metal object thudded against something softer than wood. The lamps went dark. The kitchen door eased open. For an instant, the drunk stood silhouetted in the dull orange glow emanating from the kitchen hearth. A dark shape streaked from the room. The door slammed shut. The alley went black. The drunk's protest ended in a wet gurgle as two heavy bodies struck the cobbles.

"Light," Roarke said, drawing his blade.

An insubstantial globe of blue-green light winked to life over Roarke's right shoulder. *Too late.* Roarke swore at the scene before him.

Deryk crouched over the drunk, a bloody dagger in his right hand. His sheathed sword splayed awkwardly across his thigh. A fold of his unfastened doublet flopped over the hilt. Eyes narrowed against the light, he straightened. His left hand inched toward the glint of gold visible at his throat.

Roarke sliced Deryk's right forearm. The dagger clattered against the cobbles. Blood spurted through the ruined sleeve of Deryk's doublet and shirt, and splattered the clothes of his victim.

"Caught red-handed at last."

The feeble glimmer of Roarke's witchlight painted Deryk's blond hair a pale, watery green and made his skin glow like fine marble. A slight frown creased Deryk's brow and nagged at the corners of his mouth. He resembled an aristocratic merman moderately inconvenienced by a drowned sailor.

"Roarke, you ass, how dare you try to bind me with Chosen magic?"

"It worked, didn't it?"

Deryk eased away from the corpse. "Dream on, brother. That piece of glass might have hid you from my scrying, but it won't stop me. My steel will break that fragile conceit of yours into a thousand pieces."

"Maybe. Maybe not. But you have to draw it first."

Roarke was six feet tall. Deryk was two inches taller, and he carried twenty-weight more of muscle. But Deryk had spent his whole sorry life flush with Vanyr magic and the bloody rites of the Serpent's Path. He had never been forced to earn a living by his sword—much less fight with a torn and bleeding sword arm.

Deryk feinted toward his sword with his right hand while his left reached for something hidden inside his doublet. Roarke stabbed the tip of his sword into the top of Deryk's left hand. Twisting his wrist, he dragged the edge of the blade across Deryk's right.

Deryk jerked his useless sword hand at Roarke's head. He roared a string of guttural sounds bearing little resemblance to speech.

Roarke ducked. The cursed blood flew past his head and hissed against the wall behind him. For all the fury behind the spell, Roarke's witchlight never wavered. Roarke bared his teeth. Even if it had landed, the curse would've barely raised a few blisters.

Skirting the drunk's corpse, Roarke advanced on his brother. The point of his blade aimed for the white splash of linen covering Deryk's black, black heart.

Deryk crossed his arms over his chest. He retreated, step for Roarke's step, toward Poole Lane. "Leave now and maybe I won't kill your friends," Deryk snarled.

"With what?" Roarke asked. "Your magic is as dead as mine."

Almost casually Roarke's blade re-opened the half-healed gash on Deryk's arm. The smell of fresh blood soaking the wool of his brother's doublet was better than perfume. "I could take your life here and now."

Roarke jabbed at Deryk's face, hoping to create an opening for a death blow which would disable Deryk long enough for a proper binding. Deryk flinched but kept his arms locked over his chest. Sweat sheened his forehead. It glistened in the hollow of his throat where the head of the golden snake nestled against his skin.

"I could take your tongue," Roarke taunted, his gaze fastened on Deryk's eyes, not his unprotected neck. "That would cripple your magic. Or perhaps I should aim lower and cripple your pride.

"No. I think I want your"—Roarke lunged—"snake."

Deryk was too slow to block and too proud to take a dive. But he didn't have to. His golden snake reared like a living thing and caught the tip of Roarke's blade on the flat scales of its muzzle.

Turquoise lightning exploded from the place where obsidian and gold connected. The magical bolt struck Roarke square in the chest, hoisting him in the air like hay on a pitchfork. He slammed into the wall opposite the tavern door. Roarke's dead body made a wet, sucking sound as it slid into the muck.

₮℞

"Where the hell is Deryk?"

Roarke blinked twice to clear his vision and wished he hadn't. Illuminated by the glare of a half dozen wizard lights, Gwyn's round face radiated enough anger to make Roarke's head throb. No, wait, his head *was* pounding, because thanks to Deryk's damned snake, he'd recently introduced the back of his skull to the front of a brick wall.

Splendid—two deaths in the space of what? Roarke calculated the position of the moon in relationship to the rooftops. A half hour—a new personal worst. At least he appeared to be sitting in the muck of the alley, instead of lying in it.

"Don't know." Roarke pushed the words through cracked and swollen lips. He stared at his ungloved left hand. His nails looked black against his tan. Apparently he'd been struck by lightning too. What next? Could those approaching concussions be the Old One's booted feet hammering the alley? The sound and vibrations were pure torture to Roarke's aching head. No, Jagger wouldn't waste his energy running. Jagger would Port in and hammer Roarke's head directly.

Roarke risked a glance at his next wave of tormenters. Hawke and Conlan loomed over him.

To be fair, Roarke's warrior brothers loomed over him even when he was standing. Lean, long-legged, with the kind of muscles that had on one famous occasion allowed him to wrestle a full-grown Tabar bull and win, Hawke stood nearly six and a half feet tall. Conlan was another inch taller still, not counting his braids.

The harsh light heightened the contrast between Conlan's mocha-colored skin and sardonic, white-toothed smile. In comparison, fair-haired, fair-skinned Hawke's square-jawed grin looked almost benign.

Roarke hoped that wasn't a bad sign.

"What happened?" Hawke asked.

"Deryk's snake," Roarke said. "It bit."

"Deryk got away?" Hawke frowned. "The spell should've drained his powers completely."

"Are you saying I did something wrong?" Gwyn demanded. Her hands fisted on her amply padded hips. Wisps of blonde hair spilled over her forehead and straggled from her collapsing bun. Red-cheeked and steaming from her magical exertions, she reminded Roarke of a kettle about to boil over.

"The spell worked," Roarke assured Gwyn before her frustration turned into a full-blown magical tantrum.

Conlan hunkered down next to the body by the kitchen door. "Looks like Deryk killed a drunk. One jab to the heart. Neat job, for a change." He rose to his feet and pointed to an irregular pattern of dark stains next to the storm sewer. "Your blood or Deryk's?"

"Deryk's, I think—for all the good it does us. I don't think Deryk's powers fed off the drunk's death. It was too quick," Roarke said. Too damn quick for Roarke to save the drunk he hadn't been able to chase away.

Roarke shook his head. The coronas surrounding the wizard lights shivered. Roarke's sense of smell returned in a rush. His stomach wished it hadn't.

"Before he got away, Deryk murdered a drunk," Gwyn informed Alfred DuMarc, the last person to join the group. "That should count for something."

Alfred jerked his fingers through short, brown hair matted and stiff with drying blood. Blood drenched the Lord of the Keep's blue velvet tabard and smudged his hands and face, darkening the long scar that ran from forehead to chin along the right side of his face.

"The queen," Roarke rasped, "was she hurt?"

"No. She's fine," Alfred replied. The Lord of the Keep brushed at the blood on his face. "Let's get down to business and make it official. Vanyr Roarke, did you see your brother, Vanyr Deryk, kill the man? And if you can't say for sure, would you be willing to let Vanyr Jagger inside your mind to find the true answer to the question?"

"Sure I'd let him in, but there's not much point. Even though Deryk was the only person who could've stabbed him, I didn't actually see the bastard drive the knife home. The alley was too dark, and it happened too fast."

"Not enough. Reyah's balked when we've had more. Dammit." Alfred turned back to Gwyn. "What about evidence—did Deryk leave behind a weapon or talisman keyed only to him? All I can see is evidence of a fight and a dead body allegedly killed by Deryk. We only have Roarke's word Deryk killed this man. The presence of Deryk's blood proves nothing other than the fact there was a struggle. After all, Roarke bled on the wall. Did he kill the bricks?"

"Not for want of trying," Conlan murmured. "I don't see a blade. Deryk probably took it with him."

"Without a weapon, it's not enough," Alfred said. Roarke could relate to the look of frustration on Alfred's face.

"Are you out of your mind?" Gwyn shouted. "What Roarke saw would be more than enough for any tribunal in Seshmeel. Why are you playing Deryk's advocate? He's a monster and a murderer. We need to lock him up and throw away the key. You know he killed the drunk, just like he killed the children he stole from Ragpickers Row. He sustains himself on death. When in Kalin's Hell are you going to do something about it? You're Reyah's Law. Why don't you act like it?"

Alfred flashed Gwyn a look of white-hot pain.

Hawke said, "Easy, Gwyn. Alfred's doing as much as he can. Would you rather hear the bad news from Jagger when it's too late to do anything about it? Remember, we're talking about Mommy's little darling here."

"Then we might as well set Deryk's henchmen free and go home," Gwyn said. "So Deryk feeds his magic with the hearts of innocent children. So he wants to take over Seshmeel or Hiawat and eat the life right out of the land. So we stop him again and again and again. So we endanger Isabeau of Seshmeel, the best hope for an enlightened monarchy this world has seen in a hundred years. We've still got nothing! Nothing will change, because nobody's willing to admit Deryk is a menace and force Reyah to see it too.

"I may have been made Chosen by the Voice, not by Reyah like *some* people," Gwyn spat at Alfred, "but I know shit when I smell it."

"So you can find a privy in the dark. Bravo," Roarke drawled. "Isabeau didn't die, did she?"

"No," Gwyn grumbled. "But they used some sort of sleeping powder on her, and it made her face puff up like bread dough."

"Horses do too, but that's never stopped her from riding. Isabeau knew the risks when she agreed to the plan." Roarke turned to Hawke. "Are the conspirators secure?"

"One of the mercenaries managed to impale himself on Alfred's dagger, but the rest are safe in Isolation Portals," Hawke replied. "They won't be tripping any of Deryk's Deadman Spells until we're ready for them."

"How'd you manage that?" Roarke asked. He turned to Gwyn. "I didn't think your Portal wizards were that good."

The Chosen wizard of Seshmeel wrung her hands, a sickly smile on her face. "They aren't," she admitted. "Hawke called in Jagger."

"You called in the Old One? You son of the Bitch."

Hawke crossed his arms over his chest. "If you've got a better idea, I'm dying to hear it."

"Face it, Roarke," Conlan said, "we need the Old One to finish this job. He's the only one who can unbind the spells on those idiots without killing them, and Reyah won't accept any evidence he hasn't verified."

"Fine." Roarke pushed himself to his feet. Every bone and joint creaked in protest. "As long as he's in the neighborhood, Jagger can run the bastard down too. I've had enough death for one night."

"That's not how it works, and you know it," Hawke said.

"You charge a Vanyr; you bring the Vanyr in," Roarke chanted by rote.

"You make it sound like some kind of chore. You're looking at this all wrong." Hawke raised his arm like he was about to throw it around Roarke's shoulders. A pained glance at Roarke's back appeared to decide Hawke against it.

New clothes, Roarke added to the mental to-do list which now included several hot baths with lots of soap as well as strong drink and soft, clean, vermin-free bedding. Might as well feed Hawke the straight line while he was at it.

"And how would you suggest I look at it?" Roarke asked.

"As the best possible excuse for missing Reyah's Natal Day celebrations at the Keep. No offense, Alfred," Hawke added.

"None taken," Alfred replied.

"Sounds good to me," Conlan said. "When did you want to start?"

Roarke rolled his shoulders. "Would the Third Hour of morning give you enough time to say goodbye to the barmaids at the Running Logans? I could use a decent night's sleep myself."

"Sleep!" Gwyn shrieked, reviving Roarke's headache like magic. "You aren't thinking sleeping with Deryk running loose?"

"He's not running loose. He's Porting himself to a blur to throw us off his trail. He probably won't stop until dawn. When he does, I'll find him and figure out a way to cart him back to Jagger.

"Speaking of which," Roarke said, "I can find Deryk's bolt-hole easy enough, but it may take some complicated Porting to get through whatever wards he's using these days. Have your best Portal wizard at my rooms at half past Second."

Roarke glanced at the drunkard's corpse. Someone, probably Conlan, had closed the drunk's eyes and arranged the body so it looked like he was sleeping. "And make sure your wizard brings his own rations. I'm not springing for anyone's food. I've spent enough of my own money on this rat hunt, and I've still got to pay for a funeral."

Gwyn sputtered, "Why you thrice-damned son of a—"

"Goddess," Hawke supplied. Hawke grinned at the wizard as he said it too.

₧₧

The Vanyr Tower of Reyah's Keep

By the time Deryk Ported to the apartment reserved for his use at the Keep, the power he had squeezed from Roarke's death had long since dissipated. His aching limbs trembled with exhaustion. He wanted nothing more than to sink into his samite-covered featherbed and sleep away the year. But first he needed to confound his pursuers.

Besting Roarke had gone a long way toward quelling the panic Deryk felt when his brother sprang his trap. So Roarke and the Seshmeelan Chosen bitch had gotten wind of the assassination plot and gone to great lengths to foil it. What did they have to present to Jagger when all was said and done? An aristocrat so venal Seshmeel ought to give Deryk a medal for removing him from the line of succession.

It wasn't as if Roarke could prove Deryk suborned the quartermaster general. Deryk made quite sure the man was of a mind to commit treason long before he made his approach. The privacy spell was a stroke of genius, if Deryk did say so himself. Deryk hadn't given the quartermaster general the spell. He merely afforded him the opportunity to steal it. Deryk could hardly be held accountable for what the man did with it afterwards. Or the fact such trinkets linked the bearer to their maker.

After all, tonight's attack was no more than a ploy. It served its purpose in Deryk's larger plan. A ranking member of the court, tied to the queen's fortunes by blood and a senior position in Seshmeel's army, had made an attempt on her life. Pleasant as it would've been, Deryk hadn't expected the attempt to succeed, and he was far too wily to allow his candidate for the throne of Seshmeel to be involved in the plot or appear to benefit from it.

Deryk allowed the servants to remove his garments and prepare a hot bath in front of the fireplace in his bedchamber. The servants knew better than to question the blood on his clothes.

Taking a bath in the Vanyr Tower had become an exercise in tedium since the seneschal of the Keep had banned the magically gifted from serving there. Everyone knew the ban was directed at Deryk. One day, he would revenge himself on the seneschal for the insult and the nuisance. But tonight the delay worked in Deryk's favor by providing an excuse for conversing with his inferiors.

No word of the attempted coup had yet reached the servants. The Guards of the Keep and Reyah's Thousand (who together constituted Alfred's personal army) had not been placed on alert. Deryk was the only Vanyr in the tower.

Jagger was expected to return shortly to pursue his latest flirtation with yet another mortal jade. Although Deryk considered the Old One's dalliances with mortals—particularly those without magic—beneath the dignity of a Vanyr, Deryk would've preferred to have Jagger in residence and safely occupied. Deryk was a firm believer in keeping his enemies close—with the exception of his Mother. Deryk preferred Her long gone to wherever it was She went.

Deryk dismissed the servants and eased himself into the hammered copper tub made to accommodate his godlike frame. The warm water, perfumed with sandalwood and the finest musk, caressed his tired muscles. As he leaned his head against the curved lip of the tub, his snake familiar slithered out from under the damp ends of his hair and undulated down his smooth-shaven chest. The ripple of its golden scales against his unprotected flesh excited Deryk in ways no lover ever could.

The snake settled in a relaxed coil on Deryk's stomach. The blunted arrow of its head rested atop his breastbone, just above the water. The localized, sorcerous heat of the animate gold weighed pleasantly on his belly.

"Blood calls to blood," Deryk murmured, sweeping his palm over the snake's head and neck in slow, rhythmic strokes which barely ruffled the water in the tub. Deryk felt the sibilance of the snake's pleasure shiver through his bones.

An accidental scratch, the tiniest cut—most of Deryk's victims never even knew they had fed his snake. Even fewer guessed once the snake tasted their blood, its venom could strike them dead a half a world away. Tonight a select group of Seshmeel

29

aristocrats and burghers would die, throwing the queen's government into chaos. Not all of them were traitors. But even the innocent would be implicated when they weren't around to defend themselves. Their precisely orchestrated deaths would replace every atomy of the energies lost as a result of Roarke's interference.

Rubbing faster now, Deryk recalled the contempt on the jowly face of one particular courtier as he declined Deryk's offer of patronage. The man was an under-appreciated but vital clerk of the Royal Accounts with an unacknowledged touch of mind magic. The courtier guessed who Deryk was, and still he spurned him.

Caught up in anticipation of the ecstatic moment when his first victim would release his life force, it took Deryk a little while to realize his spell wasn't working. The blood in his snake was calling to the courtier, but it wasn't getting any answer. Worse yet, Deryk's familiar had gone limp on his belly, its heat dissipated between one moment and the next.

Probably because the bathwater hadn't been properly heated. In fact, it felt downright tepid. Damned servants. Deryk was going to have their hides, literally. He snatched up his snake and stood.

The abrupt movement should've sloshed water all over the blood red carpet. Deryk meant it to. Only the water didn't splash. It froze. A thin layer of ice coated his limbs. Broad fronds of ice as clear as glass rose from the surface of the water despite the fire in the hearth.

With a strangled shriek, Deryk tumbled out of the tub. He fell to his hands and knees on the carpet between the tub and the foot of the bed. The ice encasing him broke apart, crunching and crackling like spun sugar.

Jagger was after him! No one else had the power to perform that kind of magic at a distance.

Whimpering like a frightened child, Deryk scrambled for the curtained bed. The ice waves slewed backward into the tub. The powdered frost coating Deryk's body liquefied into an army of crystal worms that wriggled across the carpet and up the sides of the tub before disappearing over its curved lip. Deryk heard them strike the surface of the water like drops of rain.

A lazy, mocking finger of steam rose from the center of the tub.

Deryk huddled under a blanket of snow tiger fur, sweating and shivering. He commanded himself to think through his panic. Maybe the Old One had pulled the stunt to see him sweat. Jagger couldn't possibly know about the Seshmeel business. Deryk had made sure the Old One would be busy on other fronts. Maybe the failure of his spell was a fluke. The others would work. They had to. Deryk clutched the head of his snake so tight he almost couldn't feel the bite of its fangs in the pad of his thumb.

But even blood magic didn't do any good. All of Deryk's targets were beyond his reach, swaddled in Jagger's magic. Guilty and innocent alike. It wouldn't take long for the Old One to unbind Deryk's Deadman Spells and send the proof of his plot to Reyah. Meddling in the Goddess-decreed stability of the Eight Lands was the one sin She would never forgive.

Deryk was dead.

He was worse than dead. With Reyah's permission—nay, with Her blessing—the Old One would confine Deryk in a hellish netherworld where Deryk would die over and over again.

The first two times Deryk had been consigned to Jagger's punishments had been bad enough. Jagger was the master of pain. Not only had he wrung the full measure of agony from each death, he permitted Deryk's body to corrupt between resurrections until the return to life became more excruciating than its end.

But this time would be worse. For this crime, Reyah would command the Old One to break Deryk completely. Jagger would savage Deryk's mind as well as his body. Deryk would be remade into a simpering lapdog.

Deryk had one chance to save himself, by creating a diversion so big, none of his brothers would have time to pursue the business in Seshmeel. Luckily for him, that chance might be near at hand. Several months before, Deryk happened to catch sight of the Keep's Chosen wizard Vallenius hurrying from the Terminus. Vallenius clutched a small, heavily warded box tight to his chest.

Deryk never had understood why the priestess who served as Reyah's Voice in Domain selected a youth barely past his teens to command the Keep's ancient magic. But Deryk found it very convenient. Vallenius's fair complexion and complete lack of guile made his face such an easy book to read. On the night in question, the shadows under the boy's eyes looked like bruises, and the set of his mouth looked too old for his face.

The Captain of the Keep's Guard—a six hundred-year-old, dark-skinned, Kushite Chosen named Willem Leopold—hailed Vallenius not far from the wizard's turret. Deryk slipped into the shadows of an open doorway.

The captain of the guard clapped a hand on Vallenius's shoulder. Peering at the haggard youth in the uneven light, Willem whistled.

"What happened?" Willem asked. "Did the Voice's monk beat you up again?"

31

Deryk watched Vallenius run an unsteady hand through his short crop of red gold curls. "No." Vallenius shuddered. "I'd rather not talk about it. You're going to have to excuse me, Willem, but I have to put something in the safe before anyone knows I've brought it here."

Neither man noticed the small golden snake sliding along the edge of the wall. Crossing his arms over his chest, Willem leaned against the wall and nearly stepped on Deryk's familiar. Willem frowned at the small box clutched in Vallenius' hands. "That bad, huh?"

Vallenius nodded "I'm sorry, Willem, but I can't say anything more. And you shouldn't either. For your own good."

With the perfect vision of hindsight, Deryk realized he should've stayed to investigate. The business in Seshmeel might have turned out differently. But at the time there were things to do and people to buy in Salentia. He could be grasping at straws, but the overheard conversation might mean the difference between freedom and being broken on the wheel of Jagger's magic.

"I wonder what was in that box," Deryk mused. A spell? An enchanted relic? Whatever it was, it had frightened Vallenius out of his wits. Which was exactly the sort of thing Deryk needed to save his skin.

Walking to Vallenius's rooms took more time than Porting, but Porting inside the Keep could be tracked. Boot soles to the floor could not. And no one would question a Vanyr out for a late night stroll. Especially when the Vanyr was Deryk.

The dusty safeguards surrounding the entrance to Vallenius's turret all but screamed the boy wizard's absence. Tired as he was, Deryk easily circumvented them. The zaihn guarding the door to Vallenius's private laboratory required a little more skill, but a sleepbearing mistwraith handled the job. The zaihn, when awakened, would identify Deryk's magic. But zaihns couldn't testify in a court of law.

"Now where would a red-haired fledgling put something that scared him spitless?" Deryk whispered, tapping a finger against his chin. Golden scales warmed against Deryk's throat before the snake wrapped itself around his hand. Deryk brought the snake's head to his lips. "Find me what I desire."

The snake slithered through the clutter on Vallenius's desk, pausing occasionally to test the air with its tongue. It stopped and hissed. Deryk followed the snake's gaze to a wall shrine to Reyah. He shifted the mirror behind the statue and revealed a small, ironbound door.

"The ubiquitous wall safe," Deryk sneered. "How gauche."

Blue bolts of magefire flashed around Deryk's hand when he touched the little door, igniting his sleeve and ruining his second doublet of the night. Deryk swore and jumped back, damping the flames. "Damnation! Where did the boy learn that?"

Retrieving his snake, Deryk examined the safe and its lingering aura. Designed to deter, not detect, Vallenius's spell proved simpler than it first appeared, but still troubling. Deryk believed boys not under his control should be forbidden such powerful toys.

Deryk muttered a counterspell. The door to the safe crumbled to dust, revealing the box Deryk remembered. Flushed with anticipation, Deryk broke through the lid and the box's magical protections in one stroke. He withdrew a copper ribbon turned and fused to form a twisted loop the size of a woman's bracelet. The metal was etched with tiny letters that ran over and around the bracelet without a recognizable beginning or end. They didn't even make much sense until Deryk picked out the words: "Body and spirit travel between the worlds…"

Laughter bubbled in Deryk's throat. He knew of only two worlds—the here and the hereafter. And he'd always wanted to raise the dead.

Chapter Three

Back at Dragon*Con

In the exhibit hall of the Marriott across the street from the Hyatt, the "Intrigue Theme" of *Domain, the Series* blared from the sixty-inch, plasma television mounted like a sacred icon behind the altar of actor Eric Bernard's personal booth. Larger than life cardboard cut-outs of Eric as Lord Alfred flanked the screen.

The cut-out on the left glared at the smaller-than-average actor grudgingly signing autographs for a line of fans that stretched past the end of the aisle. The Alfred on the right scowled at the final minutes of the last episode of the show's most recent season.

The Elder Goddess Reyah, seated behind a table in the double-wide, tulle-draped booth across the aisle from Eric, sympathized with his cut-outs. She felt ready to scream Herself.

The television screen showed a smoky interior fitfully lit by a dying fire. Dialogue identified the location as a public house in Salentia. A portly actor squeezed into a garish uniform two sizes too small folded his belly over a scarred wooden table. His pudgy fist struck a much-creased set of floor plans labeled "The Queen's Private Chambers."

"Once the royal brat is dead, nothing can stand in my way. I will take my place as the rightful king of Seshmeel," the actor said.

The flickering light lent a diabolical cast to the face of Michael Ryan as Deryk. Reyah had to give the dotty Englishman credit. On camera, he nailed Deryk's magnetic intensity, even if he was fifteen years too old for the part.

"I drink to your success," Michael purred as he lifted a tarnished silver pitcher. The foot of the pitcher clanked against one of the goblets on the table. Blood red wine splashed over the floor plans, obliterating the word "queen."

"Now that's what I call a good omen." Michael's malevolent laughter faded into the music of the show's end theme.

Reyah cursed under Her breath as She booted Her laptop. Damn, damn and double damn! Why hadn't She kept an eye on the show as She prepped for the convention? She knew the writers had some weird tie to events in Her home world. Budget and casting might skew the perspective. Production cycles might delay the broadcast anywhere from four months to a year. But since the middle of season one, *Domain*'s writers routinely, if blasphemously, scooped Her own priestesses when it came to the latest news. She meant to find out why too, as soon as she dealt with this Seshmeel mess.

The laptop winked to life to the fanfare of the main *Domain* theme. The screen paled into a multi-tiled overview of the Keep and the Eight Lands of Domain. The varied landscapes of the principalities glistened between their cloud-enshrouded borders like gems nestled in creamy velvet.

A teaser for the upcoming season erupted across Eric's plasma screen. A close-up of Eric looking grim dissolved into a shot of a ketchup-painted, bare-chested Michael Ryan standing behind an altar, a red-stained dagger in each hand.

Reyah snarled as She clicked through views of key Domain hot spots. She wished She could've learned about Deryk's plot sooner. By the time She got back to Her room last night and booted up Her laptop, She'd missed most of the action. Deryk was Porting all over the planet to throw Roarke off his scent. Meanwhile, Jagger and Alfred were up to their eyebrows in incontrovertible evidence of Deryk's guilt.

"Next!"

Reyah glanced across the aisle to where Eric Bernard's assistant held out her hand for the outrageous fee the actor charged for his autograph. Why did those sheep continue to feed the mercenary jerk's ego? He was only a pale imitation of the square-jawed, iron-thewed original, who also happened to be blessed with a *much* nicer disposition. Eric probably didn't have an iron thew in his entire body—unless you counted his conceit muscle.

Reyah moved the cursor toward a set of icons to the left of her screen and clicked on the one marked "Deryk.cam." She frowned as the laptop's screen view shifted to the broken walls of an abandoned castle clinging to the northern face of Mount Tuumb in Tambara. Once a proud fortress guarding the passage to the ancient crater known as the Plain of Elsee, the castle's lichen-covered stones tumbled down the slope of Mount Tuumb, indistinguishable from the debris of a hundred landslides.

Amid this shamble of stones and weeds, one tower remained intact at the eastern corner of the ruins. The pinks and oranges of the Tambaran sunset bled over the tower's roughhewn walls.

A Portal blinked open in the shadowed courtyard at the tower's base. Deryk's bright hair glittered in the fading light as he turned his head from side to side. A murder of crows took flight, their leaders cawing forlornly. Black wings drummed the air, but nothing else stirred. After waiting a moment, Deryk opened a Portal to a small chamber near the roof of the tower.

He set a copper bracelet on a gouged and smoke-darkened table. He crossed to a bulky, lead-sheathed cabinet at the far end of the room. His body blocked Reyah's view, but from his movements, it looked like he was checking on something inside the cabinet's topmost compartment. Reyah thought she detected a faint tremor in Deryk's hands as he closed and locked the compartment. He exhaled and slumped against the cabinet. "Snakes be praised, she's still gone."

Which of his bimbos would that be, Reyah harrumphed to herself. *Why is Deryk worrying about his love life at a time like this?*

"I can do this. I still have enough time. Today is only the thirtieth. I've still got four days to prepare for Rupert's Retreat. Perfect."

Deryk drew a chair up to the table and snapped his fingers. A handful of wizard lights sprang to life. He turned the bracelet over in his hands, squinting hard at its inscriptions. Every so often his mouth shaped a word or a string of phrases, as if trying them out for size.

Back on Earth, Reyah's stomach did a slow flip. Perfect? He thought everything was *perfect?* The situation was perfectly horrifying. Of all the things Deryk could've stolen… How, how was she going to keep Jagger from turning Deryk's brains inside out this time?

Worse yet—what if Jagger got to the bracelet before She did?

Reyah's hands clenched into fists. She knew exactly what Jagger would do if he came into possession of Her bracelet. Oath be damned—a shudder shimmied down the goddess's spine.

A flash of anger followed. She scrolled at goddess speed through past images captured by Her various cams. Several months before, the Voice had given the bracelet to Vallenius for safekeeping. How could the Voice have been so careless?

Certainly the boy was very pretty and might eventually be a first-rate wizard—if Reyah didn't kill Vallenius and the Voice for letting Deryk get his hands on one of Her most important treasures. Hadn't She told the Voice to put it somewhere safe? What had the Voice been thinking of to send it with Vallenius to...

"...My Keep," Reyah growled. "Center of My power and supposedly the safest place in My world. Well, dammit. I guess I can't punish them after all."

"This must be one of Jagger's toys," Deryk's voice muttered from the laptop's speakers. "I can't make heads or tails of it. 'Speed of light'—what's that? The rate at which a candle burns? How long it takes the magic of a wizard light to fade? Is that why it needs to be overcome?

"It doesn't matter," Deryk said. "The Servants of the Snake will make it work. I wonder if a few hundred years of damnation has sweetened Megeara's temper any."

Reyah shook Her Head. It was just as well Deryk failed to divine the real purpose of that particular trinket. Because if he did, She would have to destroy him Herself.

Another click of the mouse showed Hawke, Conlan, Roarke and a nervous Portal wizard Porting into the village on the northwest ridge of the crater. The drab little wizard kept ducking behind Hawke and Conlan as if Roarke was some kind of mad dog only the other Vanyr could keep at bay.

When Roarke mentioned Deryk, the wizard shouted, "Are you crazy? I've got a family!" Then the little coward Ported himself all the way back to Isabeau's palace on a single spell.

"Next time, don't bring up Deryk like you're talking about the weather," Conlan suggested. "Take it easy on him. Tell him he's going up against a giant Paelinorean Water Devil. At least three mortals have survived encounters with Water Devils in the last two thousand years alone."

Roarke rubbed the bridge of his nose. "Whatever. We need to get moving. Jagger is waiting for us to bring Deryk in. You know how impatient the Old One gets."

"He's keeping Deryk's people alive," Hawke snapped. "That takes a lot of magic. I'd be impatient too."

Roarke turned to Conlan. "You know this area. The Last Stand Tavern looked marginally cleaner than the Rasher's Head. Would you trust the cook to prepare a few days worth of field rations?"

"It's not like it's going to kill us," Conlan replied.

"I thought you wanted to have at least a little magic at your backs when we finally get to Deryk. Heaving my guts out tends to put a cramp in my spells. Or did I understand wrong? I thought the plan was for us to kill Deryk and ship him off to Jagger, not the other way around."

"I'd prefer it that way," Conlan conceded. "But the Rasher's Head has better ale."

Reyah drummed Her fingers on the table. This was bad, very bad. Once Hawke, Conlan and Roarke got their hands on Deryk—and She knew it was only a matter of time before they did—Jagger would not only have enough evidence to justify lobotomizing Deryk, Jagger would have Her bracelet too.

Reyah smiled grimly. She'd have to make sure Jagger got nowhere near the bracelet—or Deryk—until She had a plan. Reyah nodded. That was it. She needed a plan.

Two keystrokes and Reyah's display shifted again. She fast-forwarded through Alfred's return to the Keep and consultations with Jagger on the questioning of Seshmeel's former quartermaster general. A quick search showed neither Jagger nor Alfred had any inkling of the theft or how Deryk planned to use Her bracelet. Vallenius was cooling his heels outside the Voice's meditation room, waiting to escort her and her bodyguard to the Keep for Reyah's Natal Day celebration. The wizard wouldn't be back in his rooms for another couple of hours, at least. Reyah heaved a sigh of relief. Her luck was holding.

But She was going to need more. Much, much more. She reached into a pocket of Her caftan and pulled out a pouch of silk velvet the color of midnight. The bag shuddered. The cords wrapped around one end stretched and eased, allowing the tip of a crystal egg to nudge through the opening.

With a sigh of pleasure Reyah closed Her fingers around the egg. The strange geometry of its facets pulsed beneath Her hand. The Wishstone was as old as Her Domain—perhaps older. Extraordinarily powerful and mysterious too. Reyah didn't know where the Wishstone came from or how it worked. In four millennia of traveling the galaxies, She had never encountered another naturally occurring crystal like it.

Through some of the crystal's facets, you glimpsed flecks of what appeared to be metal sparking like fire. Through others, threads of what might have been mercury flowed like water. Tiny spheres of air appeared to move between the planes, and from some angles you could see what appeared to be a furze of bright green moss over a layer of rich peat.

The Wishstone felt strong in the manner of a living thing. Reyah passed the crystal from hand to hand, comforting Herself with its energy. She had learned, through trial and error—and stars above, had some of those errors been painful—one only used the Wishstone in times of emergency. Reyah rubbed the Wishstone against Her wrinkled cheek. If keeping Deryk in one piece and Jagger's hands off Her bracelet wasn't an emergency, She didn't know what was.

Problem was the Wishstone gave you what you wished for, which wasn't necessarily what you *really* wanted or needed. She always tried to be very careful about how She worded a wish. Being too general or too specific could prove equally catastrophic.

Reyah grimaced. Hell, at this point She'd even welcome a catastrophe. At least a catastrophe would distract the Vanyr and Her Chosen from Deryk.

"You actually agreed to go out with him?" The voice of the woman passing Reyah's booth sounded thunderstruck. "You told me last week you didn't have any time for dating. What changed your mind?"

The woman's friend answered, "I dunno. I guess I needed a distraction, you know? Geez, you act like dating is some sort of catastrophe."

Reyah sat up straighter in her chair. Distraction! Dating! That was it! She chuckled.

Dating… That could lead to courtship, which might result in marriage.

Her boys, married?

Reyah's forehead crinkled as She tried to think of a better solution. She couldn't. Maybe it *was* time for the Vanyr to settle down.

A reluctant smile tugged at the corners of Her mouth. The more She thought about it, the better She liked it. Nine women to distract Her sons. It could be just the thing She needed to get Deryk off the hook and Her bracelet back before Jagger knew it was missing.

Reyah made a mental note to spend some quality time with Deryk. He was getting out of hand and there was no way She was going to lose another son. Reyah's mouth set in a thin line. No way in Kalin's Seven Hells.

Reyah put her worry over Deryk away. She needed to get back to business. Of course, She'd have to make the women Chosen. Eternal youth would keep them around long enough to carry out their mission and prevent any inconvenient attacks of nobility over the mortal/immortal divide. She liked creating Chosen, especially when they came from other worlds. They were always *so* grateful and compliant to the goddess who made them.

Reyah stroked the egg and hummed a wordless tune. The women of Domain were too accustomed to viewing the Vanyr as gods. They fawned over them like fans here did over their media celebrities.

Personally, She thought it was rather disgusting how certain women made themselves subservient to every Vanyr whim. Take the group of women in Thrall who held all their religious rites in the nude. It was bad enough they worshipped Roarke, but the silly twits didn't seem to understand running around without their clothes on could lead to pneumonia.

But there were many other worlds to choose Her candidates from. This one, for example. She liked this one. Its mortals closely resembled the folks back home. Thanks to that charming little television show, a great many of them vicariously enjoyed the doings in Her world too. Some of them even had a little magic—like those two nice women She met last night.

Besides, hadn't the captain of the Keep's guard been complaining about the scarcity of female Chosen? She grinned. She was about to give him his wish—in spades.

Another teaser for the upcoming season flickered on Eric's television set. Reyah's newest Chosen, Donatien des Nuits, his sable hair flying and sapphire blue eyes flashing, rode hell-bent-for-leather toward the edge of a steep-sided canyon. A tow-haired girl balanced on the horse behind him, her arms locked around his waist. The girl cast a frightened glance over her shoulder at the posse of creatively begrimed stunt riders hot on their heels.

The camera cut to a front shot of Donatien. Donatien's shirt was hanging open, revealing a generous wedge of lovely muscles and crisp, black chest hair. Reyah sucked Her lower lip between Her teeth. She angled Her head for a better view, all thoughts of the Wishstone and catastrophes sailing straight out of Her brain until the camera cut away to a long shot of Donatien heading for the cliff.

Well. Reyah blew out her breath in a silent whistle. There was one actor who did justice to the original. Reyah considered the possibility of recruiting a spare.

No! Not now. She couldn't afford to be distracted. Saving Deryk from Jagger—and himself—must be Her first priority. Just because Deryk couldn't figure out the purpose of the bracelet didn't mean his demons wouldn't make it work.

"Drat the boy. The things I have to do to keep Jagger and Alfred from sending him up the river."

Reyah raised the Wishstone to Her lips. "I wish for the right nine women—"

"Excuse me, ma'am." A short, balding man tapped a finger against her counter. "I'd like to buy the silver box with the big blue stone on the lid for my girlfriend."

Reyah blinked. She was on the verge of telling the man She was closed. Then it sank in which box the customer was talking about—a silver-plated, water wyrm-scale box priced at several hundred dollars.

"And I'd like to get a couple of those earrings and maybe a necklace or two. My fiancée is a big fan of *Domain*." Noticing he had her attention, the man drew out his wallet and said the four most heavenly words in any language, "Money is no object."

Reyah set the Wishstone next to Her laptop and hurried over to the counter.

Within the Wishstone's crystal facets, fire bloomed, air and water danced, and lichen flowered. The Wishstone expanded in light and heat, and spun away to a shadowy corner of the booth. The egg whirled and glittered until it gathered the shadows in the corner around itself like a midnight velvet bag. It disappeared.

BONG

Reyah paused in the middle of verifying the customer's credit card. The customer raised an eyebrow.

"Fire alarm?" he asked.

Reyah handed him the slip to sign. "Probably one of the music booths," She said. Full of trepidation, She glanced at Her laptop. The Wishstone no longer rested beside Her computer.

The man nodded as he collected his merchandise and wandered off. Reyah stared blankly at the credit slip.

Well, shit. Somehow She'd made a wish. What was it She'd said? Something about wishing for the right nine women for Domain. She tucked the slip into Her cash box and sat down. She patted the pocket of Her caftan and was relieved to feel the Wishstone. At least it'd come back to Her. You couldn't always count on that after a wish.

Reyah opened a new window on her laptop. Maybe it was just as well She hadn't made a more detailed wish. Some of Her worst experiences had come when She'd tried to manipulate the Wishstone.

The screen of her laptop blinked. On the other side of the universe, a short, red-haired woman in a gown of pale blue silk knelt in a circular room of faceted quartz. Rainbows shifted from plane to plane across the walls. The woman's eyes were closed.

Her lips moved as if she were praying. Reyah put away Her annoyance with Her uncompleted wish. It was time to blow some smoke up Jagger's and Alfred's asses.

"*Hear me, My Voice,*" Reyah poured Her words directly into the Voice's mind. "*You must warn My Chosen to prepare, for a great evil threatens Domain. There will be pain and sorrow for all if it is not stopped. Remember: one and nine. One and nine. One to rend and nine to mend.*"

The woman in the crystal room opened her eyes. "Your Voice shall speak as she is bid, Great Mother," she said.

Reyah smiled and closed the window. "There now," Reyah cackled. "Things will work out for the best. The Wishstone always delivers. The nine I need will come soon."

"Oh wow! All the comforts of home!" a high-pitched, female voice squealed. Reyah peered down the aisle at the Immortal Productions booth. A shaggy-haired young woman, wearing thick glasses and baggy overall shorts weighted down with fan pins plopped herself in front Michael Ryan. "I'm a big fan of yours, you know," she chirped. "I wrote all the Deryk sections in the Barasheban Horde's guide to *Domain* fan fiction. I even know all your spells by heart."

"Amazing. I can never get them straight myself. Hmm, this Barasheban Horde—not familiar. Slash or hetero?"

"Slash, of course, though the guide covers everything: male/female, male/male, and I think somebody has Deryk doing it with a boa constrictor. But my group is mostly Roarke and Alfred slash. See!" The young woman spun around, giving Michael a full view of her backpack, which Reyah vaguely remembered had pictures on it. "One of the girls is faboo with Photoshop. Doesn't it look like Alfred and Roarke are actually kissing?"

Michael pushed his glasses up the bridge of his nose and peered at the backpack. In a voice pitched to carry to the back rows of a large theater, he read, "Alfred and Roarke 4-Ever." Michael chortled. "Oh, excellent!"

A burst of feminine laughter drew Reyah's attention to the mask maker's booth located next to Eric. There were four women in the booth. Reyah recognized two of them from the night before, Thea and Liz. A well-padded thirty-something brunette laced into an elaborate Elizabethan gown set an eagle-beaked mask on the counter. A tall, chestnut-haired young woman with the face of a Murillo angel offered the brunette a purple horned headdress.

A sly look crossed Thea's face. She leaned over and said something to the brunette in the Elizabethan gown which sparked a fresh burst of hilarity. Reyah noticed the four women sported large blue pins. "DoR" was inscribed in two-inch white letters in the center of each pin. Thea and Liz had worn the same pins last night.

"Hmmm," Reyah murmured, "those girls could be just what the Wishstone ordered. I'll just call them over and check."

Reyah bent Her will in Thea's and Liz's direction. Liz folded her arms across her chest and fixed her gaze on a black and silver mask. Thea stared at the same mask. She rubbed the back of her neck. Neither woman moved.

Odd. Reyah straightened in Her chair. Could it be those two had real power and not the pale imitation She usually found on this little mudball of a planet? She waited a few minutes, until Thea and Liz were relaxed and distracted by the other two women. This time, instead of trying to impose Her will, She delicately probed.

Booyah! Had She hit the jackpot or what? Wishstone material, no doubt about it. Thea was a natural healer. Almost as soon as Reyah stopped trying to force Thea and Liz into Her booth, Thea turned her attention to Anna Randall, the woman in the Elizabethan gown. Reyah "listened" in. Anna was upset over something Eric Bernard had done when she'd visited his booth. No surprise there. Eric was a prick.

Thea comforted Anna with jokes and feather light "accidental" touches on Anna's arm. Every time Thea touched Anna, the brunette's hurt and outrage eased.

This was good. This was very good. Sure, Reyah would have to give Thea a new face and body to accomplish what She had in mind, but so what? Transubstantiation was a goddess's stock in trade.

The same applied to Anna. Who, Reyah was pleased to note, was much easier to read than Thea. Not that Anna was a pushover, oh no. There was quite a strong will and sense of balance under all the purple satin and black lace of her Elizabethan gown. In a word, the lady had class. Reyah hummed with approval. Another keeper.

The oddest sensation, like someone was watching *Her*, fluttered against Reyah's perception. Reyah caught a flash of Liz asking herself *What the hell?*

Reyah chuckled. Why the little minx! Liz was a natural telepath. If they were on Domain, Liz's gift would barely qualify as pitiful. But here on Earth— Outstanding! As far as Reyah could tell, Liz was untrained. Yet somehow she had tuned into Reyah's mental frequency. And just as quickly tuned out.

The tall chestnut-haired beauty whispered in Liz's ear. Reyah pulled the name out of the dear child's head, Marisol Santiago. Marisol had a core of sweetness Reyah found most attractive. Her boys would too, bless their horny little hearts. What Reyah liked best about Marisol was She could practically walk into the girl's mind and make

Herself at home. Here was Her ticket to getting all four women to Her booth. Four down, five to go. Reyah wondered what the others would be like. She could hardly wait to find out.

ℰᏻᏣ

Reyah smiled as Marisol dithered over the collection of painted fans in her booth. "Your grandmother is a very lucky woman to have a granddaughter buying presents for her," Reyah said, lightly bespelling the words to aid Her interrogation. "Are you her only grandchild?"

"Not a chance," Marisol replied. "I've got enough sisters, brothers and cousins to fill the Orange Bowl, and since I'm the youngest, they spend all of their free time sticking their noses into my business. I've been selling real estate for six years—even before I graduated college. Last year I closed more deals than anyone else in the firm. But to hear my family talk, you'd think I was six years old. You should've heard them when I said I was coming to the con!" Marisol's laughter was as light as the retro fragrance of her Anais Anais perfume. "My brother Miguel caught me checking your web site before I left and accused me of joining a cult."

Liz arched an eyebrow. "A divinity with a web site?"

"When in Rome, dearie."

"Touche," Liz said, touching a finger to her forehead in a small salute.

"Why does your brother think you joined a cult, dear?" Reyah asked Marisol.

"Mainly because I'm one of the nine Daughters of Reyah. It's an unofficial fan club devoted to *Domain*. See?" Marisol unhooked the DoR pin from the shoulder strap of her knit top. So *that's* what those buttons meant.

"Bingo," Reyah muttered.

"Excuse me?" Marisol said.

"Clearing my throat, dearie. Is the rest of your group at the con?"

"Marisol," Liz said, the slightest hint of command in her voice, "we don't want to bore Madame Reyah. It's such a fan girl thing."

Marisol blinked and shook her head as if Liz's voice alone was enough to restore the younger woman's inhibitions. *That would never do.* Reyah patted Marisol's hand, re-establishing control. "No, no, my dear. Please, continue. I'm fascinated, I assure you."

Thea joined Liz at the counter. "Marisol will be fine. Want to go check out the corset booth? Bet they still have the matching corset and skirt you've been lusting after."

"Oh God, don't remind me. I don't think my credit card can stand the heat."

"C'mon. Live a little. Think how good it'll make you look."

"Fine, fine, you've talked me into it." Liz paused at the entrance of Reyah's booth. "Play nice," she said to Reyah. "They're our friends, and we love them."

Reyah nodded. She could take a hint. Whether or not She heeded it was a horse of a different color. She said to Marisol, "Tell me about the Daughters of Reyah. After all, I have a personal interest."

Anna and Marisol giggled.

"There's nine of us, naturally—for the eight Vanyr and Lord Alfred. I feel like I've known the girls forever, even though we all just met for the first time at breakfast," Anna said.

"Wasn't that fun? We've been trying to figure out how to meet each other for ages," Marisol burbled. "I don't know why we didn't think of a con until Liz suggested it."

"Anyway, back to the Daughters of Reyah—Thea Gardner founded the group," Anna continued. "She works for a computer help desk. She's divorced, but she didn't get any money from it, bless her heart. For her Daughters of Reyah fanfic, Thea uses the name 'Bastet', because she's a mage who can transform herself into cats—everything from a house cat to a saber-toothed tiger."

"You talk about divorce like a veteran," Reyah commented.

"I've been a through a few battles," Anna said. "That's why I chose the cyber-identity of 'Circe' for my fan fiction. There was a girl who knew how to handle men."

"Not to mention Circe was a sorceress," Marisol added. "Sort of fits in with Anna being Wiccan in real life, you know?"

"Interesting." Reyah pointed to Marisol. "What about you? What's your, er, cyber-identity?"

"I'm a weather elemental," Marisol said. "I've got this weird mojo in real life. I always seem to know when the weather is going to change or a storm is coming. I figured, why not for my fan fiction too?"

"And Liz?" Reyah asked.

"Liz is a widow." Marisol paused. "Funny how it all worked out. None of us are attached right now. Liz is the Daughters of Reyah's mind mage. Sort of like Jagger, only she came up with the idea long before they introduced him on the show. I get the feeling they're going to make him more powerful than she is, though. Liz only went in for mind-reading, illusion and some minor league telekinesis. Oh yeah, and ferrets."

Reyah wondered if she'd heard Marisol correctly. "What do ferrets have to do with mind magic?"

"Darned if I know. Liz's cyber-character likes to turn bad guys into them."

"I guess it makes sense. It'll certainly be irresistible to Jagger," Reyah mumbled.

"What did you say?"

"I said, what about the rest? You did say there were nine of you, right? Are any of the other Daughters of Reyah at the con? I'd love to meet more of My girls."

Marisol scanned the exhibit hall and pointed to one of the larger sword and armor booths. "Two of the girls are over there. The brunette dressed like Lara Croft with the double holsters on her hips—that's Sarah Blake. She calls herself 'Nemesis'. She's a lawyer in real life, so I guess it figures. Look, why don't I call them over?"

Sarah flashed a strained smile in response to Marisol's beckoning wave. In front of the booth, a shorter, much younger woman with shoulder-length blonde hair paced her way through an elaborate kata with a plastic sword.

"The one with the light saber who looks like a Buffy wannabe is Kait Williams. She's our swordmistress, 'Sekhmet'. She's the warrior with Thea's pod. That's how we're organized, in three pods of three. Each pod has a warrior, an elemental and a mage. In theory, anyway. Sarah and I work with Liz, but I usually write with Anna, and Sarah does her own stuff. She's big on Deryk. Kait and Free—"

"Speaking of Free, have you seen her lately?" The question was asked by a woman who might have seemed tall if she hadn't been standing next to the five-foot-ten Marisol. Loose curls the color of polished mahogany framed the serene features of a Celtic Madonna.

Reyah shook Her head. By this point, the tiny thread of magic coursing through the newcomer didn't surprise Her. What did surprise Her was the fact it tasted somehow familiar.

"I haven't seen Free since breakfast," Marisol told the newcomer.

"Me either," Anna added. "Did you try the *Domain* track?" The newcomer shook her head.

"While you're here, let me introduce to you to Madame Reyah," Marisol said. "Madame Reyah, this is Brigid Lawrence, Anna's warrior."

One of Brigid's elegant eyebrows lifted. Reyah knew mischief when She saw it, and She saw it in this woman's hazel eyes. Brigid made an elaborate bow. "Nice to meet you, Madame Reyah. And so close to Alfred and Deryk too."

Reyah chuckled.

"What's happening?" Kait asked as she and Sarah walked into the booth. "Isn't it almost time for the Crossed Swords panel?"

"I'll go get Thea and Liz," Anna said. "They're next door."

"We're missing Free and Pandora," Brigid said. "Have you seen them?"

"Maybe Free is still in her room," Marisol suggested.

"Too easy," Brigid said. "I was supposed to meet her and Pandora at the one o'clock Cruxshadows' panel, but those two never showed."

"I'm sure they're around here somewhere," Marisol said.

A woman's enraged shriek split the air.

"That's what I'm afraid of," Brigid said.

ℰℂ

He was perfect. Simply perfect.

From the top of his light brown hair to the tips of his sexy, sexy toes (in a great-looking pair of Birkenstock sandals), Frieda Talbot—Free to her friends—thought Stefan Warnar was nothing but sheer perfection, all six-foot-three inches of him.

Free sighed as Stefan smiled at an old lady holding out a photo of Vanyr Theron. Free loved the sparkle in Stefan's green eyes and the curve of his finely chiseled lips. In fact there wasn't a thing about Stefan Free didn't love to distraction—with perhaps the small exception of his very pregnant wife. *And yet,* Free reflected dreamily, *even Stefan's wife only proved how marvelous the man is, what a wonderful husband and lover and all-around great human being...*

"Hey chick, you in line or what?"

Free jumped. A beefy guy dressed as one of Reyah's Thousand frowned down at her. The guy stank of dried sweat and beer.

"Like, you know, if you're in line, that's cool," the guy rumbled. "But if not, why not make some room for the rest of us?"

Two acne-spotted girls wearing robes Free supposed were meant to look like those worn by the Voice's handmaidens nodded.

"Yeah, get outta the way."

"Line hog."

Free ducked her head and scuttled back. "Sorry," she mumbled. The beefy guy and the two spotty females pushed forward, followed by a horde of other fans waiting to get an autograph from the German actor.

Free didn't blame them. Hadn't she gotten to Atlanta a day early to attend a signing for Stefan's latest children's book? Hadn't she waited for over three hours to get her copy signed? Of course, she'd been standing in front of the bookstore for over two hours before he'd been scheduled to sign, which meant she got to be the first fan he saw. She'd been the first fan he saw today, too. Free glowed as she remembered Stefan's comment when she presented her most cherished photo to him.

"Ah, you come to the con too. Loyal fans such as yourself are very special, yes?"

Oh, but you're even more special, Free thought. Of course she hadn't said it *out loud,* not with Stefan's wife sitting right next to him and all the people standing in line. That would've been too embarrassing. Too personal. All she'd done was nod and move to the back of the line after Stefan handed back the photo. But now, after an hour of watching Stefan sign photos, t-shirts and almost everything else (including one overdeveloped hussy's chest, which Stefan's wife had seemed to find hilarious, but which Free found totally disgusting), Free had all but convinced herself she had said it and the actor had been flattered by the comment.

Ah, but I'm not, Stefan would've, should've, could've replied. *It is you who are the most special, fantastic, wonderful fan an actor could ever have.* Free closed her eyes and hugged Stefan's photo to her chest. Stefan's wife faded away into never-existed-land. The walking shorts and golf shirt Stefan wore disappeared, replaced by the silver-gray robes favored by Vanyr Theron.

In Free's mind, her overweight, dowdy, outer shell vanished, replaced by the slender, beautiful, vivacious, red-haired elven princess she always dreamed of being. Stefan/Theron reverently clasped Free's small, soft hand and brought it to his lips. *Ah, my lovely one,* he murmured. *I must ask you a question, a question close to my heart, a question you and only you can answer.*

Yes? Fantasy Fairy Free breathed, her dimpled knees turning to apple butter from the warmth of Stefan's lips on her creamy skin. *What is it you want to ask me?*

"Why are you still hanging around staring at SW? You were supposed to meet Brigid and me at the Cruxshadows panel over an hour ago!"

Only a minute ago Free would've said she'd do anything to get Stefan's attention. Now as Pandora Keaton's chainsaw voice ripped through Free's fantasy, she realized that wasn't true. Why, why, *why* did Pandora have to bellow loud enough to be heard three states away? Free felt the mother of all blushes staining her cheeks as most of the people standing in the autograph line—and Stefan himself—turned to look in their direction.

"Will you lower your voice?" Free whispered to Pandora. "People are starting to stare!"

"I wasn't yelling. I was asking you a question. You *promised* to spend some time with the group. But here you are again. Are you gonna waste the whole day staring at Stefan?"

"I have not spent the whole day staring at Stefan," Free hissed, trying to pull Pandora away from Stefan's table. At that moment, Free genuinely hated Pandora. How dare she come and make Free's life miserable? Oh God, oh God, oh God, now people were whispering too. Even Stefan's wife was looking at them.

Pandora dug in her heels and refused to budge. "Puh-leeze. Who's the one who boasted she was going to be the first in SW's line for the whole con? Who's the one who only stayed for about five minutes at breakfast then booked?" Pandora shook her head. "You missed out on a lot of fun, you know. The Daughters of Reyah *rawk*."

"Whatever." Free had but one goal now—to get Pandora as far away from Stefan as possible. With luck and thousands of fans clamoring for his attention, he'd forget about this incident. Free wouldn't be able to bear it if she couldn't be the first one at Stefan's booth tomorrow morning. She just couldn't bear it.

"Look, I thought we were supposed to be meeting Brigid," Free said, tugging harder on Pandora's arm. "Let's go find her. Now."

"Geez, Free, will you stop trying to pull my arm out of its socket? Gimme a sec. Before we meet Brigid I need something to drink."

"A drink is good. I'm thirsty too. Let's go get one. Now. Right this minute."

"I don't have to go get one." Pandora pulled a red and white can of soda from her backpack. "I cached a few in my pack in case of an emergency. You want one?"

"Not here," Free said, noting with relief Stefan was signing things again. "Let's go find Brigid, and I'll have one then."

"But I'm thirsty *now*. And I want to get Stefan to autograph my slash group's anthology." Pandora raised the hand holding the cola and waved it at Stefan. "Hey Stefan," she yodeled, "would'ja sign a great slash story featuring you and Vallenius? The love scenes in it are incredible!"

Free could've died. The entire world turned and stared at her and Pandora. Free grabbed Pandora's arms. "We are going to find Brigid and we're going to find her now. Get moving!" Free spun Pandora around and shoved her into the aisle.

Unfortunately, two things occurred. Pandora popped the top on her cola, and Lydia Jambon, a.k.a. Megeara the Demon Witch from *Domain*, barreled up the aisle carrying a large box of eight-by-ten glossies.

Pandora and Lydia crashed into each other. Lydia toppled into an incense and perfume booth. The box of glossies hit the floor and exploded over the aisle. The cola fell from Pandora's hand, spraying sticky brown syrup over the photos, Lydia and half the bystanders. Oily puddles of patchouli and sandalwood filmed over the cola, adding a sickly sweet smell to the mess.

Free blanched. Of all the people she could've shoved Pandora into, that pale-eyed, surgically enhanced scarecrow was the absolute worst. Fans traded horror stories about Lydia's poisonous temper on every *Domain* email list known to Free—and Free was pretty sure she knew them all. Fan boys might obsess over the way the Demon Witch's skin-tight outfits never quite covered her swimsuit model figure, but they tread carefully around the real life article.

Right now the real life article was sitting on the floor, her white spandex pantsuit covered with brown cola stains. Blue oil dripped from a bottle snagged in the rats' nest of Lydia's overpermed hair.

"My photos! Look at my photos! Do you cretins understand what you've done? Do you know how much those photos cost? Someone is going to pay for this! And I'm going to personally take it out of their hide! Who did this? Who? Let me get my hands on the sorry bastards, and I'll rip their idiotic hides from their bodies and grind them into dog meat!"

Free could've sworn she saw red sparks flying from Lydia's spooky gray eyes. Pandora began making funny little grunting noises which sounded like "no, no, no, no" under her breath.

Lydia staggered to her feet. "I'll give a hundred dollars to whoever shows me who did this!"

To Free's horror, fingers started aiming in her and Pandora's direction. Now it was Pandora's turn to grab Free's arm.

"We've got to get out of here! She'll massacre us!"

"We have to make things right," Free said. "Look at all the photos we ruined!"

"She's selling those things at twenty bucks a pop! That's a couple of thousand dollars we trashed! I don't have that kind of money, do you?" Pandora yanked Free's arm. "Come on, Free. If she catches us she'll get us kicked out of the con!"

Free couldn't take her eyes off Lydia. The actress's head whipped back and forth like a snake as she tried to follow all the pointing fingers. Free had a feeling this would be her last best chance to confess, but she couldn't move. It was like she was under one of Megeara's spells.

"She could get us kicked out of the con?" Free whispered.

"Yes!" Pandora let go of Free's arm and began to push on Free's back. "Come on, come on, *come on*! We gotta find a place to hide 'til the con people settle Lydia down!"

Free shook her head and opened her mouth to argue.

But another voice spoke before she could. "What has happened here?"

Free's heart took wing. Of course, Stefan would come to the rescue. Why had she ever doubted him? Stefan would take care of everything like he had so many times on the show. Then Free saw the shocked look on Stefan's handsome, beloved face. Her airborne heart took a nosedive straight to her tennis shoes. Free wished the ground would open up and swallow her.

"Make up your minds. Was it a man and a woman or two women?" Lydia screeched. "What do you mean you're not sure? One had red hair and the other had brown? That's all I need to know. Let me at them!" Lydia surged toward Free and Pandora.

Pandora gave one frightened bleat and ran. A bunch of other fans ran too—most notably those with red or brown hair. Free was ready to stand her ground until the absolute worst happened.

Stefan looked at her and shook his head. Free bit back a sob. He knew! Stefan knew it was her fault! Free's world fell with a crash. Unable to bear the look on Stefan's face and the thought he would now hate her forever, Free turned and ran.

Chapter Four

The Klingons led the way, shouting unintelligible war cries. A flock of black-clad, powder and paint pale Goths pelted down the aisle right behind them. Stormtroopers and chainmail-clad knights of Reyah's Thousand pounded close on the Goths' heels, followed by a swirl of terrified chiffon-, satin- and silk-bedecked females clutching their skirts in front of them.

Reyah strengthened the wards around Her booth—and not a minute too soon. The electricity started to flicker as displays crashed to the ground in the wake of the stampede. Eric Bernard and his assistant barely managed to catch his television set before it crushed them both. The corset-maker and her husband sat stunned on the floor of their booth amid a welter of fabric and overturned dummies. The mask maker cringed as two masks got caught in the cross-draft and were ground into bits of lace and feathers right before her eyes.

Another hideous shriek rent the air. The horde wailed in reply and ran even faster from the horror pursuing them. For behind them, reeking of cola, patchouli, gardenia and enough musk to gag an ox was *Lydia Jambon*.

Reyah blinked. She hadn't seen the like since the real Demon Witch Megeara attacked a small town in Thrall. The crush of humanity that'd tried to escape from the demons ravaging their homes had looked and acted much the same.

Brigid stepped in front of Reyah and scanned the herd. "I knew it," Brigid said. "I knew at least one of them had to be in the middle of this mess."

Thea rose on her tiptoes. Her eyes widened. She shouted, "Pandora, Free! Over here!"

Two women tumbled into the booth. Reyah recognized the skinny, overall-clad young woman who'd been showing Michael Ryan her backpack. An overly plump twenty-something female with chemically induced red hair followed Overalls.

"Hide us!" Overalls mewled. "She'll kill us if she catches us!"

Forgetting she was wearing a backpack, Overalls tried to dive under the table holding Reyah's credit card machine and business cards. Machine and cards went flying.

Before Reyah could protest, Marisol and Anna grabbed the arms of the plump redhead and hustled her to the back of the booth. They proceeded to cover her with every shawl and blanket on Reyah's shelves. Sarah and Kait pushed a large, carved kelan-wood chest beside Reyah's table, obscuring the ridiculous backpack and boat-sized feet sticking out from under the rucked tablecloth.

Liz, Thea and Brigid ranged themselves across the entrance to the booth, barring the only way in or out.

"Now listen here," Reyah began.

"What the hell is going on?" Sarah asked. "Why is everyone running from Lydia Jambon?"

"My fault," the plump redhead moaned. "All my fault. Now he'll never speak to me again."

"What's your fault, Free?" Marisol asked.

"We're going to get kicked out of the con and Stefan will never speak to me again, and it's all my fault!"

"Yeah," a muffled voice agreed from under the table, "it's all Free's fault."

"Where are they?" Lydia screeched. "Come back here, you fucktards! You're gonna pay!" The actress stomped past, intent on a group of fans who managed to get hemmed in by security. Two security guards, braver or dumber than the rest, muscled their way in front of Lydia, blocking her access to the crowd.

"God, what a stink," Liz said

"In more ways than one," Brigid agreed.

"Will one of you, please, tell us what happened?" Anna demanded. "Why was everyone running? What's all the brown and blue stuff on La Boner?"

"Free threw me at Lydia," Pandora stage whispered from under the table.

"Did not," Free said. "It was your fault."

"Was not. Then all Lydia's pictures fell on the floor, and my Coke spilled on them. And then Lydia fell on a perfume table, and all that stuff spilled on her and the pictures and then she got completely mad, and she said she'd grind whoever did it into dog meal and get them kicked out of the con and…"

Reyah shook Her head. This was unacceptable. She was going to have to replace four of the nine. What in the world was wrong with the Wishstone? Only five of the nine women were suitable. She'd read Sarah's and Kait's hearts. Sarah was too bitter, too damaged. Kait was too young, too feckless. And now these two. She didn't even want to contemplate what they were too much of.

"If they kick you out, they kick us all out," Thea said over her shoulder. "Accidents happen all the time. I'll be damned if I stay at a convention that would kick out fans for an accident."

"Not to mention the lawsuit I'll throw on the convention's and Lydia's butts," Sarah added.

"We'll work something out," Liz said sotto voce. "Cons have insurance for things like this. I doubt they'll be pissy, but worst case scenario, we can always hit the Atlanta Underground and make our own fun."

Reyah sighed. She should've known. Dealing with mortals was never easy. There was no way She was letting the five She wanted get away. Time was of the essence. Who knew what mischief Deryk was getting into or how close Jagger was to getting his hands on Her bracelet?

"Tell you what girls," Reyah said. "Why don't I go over and calm Ms. Jambon down? I'm sure I can persuade her to let the convention reimburse her. No one will get into trouble, and you can enjoy the rest of the weekend."

"No," Free sobbed, hiding her face behind a fistful of the best ankhoret shawl in the booth. "I'll never be able to show my face at his booth again. I want to *die*."

Reyah frowned. "Young lady, those shawls are dry clean only. You stain it, you buy it."

Marisol gently pulled the shawl away from Free's face and dabbed Free's tears with a tissue. "It's okay," Marisol crooned. "Don't cry. We'll figure out something."

"Well?" Reyah asked Liz and Thea. The two women exchanged a long look and stepped away from the opening.

Reyah sailed down the aisle. First things first. Get rid of the actress, then find a way to detach the unwanted four women. Maybe She could arrange for Sarah, Kait, Free and Pandora to be caught in an elevator at the Hyatt. They didn't call it "Elevator Hell" for nothing.

"What about my photos?" Lydia yelled. "Those photos cost me a thousand…" A calculating look crossed Lydia's face. "No six…no…fifteen thousand dollars!"

Lydia grated on Reyah's nerves almost as much as the monster she portrayed on the show. Luckily, this world's "Demon Witch" was merely petty and egotistical. The real Demon Witch had been a complete sociopath, homicidally contemptuous of any life but her own. Reyah sniffed. What Deryk had seen in the murderous hussy was beyond Her. The boy had no taste when it came to women, no taste at all.

"I'm not leaving until I catch the scum who cost me twenty thousand dollars," Lydia insisted. "And that's that."

"Can I be of some help here?" Reyah smiled at the guards and *pushed* Her will into their minds. "I'm on the con committee."

"Why thank you, ma'am," the guards chorused. "We'd be glad for your help."

Lydia's pale gray eyes narrowed, emphasizing the fact she was overdue on her Botox injections. "What do you think you're doing?"

Reyah bent Her will in Lydia's direction. Lydia didn't even twitch. "I only talk to big dogs," Lydia said. "Get the con chairman down here. Now!"

Another one? Reyah grumbled to Herself. What was it about Dragon*Con that managed to attract so many people with rudimentary magic? Whatever, it wasn't going to help Lydia. Reyah was going to take her rudimentary magic and shove it where the sun didn't shine. The goddess mentally pushed up Her sleeves and prepared to take the annoying bitch down.

"Really, dearie," She cooed, "there's no need to be rude." Reyah put Her hand on Lydia's shoulder.

And the world turned upside down.

ෂൟ

"Maybe I should turn myself in," Free moaned. "Stefan would want me to do the right thing."

"And getting kicked out of the con because of an accident is the right thing?" Liz muttered to Thea. Liz sagged against the edge of the table like she needed the support.

"You feel it too," Thea said. "It's easier to breathe when she's gone."

Liz gave Thea a startled look. "You're right. It's like there was an iron band around my head." Liz rubbed two fingers against her forehead. "I felt it last night too."

Thea noticed Liz knew exactly which "she" Thea meant. Funny, the band of iron Thea felt whenever Reyah was around circled her heart, not her head.

"Stefan wouldn't want you to be unhappy, Free," Marisol said very firmly, as if she was talking to a small child. "He'd want you to have fun and enjoy the con. You know how he feels about his fans."

"Can the pity party," Sarah said. "Stefan Warner doesn't know Free's alive and doesn't care. As long as Lydia doesn't find out it who did it, why should anyone turn themselves in and ruin the weekend for the rest of us?"

Blood drained from Free's face. "Stefan knows who I am," she whispered. "He has to."

"As if. Like he'd notice..."

"Sarah. Shut. Up."

Sarah flinched at the whip crack of Liz's voice. Free burst into tears. Not the pitiful snuffles she'd been doing before, but huge rasping sobs. It hurt Thea just to hear them.

"I thought Dragon*Con would be perfect," Free cried. "I thought it would be like our fan fiction. I thought we'd be like sisters. Why couldn't it be like that?"

Marisol supplied more tissues, while Anna rubbed Free's back, glaring at Sarah all the while. "We *are* like sisters," Marisol soothed. "Even sisters fight. This is only a little problem."

"That's right, sugah," Anna said.

"But it will never be all right with Stefan, ever again," Free mourned.

"Yes, it will. I can fix it. In fact, I can fix everything!" Pandora announced. Pandora's head popped up from behind the chest. She scrambled to her feet clutching what appeared to be a radiant crystal egg the size of an orange.

At least that's what Thea thought Pandora was holding. But Thea couldn't be certain. There was something wrong with the lights. Thea guessed someone had tripped over a wire in the stampede. Most of the overhead lights had dimmed—except for the lights in the front of Michael Ryan's booth, which sputtered intermittently over Reyah, Lydia and a couple of guys wearing headsets.

Some of the booth lights in the next aisle popped in flashes of red, and the air smelled faintly of burning rubber. The funky little lights nestled in the gauze canopy over Reyah's booth took on a blue cast.

From her post at the entrance to the booth, Brigid inquired, "What have you got in your hand, Pandora?"

"It's a Wishstone," Pandora said. "It found me under the table."

It found her? Liz rubbed her forehead harder.

"I guess something worse could've found her," Thea replied.

Name one.

"Lydia," Thea said.

You have a point.

Thea looked at Liz. Something odd had happened, but Thea couldn't quite put her finger on what it was.

"How can you make everything right with something that doesn't exist?" Free asked. "Besides, if I were going to make a wish, it wouldn't be to fix what's wrong now, it'd be to go to Domain. As Freya, Mistress of Leaf and Vine. I'd be beautiful, and Stefan would love me, and I'd be happy."

Kait frowned. "Don't you mean 'Theron'?"

Pandora shook a dusty finger at Kait. "Don't confuse her with details. I *like* Free's wish."

"As a matter of fact, so do I," Sarah said. "If I were my fan fiction character, I'd get so lucky I'd be bow-legged."

Why do I have a bad feeling about this? Thea massaged the back of her neck.

"You aren't the only one," Liz replied, chafing her arms as if she were cold.

"Only one what?" Brigid asked.

"Like Thea said, I've got a bad feeling about this wish stuff."

Brigid took a step back from Liz and Thea. "Oh. Like Thea *said*. Uh huh, okay, whatever, Liz." Brigid's expression clearly indicated something wasn't right.

"Don't be a party pooper, Liz," Anna chimed in. "I'd love to get my hands on the *real* Alfred."

"And I could have cool armor and a kick-ass sword." Kait put her hand to her forehead and pretended to swoon. "I'm in!"

"If we really could go, wouldn't that be something?" Marisol said.

"Yeah, it would, wouldn't it," Brigid agreed.

"Good! Everybody's got the same wish," Pandora said. "Now all we have to do is figure out how we want to say it."

"Not everybody," Kait pointed out. "Liz and Thea haven't said they want to go."

For a minute, Thea could've sworn she heard Liz arguing with herself. A mischievous grin spread across Liz's face. *We're going to regret this, you know.*

And your point is?

"We're in," Thea and Liz said at the same time.

"You guys are spooky," Kait complained. "Don't you think you're carrying the shared brain thing a little too far?"

"Shared brain, schmared brain. Are we ready to make the wish or what?" Keeping a tight hold on the crystal, Pandora shrugged off her backpack. She handed it to Kait. "Put this someplace safe."

Pandora set the crystal in the middle of the table. "Brig, would you move the chest? We need enough room so everybody can put a finger on the Wishstone."

"Any finger?" Liz asked as they gathered around the silk-draped table.

"Can we sing 'Kumbaya' while we're at it?" Thea said, trying to ignore the prickles of electricity emanating from the crystal. She didn't know why the crystal egg felt that way. It didn't feel evil, just…well, sparkly. Maybe there was a storm brewing, and the static electricity was what affected the lights. Thea didn't want to consider the other possible explanation her all too fertile imagination offered.

"Would you guys quit joking around? This is *serious*." Pandora took a deep breath and closed her eyes. "Let us begin," Pandora intoned. "Hear us, oh Wishstone. We, the Daughters of Reyah, wish to go to Domain—the real Domain…"

Brigid sang, "Not the fake Domain, but the real Domain."

"Hush," Anna snapped.

"The *real* Domain," Pandora repeated, "As the *real* Daughters of Reyah, with all the powers and abilities…"

"And beauty," Free interrupted. "Don't forget beauty."

"Damn straight," Anna said. Thea recalled Anna had won several beauty contests in college.

"And don't forget the youth." Sarah tapped her finger on the Wishstone for emphasis. "We want to be young too. Twenty-five, tops,"

"You got all that?" Anna asked.

Pandora opened her eyes and glared at Anna, Free and Sarah. "…as the *real* Daughters of Reyah, with all the powers and abilities and youth and beauty we wrote for our fan fiction characters and much, *much* more." Pandora cocked her head at the group. "Okay?"

"Okay."

"Wishstone, make it so."

Chapter Five

On the northern slope of Mount Tuumb

Deryk bellowed over wind and thunder: "Ricte macha klaatu. Bishta vorum, Kalinida." The clouds over his head began to spin, forming a vortex over the chanting Vanyr. Suddenly the wind died. The vortex continued to spin, growing darker and darker as Deryk held a hand over the brazier.

"With my blood, I call thee, Megeara." Deryk drew the knife across his palm, savoring the rush and burn of the cinder-laden air against the shallow wound. He pressed the cut until three drops of blood fell into the fire. "With my blood I name thee Megeara."

Another three drops fell into the brazier. "With my blood I bind thee, Megeara!" he shouted, allowing a final three drops of blood to fall. The fire in the brazier exploded upward, roaring and surging until it was a pillar of twisting flames reaching into the heart of the vortex.

Deryk fell to his knees as the tower began to shake. The clouds around the vortex spun faster drawing the seemingly endless pillar of flame upward. With another loud roar, the flame broke free of the brazier and spiraled into the clouds. Deryk chanted the invocation over and over, his gaze locked on the copper bracelet lying in the center of the hexagram chiseled into the granite floor.

Red bolts of lightning blasted down from the swirling black mass of clouds and struck the bracelet inside the magical diagram. The lightning pounded the metal band until it glowed white against the crimson heat rising from the stone beneath. The light emanating from the bracelet and the stone tiles grew brighter and brighter. After-images of impossible geometries seemed to solidify as the lightning seared down.

The wind rose again, howling insanely as it whirled around the top of the tower. The light in the hexagram intensified further. Deryk tried to shield his face, but the light passed through and around his hands. He could see the brightness through his closed eyelids, and the metallic scent of scorched earth filled his nostrils.

A thunderous explosion rocked the tower, throwing Deryk to the floor. The tower groaned and swayed, rolling the Vanyr around like a pea on a plate. Silence fell, as complete and absolute as within a tomb.

ഗ)ൡ

In the Dragon*Con Exhibit Hall

Reyah braced herself against the magic exploding around her. She couldn't believe Deryk had the nerve to activate Jagger's teleportation spell the day before Her birthday, much less that he possessed the magical ommph to cast the spell this far.

Reyah jerked Her hand from Lydia's arm. What with the red energies enveloping Lydia in front of Her and the blue energies gathering behind Her, a goddess had to be careful or She could get sucked someplace nasty.

Wait a minute. What blue energies behind Her? Reyah whirled in time to hear Overalls say, "Wishstone, make it so."

Every machine in the room went crazy. Half the overhead lights exploded, filling the air with the smell of charred plastic and ozone. The remaining lights started to strobe. Video cassettes shot from their players, spewing tape like rocket-powered spaghetti. CDs and DVDs whizzed around the room like flying saucers. Disbelieving Her own senses, Reyah twisted the pockets of Her caftan inside out. This couldn't be happening. The Wishstone had to be in Her pocket. She'd felt it there.

Scenes of Domain—the real Domain—flitted across every video screen. Hawke, Conlan and Roarke fell out of a mid-air Portal onto a table in some low-life tavern. The table collapsed beneath them. Deryk sprawled face-down in front of a column of crimson light. Alfred clung to a battlement while the Keep rocked beneath him. Theron and the priests of the Great Temple in Sevidad Reyj cast spell after spell to keep the temple from crumbling around them. Jagger stood in a circle of blue fire, his arms raised to the heavens, and howled like a wounded beast.

"What the—" Lydia vanished in blast of crimson light and a puff of heavy, musk-scented smoke.

The gauze canopy over Reyah's booth took flight and soared around the room. After an ostentatious roar of thunder, the Wishstone blinded everyone in the room with blue light. When Reyah could see again, the nine women were gone.

"Damn it, I didn't want all of them!" Reyah shouted. "How could the Wishstone do this to Me?"

The hotel's fire alarms and sprinkler system let loose. "Oh, for heaven's sake. Not on My booth," Reyah growled. She waved a hand.

The jets of water redirected by Reyah's magic pummeled Eric Bernard's booth even harder. Eric roared, "God damn it, Lydia, you stupid bint! This time I'm going to sue!"

₱₱

Electric blue light surrounded Thea. Her body felt as light as dandelion fluff, as insubstantial as mist, simultaneously incandescent and yet curiously invisible.

Eventually she became aware she was flying. Eight other presences moved along with her. The blue speck of spirit, of energy, that was Thea Gardner spun through space, soaring past planets and suns, racing past comets and supernovas.

Once a shooting star trailing a crimson tail shot past, sending the nine specks spinning around each other in a confused melee. A thought later, the blue spots containing the essences of nine women righted themselves and resumed their journey toward a blue-white gem centered in the midst of a sparkling necklace of stars. The gem and its sister planets circled a small yellow sun. *How cute*, the speck of energy that was Thea thought, *the little planet in the middle almost looks like Earth*. Then she didn't think at all because the cute little planet zoomed up and smacked her in the face.

₱₱

In Tambara

Deryk's heart pounded as he struggled to his feet. He willed himself to look at the hexagram, afraid of what might be waiting in the magic-bound circle.

"I'll be damned," he said.

Chapter Six

The Old Castle, Reyah's Keep

Alone in his turret laboratory, Vallenius thought longingly of the nice dark space under his bed. He shook his head. No, hiding under the bed was something he'd done as a child. He was an adult now. No matter how scared he was, he had to face up to his responsibilities. Somehow, he was going to have to deal with the stolen spell and the prophecy the Voice had made. He had an awful feeling Deryk was the "One to rend", but who or what were the Nine that would mend? He wasn't ready for this. He'd just passed his Adept's test. Now he was in the middle of something so big it scared the Voice away from the Keep. And she was almost as old as Roarke. Vallenius's empty stomach rolled at the thought.

And kept rolling. The young wizard's skin prickled, and the hair on the back of his neck rose. He shoved himself away from the table and ran to one of the windows. Dark energies swirled along the ley lines, poised and waiting to be called.

Deryk is casting that damned spell. Vallenius's room had been scrubbed clean of magical evidence before he Ported back from the Shadowlands. But Vallenius knew it was Deryk who stole the spell even before a footman courageously came forward and reported he'd seen Deryk, his clothing burnt and smoking, sneaking away from Vallenius's rooms.

Vallenius raced down the gallery leading to the Great Hall of the Old Castle. His magical senses filled his nostrils with the reek of blood and the thin, sharp air of the highest mountaintops. As he ran, images flared in his mind. Ley lines cobwebbed from nodes of power buried beneath the Keep. The lines shuddered and groaned.

A blood red snake of magical energy whipped against the lines. The impact knocked Vallenius to his knees. The red magic struck again. The energies of the Keep ignited. Walls of blue white light shot upward, binding with the red energies and thrusting them into the heavens. A third red coil skimmed over the light and shot into nothingness.

Somewhere in the Keep a caged beast howled in fury and despair. It sounded like a wolf Vallenius once heard in Queen Isabeau's Grand Menagerie. Only Alfred didn't keep a menagerie.

Perhaps this beast was a magical thing, because Vallenius could almost feel its heavy tread over the ley lines. Its footfalls shook the Keep to its foundations and beyond. Vallenius could almost see the beast now, tall as a man and winged like a raptor, with a pelt as black as death. The beast launched itself against the walls of light and was trapped, even as Vallenius was trapped, in the power streaming into the emptiness of heaven.

Only heaven wasn't empty. Life hurtled through the void. Toward Domain. Toward the Keep.

Vallenius didn't notice when his head hit the floor. But it hurt like hell when Willem woke him a little while later. The captain of the guard sat back on his heels and called to the blur of a face half hidden in a doorway. "Brandy and be quick about it," Willem said.

The servant bobbed his head and vanished.

"It's here," Vallenius gasped. The strange shapes of his vision reassembled themselves into coherent thoughts. "Deryk used the spell and called something terrible from someplace. I don't know where. There isn't anything higher than Heaven, is there?"

"Hell if I know," Willem said. "What happened to you? Did you fall when the quake hit? Do you remember the earthquake?

Vallenius's look of shock must have been all the answer Willem needed. The captain of the guard helped Vallenius to a sitting position. The room spun, then appeared to right itself. But the paintings on the wall to Vallenius's left hung at odd angles to the floor. Powdered plaster dusted Vallenius's robes and the area around him.

"It wasn't an earthquake," Vallenius said. "Not a natural quake, at any rate. Deryk caused it when he used the spell."

"Goddess. It felt like it shook the entire world. Is that what it was supposed to do? The spell, I mean."

"I don't think so. I think the quake was a side effect. I can't say for sure, it, but I think it was tangled up with Jagger's Portal spells. What I do know is Deryk brought something here with the spell." Vallenius clutched the front of Willem's doublet. "Maybe the thing Deryk called with the spell is the 'One to rend' the Voice warned about. And there's something else, something even more important. The 'Nine to mend'—they came too."

"You can prove Deryk cast the spell? And his magic's tied to the 'One to rend'? Yes!" Willem shouted. Vallenius's head started hurting again. "Finally, we've got the bastard tied up with a bow!"

"Put it down here," Willem called to the footman carrying a flask and a glass on a silver tray. To Vallenius he said, "Drink this. Once you've got your legs under you, we'll find Alfred and tell him the good news."

"Willem, you're not listening. We've got to find the Nine."

"There's plenty of time to find the Nine. I'm sure Reyah knows where they are. Right now, you and I need to report to Alfred."

North Tower. Roof down. People hurt. Stone fall at the main gate. Hit moat monster's tail. Complaining. Loud. Guests in Eastern Quadrant. Complaining. Just as loud.

The words tumbled into Vallenius's brain like a song progressing through a room full of bards. Only the words were all spoken in the same whispery voice. Oh Goddess, he'd nearly forgotten. Passing his Adept's test had completed the spells that bound him to the Keep. The sound of Willem's voice receded as the damage report grew longer.

"Val. Vallenius!" Willem shook Vallenius none too gently. "Did you hear me? We've got to get moving."

"Can't. The Keep is talking to me."

"Oh shit. How bad is the damage?"

"Bad. The Keep says there are people hurt at the North Tower."

"Damn. I guess Alfred will have to wait. "

ℰℐℭℛ

The magic of the Portals bubbled over Roarke's skin as he walked through the Portal Veil into the Terminus of the Keep. Roarke was amazed he'd been able to Port himself and his two brothers out of danger when Deryk let loose his spell. He still wasn't sure how he managed. Roarke hoped whatever the spell had been, it had fucked up Deryk as bad as it had him. He hadn't a clue when his senses, magical and otherwise, would return to normal.

The glossy marble walls of the Terminus and its eight arched doorways into nothingness—the Portals to the Eight Lands—looked the same as always. But... Roarke sneezed. *Dust? Mildew? Impossible.* Roarke was about to make a comment to Hawke when the cut crystal tones of an all too familiar voice distracted him.

"What do you mean I must wait for Alfred's permission to enter the Keep?" Theron demanded in a voice colder than a Gruende winter. "First, I find myself unable to Port into my chamber. Now I'm being held against my will in the Terminus. Who does that banty rooster think he is?"

Hawke sighed. "Not exactly the first voice I hoped to hear after surviving an avalanche."

"The first voice you heard after the rocks started to fly was the barmaid at the Rasher's Head inquiring after your health," Conlan said.

"Right." Hawke brightened. "Roarke, I never did thank you for Porting us directly to my favorite tavern, did I?"

"Put it on my tab," Roarke said. He strode through the ninth door of the Terminus, the mundane portal leading to the Keep.

It was like swimming against the tide. A thousand different energies pushed against Roarke's chest or tugged at the rags of his clothes. Smoke tainted the air of the Terminus antechamber.

"What happened here?" Roarke asked the nearest guard.

Theron spun on his heel, thrusting the six-foot length of his mage wand like a shield between himself and Roarke. The heavy, silver-shot blue wool of Theron's robe flared over the long linen tunic and trousers favored by the priests of Reyah-in-Hiawat. Given how much Theron relished the reflected glory of their mother's worship, Roarke could think of only one thing capable of tearing him away from a holy day ceremony. Theron must have felt the blast of Deryk's spell in the deepest cell of the Great Temple of Sevidad Reyj. Bloody, bloody hell.

Beyond Theron, Reyah's newest Chosen knight—a strapping, black-haired stallion named Donatien something or another—flashed the new arrivals a look of frightening eagerness.

"Vanyr Roarke!" The knight rubbed his hands together. "Vanyr Hawke and Vanyr Conlan too! Oh, wow! This is just too cool. Like I was explaining to Vanyr

Theron, Lord Alfred said nobody gets in without his say-so. But you guys are big dogs. We'll get you uptown in half a mo. No prob."

Roarke wondered what the hell Donatien was saying. He sounded like he was speaking Seshmeelan but the words made no sense at all.

The young Chosen gestured to the center of the antechamber, where an elderly wizard in dusty and somewhat rumpled brocade robes mumbled to himself. The wizard looked up. Peculiar blue-rimmed gold eyes assessed the Vanyr and dismissed them as unimportant. Roarke was amused. They *were* unimportant.

Theron drew himself to his full height, puffing his broad chest and tucking in his long chin for another verbal blast. Theron was famous for cowing the pious and the short. But Donatien was almost as tall as Hawke, and if anything, the Chosen seemed to brighten at the prospect of another round.

Theron's eyes narrowed until they were little more than green slivers glaring between his dark lashes. The runes inscribed on Theron's wand paled with barely contained magic.

"Hey, Roarke, it looks like Deryk tapped into the ley lines with his spell," Hawke said. The sandy-haired warrior pointed to a crack branching down the wall like a tributary of the Palknut River. A little too conveniently for accident, the gesture knocked Theron's staff right out of his hand.

"Gee, Theron, I'm sorry. Here, let me help you. Those staffs are dangerous. Hate to have it go off by accident and hurt somebody. At least not until we know what Deryk's called up."

"You don't know it was Deryk!" Theron erupted.

"Are you mad?" Conlan demanded. "We were there when he cast the spell. The world shook on its foundations. The very heavens bled."

"Lord Alfred will see you youngsters now." The old wizard croaked loud enough smother Theron's angry reply. "Follow me."

"I suppose Alfred expects us to walk?" Theron snarled. "Are you sure he doesn't want us to crawl the distance on our knees?"

"You can if you like," the oldster wheezed, "but I don't think your fancy trousers could take it. Step outside, sonny, and I'll Port you straight to Alfred. I'd do it in here but Jagger's got this place locked down tighter than Lady Yululu's chastity belt."

Theron's jaw sagged. Roarke made a mental note to find out the wizard's name and buy him a drink.

"You...you..." Theron stuttered.

"No, don't thank me. Get your keister in the Portal," the wizard admonished. "Got to get you to Alfred, you know. Lots of things happening around this old pile of stones."

Roarke tried not to laugh at the expression on Theron's face until after the Portal dark closed around him. Roarke would've made it too, if Hawke hadn't snickered first. They were still laughing when the wizard dumped them on the carpet in Alfred's office.

Alfred's office looked like it had been dumped on the carpet too. Benches and chairs lay face down or teetered against the paneled walls. A blizzard of papers drifted over every level surface. Hairline cracks laced the ceiling.

Only the portrait of Reyah the Abundant appeared undamaged. The painted goddess smiled serenely at the back of Alfred's head. All eight of the remaining jewels in the picture's frame survived intact. Five of the gems glowed as if lit from within, testifying to the presence of five Vanyr in the Keep.

Willem sat in his customary chair to Alfred's right. On Alfred's left, the Gareth Weston, the Keep's seneschal, rubbed his neatly trimmed beard and added another scrap of foolscap to the pile in front of him. A pair of burly footmen struggled to heft the Lord of the Keep's war table back into position under the windows. It might have been easier if they'd been paying attention to the task at hand, but they were too busy eavesdropping on the argument between Alfred and Vallenius.

"But we've got to look for the Nine!" Vallenius leaned over Alfred's desk, so caught up in his cause he didn't realize he was shouting in Alfred's face. Roarke wondered, *nine what?* "We've got to start mending," Vallenius said.

"Boy," Gareth warned.

"What do you think I'm trying to do here?" Alfred countered. "Repairing the Keep is our first priority. Reyah's prophecy can take care of itself."

"Reyah prophesied!" Theron bellowed. "Why wasn't I told?"

"Presumably because you weren't here," Jagger answered.

Everyone in the room jumped as if the Old One's sudden appearance in the middle of anywhere answering a question he hadn't been asked was in any way remarkable. Jagger righted one of the carved, cross-legged chairs Alfred reserved for his ranking guests. Righted it by hand, not magic, Roarke noted.

Jagger raised his soot-streaked hands to his face and stared, as if for the first time, at the scorches marring the sleeves and front of his dust-smeared black doublet.

"Damn." He reached for the decanter and glass set on a silver tray in front of the Lord of the Keep. "Wine, anyone? It's going to be a long night."

"Not if it's Alfred's wine," Hawke said with a grimace.

"I'm pouring."

"Oh. In that case."

The bitter, dishwater-colored wine Alfred favored streamed over the lip of the decanter, changing as it fell into the dense, ruby nectar of a vintage Gordo. Hawke lifted his glass in salute, took a sip and sighed. "Ah. I haven't tasted Gordo like this in years."

One of the footmen cast a desperate glance in Alfred's direction. Alfred dismissed the servants. They scuttled posthaste out the door. As a result of little alchemies like changing bad wine to good, Jagger had garnered a reputation for using the same power to change those who annoyed him into Reyah knew what.

As his former student, Roarke knew Jagger's magic couldn't achieve true transubstantiation, even under the best of circumstances. Tonight was far from the best of circumstances.

Oh, Jagger changed cheap white wine to a vintage red, and the level in the decanter never dropped, but the Vanyr mind mage hadn't multiplied the glasses to make a full round like he usually did. Instead Gareth supplied the lack from unbroken stock in the cabinets behind Alfred's desk. And when Jagger lowered himself into his chair, Roarke could've sworn the Old One paled.

"The prophecy. What was it?" Theron insisted.

"One to rend, and nine to mend," Jagger intoned in a fair imitation of Theron's ritual voice. As usual, Theron failed to recognize it. "Right, Vallenius?"

"Word for word," the wizard agreed.

"Deryk resurrected Megeara. She's *the One*." Jagger raised a hand to forestall Theron's automatic protest. "The proof is in the spell. It was made for Reyah four thousand years ago. I know every hand that touches it. *The Nine* are in Reyah's hands."

"There are nine of us in this room," Conlan pointed out.

"So there are." Jagger chuckled. Roarke hated it when Jagger played enigmatic.

"Who or what are the Nine?" Alfred asked. "Vallenius thinks we should go looking for them. Where? Meanwhile, I've got people injured, a city collapsing around my ears and a mob of the high and mighty expecting to celebrate Reyah's Natal Day with all the usual pomp."

Jagger didn't answer. His gaze wandered, unfocused, toward the row of night black windows behind the war table. Vallenius turned in the same direction. His mouth formed a perfect "O". Roarke felt the first faint prickle of magic across the nape of his neck the same instant Theron's staff started to glow. In another heartbeat, Roarke heard a faint keening in his mind's ear. The song grew inside him, from the marrow of his bones outward, until it filled him completely.

Everyone in the room began to glow. Blue light radiated from their bodies. The hundred-weight of exhaustion pressing on Roarke's shoulders blasted away. Power as pure as sunlight raced through Roarke's veins. The fragrance of roses and jasmine and spring flowers he couldn't even name captivated his senses.

A translucent sapphire curtain of Reyah's power spread across the alcove containing Alfred's war table. Behind the curtain sat Reyah and nine women. The shifting iridescence of the veil obscured all but the most basic details of face and form. Roarke couldn't believe his eyes. Reyah was going to make a Goddess-damned presentation. Didn't it figure his mother would pull something like this when he looked like a rag seller and stank like his mule.

The perfume of Reyah's divinity would probably cover the worst of the stench, but dammit, he'd been through an earthquake caused by Her stinking favorite, Deryk. Roarke was filthy and bloody and more than a little pissed. Squinting against the blue glare, he tried to assess how bad his clothing looked.

Instead of the rags he rode in with, Roarke found himself arrayed in a costly suit of heavy, forest-green, Paelinorian silk. His hands looked newly manicured, scoured clean down to the whites of his nails. The same wonder extended to Hawke and Conlan. Theron's crumpled festival robes appeared freshly starched.

The Chosen were kitted out in the close fitting hose, blue satin doublets and embroidered velvet tabards reserved for the most solemn occasions of state. Jagger wore a doublet of silver brocaded black velvet. A narrow lace of minute pearls edged the cuffs and collar of his superfine lawn shirt. The hair at Jagger's left temple had been pulled back in an intricate braid of silver wires and diamonds, exposing the row of thin, diamond decorated loops edging his ear. A stranger to the Keep might be forgiven for thinking Jagger and the three Chosen were going to a coronation.

Who are *those women?*

Chapter Seven

At first, Thea thought she'd died, and the afterworld looked like the other side of the looking glass. Thea sat at a mirror-topped table across from a row of windows framed with pointed arches of carved stone. The windows themselves reflected a veil of iridescent blue twinkling like something Steven Spielberg might dream up for the antechamber of heaven. The air was heavy with the fragrance of jasmine and heirloom roses.

To Thea's immediate left, at the head of the table, Madame Reyah occupied a gilded throne carved with plants, animals and celestial symbols. Reyah's braided crown of hair gleamed like polished silver. Her caftan had become a gown of stars so bright it almost hurt to look at it. A scepter of lapis lazuli inscribed with silver runes and topped with a sphere of pale blue crystal rested on the table in front of her. Somehow Thea knew the scepter was the true form of the old woman's silver-headed cane.

Reyah wasn't paying attention to Thea, though. The goddess—and Thea was afraid the old woman truly was—focused on the poshest Blackberry Thea'd ever seen. The casing looked like it was carved from solid blue topaz with chunks of diamonds for buttons.

Across the table from Thea sat a young woman in a white, off-the-shoulder dress. The woman's hair was the color of ruddy bronze, and her eyes were blue, but a grayer blue than the veil. For a moment the woman looked as baffled as Thea felt. Then the woman's mouth curved into a familiar smile.

"L-liz?" It couldn't be. The lissome creature facing Thea was twenty, tops—well, maybe twenty-five if it was Liz and if twenty-five-year-old Liz had been somehow transmogrified into a stunning Greek demigoddess.

Liz nodded. "If you think this is something, you'd better take a look in the mirror."

Thea lowered her gaze to the tabletop and stared into eyes the color of the very finest turquoise set at a slight angle to high, wide cheekbones. Full, rosy lips and the slightly triangular shape of the jaw gave the face a feline cast, an impression reinforced by a tawny golden mane of hair streaming past her reflected shoulders.

Thea combed her fingers through hair that seemed to go on forever. In the mirror, a long-fingered, beautifully manicured hand mimicked her motions. Thea pulled a tendril forward. The golden tress caressed her new fingers, circling her narrow wrist and slender forearm. Thea's gaze dipped lower to the reflection of a flimsy, cream silk bolero top barely held together by thin gold chains.

"Oh my God!" Thea squawked, slapping her hands over the front of her top. "Ohmigod! Liz! I've got boobs!"

"Aquiline fingers, indeed!" Madame Reyah huffed at the screen of the Blackberry. "Which one of those dingbats wrote this? I can't tell! There's too damned many names! What is this obsession you women have with cyber-names and secret identities? Don't you know how confusing that is? Who do you think you are? The Justice League?" Reyah shook the Blackberry at Thea. "There won't be any of *that* here in my world. Now what did you say?"

Thea's mouth opened and shut, but nothing came out. She felt like she'd been hit over the head with a brick.

"Oh, for Domain's sake. Close your mouth, child. Of course, you've got boobs. And very nice ones they are too. You look exactly like the lingerie model you used as your fan fiction avatar." Reyah gestured down the table. "You all must have asked to become your fan fiction characters, and here you are."

Thea glanced to her right. Seven remarkably beautiful women sat like sleeping dolls in high-backed chairs arranged around the foot of the table. Thea could almost recognize some of them.

Marisol, who sat to Liz's left, appeared much the same as she had at the con. The big difference was Marisol now wore the red satin dress she'd described for her fanfic character, "the Mistress of Sun and Wave".

Anna had to be the purple-gowned, black-haired knock-out sitting in the last chair on Thea's side of the table. She wore the silver circlet and jeweled chatelaine Anna claimed for her fictional self. There was even a filigreed silver fan hanging from her belt—Anna's version of a magic wand.

Thea knew the brown-haired, Celtic beauty in the full-sleeved, white shirt and green, leather-trimmed vest opposite Anna was Brigid. Brigid's costume was distinctive. Which made the woman sitting to Brigid's right—wearing the medieval version of Lara Croft's Tomb Raider coat—Sarah Blake. Liz had written one story where Sarah's character carried a bandoleer of small arrows like the one slung over the coated woman's shoulder.

The buff little strawberry blonde warrior must be Kait. Thea smiled. Kait would love those designer leathers and the giant sword hanging across the back of her chair. The petite nymph with masses of curling, fire engine red hair and perfect, heart-shaped face sitting between Thea and Kait could be Free in her guise of "Mistress of Leaf and Vine". Thea risked a glance under the table. Yep, the redhead was barefoot under her trailing green gown. Had to be Free, who kicked off her shoes every chance she got, exactly like her fanfic character. Had the pointy, elf princess ears she'd written for her character been translated too? Free's new hairstyle made it impossible to tell.

Where was Pandora? Thea stared at a pocket Venus with the face of a pre-Raphaelite muse and clouds of platinum blonde hair sitting at the opposite end of the table from Reyah. It couldn't be. It simply couldn't be. Could it?

Thea turned to Liz for confirmation, but Liz was checking out the coffered ceiling and the blue energy field behind Thea's side of the table. "Where is here, exactly?" Liz asked.

"Domain," Reyah snapped. "Haven't you been paying attention?"

"But where in Domain? Seshmeel? Tambara? The Keep?" Liz continued.

"O-oh," Reyah stuttered. "Why, the Keep, of course. Silly me. Put me in a time-space Portal and I get as testy as dear ol' Dr. McCoy in a transporter tube."

Liz dismissed the matter with a wave of her hand. "No harm done. I've got a couple questions, though. How did we get here, what's on the program, and when do we go back?"

"It depends on what happened in my booth after I left. What did you wish?"

Thea decided she didn't like the tone of Reyah's voice. It sounded too much like the voice of a woman who'd lost her favorite toy and was looking for someone to blame. Not at all like the sweet-natured, grandmotherly goddess on the show. Or was Thea letting the strangeness of the situation get the better of her? Thea wished she knew what Liz thought.

Liz hesitated. Her gaze turned inward as if she was searching for a memory. *How could she forget?* Before Thea could respond a cool, wordless warning brushed her thoughts. In a weird way, the sensation felt like Liz. Liz's fan fiction character was a mind mage. Oh boy. *And much, much more...*

Liz shook her head. "I'm sorry. Everything's too jumbled. If you pulled up our fan fiction on that thing," Liz gestured at the Blackberry, "couldn't you use it to connect with the security cams in the exhibit hall and tell us what happened?"

"I tried, but the combination of the Wishstone and...and a terrible spell," Reyah's mouth pursed like she'd bitten into a lemon, "cast by a, uh, rogue sorcerer scrambled everything electronic in the exhibit hall, dammit."

"What spell? What rogue sorcerer?" Thea asked, trying to remember if there were any other truly powerful bad guys on the show besides Deryk. Did Reyah mean Jagger? There were rumors the producers planned to introduce another major baddie in the next season. Had they jumped from Lydia's frying pan into a much hotter Domain fire?

"First things first. Tell me what your wish was."

Reyah *pushed* the words at Liz. It was the same force Thea had felt in the exhibit hall, only much greater and wielded with a lot less concern about collateral damage. Thea wanted to grab Liz's hand across the table, as if together they could make some kind of barrier to Reyah's invasion.

Again the cool mental whisper touched Thea. This time it carried a question. *May I come in?*

Aren't you here already?

"Tell me," Reyah commanded, pushing harder.

Liz crossed her arms under her breasts. Talk about body language. Thea could almost see a wall of ice forming in front of Liz to block Reyah's will. "Why?"

"What about you?" Reyah asked Thea, backing the words with another one of her magical shoves.

Liz extended a mental helping hand. Thea appreciated the thought, but she'd always known how to be stubborn. "I don't remember well under pressure," Thea told Reyah.

Reyah threw up her hands. "I can't believe this is happening to me! You're supposed to be grateful!"

"For what?" Liz and Thea asked in unison.

"For bringing you here!"

"But you didn't," Thea said. "The Wishstone did."

With a little help from Pandora, Liz snickered in Thea's head.

"Aha!" Reyah trumpeted. "You do remember!"

"Remember what?" Thea and Liz asked together.

For a minute, Thea was sure Reyah was going to turn her and Liz into flying monkeys. But at the last possible instant Reyah retreated into sugar-coated Glinda mode.

"I'm sorry. It was a rough day for us all, wasn't it? And I did wake you a little sooner than I should. Transmogrification can be ever so unsettling. But I can't help you settle into your new home unless I know the details of the wish you made."

Thea's chin nearly hit the table.

"New home?" Liz sounded as dumbfounded as Thea felt. "Are you saying this is a permanent arrangement?"

Several gasps from the other end of the table spared Reyah the need to answer. *How convenient,* Thea thought.

Thea heard two soft, ominous clicks. A chair thudded the carpet. The new, lethally armed Sarah backed away from the table.

"Who the hell are you people?" Sarah's voice growled from the pouty lips of her cyber-character's face. In each hand Sarah held a compact crossbow, primed and ready to fire. "Don't anybody move."

"Oh my God! It worked!" Pandora shrieked. "We're in Domain, Sarah. You've got the coat and the crossbows and everything like you wrote it!"

Pandora jumped up from the table to do a happy dance. Blonde hair, beads and blue chiffon flailed in every direction. Her chair crashed into the wall of the alcove. Sarah aimed both crossbows at her. Liz's face twisted as if in pain. Brigid punched Sarah's left elbow.

Sarah yelped and fired high. One dart buried itself in the paneling over Pandora's shoulder. The other shot between Kait and Free, straight into the blue curtain of energy. The arrow vaporized with a sizzle and puff of smoke. Liz buried her face in her hands.

"Sarah, are you out of your mind?" Marisol grabbed the spent weapons from Sarah's hands. "Those things are dangerous. People could get hurt."

"People like you," Anna said. "This is a palace, not a pigsty. Look what you did! That is hand-carved walnut, and you splintered the top half of the panel. How are you going to pay for that?"

"Damn it, Anna. You knew my ex was sending me death threats. What did you expect me to do?"

"Yeah, we look like a bunch of hitmen—as if." Kait rolled her eyes. She caught a glimpse of her new face and sleek, muscled arms. Thea wondered what Kait thought about what she saw. Charming as her new face was, Thea didn't see much of the old Kait in it.

Kait puckered her lips in an air kiss and pulled her long, strawberry blonde braid a few times. "Cool, the Wishstone slapped some glam on me. Hey, where's my sword?" Kait patted down her leathers. She pushed Anna's skirts aside to check around her chair. Kait's eyes widened. She stroked the hilt of her broadsword. "Sweet!"

Free bent over the table, almost nose to nose with her reflection. One of Free's small, girlish hands traced the image while the other stroked a delicately pointed ear. She whispered, "This is how I'm supposed to look. Now Stefan will love me. He has to."

"Hell, you're supposed to be the 'Mistress of Sorcery and Spells'. You fix the damn panel," Sarah said. "How hard can it be?"

"Not hard at all, if I say the *ra-aht* spell," Anna said, her Georgia drawl growing broader by the word. "But the only rhyme I can think of for 'repair' involves tyin' you to a chair."

"Ooh, kinky," Brigid said.

"Ladies," Reyah began.

Pandora stopped flapping her arms and spinning long enough to spit out a mouthful of hair. "Arrrggghhhh! Where did all this hair come from?"

Pandora grabbed the skirt of her filmy dress and yanked it up to face level. More beads rained over the floor. "What happened to my overalls? What happened to my Nikes? Where's my backpack? Oh no! I'm...I'm..." She dropped the skirt and lifted two handfuls of platinum blonde hair to the ceiling and wailed, "I'm *blonde*!"

Sarah slicked a strand of hair off her forehead. "And I've got black hair. So?"

Pandora put her hands to her face. "My glasses! How will I see without my glasses? I'm blind!"

"This," Reyah said, "is *not* what I wanted."

"No, it isn't," Liz said in a soft voice. The face Liz lifted toward Reyah was whiter than her dress, and her eyes glowed the unnatural blue of the magical veil. Some inner sense Thea never realized she possessed vibrated with an awareness of pain. She reached for her friend. Liz grabbed Reyah's wrist.

Time stopped when the three women touched. Reyah gasped. Thea felt blasted by a hurricane of voices.

Oh Stefan, everything is the way I always knew it could be. You will love me and cherish me and take care of me forever and ever, and I'll never have to go back to Iowa. Never. Never!

Doesn't that fool lawyer realize we could be in the Keep? Lord Alfred could be on the other side of the veil—and not that little prick of an actor, either. Oh my God. Who else is out there? Alfred always has dignitaries and nobility hanging around his office. How on earth can I make a good impression if Sarah's acting like a crazy woman, and Pandora's shrieking, and Free's rubbing her damned pointy ears like she's gone simple. They'll think we're white trash for sure!

"Liz, Thea, what's wrong?" Marisol asked aloud. Inside, Marisol was building to a scream. *Why did they grab Madame Reyah? Why aren't Liz and Thea telling us what's going on instead of staring at Reyah like they've gone crazy?*

Kait performed an elaborate kata with a sword three times too long for her. No, Thea realized with a jolt. That's what Kait saw in her mind. Brigid saw a badly blocked, execrably acted mob scene.

The din of other people's thoughts was so loud Thea thought her eardrums would burst from the inside out. She wanted to tear her hand away. The longer she held on to Liz the louder the killing noise grew, not only within Reyah's magic bubble, but beyond the energy veil, beyond the room.

"By the Hive, I can't believe what I'm seeing."

"What the hell is going on in there?"

"Now that's what I call a well-hung lute."

"Go for 'innocent' in white silk or knock 'em dead in red velvet?"

"Damn it, what's taking so long?"

Peace. The thought rippled outward like the waves spreading from a stone dropped in a pond. Silence followed in its wake. Thea and Liz faced Reyah in a space devoid of everything except light. Only Thea couldn't tell if she was standing beside Liz or inside of her. Reyah touched her thumb to the center of Liz's forehead. Thea felt Liz sigh as the agony seeped away.

When Thea opened her eyes, she was back in her chair opposite Liz, one hand holding Liz's, the other on Reyah's arm.

"That should hold you until Jagger teaches you to build your own mental shields," Reyah said.

"Should?" Liz asked mildly as she let go of Reyah's arm. Thea let go too. Reyah shifted her gaze to the other end of the table.

Marisol mouthed the words, "What's going on?" to Thea. But nobody else appeared to have noticed anything odd.

"Blind, blind, blind," Pandora moaned.

"Oh, for heavens sake," Anna said. "Pandora, you are not blind. Look 'round this room and tell me what you see."

Pandora shook her head. "I'm blind," she moaned some more. "Blind as a bat. I'll need a white cane. Or a seeing-eye dog." Pandora's face lit up. "Yeah! A seeing-eye dog! Thea! I want a golden retriever. Or maybe a Labrador. Or do I want a collie like Lassie?" Not for the first time Thea thanked her lucky stars Pandora wasn't part of her pod.

"Will you stop acting so damn blonde? You're giving me a headache," Anna complained.

Pandora's eyes popped open. "Don't *ever* call me blonde. I hate being blonde." She looked around the room. "So, I can see. Well, darn. I *can* see. There goes my seeing-eye dog."

Anna sighed. "Does anyone remember what constitutes justifiable homicide in Domain? Because in about two seconds I am going to choke the life out of Pandora!" Anna glared at Pandora. Pandora glowered at Anna.

"Can it, you two." Brigid interrupted. "Madame Reyah, are we in Domain or is this just a hell of a dream?"

Reyah beamed. "Of course, you're in Domain, Brigid. Isn't that what you wished for?"

"And much, much more," Pandora said. "But not looking like this."

"Exactly what was your wish, dear? Perhaps I can help," Reyah said.

Thea snorted.

"Gesundheit." Pandora pressed her hands together like a child saying her bedtime prayers. "Hear us, oh Wishstone. We, the Daughters of Reyah, wish to go to Domain—the *real* Domain—as the *real* Daughters of Reyah, with all the powers and abilities and youth and beauty we wrote for our fan fiction characters and much, *much* more. Wishstone, make it so."

Thea couldn't decide if she should be amused or alarmed at the look on Reyah's face. Whatever the old girl expected, Pandora's wish wasn't it.

"Well." Reyah took a deep breath. "Oh. My. How could I forget those buttons? Daughters of Reyah…"

"Yep, that's what we called our fan club." Pandora flopped a large hank of hair in Reyah's direction. "Now, will you, please, fix the way I look?"

"How long are you going to let us stay here?" Kait asked.

"What if we don't want to go back?" Sarah said.

"Ever," Free added.

Reyah took another deep breath. "To answer your questions, no. Always. And you can't."

"What do you mean? You've *got* to," Pandora insisted. "I can't be a blonde. Brigid wrote it, not me. I *told* her to take it out."

"What's done cannot be undone," Reyah said. "I didn't transform you. The Wishstone did, and you're bound by your wish."

Kait piped up, "Pandora, you know how things work on the show. Whenever something bad threatens Domain, Reyah uses the Wishstone to shape the best possible outcome. Then she sends it out into the world to make it happen. Remember how Alfred became Chosen?"

"You said this wasn't what you wanted. What did you want?" Liz asked Reyah.

Thea had a flash of insight. "Did you make a wish too?"

Another spike of temper lit Reyah's eyes before she bowed to the inevitable. "I *did* use the Wishstone," Reyah admitted. She sighed and twisted her fingers, throwing a hefty dose of little old lady wistfulness at the group. "I needed help. Remember the rogue sorcerer I mentioned? Well, he stole a powerful spell and used it to resurrect the Demon Witch Megeara."

A chorus of exclamations circled the table. Thea noticed Liz didn't join in.

Reyah sighed again. "I know it doesn't sound like much. After all, Theron and Alfred defeated Megeara before. But times have changed. My sons' hearts are in the right place, but they haven't faced a real challenge in so long they've grown complacent. And as for combining their forces for the good of Domain, well—this is embarrassing—for the last hundred years, all they've done is fight."

It was more than embarrassing, Thea realized with a shock, it was painful. It hurt the mother in the goddess that her children couldn't get along. But the moment of empathy slipped through Thea's grasp. The goddess returned to the fore. Beneath her lowered lashes, Reyah flicked the quickest possible glance at her audience.

Reyah continued, "I'd begun to despair when the Voice uttered a prophecy, 'One to rend and nine to mend.'"

"And there are only eight Vanyr!" Pandora trumpeted. "No wonder you were interested in our group."

"Since the 'one' referred to Megeara, I felt the 'nine' meant women. Very special women," Reyah said.

"Us," Liz said, a world of amusement encompassed in one small word.

"As you see, the Wishstone chose you," Reyah said. The tone of her voice implied, *And a poor choice it was, too.*

"Megeara?" Sarah growled. "Hot damn—a rematch, and this time we'll kick her ass 'til she's a wet spot on the pavement."

"Yeah!" Kait chorused. "We'll treat her like the red-headed stepchild she is."

"Megeara's a brunette," Reyah said, looking a bit confused.

"But what about my body?" Pandora demanded.

"What about home?" Marisol whispered.

"Didn't you hear a word I said?" Reyah snapped her fingers. "Pay attention, ladies, because I will not repeat myself again. I can't change your wish. You asked to come to Domain. You asked to be your fan fiction characters. You didn't say you wanted to return to your world. An entity as old and as powerful as the Wishstone takes requests quite literally—and it *always* has its own agenda. Just like on the show. For some reason it seems to think Domain needs you. The question is, are you ready to live your wish?"

"Forever," Free murmured. "Forever young and beautiful. Never going back to the hellhole I called home." Free jumped from her chair, her skirts flying around her in a flurry of green and white, and smacked her fist against her palm. "Yes!"

"No!" Marisol and Kait shouted.

Marisol grabbed Liz's arm. "We can't stay here forever. We can't!" Marisol said. "What about my family?"

"Yeah, and mine too," Kait added. Tears glimmered in her eyes. "My dad and my mom and my brother—they'll think I'm dead."

"We can't go back? Ever?" Thea asked.

Reyah turned toward Marisol and Kait. One perfect, diamond bright tear rolled down the goddess's cheek. "But I thought you loved my world as much as I do. Won't you give Domain and me a chance?" The old woman sounded unutterably sad.

Marisol's fingers loosened their grip on Liz. Her entire face softened as she gazed on Reyah. "No, no, abuelita. Please, don't be sad. We love Domain. We do."

"Damn straight," Sarah said. "Our whole lives have been leading up to this." Anna, Kait and Free added their voices to the chorus.

Marisol and Kait didn't resist Reyah, Thea mused.

She didn't even have to push, Liz answered. *Interesting.*

"I want to be here too," Pandora said. "But I want everyone to know I'm still not happy about being blonde."

ℰ℧℞

"Now they've touched our Mother!" Theron shouted, thrusting his infernal staff in the direction of the alcove. But the strange energies in the room somehow disabled Theron's spells. The runes on his staff didn't even glitter. "Sacrilege! She should blast them to ash!"

"Yell a little louder, Theron. I don't think they heard you in Paelinor," Conlan said.

"What are they doing now?" Hawke asked the question on the minds of every non-mage in the room.

"Arguing with Her." Jagger laughed. The air surrounding him shimmered, sparking rainbows from his fingertips, the diamonds and silver in his hair, and the silver designs woven into his doublet. The magic billowing through the veil danced over the protesting Theron and surrounded Vallenius in a caress as light as the bubbles of effervescent wine.

What kind of magic embraced Vanyr and Chosen in equal measure? Whatever it was, Roarke wanted it. He wanted it so badly he would do anything to taste it, even opening the doors of his mind past the point of pain. Light of every color overwhelmed him, burning away the scars of his wasted magic until Roarke felt himself reborn. The world began tonight. Nothing would ever be the same—right or wrong, sun or shadow. The material world had been transformed in a thousand ways, from the nature of Vallenius's magic to the color of Alfred's wizard lights, which in the space of an instant went from harsh yellow to the turquoise glow of reflected sky.

"Is their magic as strong as I think it is?" Roarke whispered.

"If I can feel it, it must be," Conlan said. The Chosen warriors in the room nodded their agreement. "But where would our Mother find such powerful women?"

"And why would She bring them here?" Hawke asked.

Jagger's smile spread. "She didn't. The Wishstone did."

છળ

Thirty seconds into Pandora's explanation of why a self-righteously plain person couldn't possibly want to be a platinum blonde bimbo, Reyah snatched her lapis scepter off the table. Left eye twitching, nostrils flaring, Domain's elder goddess resembled a Congressional committee chairman about to explode

Stand, Liz mentally whispered to Thea. Thea stood.

Reyah rose from her throne, which promptly disappeared. The seven women who failed to follow Liz's and Thea's example jerked to their feet like spastic marionettes. The chairs beneath them vanished. Sarah's crossbows and Kait's sword attached themselves to their respective owners with none too gentle slaps. Reyah marched forward. The mirror-topped table dematerialized in stages ahead of her.

Pandora teetered on her cyber-character's gilded, high-heeled sandals. Her cornflower blue eyes widened with admiration. "Kewl!" Pandora chirped. "They can't even do that in the movies. Was the table some kind of hologram?"

Reyah loomed over Pandora—a neat trick since Reyah couldn't have been more than five-foot-zip. Liz wondered, did Reyah even have feet under her robe? Reyah moved like a woman. Her star-gown shifted from side to side as if supported by hips and legs accustomed to swaying provocatively. But the flesh Liz had grabbed was more than flesh. It was power. Power shaped by intelligence. Reyah's material form existed solely as a vessel of her—and Reyah was definitely female—will.

Fear traced a cold finger down Liz's spine. What the hell had Liz let her friends in for? She should've stopped them from making the wish.

She'd registered the sense of power in Reyah's booth the same way she registered the prayers accumulated in a church or the fog of mourning that clung to Arlington National Cemetery. She'd known the Wishstone would do something awful or wonderful or both. Liz had nothing to lose by giving in to its magic. She had no children, and no one waited for her at home. Her husband and parents were dead. What other, peripheral family she had left ignored her as much as she did them.

But her friends weren't unattached. Liz promised herself that if she couldn't get the group out of whatever they'd gotten themselves into, she would at least do her best to protect them. Reyah wanted something specific from Thea and Liz. Liz had glimpsed as much in those brief instants when she and Thea touched Reyah. There was every chance the goddess was as bound by her wish to the Wishstone as they were to theirs. Liz hoped she could use that.

She let her thoughts brush Reyah's energies on her way to mentally grabbing Pandora's attention.

Pandora squealed, "Liz! How cool! You touched me with your mind! Do it again!"

Pretending bashfulness, Liz scuffed her sandal against the carpet. "Sorry, I didn't mean to startle you. The 'much, much more' you added to the end of the wish really did a number on me. I didn't expect to be quite this young, either. Sort of like you being blonde."

Reyah stiffened right on cue.

"But I think it might work out better this way," Liz added. "Remember the kind of women the Vanyr liked on the show? Young and curvy."

"I told you twenty-five tops was the way to go," Sarah reminded the group.

"And blonde," Thea purred behind her. Liz blessed her friend for catching on to where Liz was trying to lead Reyah. "Remember, Pandora, Roarke likes them blonde."

"Not exclusively," Liz argued.

Pandora bounced and nearly fell over. Reyah rubbed the top of her scepter against her chin.

"And Conlan likes redheads," Reyah said, eyeing Kait speculatively. Kait flashed Reyah a terrified smile.

"Yeah, he does, doesn't he?" To draw Reyah's fire yet again, Liz wrapped her words in visions of her hands tangled in Conlan's braids while his lush lips kissed their way down her body. Sure enough, Reyah was still tapped into Liz's brain.

"Conlan! He doesn't have a scrap of magic to his name. What you want…" Reyah glanced at the veil and smiled.

The back of Liz's neck tried to crawl under her hair.

"Better yet, let me show you." Reyah waved her hand. The barrier disappeared.

Chapter Eight

Deryk's Tower, Mount Tuumb

"I want twenty-five thousand dollars or someone's going to get hurt!" Lydia shrieked. Her vision cleared. She shuddered. Something was wrong. Something was very wrong.

A cold wind blustered around her. Every bone in her body ached. Instead of standing in the exhibit hall, dressing down moronic rent-a-cops and a ditsy old lady, she stood in what looked like a set for one of the Vanyr towers in Domain. Instead of being clad in a cola- and perfume-stained Thierry Mugler pant suit, she was wearing—

Lydia goggled at the sprayed-on black spandex gown with rubberized snakeskin inserts Immortal Productions' costume designers considered the ultimate in gothic slut chic.

I'm in costume, she thought dazedly. *When did I go through wardrobe?*

A man stepped from the shadows. Lydia's head snapped up. At first she thought it was Michael Ryan wearing his Deryk gear. That couldn't be right. The guy was way too young. And there was something else. Something sharper. Something…dangerous? Lydia frowned. The gold torque around the look-alike's neck slithered into life and hissed at her.

"EEEK!" Lydia squawked, taking a step back. "What the hell is going on here? Am I being Punk'd? I didn't sign a release! I'm gonna kick my agent's sorry ass!"

"Welcome, lady. I had not anticipated the pleasure of meeting you again in this life." The look-alike bowed.

"Pleasure of meeting me again, my butt," Lydia snarled. "Tell me who you are and what I'm doing here and in costume, for God's sake, or I'll tear you to shreds."

84

The man studied Lydia. "You need some time to recuperate from your resurrection. I'll release you from the hexagram when you come to your senses." He strolled to the brazier and warmed his hands over the coals.

Lydia straightened her shoulders. What the hell was this dickhead talking about? Resurrection? "Yeah, right," she said. "Watch me walk over there and fry your head on those coals." Lydia took two steps forward—and plowed into an invisible wall.

After she peeled her face from the surface of the wall that wasn't there, Lydia ran in circles, screeching threats as she tried to beat her way out of the invisible barrier. Finally, panting in exhaustion, her voice hoarse from shrieking, it dawned on Lydia's peanut-sized brain she couldn't get out. Lydia pointed one long finger at the smirking bastard.

"I'll get you for this," Lydia promised. She peered at the end of her finger. Wait a minute. She hadn't had a manicure in at least two days. Could that lovely two-inch-long fingernail be real? A poison green lightning bolt erupted from her finger and ricocheted from the barrier. Lydia screamed as the bolt struck her. She fell to the ground and writhed in agony.

The young Michael Ryan look-alike watched with a confused look on his face.

"Ah. I see you're back to your old self." The look-alike smiled. "Promise me you won't do anything…rash. Once you swear, I'll set you free." Lydia flipped the look-alike the bird. The blond man shrugged. "Your choice." He returned to warming his hands.

What a prick. Lydia scrambled to her knees and, after beating out the smoldering hole in her gown, examined her fingers. She tugged at each long, lethally pointed, blood-red nail.

"They're real! They're really, really real," she crowed. "And they do tricks too!"

Lydia rose to her feet and pointed her finger at the stone floor. Green bolts of energy spattered against the granite. Two small chickens and a frog appeared.

The look-alike cleared his throat. "My Lady Megeara, will you give me your parole?"

"What did you call me?" she croaked.

The look-alike repeated his question. "Once you do, Lady Megeara, I will release you from the hexagram."

"Megeara," Lydia whispered, wrapping her arms around herself. It finally dawned on her there were no cameras, no lights, no cables or crew standing around. There was only the night sky overhead. Flickering light from a small brazier illuminated a very dark and scary looking circular tower top. Her brain spun in circles of its own.

Megeara. He called me "Megeara". Holy shit. There's a real *Domain?* Lydia's eyes widened. Then that guy would be the real Deryk. *And he thinks I'm the* real *Megeara.*

"Where am I?" Lydia demanded.

"In the standing tower of Tuumb Castle where I resurrected you, my lady," Deryk said. "Give me your promise, Megeara. I've devised a foolproof plan to conquer Tambara. Together we shall not fail."

If she wasn't dreaming—and she'd find out soon enough—this was great. It almost made up for Immortal Productions allowing her contract to lapse. Megeara had a lot of cool tricks, and Lydia often felt the show's writers hadn't taken the character's evilness as far as it could go. Lydia promised herself she'd show this world Lydia Jambon was a force to be reckoned with. She smiled at Deryk, conveniently forgetting her fleeting impression of danger.

"Vanyr Deryk," Lydia purred, "of course I promise."

She almost laughed at Deryk's self-satisfied expression. *He thinks he's got the old Megeara back. I bet I can use that. After all, I know all about him, and he doesn't know a thing about me.*

Deryk raised an eyebrow. "So you remember…"

"I remember many things." Lydia wondered what the old Megeara could possibly know that would cause Deryk to flinch. She made a mental note to hire an assistant to do some research. "Why don't you release me?"

She smoothed the black spandex clinging to her thighs and licked her lips. "We have much to discuss."

Deryk gestured and said something incomprehensible under his breath. "Come and share my fire, lady."

Lydia stepped forward. She exhaled a relieved breath when no barrier blocked her way. She sashayed over to Deryk.

"Now then," she cooed, laying her hand on his arm. "Why don't you tell me all about your foolproof plan?"

৪০৫৪

Back in Alfred's office

The room outside the alcove was an office if the furniture, the maps on the wall and papers scattered everywhere were any indication. There were people in the room. Some of them babbled at Reyah. Reyah babbled back. Liz knew it might be important to listen, but all she could do was stare at the man in the black and silver doublet.

He was so beautiful it made Liz's heart ache to look at him. At the same time, she couldn't quite believe he was real. A lustrous mane of raven black hair framed a strong, cleanly chiseled, young face with eyes an impossible shade of purple. Liz thought of violets and amethysts. Amethysts, because no man should be compared to a flower; violets, because there was nothing cold or hard about the expression in the man's eyes when they looked at her.

Er, looked at the group. *Get a grip,* Liz commanded herself. Her breath quickened. Damn, but wouldn't she like to.

She guessed the man stood about six feet tall. His opulent doublet highlighted the breadth of his shoulders. Black silk hose displayed long, splendid, muscular legs, leaving nothing to Liz's imagination. *Nothing at all. Oh my.* Liz wondered what his chest and arms looked like under all that stiff velvet and what kind of music his long-fingered hands might play on a woman's body.

Gah, Thea's mind voice drooled. *Simply gah. If that's Reyah's idea of an "Old One", I'm applying for my senior citizen card right now.*

Jagger? He couldn't be Jagger. So what if he was wearing black? First of all, he was too young—twenty-five tops, to quote Sarah. On the show, Jagger was played by fifty-something rock star Phil Richards, who had a beak of a nose and lips that reminded Liz of exploded balloons. This man's nose was thin and classically straight; his lips perfectly drawn. As Jagger, Richards ponced around the countryside in a teased, white rat's nest of a wig. This man's hair was so black it was almost iridescent. The only thing even remotely gray about this Jagger was the silver and crystal ornament braided into his hair.

The faintest smile played over the man's mouth. Or was it a smirk? It was almost as if he heard her thoughts. *Uh oh.* What if Thea was right? Whatever he looked like, Jagger was the primo, numero uno mind mage of Domain.

Oh. Shit.

"Who's the hottie in black, and do you think he'd be interested in wild monkey sex?" Sarah asked.

"Thea thinks he's Jagger," Liz said.

"No way!" Pandora said. "He's not old enough."

"Of course he's old enough," Reyah snapped. "He's over four thousand years old."

"Gee, he doesn't look a day over two thousand," Thea murmured.

"Twenty-five hundred, tops," Liz replied. They both cracked up.

Jagger smiled for real. Liz bit her lip. He couldn't be that beautiful. Nothing in heaven or earth smiled like *that*. Maybe what she saw was an illusion or some form of glamour. According to folk tales, you could only see through fairy glamour out of the corner of your eye. It was worth a shot. Liz shifted her attention to the rest of the men in the room.

The extras in the scene turned out to be Theron, Hawke, Conlan and her personal favorite, Roarke. *Yikes!* Her brain *had* gone south. The four Vanyr looked like the actors on the show, only better. Liz liked the easy way the big warriors wore their silk and jewels. Most of the guys in her old agency couldn't carry off a business suit. Theron, on the other hand, lost big points for the all-too-obvious poker sticking up his ass.

Even tricked out like a Renaissance aristocrat, Roarke remained as lean and lethal as the rapier he wore at his hip. The elegant, ascetic lines of his face, his somber hazel eyes, his mobile mouth...only the slight bump on the bridge of Roarke's nose saved him from looking like a manga wet dream. His short hair didn't help. The wayward, dark-brown strands practically demanded a woman run her fingers through them.

Damn. It appeared Roarke did prefer leggy blondes. His thickly lashed eyes focused on Thea like she was his first meal after a long spell of starving. Thea edged close. Her breath tickled Liz's cheek.

Where is it? Thea demanded.

Where is what?

The spot, the smudge, or whatever it is they're staring at.

Thea, have you forgotten your transformation?

Transformation? You mean he's looking at—oh, shit—"boobs", right?

Not to mention all the leg showing through the slits in your transparent harem pants.

Damn it, Liz! Thea blushed so hard, so fast, she radiated red all the way down to her navel. If Thea's idea was to fade into the woodwork, it wasn't working.

Hawke wiped the side of his mouth. Catching Liz's gaze, the blond Vanyr winked at her. Liz winked back. She flicked another sidelong glance at Jagger. Still gorgeous, damn it. Obviously, she was doing something wrong.

On the other side of Jagger, Alfred DuMarc, Gareth Weston, Willem Leopold and Vallenius bowed deeply to their goddess. Eyeing again the hose that seemed to be the current fashion, Liz could well understand why the men were Chosen. But good grief, Alfred was short. Standing straight enough to break, the Lord of the Keep had to be five inches shorter than Jagger.

"All right, ladies, let's have some order here." Reyah prodded her fan club into the ragged semblance of a chorus line.

Liz was tempted to beam the thought "One, two, three, kick!" at Brigid but refrained. Reyah's "boys" also seemed to be lining up for some kind of formal introduction.

Interestingly enough, Alfred led this Domain version of a receiving line. Vallenius, Gareth and the avid Willem stood behind the Lord of the Keep's right shoulder. If Domain reflected the TV show—or vice versa—the Vanyr followed Alfred in order of birth. Jagger came first, then Theron, Hawke, Conlan and Roarke. Despite their position in line, the Vanyr didn't bow to Reyah, Liz noted.

"My sons, Lord of my Keep and my Chosen Champions, I bid you greet my daughters." Reyah's voice boomed, the sound of it echoing everywhere at once. A heavy blast of jasmine, roses and lily of the valley flooded the chamber. Liz's eyes watered. She barely suppressed a sneeze—a problem Alfred appeared to share, despite his best efforts to hide it.

"Lady Pandora, Mistress of Mayhem," Reyah intoned.

Pandora's dainty ankles bowed in and out as she tried to maneuver both her feet and her high-heeled sandals across the floor at the same time. Pandora wasn't any worse at it than most five-year-olds. She might've even gotten close enough to Alfred to pump his hand if she hadn't tripped over the pattern in the carpet.

With a squeak of dismay, Pandora fell on Alfred in a blizzard of jangling, dangling necklaces and trailing chiffon. Her platinum blonde hair swamped the Lord of the Keep like a tidal wave, and he was short enough it nearly dragged him under. Sneezing and blushing, his arms extended like he didn't dare touch the divine klutz attached to his chest, Alfred fell backward into Gareth's arms.

As practical as his character on the show, the seneschal righted the Lord of the Keep. Gareth began disengaging Pandora's hair and scarves from the epaulets, gold braid and other fripperies of Alfred's fancy blue uniform.

"Lady Pandora," Gareth said, "with your permission, and if you'll hold still for but a moment, I'll get you both free."

"No prob." Pandora's voice was muffled by hair and fabric. "This happens to me all the time. Trust me, I know what to do!"

Yes, Liz agreed, this sort of situation probably did happen to Pandora a lot—but Liz was willing to bet never with long hair. Pandora shoved against Alfred's chest and yanked herself free.

Alfred fell backward into Gareth's arms, decked with tufts of blonde hair but minus one of his medallions, which dangled over one of Pandora's ears. Clutching her head and shrieking, Pandora attempted to back-pedal. Once again she tripped over nothing. Pandora let go of her head and started wind-milling her arms. She wobbled back and forth on her three-inch heels.

Brigid, Hawke and Willem rushed to help. Willem tripped over the fringe of a carpet and somersaulted across the room. Brigid hooked an arm around Pandora's ribs and heaved. Pandora flopped forward. Hawke reached out to catch her. His hands landed on her breasts. Pandora squealed in outrage.

Hawke jumped back like he'd grabbed a burning coal. A chair collapsed into the back of Hawke's legs, propelling Hawke into Alfred and Gareth. The three of them staggered into Vallenius. All four fell to the floor.

"Pandora, how could you?" Anna moaned and wrung her beringed hands.

Sagging like a temperamental tabby in Brigid's grasp, Pandora glared at Hawke. "Some people should learn to keep their hands to themselves."

"I don't think Lady Pandora likes you," Conlan stage whispered as he pulled Hawke to his feet.

From under the still prone Alfred and Gareth, Vallenius squeaked, "Thank you."

"How could Lady Pandora not like me?" Hawke asked. "She doesn't even know me. Yet." Hawke proffered a roguish bow in the women's direction. Alfred, Gareth and Vallenius popped off the floor. None of the three seemed surprised.

It will get better, Reyah's mind voice promised the universe.

I know. A masculine voice as dark and tactile as velvet stroked Liz's inner senses.

Tickled in spite of herself, Liz shook her head. *Ahem. I didn't invite you in.*

Yet.

Brigid spat out a mouthful of Pandora's hair. "Hi. I'm Brigid, Mistress of Battle and Confusion. It's totally iced to meet you guys, but I've got to find a safe place to put Pandora."

"Oh, put her over here," Reyah said. The gilded and carved chairs re-materialized in the alcove.

"Groovy." Brigid dumped Pandora in the nearest chair.

"I'm not a bundle of laundry," Pandora objected.

"You will be if you don't quit wriggling," Brigid said.

"Lord Alfred, whatever must you think of us?" Anna's voice throbbed with chagrin.

"Lady Anna, Mistress of Sorcery and Spells," Reyah said.

Anna started to curtsey. Liz could tell the instant Anna realized Reyah had called her by her real name. Anna stopped and glared over her shoulder at Reyah. *Uh oh,* Thea's voice said in Liz's head. *Looks like there's gonna be Mutiny from Lady Bounty.*

"That's Lady *Circe,*" Anna said.

"No, it's not," Reyah replied. "I'm not putting up with that nonsense. You're Lady Anna, period."

Anna pressed her lips together. She nodded and turned back to Alfred. Head held high, she swept the Lord of the Keep a curtsey deep enough to qualify as obeisance. The only problem was Alfred was unprepared for the honor—or the effect of the full white breasts displayed cleavage-first by Anna's maneuver.

Alfred's eyes bulged. He wet his lips a few times before he managed to croak, "My gracious lady, the honor is mine. Please, rise."

He extended his hand. Reyah cleared her throat. Alfred dropped his hand and bowed again. Liz wondered if anyone else noticed Reyah's little rebuke. Anna hadn't.

I am not going to curtsey to Alfred—or to any of them, Thea mentally told Liz.

It finally occurred to Anna the object of her lust was not going to offer her his hand. She rose and favored each Vanyr with a melting smile, a practiced dip and honeyed "hello" before joining Pandora and Brigid. Theron muttered something that turned Jagger stone-faced and close-minded.

With a mental shrug, Liz replied, *You're not supposed to curtsey, Thea. Thanks to Pandora and the Wishstone, we're Reyah's adopted daughters, not her servants. The Vanyr don't bow to their mother, much less to each other or the Chosen.* A fine point of precedence Kait, Sarah and Marisol missed, thanks to Anna's fractured protocol. Liz never realized how peculiar repeated curtseys looked without a skirt to hide the squat.

At least Sarah's trailing coat hid the worst of her wobbling derriere. The creaking of Kait's very new leather pants added a nice touch too. None of the preening tomcats in the room seemed to notice, though.

You know, a girl could have a lot of fun around here, Liz mused to Thea.

"Lady Frieda, Mistress of Leaf and Vine."

Some things never change, even if you're in a galaxy far, far away, Liz thought. The Wishstone transformed Free into possibly the most beautiful woman in the universe, certainly the most beautiful woman in a room full of extraordinarily beautiful women. But like Pandora, Free's mind hadn't caught up with the transformation of her body.

Head down, Free minced forward, her skirt held high enough to expose her delicately arched feet and a significant length of well-turned ankle. Free seemed to have no idea of the potential effect of this maneuver in a society where a lady's skirts obscured the fact she had feet, much less legs. Instead, Free bobbed in Alfred's general direction. She replied to Alfred's and Jagger's greetings with little more than a mumbled "hi."

Uh oh, Thea whispered in Liz's mind as Free side-stepped to Theron.

A wide-eyed, enraptured Theron who homed in on Free like iron filings to a magnet. Still holding his wizard's staff, Theron made a deep, graceful bow and caught Free's right hand on the upswing. She didn't resist his familiarity, but she didn't raise her eyes from her feet either.

"Little flower." Theron brushed his lips over the back of Free's hand.

Free's gaze zoomed from the floor to Theron's face. "What?"

"'Frieda' means 'little flower' in old Hiawati," Theron explained. "And I vow I've never seen a rose as fair in all of my Mother's kingdoms."

Free stared at Theron. Her cheeks paled. Her lower lip quivered.

This is going to be a disaster, Thea echoed Liz's thoughts. *She's terrified. Liz, we've got to do something.*

Here goes nothing. Liz's thoughts enveloped Free like a protective cloak. When Free didn't object, Liz settled gingerly into her friend's mind.

Oh, Stefan, I mean, Theron, you're so young here, not quite as young as me, thank goodness, but your beautiful eyes are so wise, so understanding. They seem to see into my very soul. Do you see the love there, Theron? Do you know how I've dreamed of this day? Oh my darling, Stefan—I mean,

Theron, of course I knew you'd find a way to bring me to you. Who else's magic is powerful enough to cross the gazillion miles separating us?

"Thank you," Free whispered.

"You're a lot shyer than your sisters," Hawke said.

"And what have you done to make the lady feel welcome?" Conlan rumbled. He sank to one knee and extended his hand. "I am Conlan, Lady Frieda. Now and forever yours to command."

Hawke didn't stare; he gaped. Roarke's features settled into a more calculating expression. Jagger wore no expression at all.

Oh wow, who knew Conlan could be such a gentleman, Free thought. *I don't remember him being like that in the show. I mean, he's just a jock. Stefan was never into sports, thank goodness. I bet Conlan gets his manners from hanging around Theron. See, I knew Theron was a good influence on all the people around him.*

Throughout Free's internal monologue, Conlan gazed deep into her eyes, waiting patiently for some recognition of his gesture.

"Thanks," Free said. She brushed her fingers against Conlan's hand and shuffled toward Roarke.

Free, don't you dare! Liz's mental voice barked. *Quick—say something more to Conlan! Look at him, for God's sake. He damn near handed you his heart on a platter. You don't walk away from a gesture like that.*

Stupid conscience. I said "thanks" and touched his hand, Free answered. *What more do you want? It's not like he's upset about it or anything. Besides, I don't like jocks. I'm only interested in Theron…and maybe a little bit in Roarke. I hate it when my conscience talks like my aunt! I'm Freya, no matter what Reyah says, and Freya belongs to Stefan, I mean Theron, and that's that.*

Nice try, Jiminy Cricket, Thea commented in Liz's head. *Who knew you and her conscience sound like her aunt?*

Conlan rose, his face shuttered.

Liz glanced at Reyah, who shrugged. Not that Liz expected her to do anything, but…

"Lady Elizabeth, Mistress of Mind and Illusion."

Liz walked up to Alfred. In her three-inch heels, they stood eye to eye. Liz lifted her chin. The corners of Alfred's eyes crinkled as he bit back a smile. He and the other Chosen offered bows only a hair less deep than those they offered Reyah herself.

"Please, accept my heartfelt welcome to Reyah's Keep, Lady Elizabeth. I am honored to make your acquaintance."

"And I am honored to meet a man who lives up to the title of Reyah's Chosen Cavalier." Translation: *Way to go, Alfred.* Liz smiled at the Lord of the Keep and the Keep's Chosen before turning her attention to the Vanyr. "Gentlemen, I trust you'll help a stranger here. How does a daughter of Reyah greet one of Reyah's sons?"

"As an equal." Jagger's voice poured over her, as rich as chocolate and twice as sinful. He raised his hand.

Liz imitated his gesture. Energy fizzed across her palm as it neared his. A white light sprang from their fingers and formed a cat's cradle of electricity that sizzled through her. She'd never felt anything like it. It was as if someone had injected pure sunshine into her bloodstream. Liz giggled. She couldn't help it.

Jagger's smile was sunshine too, as light-hearted and open as the joy humming through Liz's veins. Liz would have to be stone not to respond to it. "What is it?" she asked in awe.

"Magic."

"Is it always like this?" Bright, fresh, as alive as the heart racing in her chest.

"I should say…"

"You should stop this instant!" Theron pounded his staff on the carpet. "Lower your hand, woman. Sharing magic in public is not only unseemly, it is an insult to our Mother and our status as Her Sons. Show proper respect to your betters. Curtsey as your sisters did."

Liz raised an eyebrow. Her initial impression of Theron had been right on the money. He was a pompous bastard with an exaggerated opinion of his own importance. After years of working with Congress and the military, she knew how to deal with the type. She said, "Theron, do you bow to your brothers?"

"Brothers!" Theron thundered. "Listen to me, you insolent baggage, we aren't your brothers."

"Theron!" Reyah bellowed. "You will not make an ass of yourself in *my* presence. What part of 'Greet my daughters' didn't you understand? They are your equals. Insult these women, and you insult me. Apologize. Now."

Theron's face purpled. Time for damage control. Liz said, "I guess this situation is a bit of a shock for everyone—excepting Reyah, of course. I'm sure there was no harm meant on any side."

Jagger inclined his head. "As politic as she is lovely, Great Mother. We are doubly blessed."

Hawke's blue eyes twinkled. "Yeah, she's almost as slick as you, and she just got here. Lady Elizabeth, would you permit a lowly warrior to kiss your hand? I should warn you, though, I'm not feeling the least bit brotherly. Pardon me for moving fast, but being the eldest, Jagger usually gets first shot at the most beautiful women. Why don't we get together later? I'll show you my magic lance. It's famous throughout Domain."

"Ther-on. I'm waiting," Reyah said.

"For Goddess' sake, Theron, spit it out and get it over with," Hawke muttered out of the side of his mouth.

Theron squeezed his staff so tightly, Liz was afraid his knuckles would split the skin. Staring hard at a point somewhere over Liz's left shoulder, he said, "Lady Elizabeth, forgive my misunderstanding of the situation. I will not make the same mistake again."

Reyah's not being fair! I'm sure Stefan, I mean, Theron, didn't mean it the way it sounded, Free's mind voice rang in Liz's inner ear. *He was probably trying to protect Liz from Jagger.*

Liz decided Free no longer needed help to overcome her fear of the Vanyr and shut "the Mistress of Leaf and Vine" out of her mind. "Thank you, Theron. Apology accepted." Not believed, but accepted.

"Thanks," Hawke mouthed at Liz.

"Conlan, I've so looked forward to meeting you." Liz extended her hand. Conlan went through the motions of kissing it. Mentally, Liz flinched from the unhappiness radiating from his touch. *Is he suffering from Free, Theron or both?* Liz asked herself. *Whatever, maybe I can help. Hawke's not the only one who can do outrageous in a good cause.*

"I've heard about your expertise with your weapon." Liz paused. "And they say you're pretty good with a sword too."

A smile tugged at the corners of Conlan's mouth. With mock gravity, he said, "Indeed, Lady, from what source did these tales spring?"

Kait called out, "The TV show, of course. You and Hawke are the baddest badass warriors on the planet."

"Were," Sarah corrected. "There's a new badass in town."

Oh, give me a break, Thea said in Liz's head.

"Tee Vee?" Vanyr and Chosen asked.

"It's a kind of scrying device," Liz said. "It uses glass and light instead of water."

"Could you teach me that spell?" Vallenius blurted out. Gareth shushed the young wizard, cuffing Vallenius lightly on the head to emphasize the point. "Oh. Excuse me."

"Perhaps another time," Liz offered.

Jagger laughed inside her. *Will you teach me too?*

And he still looked good.

Damn.

Chapter Nine

"Roarke, your reputation precedes you," Lady Elizabeth said.

"Are you sure it wasn't his nose?" Hawke quipped.

Lady Elizabeth chuckled.

Roarke marveled at the strength of her power. Was there no limit to these women's magic? The wizardry bred to the bone of Lady Anna had stunned him. The elemental gifts of storm and vegetation flowing from Lady Marisol and Lady Frieda awed him. But this... In scope and strength, her magic matched Jagger's, but it wasn't the same. There was none of Reyah's treacle sweet or Kalin's bitter in Lady Elizabeth's bracing energies. Her magic tasted as clean as the white fire Jagger drew from her hand.

Roarke glanced at the lovely blonde waiting beside Reyah. It was obvious Reyah was saving the best for last. How powerful would the blonde's magic be? And of what kind? Something in Roarke yearned toward the blonde. Even though it hadn't been displayed, he could almost feel her magic, taste it. Taste her. She'd be sweet, as sweet as the Adaban peaches he'd craved as a child. He could almost feel her petal-soft lips against his.

Where had that thought come from? Roarke didn't have time for that kind of distraction. What he needed was help, of the magical sort. He needed mages, powerful mages who could help him expose and destroy Deryk.

Despite the smiling woman standing in front of him, Roarke's gaze returned to the blonde.

Lady Elizabeth cleared her throat. "Thea will be here soon enough," she said, an amused smile on her face. "I promise to move along as soon as you've said hello."

"You'll have to pardon him, Lady," Conlan said. "I understand his nursemaid dropped him on his head quite frequently when he was young."

Roarke flushed and raised Lady Elizabeth's hand to his lips. "I beg your pardon, Lady. Truly, it is an honor to meet you."

Roarke tugged at the collar of his doublet. Kalin's balls, what was wrong with him? This woman had power he could only dream of, and he had insulted her. If he didn't watch it, his dream of taking down Deryk would remain only a dream.

"Gentlemen, please, drop the formalities. My friends call me Liz." The redhead tilted her head in Alfred's direction. "And that applies to everyone in this room."

Delighted smiles bloomed on the Chosens' faces. Theron sneered, naturally. From the corner of his eye Roarke saw Reyah open her mouth as if to comment. The goddess glanced at Jagger and folded her lips shut. Roarke would've given his left arm to know what his mother was thinking.

"Speaking of formalities," Liz continued. "You guys are dressed to the nines. Did we interrupt a party?"

Hawke slanted a look at Reyah. "After a fashion. Tomorrow is our blessed Mother's Natal Day. All of Domain will be celebrating."

"If Alfred can get the damage from the earthquake fixed in time," Conlan added.

Kait broke off a conversation with Sarah to ask: "Earthquake? What earthquake? There was an earthquake?"

"But it can't be Reyah's Natal Day. Reyah's born in the spring." Pandora tugged on Brigid's sleeve. Roarke could almost hear the fabric getting ready to tear. "Remember the show. Monday is Labor Day—oopf! Bri-gid! Why'd you poke me with your elbow? That hurt!"

"Ladies!" Reyah rapped her scepter against the arm of her throne. "Explanations later. Shall we finish?"

With an impish grin for the Vanyr and a wink for the lithe beauty Reyah saved for last, Liz took her seat.

Reyah intoned, "Lady Thea, Mistress of Magic and Change."

Roarke's brain ceased to function. The way Thea walked was an invitation and a challenge all in one. That mouth-watering, brain-numbing walk made Roarke ache in places he'd forgotten he had places.

Danger. Roarke shook his head and glanced at Jagger. Had the Old One said something? Thea stopped in front of Alfred. A thick tress of tawny gold hair slipped over her shoulder and curved under one breast. Roarke's hands clenched into fists as the urge to touch Thea, to follow the strand of hair with his fingers, became almost overwhelming.

Yes, oh yes. Damned dangerous.

Thea accepted Alfred's greeting with a friendly smile. "And I'm Thea," she said. Roarke sourly noted Willem, Gareth and that pup Vallenius were in danger of falling over their tongues. Thea didn't seem to notice. She turned to Jagger.

"Will the magic work for me too?" Thea raised her hand.

Jagger smiled. "Why don't we find out?"

A ball of blue energy spun between Thea's and Jagger's hands. Softer than the crackling white energy Jagger had shared with Liz, but still strong. The floor beneath Roarke's feet trembled. By the stars, more than strong. Roarke felt every fiber of his being vibrate to the song of Thea's magic. He felt energized, he felt alive. He felt...whole.

"I'll be damned, the Magic of the Two," Hawke exclaimed. "I didn't think it existed anymore."

"The Magic of the Two hasn't been seen in centuries," Roarke objected.

"Fascinating," Conlan said.

"Stop!" Theron shouted, thumping his staff against the floor. "What're you playing at, Jagger? There is no such magic!"

"Theron," Reyah growled. "One more word and I swear I'll unmake you."

Behind Reyah, Frieda gripped the arms of her chair and shot the back of Reyah's head a murderous glare. Roarke prayed Theron would open his mouth and do Domain a favor. But he didn't. Roarke hoped all the bile Theron was swallowing would eventually choke the sanctimonious prick.

"Oh wow," Thea breathed. She looked over her shoulder, a mischievous smile lighting her face. "This magic stuff is all that and two bags of Doritos." Her sisters, even Frieda, burst into laughter.

"I'm not sure what 'Doritos' are, but I know how to make it even better," Jagger teased. "Let's try two hands and see what happens."

Thea chuckled. "This was pretty earth-shattering. I think we might want to save two hands for a later date."

Jagger bowed. "I live for that day, Lady."

Roarke nearly burst out laughing when Thea stepped in front of Theron. "You might want to do something about your blood pressure," she advised. "And *you* can call me Lady Thea."

Theron's staff quivered. Roarke would've been willing to wager serious money Theron would have splinters all the way to the bone once he let go.

"You're cruel, Lady," Hawke complained when Thea stopped in front of him.

"I am?"

"You made a date with Jagger before giving the rest of us a chance. You don't want to step out with an elderly mind mage, do you?"

"Oh, I don't know," Thea said, grinning at Jagger. Jagger blew her a kiss. "He looks like he'd be able to keep up with me. Besides, I never said when we'd meet."

"I can rectify that right now," Jagger said.

"Hush, Jagger, you had your chance. Thea, will you do me the very great honor of accompanying me to tomorrow's celebration? I can show you things no one else can."

"Or would want to," Conlan said.

Roarke rubbed his damp palms against his thighs. When the hell were Hawke and Conlan going to step back and let Thea get to him? And, dammit, there was Jagger jumping into the conversation again. Greedy bastards. Still—Roarke's gaze lingered over Thea's lush figure—he doubted he'd be able to tear himself away either.

"And last, but I'm sure not least, Roarke." Thea's voice jerked Roarke from his reverie. She extended her hand. "I'm very pleased to meet you."

"The honor is all mine, Thea." Roarke took her hand, intending to lift it to his lips. Turquoise lightning seared through his veins, awaking the withered seeds of his magic into painful, ecstatic life. Where Liz's magic had been the cool, brisk, freshening winds of the high plains, Thea's was the warm, ripe, sensuous magic of a summer afternoon. Goddess, there was so much of it. So much magic it almost took his breath away.

Was taking his breath away. Roarke tugged at his collar. He couldn't breathe. *Why couldn't he breathe?*

Thea snatched her hand back. "Roarke? Are you all right? Did I hurt you?"

Roarke struggled to catch his breath. He didn't like the speculative looks his mother and Jagger wore. Roarke simply hadn't been prepared for the extent of Thea's magic. That was all. "No Lady, it wasn't you, I swear. I'm afraid I'm a bit weary after the day's events. It all caught up with me."

"Are you sure?"

100

Roarke savored the concerned look on Thea's face. "Absolutely. You needn't worry about me, my lady."

Roarke braced himself and took Thea's hand again. This time her magic coursed no less strongly, but far less painfully through him. In a calculated move, Roarke turned her hand over and pressed a lingering kiss on the creamy skin of her wrist. "Unless, of course, you want to."

Thea's eyes widened. "I think you're all right," she said, taking step back. It wasn't quite the reaction he would've liked, but it was better than no response at all.

"Roarke recovers quickly," Jagger remarked. "He's quite the survivor." Roarke debated the wisdom of running Jagger through with one of the swords decorating Alfred's walls. But Roarke knew the sword would be at his own throat before he even had it off the wall. He tamped down his rage and did what he did best. Waited.

"Surviving is a good thing," Thea said. "I'm all in favor of it." She turned and walked away.

Roarke licked his lips. The sight of Thea walking away was just as good as Thea walking toward you. Lost in admiring the sway of her slender hips, Roarke nearly jumped out of his skin when the doors to Alfred's office burst open, and the young stallion from the Terminus galloped in. Four of Alfred's personal guards, their pikes leveled as if they were charging into battle followed.

"Lord Alfred," Donatien brayed. "A new tower has appeared on the east side of the Keep!"

"*Protect!*" Reyah commanded.

He almost missed the change. Thea's form blurred. A tawny panther with startling turquoise eyes crouched in her place. The panther roared and swiped at Donatien. The attack's physical and magical weight sent Donatien spinning into Hawke and Conlan. Hawke bundled the Chosen behind him.

Sarah sprang from her chair and back-flipped to the nearest guard, catching him under the chin with her feet. The guard staggered backward through the doors, struck his head against the wall, and tumbled to the floor. Kait whipped out her sword and chopped the second guard's pike into kindling. Sarah kicked the unfortunate guard into unconsciousness, neatly landing him next to the first. The last two guards hesitated, lowered their pikes and backed away.

Reyah wore a cat-who-ate-the-thrallingbird smile. Leaning forward, Roarke glanced at Jagger. The Old One displayed no expression at all—a sure sign he was furious. Roarke wondered why. Reyah staged stunts like this all the time.

On Alfred's signal, Willem barked, "Guardsmen, stand down!"

Theron raised his staff, then, with a sidelong glance at Reyah, lowered it. Kait pivoted. Her sword pointed at Theron's heart. Sarah aimed both of her miniature crossbows straight at Theron's throat. Brigid moved in front of the panther.

The rest of the women formed a protective crescent in front of Reyah. The panther's head jerked as if she were straining against an invisible leash. Growling, the big cat turned her back on the commotion and stalked to Liz's side. Brigid followed. Liz's eyes glowed Goddess-blue. The bleak line of her mouth eased when she rested her hand on the panther's neck. Next to Liz, Anna began to chant to under her breath.

So that's what the "change" in "Mistress of Magic and Change" meant, Roarke thought. *Thea's a Shifter like Reyah's Firstborn. And she doesn't look pleased that Reyah caused her to Change.*

"Here, Brigid," Reyah called. "Take this."

Reyah's scepter flew through the air, changing into a tall staff in mid-flight. Brigid plucked the staff from the air. "Thanks," she said. "It's, um, very nice."

A glow rose from the three women standing closest to Reyah. Frieda, Marisol and the unsteady Pandora clasped hands. Marisol's red satin dress seemed to melt into the fiery outline of a massive sun. Its orange and crimson corona lashed the air. A gust of wind roared around the room, hotter than any smithy's forge. Roarke could feel power building, building, building.

Vallenius groaned. The young wizard looked as if he were about to pass out.

"End it," Jagger said. "The Keep and its wizard can't take any more."

Reyah pouted. "Jagger, you're no fun anymore. But you have a point. Enough, My daughters. All is well."

The cat shivered. Once again Thea stood next to her sisters. Blue wisps of power shimmered and dissipated in the air. Liz took a deep breath as Kait and Sarah lowered their weapons. Frieda, Pandora and Marisol unlinked hands.

"I can't believe what She just did," Thea growled. Roarke sympathized with her fury.

Liz put her arm around Thea's shoulders. "Shh. Is everyone okay?"

Anna and Brigid nodded.

Marisol put a hand to her head. "Oh my God. I felt as if I was going to burst into flame."

"We were great!" Pandora exulted. She tottered toward Kait and Sarah. "Thea, your cat was past badness! And man, Marisol, your sun magic hoodoo was kicking! I love it! We did it! We *are* the Daughters of Reyah, *just* like we wrote. Isn't that the coolest?"

"Positively icy," Kait cheered before engaging Pandora in an elaborate hand-slapping ritual.

"*The new tower will be My daughters' home,*" Reyah said. Her outline wavered, sparking with tiny blue-white flares. Her image began to fade. "*It is My gift to them as they are My gift to Domain. I charge you, My Vanyr and My Chosen, to honor them as you would honor me. But above all, I charge you to guard them well and aid them to unlock their potential, for the fate of Domain rests in their hands.*"

Reyah vanished in a final cascade of light.

"Bitchin'! The special effects around here are out-*ra*-geous!" Pandora exclaimed.

Chapter Ten

Deryk's tower, Mount Tuumb

Lydia sighed in relief as Deryk threw open a door, revealing a luxurious room warmed by a roaring fire. *Thank God.* It'd been cold on top of the tower. Lydia made a mental note to find the nearest purveyor of haute couture as soon as possible. Something in velvet or fur for outerwear, with a nice heavy silk for formal occasions. Of course, she was going to have to give some serious thought to daywear, lingerie…

"I prepared this room especially for you, Lady Megeara," Deryk said.

Lydia blinked. For a moment she'd forgotten Deryk was there.

Deryk slid a hand down Lydia's arm. "A warm and safe haven for us to discuss our partnership and other things," he said, doing his best to blow in her ear.

Lydia let Deryk's familiarity slide. After all, they were still in the negotiation stage. She'd done more than her fair share of casting couch deals.

Exhaling a slow, deep breath, Lydia lowered her woolly eyelashes as if she couldn't imagine anything she'd rather do than be closeted in the same room with Michael…er, Deryk. Lydia hoped this Deryk was more interesting than the wimp who played him on the show. Why couldn't the writers have set Megeara up with a really cool villain and not some mama's boy?

"Such a deep sigh," Deryk murmured. He planted a wet kiss on the back of Lydia's hand. "I hope it indicates pleasure with your new home…and host."

Lydia resisted the urge to wipe her hand on the back of her dress. *Ick*, the creep had used his tongue.

Deryk smiled at her in a way he probably thought would make an ordinary woman dizzy with pleasure. Lydia smiled back. Unfortunately for Deryk, the word "ordinary" had never applied to Lydia in her entire thirty-eight—er, thirty-two years of life. "Obstinate", "obdurate", "obstreperous" and "obnoxious" maybe, but never "ordinary".

She needed to keep Deryk hot for her. Sparing him one last smoldering glance, she turned her attention to the room.

A small table for two was set with crystal and gold. Light from a chandelier gilded platters of bread, fruit and cheese. Facing the fireplace was a large, high-backed wooden bench softened with plush, multi-colored pillows and several thick, black fur throws. Another fur throw, snowy white flecked with gold, lay on the floor. A four-poster bed stood in one corner of the room, its crimson satin coverlet drawn back to reveal ivory silk sheets, embroidered in gold and edged with lace. To the left was a tall armoire. Lydia's fingers itched to open the doors and see what Deryk had inside.

"Not bad," Lydia drawled. This was a good start. Not fantastic, but good. A lot would depend on the kitchen and maid service. Lydia flicked an imaginary speck of lint from her sleeve and yawned. "A bit small, but I suppose I can make do."

Deryk smiled tightly and gestured toward the table. "Shall we have a glass of wine, my lady? Let us toast your return and our ultimate victory."

Lydia permitted herself a small mental smirk. She was getting under his skin. Good.

Deryk poured copper-colored wine into two crystal goblets. With an elegant bow, he handed a goblet to Lydia. Deryk raised his glass. "Here's to a successful partnership."

Lydia returned Deryk's smile with interest. "I love success," she cooed as she clicked her goblet against his. Lydia sauntered to the sofa. "Tell me, Deryk, darling—" she patted the cushion next to her "—you mentioned something about conquering Tambara?"

Deryk sank down beside her, a self-satisfied smile on his face. *Better enjoy feeling like you have the upper hand, bucko,* Lydia thought. *When all the shouting is done, I'll be the one with top billing and you'll be nothing but "Villain Number Two".*

Chapter Eleven

The Daughters' tower, the Keep

"Liz, where are you?" Thea called from the foyer. "Holy cow. Your room looks a scene from a 1930s' movie."

Liz agreed. She'd thought exactly the same thing the moment she'd walked in the door. Ivory-on-white damask covered the walls and tented the ceiling. Twinkling wizard lights danced among the crystal prisms of the room's chandelier and sconces. Along the outer wall of the room, cascades of inky black velvet embroidered with stylized gold and silver wolf heads alternated with tapestries depicting semi-naked men in martial poses. More gilt-embroidered black velvet shrouded a canopy bed large enough to accommodate an intimate, lay-down orgy of six. Facing the foot of the bed, a massive blue-veined marble mantel seethed with satyrs and nymphs.

Thea sank down on a white velvet covered chair. "This is way beyond our fan fiction."

"You got that right. And you ain't seen nothing yet." Liz threw open the door to the nearest armoire. A rainbow of rich fabrics ballooned out of the opening.

Thea chuckled. "Girlfriend, your inner clotheshorse must be doing a major happy dance."

"Roger that. But let's not forget the bling, shall we?" Liz moved to a lacquered cabinet on a matching stand and pulled open a few of its drawers at random. Velvet sacks bulged with jewelry, loose gemstones and fat purses of gold coins, each bearing the imprint of a different monarch. "What did you get?"

"Blue," Thea crooned. "Every shade of my favorite color you could imagine."

"Did you get the clothes and other goodies too?"

Thea grinned. "In spades. I'm still trying to figure out what I'm going to do with all the shoes."

"Duh. You wear them." Liz draped herself over a chaise. She felt a little headachy. She probably shouldn't have taken Alfred up on his offer of a glass of wine. But it had been such a relief to lose Reyah, and the wine Hawke called Gordo had tasted marvelous. Besides, she'd feel fine as soon as she ate. "One thing you gotta say about Reyah—she gives good bribes."

Thea snorted. "She needs to. I'm still mad about her little demonstration of shock and awe in Alfred's office."

"Yeah, it bothers me too. First she yanks us around like puppets, then she gives us the Enchanted Castle, Domain-style. What's next?" Liz rubbed her temples.

The slight pressure refused to go away. Were Reyah's shields breaking up already? No, it didn't feel like an invasion. It felt familiar, like…Marisol? Specifically, like an upset Marisol.

"Thea, we've got trouble in Whoville."

"What kind of trouble?"

"I'm not sure." Liz slipped out of the room onto the landing. She craned over the staircase.

"Liz," Kait huffed from two flights down, "is Thea with you? You guys've got to get downstairs. World War III is breaking out in the living room. I think it's going to take both of you to stop it."

"Coming," Liz called to Kait. "I *knew* this was going to happen."

"So speaks the mind mage. I wish they'd waited 'til we learned how to Port. All these stairs are killing my calves."

♾♋

"Oh, for Pete's sake, Free! Give me a break! Every other word out of your mouth is Theron, Theron, Theron."

Anna's voice rose up the stairwell. Liz didn't need to be psychic to hear the frustration rising with it. "I'm sick to death of hearing about Theron…or should I say 'Stefan' since your tiny brain can't seem to separate the two? Of all the Vanyr you could choose, why does it have to be that dickhead Theron? Don't you have any taste at all?"

"Free, Anna's right. Why do you want to be with somebody like him?" Marisol asked. "Dios, the man is horrible. Sure, Stefan Warner is a great guy, but this Theron is nothing like the TV show or Stefan. He's got a stick up his ass. You can tell he thinks he's better than anybody else. You'd be better off back home, with a real man like Stefan, not this jerk."

The tower's ground floor entrance hall spread in a large arc from the mouth of the central staircase. Boule sideboards, velvet-padded settees and rose-enameled porcelain stoves flanked the arched double doors leading into the Keep proper. Six battling beauty queens formed a shifting, multi-colored mass in front of the sideboard to Liz's left.

I give 'em five minutes before the fur starts to fly, Thea remarked. Thea joined Liz on the third step up from the bottom of the stairs. *Securing the higher ground just in case, Liz?*

Liz shook her head. *You'd think they'd be too tired to fight. I sure am.*

"At least Theron paid attention to me. Even with Reyah getting my name wrong, he kissed my hand and called me a 'little flower'. That's more than you got from that pipsqueak Alfred," Free snapped at Anna.

Sarah zoomed in on Marisol. "Oh, now you want to go home for Free's sake. Why don't you admit the real reason you want to go home, Marisol? You're not the center of everybody's universe anymore. You're just one of the girls. How does it feel not to be the prettiest woman in the room? How does it feel to have some competition for a change?"

"Sarah," Brigid growled. "Stop it. This has gone far enough."

"Shut your face, Brigid. I suppose you want to go back to your stupid little dead-end job in Seattle. You were never going to make it as an actress. Everyone knows if you don't hit it big by thirty, you never will. All you were doing was screwing off your chances for a real career."

"Sarah, that's not fair!" Pandora chimed in. "I'm sure Brigid didn't want to be changed any more than I did. Who wants to be a bimbo in skin-tight pants and thigh-high boots?"

Free whirled around. "You do, you hypocrite. I saw the way you stared at Donatien and the way he stared right back at you. Do you think he would've looked at you if you still wore a stupid butch haircut and those dumb overalls?"

"Looks aren't everything," Marisol protested.

"How would you know?" Free, Sarah and Anna shouted.

Marisol flinched and backed toward the nearest stove. Her hunched shoulders and shaking head reminded Liz of a cornered animal.

Even a cornered rabbit fights back. The air around the Mistress of Sun and Wave began to vibrate. Liz tasted the same heat and rapidly multiplying energies that had nearly exploded Alfred's office, but this time there was no Elder Goddess to control them.

"That's enough," Liz roared over the squall of voices. "*Enough!*"

The power in Liz's voice resonated through the air. The veneers on the furniture buckled and popped. The stemware on the sideboards shattered. The fisheye mirrors hanging on the brocaded walls crumbled. Porcelain bowls of potpourri imploded, releasing their spicy, citrus perfume in a sinus-searing rush. Liz glanced at the stove behind Marisol and held her breath.

The stove didn't crack, thank God. Liz didn't want to think about broken fireboxes or what might've happened if something fragile—a mortal servant, for example—had been in the room when her power sang. At least, she appeared to have shaken Marisol out of whatever Marisol had been about to do.

"Liz?" Kait's uncertainty shivered across Liz's back.

Liz forced herself to relax the unfamiliar magical muscles fisted around her "command voice". It was like untying knots in the dark. *Great. Just when I need to talk some sense into this bunch, I find my voice is a lethal weapon.*

It always was, Thea answered in Liz's mind. *Only now it's got a lot more firepower. Don't worry, I've got your back.*

It's my front I'm worried about, Liz thought as she marched down the remaining steps.

"Stop it," she ordered. "All of you. We've got trouble enough without fighting among ourselves."

"What do you mean, 'trouble'?" Pandora said. "The only trouble around here is certain people with bad attitudes."

Pandora glared at Free. Free glared back.

Liz clapped her hands together. "Pay attention, ladies. Have you forgotten we're supposed to take out the Demon Witch? Or that we haven't got a clue how to use our magic?"

"So? Jagger said he'd teach us," Anna said.

Liz swore under her breath. "And what do we do 'til then? Throw flowers?"

Anna sniffed. "I don't know what you're worried about. It's not like we're going to have to take out the Demon Witch tonight. 'Sides, all I need is a few remedial lessons. I pretty much know how to use my magic."

"For crying out loud, Anna, look at what I did to this room," Liz said. "Do you think I wanted to trash the furniture? All I wanted to do was get your attention."

Thea joined the fray. "Anna, if you 'pretty much' know how to use your magic, why don't you give the rest of us a small demonstration. Any old spell will do."

"I could...no, I can't." Anna flounced to a chair. "Damn you, Thea. I *hate* when other people are right."

"Our magic can't be screwed up," Pandora whined. "I was counting on you guys to do something about my hair." Pandora grabbed a hank of hair on either side of her head. She flopped the tresses up and down. "Look at this stuff. What if I roll over in the middle of the night? I could suffocate!"

"Now there's a happy thought," Anna said.

"Oh for heaven's sake," Marisol said. "It's only hair, Pandora. Cut it."

"Why didn't I think of that? Hey, Brigid, gimme one of your knives."

"No!" Brigid and Marisol shouted together.

"Let me find some scissors," Brigid said. "There's got to be some around here someplace."

"Liz, don't let her do anything until we get back," Marisol added, racing up the stairs after Brigid. "Curly hair looks awful if you don't cut it just right."

"And you wouldn't want to run into Donatien looking anything less than your best," Free said snidely.

଼ଓଃ

In another part of the Keep

Blue light spilled from between the doors of a large cupboard in a corner of the Lord of the Keep's private library. The cupboard began to rock back and forth. It fell forward. The crash shook the room. Half-smothered curses seeped from the interior of the cupboard. A rhythmic pounding shook its back. There was a splintering sound. Pieces of wood flew across the room. The glowing tip of a staff ran around the perimeter of the hole, smoothing away jagged edges.

"Deplorable! I must speak with Reyah about Jagger's unconscionable laxity regarding the upkeep of the Portals." Theron climbed from the back of the cupboard. He sneezed. "If the College of Wizards ever found out I Ported into a cupboard I'd be a laughingstock. Me, Reyah's son!"

Brushing the splinters from his robe, Theron looked around for the shelf where he'd last seen the Keep's copy of *The Arts of Love*. It wasn't there. Neither were most of the shelves. Books and scrolls lay helter-skelter on the floor, covered with plaster dust and broken furniture.

"Goddess, but this place is a wreck. I don't care what Gareth says; an earthquake is no excuse for slovenliness. It's going to take me forever to find that damned book."

A triangle of white covered with oddly shaped letters caught Theron's eye. Theron reached under a pile of crumpled scrolls and lifted what looked like a flour sack. The strings tying the top of the sack had come undone. Theron's eyes widened.

"What have we here?" Theron eased a stack of papers from the cotton bag. "I've never seen…"

"This way! The crash was in here!" Voices resounded outside the door.

"Shit," Theron swore.

ᏚᎧ

Vallenius skidded to a stop outside the library door. The Keep was nagging him blue over someone in the library. Val wondered if he'd ever get used to the voice whispering in his head. "The Keep says there's an intruder in here."

Willem reached for the door.

"Wait!" Val grabbed his hand. "The room is warded!"

"I thought Jagger released all the wards. When did he put them back up?"

"He didn't." Val traced the release spell with his hands. "I did. I was worried about looters so I put a few back up."

"Stand back." Willem drew his sword and eased the door open. He peered into the room, then stepped inside. He called to Val a moment later. "No one's here now."

At first glance, the room looked the same as it had when Val warded it an hour earlier. Then he saw the busted cupboard. Val picked up a chunk of the cupboard's back. "Why would looters chop up this cupboard? It's never locked. The librarian only used it to store supplies."

"My question is, how'd they get in?" Willem prowled the room. "I know your wards. Anyone opening the door would have been blown halfway down the hall."

"This doesn't make a lick of sense," Val grumbled. "There's no way a looter got through the door. So, how'd they get in?"

"Hell if I know. I've got this entire wing under lockdown. No one should've been able to get past my guards or your magic."

Val paced the room, tracing a scrying sigil over and over. One of the sigils suddenly glowed blue. "You're not going to believe this. It was a Portal."

Willem folded his arms across his chest. "Didn't Jagger shut the Portals down?"

"Don't ask me. Nobody tells me anything, especially Jagger." Val poked at the remains of the cupboard. "You know what else is strange? This tastes like Vanyr magic."

"Deryk?" Willem asked. Val shook his head. "Why would one of the others need to sneak in? They've got free run of the Keep."

Val turned in a slow circle. "All I know is what the Keep tells me and what I feel. A Vanyr Portaled in here and busted up this cupboard."

Willem brushed a hand over his head. "Jagger used a lot of magic tonight. Not to mention the fireworks from Reyah and Her lovely Daughters. Maybe that's what you're feeling."

"It wasn't the Daughters. Their magic is different from Vanyr magic. *Very* different."

"I'm calling for backup." Willem walked to the zaihn hanging by the door. He said the activation word. The zaihn's eyes opened. "I need four guardsmen to the Lord's library. Priority."

The zaihn repeated Willem's orders and closed its eyes.

"Can you tell if anything is missing?" Willem asked.

Val raked his fingers through his hair. He was almost ready to pull it out by the roots. "Only the librarian would know if anything's been taken. I hope he's all right. I would've thought he'd be here by now."

"Don't worry, once we're certain nobody's hiding in a closet—"

"Kalin's balls! I knew I forgot something!" Val grabbed Willem's arm. "There's one place your guards don't know about."

"Damn, you're right." Willem checked the hall. "Good. Tanak's on the ball. Here they come."

Four uniformed guards double-timed into the room. Willem pointed to the tallest man in the group. "Burfel, you guard the door and make sure no one comes inside. Ferd, find the librarian and bring him here if he's not too banged up. The rest of you search the wing. If you find anyone, bind them and take them to Tanak. All right, Val, let's check out our hunch."

A few moments later, a window swung open. Theron hoisted a leg over the windowsill. "Thank the Goddess they finally left. I don't think I could've held on much longer." With a muttered chant and a pop of displaced air, a Portal opened. "And now, back to my room to see if what I've found is as good as I think it is."

As soon as Theron vanished, one of the built-in bookcases swung forward. Val and Willem emerged from the secret passageway connected to Alfred's bedroom.

"Theron?" Willem asked incredulously. "Why the hell is *he* sneaking around? There isn't anything in here he hasn't seen before. Hell, according to him, he wrote half of it."

Val frowned. Skulking around like a cat burglar wasn't Theron's style. The pompous Vanyr generally got whatever he wanted by beating people over the head with his "I'm Reyah's son" routine.

"He must've found something," Val said, "because he sure looked pleased with himself when he Ported out."

"Yeah," Willem agreed. "He did. We'd better report this to Alfred."

₧₧

Back in the Daughters' tower

Brigid, Marisol and Pandora were still arguing about the best way to cut Pandora's hair when Liz sensed a Portal opening outside the double doors leading to the Keep. The parted space bloomed like a dark rose inside her mind. Ripples of energy fluttered outward from the opening, resonating against a host of people.

The energy seemed to throw some kind of mental spotlight on the crowd. For a moment, Liz was thirteen, caught in the mob of her first stadium rock show. Masses of people shoved every which way, frantic for a glimpse of celebrity. She could almost hear them chanting for the band to take the stage.

Only this mob wasn't pitting their weight against barricades manned by gun-toting policemen. They were swarming the guards of the Keep, demanding to see Reyah's Daughters. Liz's new-made sisters. Her.

"Liz, what's wrong? Is Reyah's shielding breaking down?" Thea whispered.

With a start, Liz realized her cheek was pressed against the door. Liz took an unsteady step back. "No, I'm fine. You'd better get away from the door. I think they're bringing the food Alfred promised us."

"Food! It's about time!" Kait caroled. Kait, Sarah and Anna yanked the double doors open before Liz could stop them.

The mob outside roared. The sound boomed through the doorway, sending the three women reeling. Gareth and a train of servants toting wicker trunks raced into the room.

"Bolt the door!" Gareth yelled.

Two burly guardsmen threw their weight against the doors. But it took the added muscle of Brigid and Sarah to hold the doors closed long enough for Thea to throw the bolts. The doors were four inches thick and laced with patterned iron, but Liz could still hear the crowd's howls of frustration.

"What the fuck going on?" Sarah swore.

"Word of your arrival has spread throughout the Keep. Everyone is eager to meet you," Gareth said.

"That wasn't 'eager'," Brigid said, "that was extreme."

Free peeked from behind the settee. "They can't get us, can they?" Liz could almost hear Free's teeth chattering.

"Not through those doors, Lady Frieda," Gareth assured her.

Guardsmen took up positions on either side of the door. Gareth glanced around the room, his gaze lingering only an instant on the splintered glass and ruined sideboards. "Would you like the servants to lay out the meal in here?" he asked.

"There's a dining room through there," Anna said, waggling her hand in the direction of the archways flanking the staircase.

Gareth turned to a superior looking servant wearing a dark blue tabard emblazoned with the Reyah Hand and Eye motif. "Yeves, please, set out the ladies' supper in the...er...dining room."

Yeves nodded. The kitchen staff bustled toward the opening and the polished stone table beyond. Liz's empty stomach rumbled at the glorious aroma of fresh-baked bread and the hints of herbs and roasted garlic wafting from the covered dishes.

"If you'll excuse me, ladies," Gareth said. "I'm calling for back-up."

"How?" Thea asked.

"Is there another way out of the tower?" Liz added.

Gareth shrugged. "I wouldn't know. This tower is as new to me as it is to you. With your permission, I'm going to use your zaihn."

"We've got a zaihn like the ones on the show! How cool!" Kait exclaimed. "Where is it?"

Gareth pointed to a larger version of the stylized masks decorating Liz's room. She gave herself a mental headslap. And she called herself a *Domain* fan. She should've made the connection.

Whoa. Talk about all the conveniences of home—we can use the zaihns like intercoms. Thea's mental remark made Liz smile. Liz'd been thinking the same thing.

Anna, *Domain* canon diva, eyed the mask. "What's the activation word for this zaihn?"

"Your zaihns are too new to be keyed," Gareth said. "I'm going to use my emergency Seneschal Protocol."

Liz chuckled to herself. Emergency protocol—didn't it figure emergency protocols would be universal?

"Seneschal Weston," Gareth said to the mask. "Zakhar Blue One. Wake!"

The mask opened its eyes. "Yes?"

"Cool!" all nine women squealed. Liz felt like such a fan girl, but it *was* cool.

"Where's Vallenius?" Gareth asked.

"With Captain."

"Good," Gareth said. "Tell Willem we need crowd control at the new tower soonest. Vallenius is needed too. That's all."

After an instant the zaihn said, "Done." The zaihn's eyes closed.

"Far out," Brigid said. "I hope our zaihns do as many tricks as Val's."

"How do you know what Vallenius's zaihn can do, Lady Brigid?" Gareth asked.

"Call me Brigid, 'kay? We, um, used our scrying device." Brigid winked at Liz.

"If there's an emergency, can we use the same protocol?" Liz asked.

"No," Gareth said. "But I'll have Vallenius come by after the ceremonies tomorrow. He'll help you set up your zaihns then."

"Tomorrow! Tomorrow!" Anna cried, her Georgia drawl thicker than usual. "Oh my God, tomorrow!"

Free, Marisol and Kait jumped. Anna's yelp brought Yeves out of the dining room. The servant looked down his long nose at Anna. He couldn't help it, Liz reflected. He was five inches taller than Anna, and Anna was wearing heels.

Here it comes. Thea's mind voice held a certain morbid satisfaction. *You can't keep a good Scarlett down.*

Isn't Alfred a little short to carry Anna and her bodacious ta-tas up the stairs of Tara, I mean, the tower? Liz responded.

"Where are my priorities?" Anna asked the ceiling. She fluttered her long eyelashes in the seneschal's direction. "Gareth honey, would you mind taking notes?"

Gareth glanced at Yeves. Yeves drew a small, hinged tablet and stylus from under his tabard and waited. Anna paced the room. Her satin skirts shushed with every step. Her perfume drifted after her. When she passed Liz, the spicy scent momentarily overwhelmed the aroma of the food. Liz didn't remember Anna's perfume being as strong at the con. Maybe the translation had something to do with it?

The fascinated gazes of the guards trailed the voluptuous brunette like puppies chasing a bone. Liz's stomach rumbled again. She hoped Anna wouldn't take too long. Their last meal had been a universe away.

"First." Anna held up a finger. "We need tomorrow's schedule and expected attire for each event. Second—and as important—we'll need servants. At the very least, lady's maids to assist us in dressing tomorrow. And the day after, I'll want to interview servants to manage the daily upkeep of our tower."

Yeves looked up from his tablet and regarded Anna with something close to approval.

Anna paused in front of a guardsman and ran a finger down the front of his tunic. "Oh my. Aren't you the cutest little moon pie?"

The guard flushed bright red. He tried to look anywhere but at Anna's overflowing bodice. He didn't succeed.

Anna's eyes sparkled like sapphires. It was plain she adored being young and beautiful again. The black-haired sorceress turned and tapped a rosy fingertip against her cheek. She marched up to Yeves. Yeves blandly returned Anna's expectant stare.

"Finally, we need a superior major-domo," Anna said. "Someone we can trust to make sure we have perfect service at all times. Someone who'll be able to handle all the perks that come with working for nine, very, very generous goddesses."

Anna waited. Yeves pursed his lips and surveyed the room. He nodded. Anna beamed.

"I think that's it," Anna said. "For now."

Gareth coughed back a chuckle. "As you wish, Lady Anna."

"By the way, Yeves honey chile," Thea cooed in an exaggerated southern drawl. "There's one more thing. We'll need at least two hunky footmen named Ashley and Rhett."

"Thea!"

ᔥᔥ

The Vanyr Tower, the Keep

Theron latched the door to his room. A quick gesture activated his wards. He pulled the sack from under his tunic and placed it on his desk.

He snapped his fingers. A pair of wizard lights appeared at his favorite angle for reading. He settled into his chair and pulled a sheet of paper from the sack. *How unusual. I've never seen paper this thin. And the edges are so sharp, almost as if... No. Impossible.* Nothing he knew of could produce edges so uniform.

Theron ran a finger down the smooth page. No human hand could script this finely, this evenly. The symbols resembled nothing Theron had ever seen before.

"Where did this come from?" Theron muttered. It was too strange, too odd to be of Domain. Whatever this was, he was willing to bet it belonged to the women. Theron stroked the paper again. Maybe these papers could tell him more about Frieda and how to win her.

Not only win her, but bind Frieda's beauty and power to him for all time.

Unfortunately, he wasn't the only one who wanted the lady. Conlan's actions in Alfred's office had pointed out the need for Theron to act quickly if he hoped to secure Frieda's affections. In a way, this bothered Theron. He was accustomed to women pursuing him. In fact, it'd been several centuries since he'd had to ask a woman to lie with him.

But in this case, there was no help for it. He was going to have to woo the lady.

An image of his body joined to Frieda's, passion and magic rising like perfume through the air, flitted through his mind. Theron turned back to his desk, quieting himself with slow, even breaths and whispered chants until he could apply the Vanyrs' inborn Gift of Tongues to the unfamiliar symbols on the pages before him.

The very thought of the Gift of Tongues exerted a calming influence. It reminded Theron, although his power sometimes faltered before Reyah's most talented Chosen, his position as Reyah's son granted him status and abilities to which the once mortal Chosen could never aspire. That should count for something in his pursuit of the lissome, red-haired beauty. *It must,* Theron assured himself as he mouthed the words on the top sheet of paper.

"'Vanyr Be Mine' by Pandora." Theron tapped his chin. Since it seemed to be written by one of Frieda's sisters, perhaps there would be merit in reading it.

Conlan threw open the door to the tavern. The strong, virile warrior clutched his chest and gasped in astonishment. There, wearing a comfy pair of overalls and a really cool pair of Nikes, was the girl of his dreams. There, across the smoke filled room, was the fun-loving gal who haunted his restless nights and possessed his lecherous thoughts during his adventure-filled days. There, slurping lustily from a flagon, was the bespectacled elemental who made his turgid manhood ache at the mere thought of the touch of her aquiline fingers.

Theron drew in a deep breath. Now this had real possibilities. He traced a sigil. A mug of tea and a plate of Thrallish Delight appeared on the desk. Theron squinted at the page. What, in Kalin's Seven Hells, were "overalls" and "Nikes?"

Conlan rushed through the crowd of revelers, ardently anxious to meet the dream damsel who, despite a crooked front tooth and a few other, not really noticeable flaws, rocked his world. Conlan punched out two guardsmen, three sailors, five knights and a nerdy law clerk who stood between him and heaven. Conlan wiped his chin. Boy, did this chick make his mouth water.

"Hello there, tall, dark and hunky," Pandora gargled. "Buy me a drink?"

☜☞

The dining room in the Daughters' tower

"You will be here first thing tomorrow morning, won't you?"

"Yes, Lady Anna," Val said, inching toward the shimmer of the Portal he'd opened in front of the windows.

"And you won't forget to bring Yeves and our servants with you, right?"

"No, Lady Anna," Val answered.

"Good. Now let me think, is there anything else?"

An arm reached through the Portal and grabbed Val's collar. The arm hauled Val through. The Portal immediately closed.

"Well!" Anna huffed. "How rude! I wasn't done!"

"You are now," Liz mumbled around a mouthful of what tasted very much like baby green tomatoes pickled with garlic and sweet onions. Only the small, thin-skinned fruits were yellow, and the garlic flavor appeared to derive from what looked like diced green jalapenos. She was in gustatory heaven.

"What is this stuff?" Free inspected the platter of sliced meats, a dubious expression on her face.

"I don't know. But some of it's blue." Kait grimaced.

"What does blue meat taste like?" Free asked

"I don't know. Why don't you taste it?" Kait replied

"No, you taste it."

Anna sighed. "I'll taste it, all right?" She put a piece of the blue meat in her mouth and chewed. The other women waited.

"Yum. Now that's what I call finger food," Anna said, spearing another slice. "Ya'll should try some."

Sarah, sitting to Liz's left, looked doubtfully at the plate. Sarah took a tiny bite of the meat. She smiled in relief. "Anna's right. It is good. Sort of like grilled chicken."

"There is no way I'm eating blue meat. Blue Jell-O, maybe. Blue meat, never." Free eyed the large trays with the gravest misgivings.

Avid curiosity wiggled across Liz's awareness. Liz couldn't be sure, but she seemed to feel something behind the drapes drawn over the windows. As she watched, the drapes shifted, but not from any wind. The windows were closed. Liz nudged Thea.

Thea followed the direction of Liz's gaze. A sneeze rippled the drapes.

"Gesundheit," Pandora said to Kait.

"I didn't sneeze," Kait said. "I was going to say 'God bless you' to you."

"I didn't sneeze," Pandora said. "If you didn't sneeze, who did?"

Thea pointed to a small pair of feet peeping from under the edge of the drapes. Sarah rose from her chair. Liz cleared her throat.

"You probably heard a guard out in the hallway or something," Liz said loudly.

"Yeah," Pandora said as Sarah crept toward the window, "must've been a guard outside."

"Gotcha!" Sarah reached behind the drapes. "Ouch!" Sarah jerked her hand back. "She bit me!"

A young girl wriggled out of Sarah's grasp. The girl tripped and sprawled on the floor. Large pansy brown eyes stared at Sarah, who glared back.

"All right, missy," Sarah said. "What are you doing hiding in our tower?"

The girl—an exact double of Ember Weston, Gareth's adopted daughter on the show—gulped. Liz felt a surge of fear from her. Not one of the adult faces turned toward Ember was smiling. She sat up and pushed a strand of dark brown hair back from a gamin face sprinkled with freckles.

"Um…" The Ember look-alike rose to her feet and brushed off her breeches. She looked warily at Sarah. "I was just…"

Pandora smiled. "You wanted to see the nine women everyone was talking about, right?"

"Right!"

"Does Gareth know you're here, Ember?" Brigid asked.

"How did you know who I am? Wow, you *are* magic ladies, aren't you? I mean they all said you were, but grown-ups exaggerate all the time."

The distant tolling of a large bell drifted into the room. Ember shuffled her feet. "You won't tell my dad, will you? He'll be awfully mad at me and the guards who snuck me in." She turned a woebegone gaze on Pandora, who true to form, melted like candy in the sun.

"Of course we won't tell him," Pandora promised.

Thea studied the small figure dressed in a smudged and torn yellow tunic, grubby brown breeches and even grubbier half boots. "I'll make a deal with you, Ember," Thea said. "You answer some questions about the Keep, and we won't tell anyone you were up here. Deal?"

"No snitching?"

Thea nodded. "No snitching."

Ember grinned. "Deal." She plopped on a chair next to Pandora. "May I have something to eat? I'm starving." Pandora handed her plate to Ember, who attacked it like she hadn't eaten in a week.

"All right, about the Keep, let's see." Ember took another bite of Pandora's sandwich. "My dad is Sir Gareth Weston—but you knew *that*. I'm almost twelve years old, and they keep trying to make me dress up in girly clothes, and I hate having to dress like a girl, and I heard all about one of you becoming a panther, that's great, and I wonder if I could learn to do that, because then I could scare dumb ol' Sir Arbon, and my dad is seneschal, which means that he sort of runs the Keep for Lord Alfred, who's a nice guy like Sir Willem who lets me hang around the practice yard, and sometimes Willem lets me use my slingshot on the pells…"

Chapter Twelve

Outside the Daughters' tower

Crumpled, dusty and smelling like a barracks in summer, the twenty guardsmen manning the barricades outside the Keep's newest tower represented the Daughters of Reyah's last line of defense from rabid hordes of novelty-crazed nobles. Naturally, the guards were dying of curiosity too. They surrounded Roarke and pelted him with questions.

"Vanyr Roarke, there's been all sorts of rumors 'bout what happened when Reyah brought Her daughters to the Keep. You were there. 'Tis true one of them turned into a tiger and ate Sir Donatien?" the youngest guard asked hopefully. The soldier was almost as tall and broad in the shoulders as Hawke, but dough-faced, with a nose broken once too often for the healers to fix.

Roarke suppressed the urge to rub the bridge of his own nose. He shifted the weight of the hamper he'd brought with him to his other hip. Jagger chose that moment to appear in the middle of the brightly lit area between the barricades.

"At Reyah's behest, the Lady Thea demonstrated her shapeshifting abilities for the Vanyr and some of the Keep staff. But no one was in any danger," Jagger said. "In fact, the lady was a regular pussy cat. Ah, Roarke, once again, great minds do think alike."

Roarke closed his eyes and prayed for strength. Jagger carried a linen-covered basket from which protruded the distinctive bottles of Seshmeel's premiere sparkling wine.

At least it wasn't a Peninsular red. Roarke thanked the stars for small favors. And Jagger wouldn't have covered the basket if he'd brought cinderberries, would he? Then again, Jagger wouldn't have stolen the delicate, fleshy pink fruit from Theron's winter garden, either.

One of the tower doors flew open. The guardsmen gasped. Roarke cursed. *Who'd let a boy in the tower?* Roarke's gaze dropped from the back-lit corona of short, fair curls to a tight shirt and even tighter pair of breeches straining against the kind of assets no boy would ever own.

"Ooops," the blonde vision said in a breathy, little girl voice.

"Lady Pandora?" Jagger sounded like he didn't believe his eyes either. The Old One shouldered his way into the tower's receiving room. *Close the door*, his mind voice ordered Roarke. *We don't want them to see Ember.*

Roarke couldn't see Ember, and he was in the receiving room, but he wasn't about to argue the point. The merchant in him was too busy calculating the value of the room's contents. Even damaged, the amount was staggering.

"Vanyr Jagger," Pandora burbled. "This is great! I was about to call Val, but you're even better at Porting than he is. Ember, look who's here. Ember? Em-ber!"

Jagger dropped his basket on a chair and strode toward a linen-covered service table topped by a large samovar. "Ember Weston, I would know your mind in a crowd of thousands. You might as well come out."

Ember backed from under the tablecloth, pausing before the linen cleared her shoulders. Jagger's lips twitched as if he were fighting a smile. "All the way, sprig," he coaxed.

The reason for Ember's hesitation became clear the instant her head came into view. It looked like someone had sawed off the child's braids just above her ears. Tufts of dark brown hair, some of them no longer than a finger's breadth, stood out in every direction from her scalp.

"Ember, who did this to you?" Whoever he was, Roarke would murder the bloody swine with his bare hands.

Ember thrust her chin into the air. "Nobody. I did it to myself. If Lady Pandora can wear her hair short, why can't I?"

Roarke could think of a thousand reasons why the adopted daughter of the Keep's seneschal, who often shared the dais with her father and other ranking officials of Alfred's court, couldn't and shouldn't. But Ember's lower lip was quivering.

Roarke surrendered to the inevitable. "It's nothing that can't be mended, poppet. Right, Jagger?"

"Gee, maybe it is a bit uneven," Pandora conceded. "I'm not as good as Marisol or Brigid at cutting hair. Why don't I take her up to them?"

"No need. Come here, sprig," Jagger said, dropping to one knee. He ran his hand over what was left of Ember's hair. The strands lengthened until they reached the level of Ember's chin. "That should do it. You know, you and the Lady Pandora could very well start a new fashion with this."

"You think so?" Ember asked in a watery voice.

"You look much better now, poppet," Roarke assured her, hoping Gareth saw things in the same light. Ember rewarded him with a weak smile. "Now we need to get you back to your room. If your father finds you missing tonight of all nights…"

"Not to mention Lady Havasham," Jagger murmured.

"Oh bother. The old grouch'll have my head. Did she send you?"

"No," Jagger said.

"Good. She's still sleeping off her joint medicine."

Roarke vowed he was going to have a talk with Gareth about Ember's latest governess as soon as possible.

"But I guess I better get back, anyway," Ember continued. "I don't want Dad to worry. I bet he's heard the strange stuff people are saying about the Daughters of Reyah. But those stories are silly. Thea wouldn't eat anybody."

Not unless he were very lucky, Roarke thought.

"Not unless they deserved it," Pandora said. "Especially once Thea knows what she's doing."

Ember straightened and made a big show of patting her breeches. "Oh darn, I don't have my slingshot. Where did I have it last? I remember showing it to you in your room," she told Pandora. "Do you think I left it there?"

"I don't know. Why don't I go check?" Pandora volunteered.

"A very good idea, Lady Pandora," Jagger said, edging his words with the lightest hint of force. "Ember's slingshot has a history of losing itself in the strangest places. I've known it to take *hours to find*."

Pandora bobbed her head in agreement and trotted up the stairs, her footing more secure in felt slippers than it had been in heels. Perfectly at ease with the effect of

Jagger's words on others, Ember waited until the winding staircase hid Pandora from view. She pulled the missing slingshot from under her tunic.

"I know I'm not supposed to fib, but I needed to talk to you," Ember confided. "I don't know where they're from, but the Daughters of Reyah aren't from Domain. They don't know how we do anything here. But they're nice ladies, so you'll help them, right?"

"Of course we will, sprig," Jagger said. "Now I think it's time you went to bed."

Roarke barely noticed Ember scampering through Jagger's Portal. Not from Domain? Where else was there besides Domain?

ഇൽ

The eighth floor of the Daughters' tower

"The Spa," as Thea dubbed it, occupied most of the eighth floor of the tower. Thea rested her arms on the lip of the pool and tried to determine if the mosaics circling the walls told a story or were only pretty porn. A large brass orb, pierced all over in a pattern of stars, diamonds and circles, hovered near the apex of the vaulted ceiling. Some of the piercings were inset with precious gems, and the combination cast a mandala of soft, multicolored light over the room.

Chaises and chairs were arranged to take advantage of the heat from the room's twin fireplaces. Etched glass screens on either side of the entrance concealed shelves with robes, towels and other supplies, and a small lavatory. Lanterns pierced like the chandelier gave off a diffused light, reinforcing the intimacy of the room.

"Mind if I pour a little of this in?" Liz lifted a stoppered, cut crystal bottle from a gold-plated tray sitting near the edge of the pool.

Thea gave Liz a thumbs up. Liz trickled a thin stream of lavender-scented oil into the heated water. A tidal wave of bubbles immediately foamed over the surface. Liz and Thea scrambled out of the pool.

"What on earth was that stuff?" Thea asked.

"Um, I don't know." Liz poked at the foam. "Mr. Bubble never did this at home."

Suddenly the absurdity of two grown women hovering naked at the edge of the pool, spooked by a blizzard of bubbles hit Thea. She started to giggle.

After a startled glance, Liz joined in. "Oh, what the hell," Liz burbled between gusts of hilarity. "I doubt it'll hurt us. Let's get back in before we freeze."

"Yeah. But no more experimentation with the goodies. Let's let Pandora or one of the other girls turn themselves purple or into frogs or whatever." Thea gratefully slipped back into the warm water.

"Works for me. Where were we?"

Thea fought her way through huge drifts of bubbles to a seat next to Liz. "Still bitching about Reyah."

"Right." Liz chuckled. "We could gripe all night and most of next week. Unfortunately, bitching's not getting us any forwarder. Yes, she indulges in mind control. No, she's not telling us the whole story. But try convincing Pandora it isn't for our own good."

"Try convincing any of them." Thea pushed at a drift of bubbles tickling her nose. "I don't think it's even registered this Domain isn't the same as the TV show."

"Ain't that the truth. Alfred's office never looked so good." Liz sighed. "Neither did Jagger."

"Makes you wonder what else is different, doesn't it?"

Liz nodded. "Big change of subject here. I've been dying to ask all night. What did it feel like when you went cat?"

"That's kind of hard to answer. I didn't have time to feel anything. One minute I'm walking away from Roarke and boom! Reyah says, 'Protect', and I'm wearing fur. And I'm hungry. God, Liz, I don't like to think about the hungry part."

"I can imagine. Nasty."

"You don't know the half of it. The next thing I know I'm back into my own skin standing between you and Brigid. It was lightning fast and my brain couldn't keep up. Liz, I'm scared. If I can't control my shifting, what about my magic? I know I can work miracles, but I don't know how. It's like I'm sitting on top of the world's biggest power plant, and someone else's hand is on the switches."

Liz sank down to her chin. "We'll work it out," she promised.

Thea debated for a moment with herself. "Since we seem to be having true confession night, there's something else I think you should know."

Liz raised an eyebrow. "Should I be scared?"

"I...don't know." Thea scooped up a handful of water and let it trickle through her fingers. "You remember the reaction Roarke had to my magic?"

"Yeah. He looked like he was about to have a heart attack."

"He did, didn't he? Well, guess what? I reacted to him too."

"His magic or him? I didn't feel a lot of magic when we touched."

Thea shook her head. "No, it definitely was his magic." Liz looked unconvinced. Thea laughed. "Okay, some of it was him. Liz, I never felt anything like that before—not even when Jagger made my magic dance."

"Very poetic. Magic dancing. I like the imagery."

"Liz!"

"All right, all right, just trying to keep things light. We've had enough angst for one night."

Thea didn't answer.

Liz sighed. "What did you feel?"

"Like a missing part of me snapped into place. Like I would go to the ends of the universe for this man, do anything he wanted to make him happy."

"Oh damn, not good."

Thea closed her eyes. "No. Not good at all."

೮)03

In another part of the Daughters' tower

Jagger climbed the stairs, his basket trailing in the air behind him like an obedient puppy. There were times when Roarke truly hated the Old One. Following Jagger and his levitating hospitality gift up an endless staircase while hauling a hamper that weighed as much as a baby potlyii happened to be one of them. But he had to admit, Jagger's "hide me" spell was very useful. It allowed them to do a little discreet snooping without being noticed.

A panoramic fresco of Domain's legendary heroines—all looking remarkably like the Maiden Reyah—covered the walls of the fourth floor landing. The battle scenes appeared to be keyed to the carved lintels Roarke guessed belonged to the first of the women's private rooms. The teak relief of swords and knives would suit Kait, while Ravenwood whips and arrows recalled Sarah. It followed the flowering staff and tankards carved in kelan wood over the third door belonged to Brigid.

Brigid was the only one of the warrior women occupying her chamber. A wing of hair, the color of autumn oak leaves, hid Brigid's face as she wrote in a slim chapbook. The isolation heightened the scritching of her pen strokes and the tang of ink that followed each jab of her feather pen into the inkwell.

A scholarly warrior, Jagger remarked. Normally Roarke would've resented Jagger's intrusion in his mind. But like the "hide me" spell, mental conversation had its uses. Jagger continued, *Some would call it an ideal match for a swordmaster of your history and temper.*

A match? Roarke sputtered. *Is this your thought or Reyah's?*

Jagger didn't answer.

The murals on the next landing depicted the abundance of Domain, from the flowers and fruits of Kush and Paelinor to the wheat fields of Seshmeel. Brown-striped savannah tigers raced herds of spiral-horned antelopes across the plains of Thrall. Elsewhere, miners plundered the riches beneath the sere hills of Hiawat, seemingly within sight of Reyah's great temple in Sevidad Reyj.

The scenes made no sense as geography, but the breadth and scope of this vision of Domain spoke to Roarke. He knew the chase across the savannah would end in death. Likewise, the Hiawatis refined their precious ore in conditions of poisonous squalor. Yet Domain encompassed so much, and it could be so much more—for mortals as well as Vanyr and Chosen.

Jagger folded his arms across his chest. The sight of Jagger's unencumbered arms reminded Roarke of the jagged ache between his shoulders and the tightening muscles in his calves.

Disgusted, Roarke lifted the basket to his shoulder in much the same way he used to carry baskets of coal for his foster father's jewelry forge. He waited for Jagger to make a snide remark about serving boys, only to be irritated when Jagger didn't appear to notice.

In the first room off the landing, Frieda sat at a flower-strewn dressing table, transfixed by her image in the large, flat mirror. She brushed her curling red hair back from her strangely pointed ears. Each stroke released a fragrance as sweet as the roses and lirian flowers climbing up the legs of the table.

"They'll see," she told her reflection. "Theron is too like Stefan. I know it. He's exactly like he was in my fan fiction. He called me 'little flower'. They're just jealous. Conlan didn't even look at Liz or Thea until they made him."

Jagger shook his head. Roarke couldn't blame him. Roarke pitied any woman who nurtured romantic visions of Theron. They moved to the next room.

"Do you think our families think we're dead?" Kait asked in a low, miserable voice. The small, leather-clad warrior sat lengthwise on a padded bench at the foot of Marisol's bed. Kait's arms were wrapped around her legs, her cheek pressed against her knee.

Marisol tied a silk robe around her chemise and sat behind Kait. "I don't know, Kait," she said. She put her arms around the smaller woman. "But I've been thinking a lot about it, and I think what we need to do is talk to Jagger."

"Jagger?"

"He's Reyah's oldest son and he's the most powerful mage in Domain. If anyone can get word to our families, I bet he can."

Jagger turned away. The Old One's jaw was clenched so tight, Roarke felt like his own teeth would crack.

Jagger ducked into a doorway surrounded by carvings of small boxes and scattered trails of faceted gemstones. He stopped short. A softly snoring, fully clothed Pandora lay curled in the middle of a huge bed veiled in uneven layers of dark purple lace adorned with jeweled bats, spiders and owls. Clutched to Pandora's chest was a red-painted sling shot.

What the hell? That looks like Ember's sling shot.

Chaos afoot. Jagger laughed. *All hail the Wishstone, in Domain and in the heavens, forever and after, amen.*

What did Jagger mean? Roarke worried the thought until he reached the next landing. All the opulence and luxury he'd seen paled before the lavish display of diamonds, star sapphires, rubies and topazes set directly into the walls.

Interesting. What do you make of this? Jagger pointed at the gold-washed mural.

It looks like Syder's Primer, Roarke said. *Why would mages as powerful as the Daughters of Reyah need to see the lowest level text on magic every time they stepped out of their personal chambers?*

Did you ever consider the possibility Ember might be right?

If Ember were right, and the Daughters weren't from Domain, where would that leave Roarke? Watching Deryk get away with murder, that's where. After feeling her power in Alfred's office, he'd been counting on convincing Thea to work with him to defeat Deryk. But if she didn't know how to use her power... Thea didn't strike Roarke as the kind of woman who would hand the reins of mind and body to another mage. She would have to be wooed—a not entirely unpleasant prospect. Roarke fought back a grin.

But wait, maybe Jagger has the same idea. Shit, shit, shit, shit, shit.

The doorway to Anna's apartment was marked by lotus blossoms carved from rose quartz. Clutching a bundle of velvets and beaded brocades to her chest, the black-haired sorceress bustled between a wall of cupboards and her barge-sized bed. Her lusciously rounded ass jiggled nicely under the sheer silk of her chemise. Pity her breasts were invisible behind all the fabric she carried.

"I wish I knew what they were wearing to tournaments in Domain this year." A small, horrified gasp escaped Anna's ripe, red mouth. "I had a *dreadful* thought. What if Lord Alfred wants us to wear our cyber-clothes?"

Sarah snickered over the rim of her wine glass. "Afraid of being seen in the same dress twice?"

Old Tambaran joke—How long can two women talk about clothes? No one knew, because the conversation began when Reyah created the first mortal woman and hadn't stopped since. Roarke and Jagger backed out of the Anna's room as fast as they could without running into the furniture.

Roarke didn't mind. He wanted to get to Thea's room. But Thea wasn't there. Her small vest and revealing trousers were neatly folded on a strange but sumptuous velvet-covered settee. The door to one cupboard hung slightly ajar. An echo of her perfume wafted from a bowl of lavender on her dressing table.

She's so obvious.

Roarke's head whipped around. *Who? Thea?*

No, you ass. Reyah. Jagger angled his head toward the ceiling.

Roarke squinted at the ornate cornice. *Reyah gave Thea a cornice decorated with seashells. What's obvious about that?*

Not seashells. Horns, ram's horns.

Roarke wondered if Jagger was finally going senile. *What have you got against decorative ram's horns in a lady's room?*

Jagger sighed. *Never mind.*

Entering Liz's room was like stepping inside an iceberg, despite the heat radiating from beneath the floor. *Wonder why Reyah gave something like this to Liz? Liz didn't strike me as cold.*

She's not, Jagger said, his mind voice clipped and hard. He stared at one of the faded tapestries decorating the walls. The style suggested the weavings dated from the period known as Reyah Triumphant—the first century after Reyah and Her two eldest sons defeated Her Opposite, the Great Evil known as Kalin.

Too few images in any medium survived from the period for Roarke to identify who or what the tapestries depicted, but there was nothing objectionable about any of them. In the one preoccupying Jagger, a nude man cowled in the skin of a large gray wolf balanced in the basket of a runaway chariot and aimed an arrow at the viewer. The wolf's head and the angle of the arrow left the man's face in shadow. The prow of the chariot discreetly hid his nakedness.

"I live to serve," Jagger ground through his teeth. "Let's get this over with."

Roarke was so startled, it wasn't until they were halfway up the next set of stairs he realized Jagger had said the words out loud.

Chapter Thirteen

Deryk's tower, Mount Tuumb

Lydia opened her eyes at the sound of the door closing. *It's about time.* She shoved a couple of pillows behind her back. *I thought he was never going to leave.* She pushed her hair away from her face.

It had gone pretty much as she expected. Once Deryk had skillfully (he thought) maneuvered her to the bed, he couldn't wait to brag about his "big plans" for conquering Tambara. All Megeara had to do, Deryk said, was to hide in the tower for a few days—four at most—and Deryk would have everything ready to obliterate the royal house of Tambara.

"And how do you propose to do that?" she asked, eager to poke devil red fingernails through yet another of Deryk's grandiose schemes. Poking holes through Deryk's schemes had been Lydia's favorite part of the show. "Rupert's so paranoid he never lets more than two relatives stay in the same city overnight."

Deryk had cocked his head like some exceptionally stupid bird at the word "paranoid." But he soon forgot his confusion in his overriding need to get one up on Megeara. Again, like on the show.

"Forgive me for bringing up what must have been an unpleasant experience, but being dead seems to have scrambled your wits. How could you have forgotten Rupert's Retreat?"

"Rupert's Retreat?" she echoed in a faltering voice.

"Rupert's Retreat—Rupert's tri-annual attempt to commune with the warlike spirit of his namesake, Rupert I, the first of his louse-ridden line. The one who got his sorry ass kicked by marauding tribesmen and spent two and a half years hiding in the Elseean Hills until the tribes ran out of wine and went home."

"Of course, *that* Rupert. And the retreat's happening this year? Oh, I must have lost track. Time runs together in the afterlife," Lydia choked out.

She didn't need to worry. Her ignorance restored Deryk's sense of superiority. His too sharp teeth nipped her breast, and he mumbled into her nipple like it was some kind of clip-on mike.

"In two days time, the first of Rupert's outriders will enter the Elsee Gap. A day after that, Rupert, his brothers, his uncles, his cousins and every important noble in Tambara will be huddling in flimsy silk tents in the middle of the mud and rain, praying for someone to put them out of their misery. I will be only too happy to oblige."

"Yeah, you and whose army?" she asked, prying Deryk's head from her breasts.

Deryk rose to his elbows and gave his partner another healthy gust of wine breath. "Several armies, actually. I own all the best outlaws in Domain, sweetling. By this time tomorrow, they'll be poised in the Elseean Hills waiting for my signal to sweep in and seal Rupert's fate. Between your demons, and my magic and tactical expertise, we'll own Tambara in no time."

Deryk slathered his tongue over Lydia's lips.

She opened her mouth for another round of tonsil hockey. Taking her acquiescence as an invitation, Deryk began making love to her again.

Deryk pawed and grunted, his breath hot and unpleasantly wet on her skin. Meanwhile, the pistons of Lydia's brain pumped harder than Deryk's hips. *He expects me to control demons? Demons!* She moaned on cue and raked her nails up the backs of Deryk's thighs.

Now Deryk had come and gone, and she sat in the middle of the bed amid a welter of silk and velvet and pondered what to do. Deryk said he'd be making his move in three days, maybe four. Lydia scratched under her arm. *I know I can do magic. Sort of, anyway. How hard can it be to call a demon?*

Another thought struck her, and she frowned. *Wait a minute. Doing magic and calling a demon aren't exactly the same thing. Wasn't that what the scriptwriters kept arguing about? I remember they gave me a bunch of gibberish to yodel, then special effects went to work.* She stared at her hands. *I don't think chickens and frogs will be enough to convince Deryk I'm the real Megeara.*

She uncurled from the bed and walked to the window. The moon was huge. Was the moon here closer than the one back home?

She'd never seen moonlight quite so bright. Lydia could almost count the fleas infesting the dilapidated hovels crouching at the far edge of the plain. Moonbeams spotlighted a cloak-wrapped figure creeping through the shadows of the ruined courtyard.

"What the hell?"

The figure scurried into a nearby corner. A man's face stared up at her window. It wasn't much of a face. In fact, it reminded her of a weasel. A very frightened weasel. The weasel peered at the tower. She didn't move. Finally, with a small shrug of his shoulders, the weasel scuttled out of the corner.

Lydia folded her arms across her chest and *humphed*. The weasel was obviously an AWOL servant who hoped to sneak back in before anyone noticed he'd been gone. Sure he was scared, but not scared enough to keep from going over the wall when he shouldn't.

It was clear she was going to have to show Deryk's servants what it meant to serve a Demon Witch. A good tongue-lashing and perhaps a teapot or two tossed at the man's head would show him, and the other servants, who was boss.

"Well, well, well. What have we here? A little coney come looking for a bit of cabbage from Deryk's garden?"

Lydia jumped. Deryk's voice—as smooth as polished steel and as sharp as an adder's tongue—slid through the window.

The weasel screamed. And screamed and screamed and screamed. The shrill unpleasant sound grated on her ears. She couldn't understand why the sorry little bugger just stood there and shrieked his throat raw.

Wait a minute. She frowned. This was way weird. Why *hadn't* the fool run for the hills already?

Tendrils of darkness slithered up the weasel's legs, and over his arms and torso like living ropes. The dark ropes held the weasel in place as firmly as a fly caught in a spider's web.

And the weasel was no servant. Pulled by Deryk's magic out of the shadows, the too-bright moonlight revealed the weasel's cloak was nothing more than a few rags stitched together. The rest of the man's clothing hung in tatters.

He was nothing but a half-starved peasant. His face wasn't only thin, it was gaunt, all hollow eyes and cheekbones. Lydia recognized starvation when she saw it. One of her first roles had been in a movie about the Donner expedition.

Deryk strolled into view.

Again Lydia was struck by the sense of deadliness she'd felt when she'd first looked at the real Deryk, the Deryk who now loomed like Death in a red cloak over his hapless victim.

Deryk lifted a finger. "Sssh."

The man's shrilling ceased.

"That's better." The smile that curled across Deryk's face sent cold shivers down Lydia's spine.

"Welcome, my little coney. You don't know how glad I am you came to call tonight. You see, I've had a busy evening." The light, pleasant sound of Deryk's voice made her skin crawl. "Now, I know you're wondering, what does Deryk's busy night and his pleasure at an unexpected guest have in common with me?"

The sorcerer put a hand to his throat and caressed his golden torque. Fear pooled in the pit of Lydia's stomach. Something bad was going to happen. Something really, really bad.

But Deryk didn't do anything. He simply stood there, talking.

"It's like this, my little coney. I worked a major spell tonight. Do you know what kind of blood and power that takes? Of course, you don't, but that's neither here nor there, is it?"

He's talking about me, Lydia realized. *He's talking about the spell that brought me to Domain.*

"Oh, I performed wonders tonight. There may be hell to pay with my Mother in the days to come. But if I play my cards right, even She will have to back off and give me what I want. Aren't mothers a pain in the ass? I don't know about yours, little coney, but mine's a total bitch.

"Where was I? Oh yes, telling you why I'm so pleased you came to…'steal' is such an unpleasant word, isn't it? Let's call it a visit, since it's quite obvious you won't be stealing anything from *me*.

"You see, my little coney, I'm a far bigger thief than you ever dared dream of. Indeed, you could well call me the king of thieves, for I plan to steal it all—Tambara, Seshmeel, Paelinor. Everything. In fact, with a Demon Witch under my thumb, I've decided I'm going to steal the biggest prize of all—my Mother's entire world. I will become a true god."

Lydia closed her eyes as the tower spun around her. Take Domain? From Reyah? The man wasn't crazy; he was completely and certifiably insane.

Deryk chuckled—a small, delighted sound that was the most evil thing she'd ever heard. Almost against her will, Lydia's gaze returned to the two men in the courtyard. She suddenly understood how the scene read. Cat and mouse. Predator and prey.

"Now I've shocked you," Deryk told the peasant, "and strayed from my original subject again. It must be my good mood—despite the inferior sex I had earlier—making me so talkative. Back to business, my coney. Though you might not think it, I *am* glad you came. Calling and entertaining a Demon Witch leaves one feeling—" Deryk touched a gentle hand to the peasant's face "—peckish."

Deryk's crimson magic blossomed from the peasant's face. Two shocked seconds later, Lydia realized what she thought was magic was actually blood, lots of blood. It sprayed from the peasant's right eye as Deryk's torque, now horribly alive, slid deeper and deeper into the peasant's skull.

Blood oozed down the peasant's face. Lydia's stomach twisted and flipped. The snake's head burst through the peasant's left eye in another spray of blood and gore.

"No," Lydia whispered. "No."

"Yesssssssss…"

Deryk knelt in front of the peasant, arms outstretched. A blade gleamed wetly in his right hand. His cloak lay on the shattered pavement behind him, his body bare from the waist up. Blood spewed over Deryk's chest, painting dark designs that glowed and shimmered, before being absorbed into his skin.

Lydia couldn't understand where all the blood came from. Blood didn't gush from cuts like water from a tap. But this blood did. The peasant's body shrank as it lost its fluids. One last spatter of blood evoked another sibilance of pleasure from Deryk. The dead peasant hung like a shriveled bug in the web of Deryk's magic.

Deryk stretched like a satisfied cat. With a flick of his fingers the strands of magic vanished and the peasant's corpse hit the ground with a dusty thud. Lydia watched Deryk raise the knife to his lips and lick away the blood.

"*Ick*," Lydia whispered. Her eyes rolled back in her head. She fainted.

Chapter Fourteen

The eighth floor of the Daughters' tower

Steam spiraled into the sultry air of the tower's bathing chamber. Liz moaned. "We need to get out, you know."

Thea yawned and stretched. The hot water had eased muscles she hadn't known were tense. "You're right. Tomorrow promises to be a *long* day."

"Tell me about it," Liz said. "Wonder if there's any wine left over from dinner?"

"Ahem."

Thea's head whipped around. Roarke and Jagger stood inside the entrance to the room.

"Who let you in our tower?" Thea demanded, doing her best to hide underneath dissipating bubbles.

"Lady Pandora," Jagger answered. "She told us you were still awake and on the top floor talking. She thought you wouldn't mind if we joined you. We didn't know you were bathing."

Liz frowned. "You're a mind mage and you couldn't tell?"

"Not without intruding on your thoughts. That would be rude," Jagger said.

Thea couldn't be sure, but it sounded like Roarke snorted.

Liz arched an eyebrow at Roarke. "It sounds like you don't agree."

Roarke shrugged. "Seldom, but in this instance he's telling the truth. If we'd known you were bathing we wouldn't have climbed eight flights of stairs."

"You didn't Port?" Thea asked.

"We didn't know where we were going," Jagger said.

"You have to know where you're going to Port? But what if—" Liz stopped. "Wait a minute, turn your backs. Better yet, would you mind going outside and waiting on the landing a minute?"

"What?" Jagger and Roarke looked confused.

"We need to put on some clothes," Liz explained. "We want to talk to you about Porting."

୫୦୦୪

"I'll be damned," Jagger said. "I just realized why this room looks familiar."

He stood. The men had discarded their doublets some time ago, but Liz hadn't finished admiring the play of muscles beneath the damp lawn of Jagger's shirt. She nibbled another cinderberry. Maybe later she'd be biting into something more substantial.

"Roarke, do you remember the winter retreat the kings of Tambara used to have outside of Pilnerchek?" Jagger asked.

Liz wondered why Roarke shifted in his chair at the mention of the town's name. "Ye-es." He drew the word out as if he wasn't sure he should admit it.

"When the king's engineers excavated the foundations of the palace, they found some pre-Triumph mosaics. That means they were older than me," Jagger explained. "And almost as good-looking."

"You shouldn't run yourself down like that," Liz said.

"I can't help it. I have a very self-effacing nature." Jagger extended his hand to Liz. She steeled herself for the trumpet burst of joy they'd shared in Alfred's office. But this time, the sensation was one of luxuriant warmth. Nevertheless, it raised goosebumps under the lace-edged sleeves of her nightgown. His magic zipped along her veins like an electric current.

Liz followed Jagger to one of the fireplaces. He pointed to a vignette of a parrot and a capering monkey a little to the right of the mantelpiece. There were subtle differences in the tiles on either side of the grout line running through the monkey's chest and shoulder. The shift seemed to travel all the way up to the molding. Another faint dividing line swept along the monkey's tail. Now that she knew what to look for, Liz could detect the signs of a masterful repair in other sections of the wall.

"Looks like She made an exact copy, right down to the repairs," Jagger said. "The king—I think he was a Rupert…"

"They're all named Rupert in Tambara," Roarke remarked, "including half the women."

"Even though the king was something of a prude, he was so impressed with the beauty of the workmanship, he imported craftsmen from the Peninsular States to restore the mosaics. The king installed them in a bathhouse to which he would retreat on his birthday. There he would indulge in every pleasure depicted in the tiles. Of course, being a prude, he would fast and scourge himself for ten nights afterwards. And no one ever knew the reason why except the acolytes of Reyah the Abundant who served as his concubines for the night."

"A fiction the Bard's Guild uses when they want to embarrass the royals of Tambara," Roarke scoffed.

"You think so?" Jagger asked, his gaze lingering on Liz's mouth.

The light from the orb painted Jagger's inky hair with highlights of midnight blue, purple and the darkest bottle green. If Liz looked beyond Jagger's shoulder, the monkey's tail pointed to a pair of lovers. The man traced a line of gold between the woman's breasts all the way to her groin. Was that what Jagger wanted her to notice?

You are so bad.

Jagger didn't reply. He lifted her hand and led her through a dancer's turn that left her facing the pool. A lock of his hair brushed her shoulder, and Liz felt a charge through the silk of her gown all the way to the tips of her toes.

"Do you remember what else the bards said about the pool?" Jagger's words ruffled Liz's hair. They ruffled something else too, something not quite physical but not quite spiritual either. *Magic.* This was magic they shared with no one else. The wonder of it enveloped Liz like a cocoon.

Even Roarke's wry voice couldn't break the spell. "They said the king's playmates would make the waters dance. Of course you could do that anyway."

"So could you," Jagger said.

Jagger let go of Liz and approached the pool. He peered between the gaps in the lavender-scented foam. "I saw it only once, after the king died and the bathhouse was boarded up. But as I remember there was a circle of raised tile stars in the center of the pool. The stars were connected by gears and counterweights to a series of pre-spelled talismans controlling jets of air or water."

"Reyah must've loved that," Roarke said, his voice unaccountably bitter.

"Why do you think the pool was demolished as soon as the king died?"

"But if the pool was demolished, how…" Thea's wide-eyed gaze swept the room.

"Not how. Why." Roarke's eyes narrowed. "What's She up to?"

Jagger didn't answer. Instead his half-boots blinked off his feet and reconstituted themselves next to his doublet. It was the strangest thing Liz ever saw in her life. Roarke made a strangled noise in the back of his throat. She guessed this kind of graduate-level Porting was a bit beyond him.

"You're not going in the pool," Thea protested. "Not in tights!"

"Don't worry, I'll change. I want to see how closely this pool matches the one in Pilnerchek."

"Change into what?" Liz said. "Wait, considering my ferrets, I don't want to know."

"Ferrets?" Roarke asked. "Is 'ferrets' a fashion where you come from?"

Thea and Liz burst into laughter. "Ah, no," Liz said. "They're animals. You might call them a quirk of my magic."

Roarke shot her the kind of look that said, *You and I need to talk.*

Jagger dove into the deep end of the pool. As his body streaked beneath the surface, his tights morphed into what looked like a Speedo.

"Show-off," Roarke told the spot where Jagger disappeared. Roarke added for Liz's and Thea's benefit, "Jagger can change his clothes as easily as he changes his wine."

Thea padded to the end of the pool where Jagger went under. "How did you do that?"

Jagger's head and shoulders emerged in the center of the crescent-shaped pool. "I'll show you later," he promised. "Watch this."

Choppy wavelets obscured Jagger's movements, but Liz could've sworn he was trying to recreate the steps of a dance. He took another step and water fountained from the deep end of the pool. A quarter-turn and a matching fountain jetted from the other side. With a sly glance in Liz's direction, he stepped forward, and a half circle of sparkling water whooshed upward like a giant Elizabethan ruff.

The water level of the half-circle dropped abruptly, spraying Jagger with hundreds of tiny droplets that glittered like diamonds. He blinked the water from his lashes and grinned at Liz.

Will you join me?

Liz's heart lurched against her ribs. She thought it would shatter. She wanted to leap feet first into the deep end of the pool and attack life with all the ferocious glee of

Johnnie Devereaux's outrageous Yankee wife. But the thought of her dead husband was enough to make Liz sick with an irrational sense of betrayal.

She knew it was irrational. Johnnie would've given his left nut to be part of an adventure like this. The thought he couldn't was a wound in her heart that might never heal.

A shrill, insistent inner voice demanded, *And if it doesn't?*

Liz hated that voice. It came from somewhere deep inside her lizard brain, and it never let up. It nagged her into breathing. It forced her to eat and work and go through all the motions as if her heart hadn't died along with Johnnie and the rest of his flight.

Jagger waited, fanning his arms below the surface of the water. Plumes of water rose and fell in a graceful display Liz suspected owed nothing to the mechanisms of the pool. Roarke chuckled at Thea's *oohs* and *aahs*.

Liz moistened her lips. What should she do?

Her flagging courage needed reinforcement. Reinforcements...yes! Liz reached out to Brigid, pulling up the image of her friend sitting at a writing desk four flights below.

Brigid, listen to me. You need to get the rest of the girls and come up to the top floor. Jagger and Roarke are here, and Jagger's got the pool doing tricks. It's the most amazing thing you'll ever see.

What! Brigid squawked in Liz's mind. *Roarke and Jagger! We'll be right up!*

Jagger's grin returned. *Minx.*

"Of course," Liz said out loud. She gathered up her nightgown and descended the stairs into the shallow end of the pool.

∞∞∞

Thea grabbed Roarke by the arm. The shock of his magic shook Thea to her core. She forced herself to ignore it. "What the hell is going on in there?"

Thin jets of water arced over Liz's progress like an aquatic version of swords raised over a bridal procession. A veil of water formed an impossible canopy over Jagger's head. The eyes of both mind mages glowed with the same intense blue light as the magical barrier in Alfred's office.

Roarke whispered, "I don't know. I've never seen magic like this before."

"*Liz!*" Thea called inside and out. *Liz, for God's sake, answer me.* For the first time since Pandora took possession of the Wishstone in Reyah's booth, Thea couldn't get any sense of Liz's thoughts. The long pins holding Liz's hair in place fell into the foam. Shimmering copper tendrils snaked down her back. Jagger's hands plunged into the heavy coils, dragging Liz to him like a sea god taking possession of a Nereid.

The mindless look of passion on Liz's face scared the hell out of Thea. It was so not Liz. And for Liz not to answer Thea's panicked mind and voice calls...

Thea watched the water in the pool begin to glow as blue as Jagger's and Liz's eyes. Was Jagger using his magic to seduce Liz?

Thea's temper exploded.

"Now wait one fucking minute! Jagger, back off!" Thea stormed to the edge of the pool.

Roarke tried to head her off. "Thea, listen to me. You can't go into the pool until we know what's happening. It could be..."

Thea shoved Roarke out of the way, hoisted the skirt of her nightgown and stepped off the edge of the pool.

"Dangerous," Roarke said.

೮ാ

Jagger's kiss plundered Liz's mouth. His tongue was everywhere, stroking, probing. Liz savored the lingering taste of wine and cinderberries as she drew his tongue ever deeper inside. Her hand cupped the clean edge of his jaw, palmed his cheek.

Liz had thought being held by Jagger would be awkward. Johnnie had been five-foot-ten, with the barrel chest and bulky arms characteristic of most pilots. Jagger was at least two inches taller, his arms and legs longer, his form more refined. Yet when he wrapped his arms around her everything fit like the tumblers of some cosmic lock clicking into place.

The heat of his hand branded the small of her back. He cupped her buttocks, pulling her forward, upward. Liz ground her body over his chest and flat, hard stomach and the sex characteristic that had gone straight from primary to cocked and ready to fire. Liz whimpered in frustration at the heavy layers of sodden fabric bunched between them. She wanted his skin roughing her exquisitely sensitized nipples. She wanted his hands tangled in the curls at the junction of her legs. She wanted him, now, in a way she'd never wanted anything in her life.

Jagger's answer flowed into her mouth like the deep rumbling of the tide. Her nightgown parted up the front and melted into the blood-warm water. The sleek contours of his naked back felt like living satin beneath her hands. Her legs wrapped around his waist; his hands spanned hers.

Liz could no longer distinguish where she ended and Jagger began. They were caught in a maelstrom, their separate identities and bodies spinning into one.

Round and round and round they spun between a violet-colored sky and amber-colored grass. Faster and faster they whirled toward the light green sun. The relentless beat of their wings lashed the air, crushing the grass beneath them and fanning the scent of freshly cut sage across the plain for a hundred miles in every direction.

ဆာ

The water was electric, but not in the way Thea expected. It tingled against her hands and the parts of her legs not swaddled in waterlogged silk. Soaked, her diaphanous nightgown weighed a ton and seemed to be pulling her every which way except toward the waterworks exploding around Liz and Jagger. Something large hit the water behind her, and she nearly went under.

Roarke grabbed the back of Thea's gown and hauled her to the surface of the fizzing water. He pulled her around to face him.

"What did you do that for?" he demanded. "I'm trying to save you, and you damn near knocked me off my feet,"

"*I* knocked *you* off your feet? Who was the one who slammed into the water like a ton of bricks?" Thea's question ended on a shriek as a blast of cool air registered on her exposed throat and the tops of her breasts.

"Give me a break, love. I slipped over the side specifically so I wouldn't swamp you." Roarke rubbed the bridge of his nose like a man trying to jump-start his brain. "Wait. Things didn't get crazy until my feet touched bottom. The water boomed, and...shit, it's the pool. Thea, we've to get out of here. Now!"

Thea pulled in the opposite direction. Couldn't he see Liz was in trouble? "Not without Liz I'm not."

"Liz is the least of your worries." Roarke dragged Thea back into his orbit. "Just because the lucky bastard has her right where he wants her doesn't mean he's going to hurt her. Jagger never drains the magic from his sex partners. He doesn't have to."

"What!"

Thea flailed her arms in an effort to get away. They both lost their footing and submerged in a welter of arms, legs and fabric. Roarke lurched to the side of the pool, taking her with him. One of the underwater benches caught her on the shins. Roarke grabbed her before she went under. Thea clung to him, heat spearing through her body at every point of contact.

"Are you all right?" he asked in a voice rough from coughing water. "I don't want to hurt you. Kalin's balls, but I'd never forgive myself if anything happened to you. You're so beautiful. So damned heartbreakingly beautiful."

His gaze dropped. Beneath the all but transparent silk plastered across her breasts like a second skin, Thea's nipples beaded into tight, aroused buds. At the same time, almost forgotten sensations unfurled deep within her belly.

"I want you." Realizing she'd said it out loud, her traitorous body blushed so deeply she could feel her expanding capillaries all the way down to her bones.

"Oh love, don't be embarrassed." Roarke's hands skimmed the fabric of her sleeves, over her exposed throat. He framed her face with those clever, capable hands. "I love the way you respond to me. Inside and out. Mage and woman. You make me feel unbroken. I'd forgotten what it felt like to be whole."

Tiny drops of water dewed his sooty eyelashes. Mesmerized, Thea watched the droplets glitter as his eyelids lowered to half mast. His lips grazed her forehead and trailed down her nose. By the time their lips met, she was combing her fingers through the soft spikes of his wet hair. His kiss deepened. The animal within her stirred, but in a different way than she'd experienced before.

Cats were such possessive creatures, Thea realized as Roarke's tongue flicked against each corner of her lips. Her fingers clenched in his shirt, piercing the taut fabric like claws. She tried to take a proper bite but completely lost track of her intention when his mouth began to play over her throat.

He seemed to draw her pulse inside of him. His hands cupped her breasts. His thumbs traced lazy circles over the puckered skin surrounding her nipples. Thea moaned from the excruciating pleasure.

The purr of Roarke's laughter resonated through the deepest, most secret cavern of her soul. His hands moved under her arms, and the next thing she knew she was standing on the bench, staring down at him.

The sudden absence of warmth prickled her skin. Her lips felt impossibly swollen. She wasn't sure she liked the cocksure way he grinned at her or the disquieting glints in his turquoise eyes.

"But you don't have turquoise eyes," Thea said.

"Mine." He smoothed the damp silk over her right breast. "All mine." He stroked with hands, lips and teeth until she was ready to scream like a cat in heat.

Thea drew in a great shuddering breath. She almost choked on a thick perfume of orange and sage. Helplessly, she started to cough. The sudden jerking of her chest caught Roarke unawares, and he nipped a little too deep. Thea gasped and reached for the lip of the pool to steady herself. The shock of contact with the cool tile made her start coughing all over again.

Roarke's head tilted over the elegant, bronzed column of his neck. Turquoise light flickered like a wind-blown veil over his hazel eyes.

"Don't move away from me, love. I promise you we aren't done yet." The music of his voice ached with sadness. "Don't you see? I have to bring you to the point of frenzy or I won't be able to ride your magic."

Pain exploded in Thea's head. In her heart. She scrambled out of the pool and crouched at the edge. Her nightgown wrapped itself around her like a mummy's bandages. She didn't care. The hair on the back of her neck bristled like it had the instant before she shapeshifted in Alfred's office. But she couldn't, she *wouldn't* let the cat take over. "Is that what this is all about? You and Jagger lured us into the pool to steal our magic?"

Roarke shook his head. He moved closer. The turquoise light in his eyes wavered, revealing flashes of the natural hazel color beneath.

"No. No. Not Jagger. He doesn't need it. I don't want to steal your magic, love. I only need to borrow it. Goddess, but I need it. I need your magic to help Domain. Believe me, you'll have it back before you miss it."

"You bastard! You're just like my ex-husband!"

Thea slapped Roarke so hard she felt his cheek crack against her palm.

Roarke's head jerked. The last of the turquoise glow drained out of his eyes. He pressed his hand against his cheek, only to draw it back as if stung.

"Bloody, bloody hell. Thea, what's wrong?"

"You know damn well what's wrong. You said it! You want to control my magic. You want to control me! Well, I've been there, you jerk, and I'm not going back. No man is ever, ever going to use me again. Not for my contacts. Not for my money. And damn it to hell and gone, not for my magic. Read my lips, Roarke. If you want my power, you're going to have to take it. And the only way is over my dead body."

"But, don't you understand, I need—"

A red haze clouded Thea's sight. She raised her arm to hit him again. She wanted to beat his fine-boned face into a bloody pulp. But Roarke caught her wrist before she connected. Thea fell back on her heels to pull herself free. Ready to claw herself free.

Only she already had—clawed Roarke that is. His wet hand slid down her arm, leaving trails of watered blood. The water dripping down the side of his torn and rapidly healing cheek was pink.

೮೧೦೩

Liz nuzzled his warm throat, memorizing all over again the beloved scent of bitter orange and sage. She'd bought the bath oil for him the last time she was in San Francisco, and she would've sworn on whatever holy book you wanted there was nothing more intoxicating than the sweet bite of citrus and sage rising from Johnnie Devereaux's damp skin.

Her eyelids heavy with pleasure, she lapped the faintly salty water clinging to his collarbones. His hand traced a feather light pattern down her spine. She arched her back, stretching throat and chest so there would be more of her to kiss. His mouth blazed a new trail of sensation between her breasts. Liz fisted her hands in the dark river of his hair.

Hair? Too much hair.

As far as Liz knew, Johnnie had never worn his hair long in his life. Lately, to be honest, it had begun to thin on top. But her hands combed through hair—heavy ribbons of hair trailing all the way past his shoulders.

She opened her eyes and stared at the black-haired, amethyst-eyed stranger holding her. He wasn't Johnnie. He was touching her like Johnnie with slender fingers too long for Johnnie's square-shaped hands. He was kissing her like Johnnie. He even smelled like Johnnie. But he wasn't her husband.

Her husband was dead.

"No!" Liz howled, slamming her fists against Jagger's broad shoulders. She thrashed and tried to wriggle out of his grasp, but his hands and arms seemed to be everywhere at once. She couldn't land a decent kick no matter how hard she tried.

"Lizzy, for God's sake, babe, calm down. Tell me what's wrong," Jagger pleaded in a ghastly echo of Johnnie's South Carolina drawl. "Please."

"You forget yourself, Consort. Release me!" Liz commanded.

"Mistress?" Jagger asked.

Liz drew a grim satisfaction from Jagger's unsteady breathing. *Quite right, the inferior male had gone too far and needed the reprimand.*

Jagger's eyes widened.

"Woohoo!"

"Hey, guys!"

"Make room for baby!"

"Come on you two, it's time to share!"

Four huge splashes rocked the pool as Anna, Marisol, Sarah, and Brigid jumped in. Free slipped into the water a moment later. Jets of water whooshed in every direction, startling Jagger enough for Liz to wiggle free.

She barely got away in time. Marisol and Sarah each latched on to one of Jagger's arms, apparently willing to tear him apart for a kiss.

"Couldn't happen to a nicer guy," Liz mumbled as she half floated, half drifted to the nearest underwater staircase.

Her mind had been invaded, her most precious memories robbed, and with them, it seemed, Jagger had taken the last bit of her strength. She staggered up the first two steps and couldn't go any further. The only thing keeping her upright with her head out of the water was the desperate pressure of her fingertips in the seam where the lip of the pool met the floor.

If she was in this state, what had happened to Thea? At first Liz couldn't find the blonde knock-out Thea had become. Free, Anna and Brigid surrounded Roarke. Weirdly enough, it sounded like he was trying to warn the women about a truth spell, but Liz didn't trust her ears or anything else at this point. Furthermore, none of them seemed to care.

Thea appeared. "Quick, take my hand." Her hand trembled. When Liz clasped her arm, she felt the fear rippling beneath Thea's skin.

Liz realized there was something left inside her after all. She hauled herself out of the water mostly on her own power and wrapped herself in the robe Thea offered. Thea's shudders were growing more visible. What the hell had Roarke done to her?

Liz figured she had enough energy to get them both behind the privacy screens where the dry robes and towels were stored, which might help Thea's physical chills. She wished with all her heart she knew how to Port.

Jagger disentangled himself from his admirers and swam a few strokes closer to their side of the pool. "Lady Elizabeth, wait. We need to talk."

To Liz's fury, the sound of his undisguised voice still had the power to make her toes curl. "*Talk?* Is that what you call it?" she asked. "I think we've done quite enough of that for one evening. Besides, you've got all these other women who want to 'talk' to you now."

"Damn it, Liz, you were in my mind as deep as I was in yours."

"Go to hell," Liz said.

Sarah burst from the water in front of Jagger. He opened his mouth, only to have Sarah wrap her arms around his neck and lock her lips to his.

Chapter Fifteen

The next morning: the Guards' Ready Room in the Keep

"Squads Six, Ten, and Fifteen—you have crowd duty at the tournament. You know what to watch for—pickpockets, cutpurses…"

Sir Donatien des Nuits, newest Chosen Knight of the Elder Goddess Reyah, stood at rigid attention behind the Keep's captain of the guard. Don stared at the back of Willem's head and wished he could reach down and scratch his balls.

His own balls, Don hastily amended, not Willem's. After all he wasn't *that* kind of guy. A bead of sweat trickled down Don's back. It never failed—whenever he got worried or nervous his balls itched. Right now the ol' family jewels felt like a thousand ants were crawling around in his codpiece.

But Don knew, especially after last night's fuck-up, if he even rubbed his thighs together Willem would not only have his balls for breakfast, but Gareth would have Don's guts for garters too. He knew this for a fact because Willem and Gareth told him so—in excruciating detail—right after his ill-advised gallop into Lord Alfred's office.

Don considered himself the uber-pro when it came to ass-chewings, especially considering the number he'd received from his parents and bosses over the years. But even he had to admit Willem and Gareth took ass-chewing to an all-time painful high.

He couldn't understand what the BFD was. Everyone had been shouting about the Keep being under attack. Then a big tower appeared. How was he supposed to know Reyah created it for nine hot babes?

Don sighed. What he did know for certain sure was, after last night, his ass was grass, and Willem was his own personal lawnmower.

"Knights Jelamas, Trebyth and Lendag, you'll be taking Squads Two, Eight, and Twelve and working the blue quadrant. Jelamas, Trebyth, I know you're disappointed you won't be able to kick ass like you did at Midwinter Melee. I know I am. I had good odds on both of you," Willem said.

Most of the guys in the room laughed, including Jelamas and Trebyth.

"But the way things are going, you'll probably see action anyway," Willem continued. "There were over three hundred people lined up outside the lists before dawn. The wizards expect to finish repairs and open the auxiliary seating areas by mid-morning, but with the Daughters' presentation, we're not sure that will be enough."

Hurry up and get to the good stuff, Don thought impatiently. He was tired of listening to Willem drone on and on about assignments. He wanted to hear the names of the knights participating in today's tourney. He fully expected to be part of the Keep's team. When it came to kicking armored butt, Donatien des Nuits was the best, and everyone knew it.

Why just the other day he'd managed to knock Sir Tanak ("the Tank") off his horse—a feat no one, not even been-there-done-it-all-millennia-ago Willem had ever managed to pull off. Don gave himself a mental pat on the back.

Yeah, Willem *had* to put him on the team.

"There have been some issues raised about guards refreshing themselves at the stands closest to the royal boxes…"

Bored to tears, Don's gaze wandered around the room. A mirror on the back wall, used by the guardsmen to check their uniforms, caught his eye. His mirror image grinned cockily back at him. His dark blue uniform fit him like a second skin. You could shave yourself in the polish on his boots and, if he did say so himself, he had the coolest codpiece in the room. Damn, but he looked good. Don congratulated himself on being the studliest dude in the Keep.

Willem walked between Don and the mirror.

Don shrugged. Okay, he wasn't the *only* studly dude in the Keep. Some of the Vanyr weren't bad looking either, he guessed. Still, he was one of the top five percent and that rocked too.

Considering what he'd once been…Don's vision blurred as he remembered another time and another place.

སྃ

A man sat in front of a computer terminal in a small, cluttered apartment. Despite his youth, his lank, brown hair was starting to recede, and his shoulders bowed as if with age.

Posters of Mandy, the winsome pirate introduced in the second season of *Domain*, and publicity stills of other stars from the television series lined the walls of the room. Shelves full of *Domain* memorabilia flanked the computer. To the man's right, a printer chattered.

Donald Kritchenstern, computer programmer, Internet junkie and devoted fan of *Domain, the Series*, cleared his email and logged onto the *Domain* Forum. The corners of his thin mouth drooped as he read the various posts. Nothing was hopping. The only thread on the board dealt with what stars had signed up for the *Domain* track at Dragon*Con.

God, he was sick of hearing about it. Dragon*Con was seven months away, for crying out loud. Even Pandora, his online friend from that crazy bunch of women fanfic writers, did nothing but natter on and on about it.

Don's printer spat out another sheet. Thank God, he had hacked into the Daughters of Reyah's private Web site. Reading their erotic fan fiction was as close as he'd gotten to lucky in years.

He patted the growing stack of paper by his mouse. The Daughters had recently posted more stories, and he planned on reading every one. He looked over the Forum one more time. Didn't these dorks have anything else to discuss besides Dragon*Con? Too pissed off to fake the serenity of his cyber-character, he typed in a new message.

"In Search of Another Topic…Hey, peeps, Atlanta is not a BFD to the peeps not going to the con. Who wants to gab about the rumor there's a new Chosen waiting in the wings? Ten PayPal bux says it's a warrior and not some weenie mage. Put your money where your email is, Brother Donatien."

Don pressed the send button and sighed. He wished he could afford to go to the con, but with his car in the shop for a new transmission, there was no way.

Exiting the Forum, he reached across his desk and plugged in his joystick. Six months earlier an anonymous post had appeared on the *Domain* Forum advertising an online game based on the television show. It only took an hour's session for him to become hooked. Lately, he admitted to himself, he spent more time in the game's virtual reality than he did in the so-called real world.

Five minutes later, Don, wearing the cyber-personality of a lone-wolf knight, strode through the virtual landscape. He called the knight "Sir Donatien" as both a joke and a challenge. He didn't know how many of the peeps on the *Domain* Forum played the game, but no one had recognized the scholarly (at least in so far as *Domain* trivia went) Brother Donatien from Immortal's B-board in the cyber-person of his ultimate warrior. Which went to show how dicked in the head everyone on the board was.

He wondered when or if he should bring "Sir Donatien" out of the closet, so to speak. Was the respect and envy of Forum gamers worth the price of losing Brother Donatien? Don scratched his balls.

Damned if he knew why he was keeping his warrior a secret. It wasn't as if anyone gave a shit one way or the other. Still, he needed to make up his mind—and soon. One last quest stood between "Sir Donatien" and the game's ultimate prize—elevation to Chosen status.

Don walked his character bold as brass through the front gate of the bad guy's castle. It still pissed him off he wasn't the first to try his luck here. Three people had made it to this level before, but he decided they didn't count. The bozos who'd gotten this far had played computer-generated, wizard weenies who relied on gimmicks and tricks to get ahead. All three claimed a guy couldn't make it this far on guts and brains and strength alone.

Okay, cyber-strength, he amended. But it was still his own skill. And his own determination. You couldn't conjure those up.

"No magical shortcuts for me," Don promised his monitor. "No way, Jose. I'm gonna win the prize the right way."

Time ceased to exist. "Sir Donatien" chopped his way forward, only pausing to drink the healing potions he had stockpiled before trying to defeat the last and hardest foe of the game. Slowly, surely, his character slaughtered his way closer to the final battle.

Midnight came and went. Three times his character died. Three times he replenished his healing potions and went back in. His alarm went off at seven a.m. He threw a crumpled beer can at the clock and continued the game.

Finally, somewhere near noon, the virtual character known as Sir Donatien stepped into the room containing the final, nastiest, most difficult monster of the game. Another three hours later, the monster known as Kalin lay dead at the knight's feet.

"Yes!" Don fell off his chair onto the floor and kicked his feet with joy. His feet were about the only part of him he could still move. His fingers wouldn't straighten from the death grip they'd had on the joystick. His butt had lost all feeling hours ago.

Still, he'd beat the game as a warrior—something everyone on the game list insisted couldn't be done. He had to tell somebody, he decided.

"I'll tell Pandora," he said aloud. "Maybe this way I can convince her to play the game too."

Music swelled from the six-foot-tall speakers he'd jury-rigged to his computer. A woman's voice, chiming like a thousand bells, issued from the speakers. "To claim your place as one of Reyah's Chosen, place your hand upon the screen."

Don glanced at the clock. He'd been in the game for nearly twenty-four hours! He flexed his cramped fingers until the needle jabs of returning circulation dulled. He picked up the fan fiction he'd printed before settling into the game. Time to put away the print-outs, turn off the computer and get some sleep. God only knew what excuse he'd give his boss for missing work again.

The woman's voice rang from the speakers again. "You must place your hand upon the screen to become one of Reyah's Chosen."

He eyed the handprint displayed on the monitor. He'd said he was going to win the right way. That meant going the distance. *What's five more minutes before I call the office and get to bed?*

He splayed his aching right hand over the screen. Light outlined his hand. He tried to pull away, but he couldn't move.

The woman's voice said, "You have been deemed worthy. Do you wish to enter Domain as a Chosen Knight? Answer carefully, for once made your wish cannot be undone."

Don stared at the screen and the light irradiating his hand. This was right out of *The Twilight Zone*. A loud belch rumbled from his chest. Eight empty beer cans sat next to a plate scummed with dried chili. That was it—the chili had gone bad, and he was hallucinating.

"If I'm tripping what do I have to lose?" he sniggered. "Sure thing, Reyah, I wanna be a Chosen Knight. Hit me with your best shot."

His sarcastic laugh changed to a scream as the glow swarmed up his arm and over his body. Exploding blue light blinded him. The room whirled under his feet. When his head stopped spinning, he found himself standing in a field full of blue flowers. The air smelled like a perfume counter at Christmas. A naked babe with the most bodacious tatas he'd ever had the privilege to leer at smiled at him.

"Welcome to Domain, newest of My Chosen. By what name will you be known in your new life?"

153

"Donatien!"

Don jumped, startled from his daydream. *Oh shit.* Willem and Gareth were both frowning at him. *Now what had he done?*

"Woolgather on your own time," Willem said. "You've been given your assignment."

Don grinned. "You read the tourney list already? All right! Whose colors will I be wearing: Seshmeel's or Tambara's?"

Willem raised an eyebrow. "What does the tourney have to do with your assignment?"

"Come on, Willem, don't be a dweeb, man. You know I knocked the Tank on his ass."

The room went totally silent.

"What. Did. You. Call. Me?" Willem's eyes were like two chunks of frozen double decaf chocolate expresso.

"Oh, fuck. I mean, sorry, Captain, sir. I, er, lost my head," Don sputtered.

"Call me by my given name again," Willem said through his teeth, "and you *will* lose your head, because I will personally remove it for you. Dismissed."

Sweat beaded Don's forehead. "Captain? Sir, would you mind telling me again what my duties are? I, er, couldn't hear you the first time."

"Interesting," Willem drawled. "A deaf Chosen. A first for the Keep, wouldn't you say, Gareth?"

Gareth stared at Don, a bogus expression of astonishment on his bearded face. "Truly. Shall we put him in a tent and charge people a zhin apiece to take a look? Goddess knows the Keep's coffers could use the money."

The thousand ants on Don's balls suddenly doubled in number. The guards and knights still in the room snickered. His face flushed crimson. He would not scratch his crotch. He wouldn't.

"Let me say this slowly and clearly." Willem folded his arms across his chest. "You will go to your quarters. There you will find the dress uniform the Keep's wizards have provided. After putting on your uniform, you will report to Lord Alfred's office."

Don's eyes widened. "I have to wear the tights?"

"One more question and I'm going to kick your sorry ass all the way to Paelinor. Have you got that, soldier?"

"Sir, yes sir!"

154

"Good. Now move!"

"Sir, yes sir!"

Don practically ran from the room. Once he'd put a few hallways between himself and the irate captain of the guard, he stopped, took a quick look around and scratched his itch.

Despite Willem giving him a hard time, and even despite not making the cut for the tourney, Donatien, a.k.a. Don Kritchenstern, was having the time of his life. The erstwhile "Brother Donatien" glanced down at his muscular frame, half expecting to see the concave chest and spindly legs of his former self.

He gave his crotch one last satisfying scratch and sniffed his pits. After all the sweating he'd done, he was rank. He'd better bathe before reporting to Alfred, or he'd get his ass chewed for *that*, too.

He headed for the baths. Sissy tights or no, life was *good*. No more mainframes, servers or coding boring documents for him. He was in Domain to stay.

His footsteps slowed. Only one thing still connected Don with his old life, one thing which inexplicably followed him into Domain. And he'd hidden it in the safest place in the Keep.

Chapter Sixteen

Deryk's tower, Mount Tuumb

Lydia was holding body and soul together just fine until she ran out of napkins.

So she did what any displaced drama queen fearful for her life would do under the circumstances—she had a screaming, rampaging fit. Once she'd shrieked herself hoarse, broken some crockery and ripped several pillows into shreds, she felt much better. Finally, staring around at the mess she'd made, inspiration struck. She gathered up some of the feathers, wrapped them in the remaining two napkins and used them to stuff the toes of the boots she'd found in Deryk's armoire.

Lydia stared at her reflection in the mirror hanging near the bed. (Superstitious in the extreme, Lydia'd been quite careful not to break the mirror during her tantrum.) The combination of goth slut gown and bright crimson velvet and gold-embroidered robe was bad enough. But the oversized purple suede half-boots were truly hideous. She didn't have a lot of choice, fashion or otherwise. There was no way she could do a nature hike in four-inch spike heels, and she knew it.

The minute she'd woken from her faint, she'd sprung into action. The way she saw it she had two choices—remain in the tower and hope like hell Deryk wouldn't slaughter her like the peasant, or make a run for the village across the plain and pray she could bribe or buy her way to the nearest large town.

The first thing she'd done was check out the armoire. Surely Deryk, in anticipation of bringing the famous Demon Witch back to Domain, had stocked up with the latest in designer wear and accessories. Unfortunately, the only things the armoire contained were three garish robes, purple boots and a couple of pairs of moth-eaten socks.

156

What was it with men and holey socks, Lydia wondered irritably. She hadn't met one yet who didn't have a drawer full of the things. After a few choice words about the size and staying power of Deryk's dick and his execrable fashion sense, she grabbed the boots and the robes. Escaping from a psychotic killer was more important than looking good.

She stuffed two pillowcases with the best of the gold and gem-encrusted doo-dads lying around the room. She carefully wrapped the breakables in the heavy linen napkins she found in a drawer. After a bit of thought she grabbed another pillowcase and tucked in the other two robes and her designer boots. After all, magicking up chickens and frogs wasn't going to pay for a place to stay or a good pair of hand-made shoes.

Besides, Deryk owed her. What she was taking from the tower was only a small percentage of the sum she fully intended to collect out of his miserable hide.

Lydia adjusted the heavy velvet robe over her shoulders and wished, not for the first time, she could grab her trusty cell phone and call for a cab. Still, she reasoned, there was bound to be a Portal down at the village. On the show, the damned things littered the landscape. After one last look around the room to make sure she hadn't missed anything worth pawning, she opened the door and clumped down the stairs.

With luck, Deryk would be gone long enough for her to get to one of the capitals of the Eight Lands—Lydia never could remember their names—and find a nice little condo close to some good shops. Hell, once she was safe, she figured, with a couple of days of practice, she'd be calling up demons and Portals as easily as she did her agent and masseuse back in L.A.

Then Deryk and anyone else who thought they could mess with Lydia Jambon had better watch out.

$\wp\mathrm{O}\mathrm{C}\mathrm{R}$

The Dragon*Con Exhibit Hall, Marriott Hotel

"You know, we might survive this after all," Doug, the corset seller, said as he handed Reyah the boxed salad She'd ordered for lunch. "I'm amazed at how little stock we actually lost. I thought we were all goners. But the only booth totally trashed was Eric Bernard's. And he's no loss."

"Darling boy, don't you know there's a Divine Providence watching over this convention?"

157

Doug smiled. "I think it's more on the order of dumb luck, myself, but whatever it is, I hope it keeps working.

"Speaking of which, Morgana and I were talking to a few of the other dealers this morning," Doug said. "We're planning to get together after the hall closes tonight and raise a glass to Providence or the Goddess or whoever was responsible for saving our butts. Would you like to join us?"

"Aren't you the sweetest thing? As it happens, I'm free this evening, and I can't think of anything I'd rather do than share your libation."

Well, Reyah *would* be free and very soon. Natal Day or no Natal Day, this offer was too good to resist. She estimated there could be as many as twenty people raising their glasses in Her honor.

Translation: twenty potential worshippers pledging themselves to Her of their own free will without incentive or obligation on Her part. What a coup! Reyah had been trying to set up an Earth franchise for ages, but the local cults were so prejudiced against outsiders. This could crack the market wide open. If ten or twelve of them went the distance, she could be set on this world for a millennium, maybe two.

It wasn't as if She needed to be present at Her Natal Day celebrations. Jagger could project an avatar of Her for the occasion. It wouldn't break Her heart to miss the fawning and scraping of the second string bootlickers currently polluting the air of Her Keep.

Perhaps She should suggest Jagger ask Liz to assist in projecting Her avatar. What a great idea! It would make things much easier for the dear boy, and by now Liz should be ready and willing to walk through fire for him.

If Liz could still walk, that is. Reyah snickered and opened the Keep browser on her laptop.

At first Reyah thought there was something wrong with her zaihn directory. A vision of Thea being laced into a blue satin corset filled the eyes of the zaihn labeled "LizWebcam1".

Reyah zoomed out. A gown of iridescent turquoise and gold brocade flowed across the counterpane of Liz's black-curtained bed. The drapes had been drawn back from the room's tall, center-latched windows, flooding the chamber with light. Strong, searching light which nevertheless managed to bend around a certain someone in servants' livery trying very hard to hide behind Thea.

Reyah shifted her view to another zaihn. A short, pert-faced ladies maid stepped out from behind Thea. The maid crossed her blue-rimmed, brandy-colored eyes and stuck out her tongue at the "camera".

Reyah chuckled. "Well, well, well, look what the cat dragged in."

Liz swept into range. Unlike Thea, Liz was dressed, wearing a beaded silk corset and belled skirt sans chemise—very fetching for a ball but highly impractical for an outdoor ceremony on the first day of a northern spring. Reyah was about to express her disappointment in Liz's fashion sense when the redhead picked up a full-sleeved, velvet jacket the same coppery peach shade as her skirt.

The maid's gaze lingered on Liz's lithe figure as the mind mage smoothed the jacket over her corset. The maid appeared to be considering something Reyah hadn't planned for. Reyah boosted the volume on her computer.

And got blasted by a series of concussive brays. It sounded like a foghorn crossed with herd of giant camels.

Thea mouthed, "What?"

The maid had to shout to be heard. "Moat monster."

The former Earth women exchanged excited glances. Liz darted to the pair of windows closest to the Great Gate of the Keep.

Reyah rubbed her hands together with glee. From the way Liz moved, you'd never suspect she'd spent the night in the arms of Domain's most fabled lover. Who would've thought that little slip of a thing would have so much stamina? Jagger was probably halfway in love with the girl already.

And he'd probably fall all the way once he got a good look at the back view, Reyah noted as Liz leaned over the window sill.

Reyah switched cams to see what was happening outside the tower. The scaly coils of the moat monster's tail thrashed the murky waters of the moat close to the Great Gate. A mob of what might have been a thousand or more crowded the moat's outer bank. A few people had fallen in and were attempting to put as much distance between them and the giant reptile as possible.

A troop of the Keep's Blue Guard, their halberds crisscrossed to create a living wall, blocked the road to the bridge connecting the Great Gate to the surrounding countryside. Chosen Jelamas and his mortal lieutenants tried to urge the crowd back. Neither Jelamas nor his men appeared to be having much luck.

Alfred stood in the middle of the bridge. His eyes were locked on the moat monster, whose head and neck were hooked over one of side of the bridge.

Vallenius stood beside the gate. His hands traced sigil after sigil, but each one vanished as soon as the figure was complete. More guardsmen stood at his back, apparently to protect the young Adept from the people pushing against the Gate's massive iron portcullis.

With a bellow, the moat monster reared. Its giant head snaked toward a richly dressed man clambering over the outside of the bridge. Dirty moat water streamed through the gaps between the monster's razor-edged, six-inch-long teeth.

The man screamed as he fell back into the soupy water. One prehensile coil of the monster's serpentine body slapped the water near where the man submerged. The movement created a wave which allowed one of the people on the outer bank to snag the hem of the man's cloak.

The moat monster seemed to think this good deed merited a special reward. Neighing as if he wanted to be petted, the moat monster playfully batted the side of his head against Alfred's shoulder. The Lord of the Keep went down like a nine pin.

"Oh, Spot, not again! We're in enough trouble, already," yodeled an all too familiar, high-pitched voice.

The moat monster keened piteously. Reyah plugged in her headphones in order not to alarm the nearby booths.

She couldn't believe her eyes. The monster was twined around that dingbat Pandora. Looking at Pandora's cropped hair, her butt-cupping, electric blue pants and hooker boots, Reyah was tempted to wail herself. Where in Kailin's Seven Hells had Pandora come up with such a trashy outfit? She hadn't pulled it from any of the wardrobes Reyah provided.

"No, Lady Pandora, you're not in trouble," Alfred said as he got to his feet. "Neither is the Guardian, I swear. However, it's very dangerous to have the Guardian on this side of the Keep with so many people around."

"Someone's in trouble!" yelled the mud-slimed, red-faced, bridge climber. His right hand was tucked under the rags of his once splendid, fur-trimmed left sleeve. "That thing nearly took off my hand!"

"Too bad he didn't aim higher," Alfred growled. "Ambassador, your diplomatic status is the only thing keeping me from clapping you in irons. One more word from you, and even that won't save you. That goes for the rest of you too."

Alfred's voice, trained on the battlefields of the Rider Wars, carried easily over the protests of the mob. "If this crowd hasn't retreated to a position at least twenty feet from the banks of the moat by the time I count ten," he said, "I will order Vallenius to start Porting people at random. Chances are very good those who are Ported will never see their homes again.

"One…"

The crowd was twenty paces away by the count of nine. Vallenius droned another iteration of the spell designed to send the moat monster to its lair on the other side of the Keep.

Pandora patted the notebook-sized scales on the monster's neck. "I can't figure out why these guys are acting so crazy about you swimming around, Spot. I mean, I know you're a good guy. The writers' on the show made it clear on at least four episodes."

Pandora's eyebrows drew downward in the world's prettiest frown. "You know, though—the CGI they used didn't look anything like you. I'm going to have to write a letter to TPTB."

Reyah shook Her head. The Wishstone had a lot to answer for.

Back on the drawbridge, the hideous spawn of a sea serpent and a Paelinorian water devil made a wet gargling noise very much like the sound of a dying car. Pandora scratched the underside of the monster's second chin. The moat monster's eyes closed from the bottom up. It rumbled something perilously close to a purr.

Another hyacinth-colored sigil disappeared in a puff of blue smoke. Vallenius's shoulders slumped.

"I don't understand it," Vallenius said. "That spell has been used to control the Guardian since Reyah's Firstborn raised the Keep in Her Name. It's never failed."

"Who's the guardian?" Pandora asked.

Alfred, Vallenius and most of the crowd gaped at her.

Pointing at the moat monster, Vallenius said, "He is. He guards the Keep. That makes him the Guardian. It's his name."

"Well, he may be the guardian of the Keep, but that's *not* his name," Pandora said.

"Lady Pandora, I don't mean to contradict you, but you're wrong. The spell has always worked before using the name of 'Guardian,'" Vallenius protested.

"It's not working now," someone in the crowd shouted.

Alfred grasped the top of his head as if he was afraid it would fly away.

"If the Guardian's name isn't 'Guardian' what is it? What do *you* call him, Lady Pandora?" Alfred clarified.

"He said his name was 'Spot.'"

"Use it," Alfred ordered Vallenius.

ℼℙ

Reyah massaged Her temples. Nothing was going the way it should. First, a certain party was putting the moves on Liz as well as Thea. That was enough to throw Her cunning plans to hell and gone. Then Pandora went and renamed the moat monster, and it *stuck*! The last thing Domain—or Her sons—needed was a dingbat wielding wild magic.

Reyah took a deep, calming breath. There was no point in getting worked up over what might be nothing. Just because Pandora scraped Reyah's last nerve didn't mean Jagger couldn't handle the twit.

A sense of foreboding settled over Reyah. All things considered, it might be a good idea to check and see what everyone else was doing.

Back in the Daughters' tower, Anna was bossing the servants around like she owned the place. No surprises there. Reyah had read Anna's fanfic. Reyah clicked on another zaihncam. Brigid, Frieda and Marisol stood on the observation deck of the Great Gate's South Tower. From their vantage point, the three women had a fine view of the moat monster fiasco.

Another flurry of excitement occurred when the exhausted Vallenius failed to Port Pandora back to the Daughters' Tower. Alfred solved the problem by dispatching an "honor guard" to escort the dingbat to a Portal mage inside the walls.

It was a sound tactical decision on Alfred's part. Nevertheless, Reyah knew the Keep's youngest Adept would pay for his failure as soon as the story got around to the wizards under his command. There was little affection for Vallenius among the senior members of Domain's magical community. Those wizards were so jealous they hadn't been Chosen they peed green. Reyah shrugged. All Vallenius had to do was wait a decade or two, and most of the older ones would be dead. It was one of the advantages of being Chosen.

Another click of the mouse revealed Kait and Sarah with Hawke and Conlan on the far side of the tournament stadium. Reyah heaved a sigh of relief. Oh good. For once something was going right. With any luck, the two Vanyr and the warrior women would be inspired to do a little private one-on-one. Now those were exactly the sort of matches Reyah had in mind.

Speaking of matches, though, where were the rest of Her boys? Reyah clicked on the macro Jagger had installed to allow Her to check on the Vanyr in the Keep.

There was Theron, using his scrying bowl to spy on Frieda. Reyah's upper lip curled. While it wasn't exactly a match She'd normally promote, She had to admit those two limp sponges were certainly lugubrious enough to suit each other.

Click.

Dressed for the day's ceremonies in black and jet, Jagger dictated a letter to one of his agents. Jagger, his secretary and Reyah knew the missive would be in the hands of every monarch and guild head in the Eight Lands by evening prayers. Reyah turned up her speakers. And did Reyah detect a hint of a more than academic interest in Jagger's description of Liz's powers? Reyah smiled. Of course, She did.

Click.

Roarke sprawled, semi-comatose, in his copper tub. Every so often he grunted at a article of clothing his valet offered for inspection. Reyah wondered which of Roarke's fan girls had taken him out for a spin—and wrung him dry. As long as it hadn't been either Liz or Thea, Reyah didn't care.

Click.

Click.

Click.

There weren't any other Vanyr in the Keep. That left three of Her sons unaccounted for. She wasn't worried about Fynn and Aleks. But where was Deryk? She chose another macro.

Click

Deryk stood at the edge of a large campsite hidden among the giant trees of Kush's Old Forest. Hard-featured villains dressed in bits and pieces of ill-fitting armor lounged around the ragged clearing. Some swilled ale, some sharpened swords or knives.

"Outlaws," Reyah muttered to Herself. "Drat the boy! First the spell and now this. And I bet he didn't get me a present either."

A huge man, muscled like a gorilla and almost as hairy as one, belched. Bracing himself on a nearby keg of ale, the giant heaved himself to his feet and sauntered a little too carefully over to Deryk.

Deryk nodded at the brigand and held up a bag of coins. "I have a job for you."

The brigand smiled. "Who do you want killed now?"

Deryk gestured toward the camp. "I want you to move your men to the Plain of Elsee. There's a swineherd's hut across the plain from Mount Tuumb, about two zakkans west of the village. Kill the swineherd and set up camp on his holding." Deryk tossed the bag of coins to the brigand. "I'll have a Portal waiting in the clearing by Kala Falls in three hours."

The brigand opened the bag of coins and peered inside. "Make it four hours. My men are tired."

The bag fell to the ground, coins spilling onto the dirt as the brigand clawed at his throat.

"Your men are drunk," Deryk said, "and you forget who you are dealing with." He traced a red sigil in the air. The brigand's face purpled, and he fell to his knees.

"Three hours," Deryk said again. He slashed a finger through the sigil. The brigand gasped and began to draw in great shuddering breaths. "Don't disappoint me, Terba. Unless you find the prospect of being slowly turned inside out enjoyable. I know *I'd* enjoy it."

"We'll be there, milord," Terba croaked.

"Excellent." Deryk Ported.

By Kalin's tiny prick, what fool scheme was the boy up to now? From the timing, Reyah suspected he planned to stage a coup—or worse—during Rupert's Retreat. Hell and damnation, there'd be no distracting Jagger or the rest of them if Deryk did take out Rupert.

Reyah had no intention of letting Hawke, Conlan, Roarke or Jagger get their hands on Her precious boy. She needed a little more time to allow one of the women to help Deryk mature into the man Reyah knew he could be. All it would take was the right woman.

Unfortunately, Deryk probably wouldn't recognize the right woman if she walked up and bit him on his pink and white tush. Look at all the time he'd spent with that awful Megeara.

Wait a minute. Speaking of Megeara—or at least of the wannabe actress Deryk thought was going to fill the original Demon Witch's spike-heeled boots—where was Lydia Jambon? Reyah's fingers flew over the slick titanium keys of her laptop.

Lydia hadn't been with Deryk when he Ported into the outlaw camp.

That wasn't good.

Reyah replayed the scene of Deryk and Terba. She sighed with relief. Deryk wasn't pulsating with the forbidden power he gained from devouring someone else's magic.

That was good.

Which meant Lydia was probably still alive.

Which was good too.

Or was it?

With no little amount of trepidation, Reyah clicked on "Alt.Tuumb.cam".

You couldn't miss the screaming crimson and gold of Deryk's second best mage robe against the winter browns and early spring greens of the Elsee Hills. Late morning sunlight glinted off the metallic threads of the robe and the shiny red lacquer of Lydia's mandarin-length fingernails. You could almost hear the strains of "Thus Spake Zarathustra" in the croaks of the mud toads gathered around Lydia's hideous purple boots.

Puzzled, Reyah watched Lydia drop two overflowing pillowcases to the ground and stretch her bony fingers to the pale, cloud-strewn sky. Whatever was the wench doing?

"Mememememememe," Lydia caterwauled. The toads croaked in time. Lydia cracked her knuckles and spoke to the frogs. "From the top, boys:

I am Lydia

Lydia I am

I want to call

A demon on the lam

I want to have one

That's mean and bold

I want to have one

That'll do what it's told

I am Lydia

Lydia I am

Send me

Send me

My demon on the lam!"

This couldn't be happening. It shouldn't be happening—not with Lydia's wretched excuse for a spell—but something was taking shape in the air about ten feet from where Lydia stood. It was the height and shape of a tall man, but with a strange, bulbous head and a giant fin sticking out of its spine. The thing's features grew denser and more distinct with each repetition of "*I am Lydia, Lydia I am*".

Chapter Seventeen

Reyah hit Her "Delete" key so hard it shot through the computer, the tablecloth and the table before vaporizing in a puff of metallic-scented smoke. In Domain a silver bullet ripped through Lydia's half-formed demon. The demon disappeared. The recoil from her broken spell tumbled Lydia into a nearby bush.

Reyah pressed Her fingers to Her throbbing head. This was not happening to Her. It couldn't be. Especially not now, when She was closer to an Earth franchise than at any time since those damned Greeks had figured out She wasn't their mother goddess. Where in Kalin's Seven Hells did a two-bit hambone get the kind of power necessary to call a demon?

Where in Kalin's Seven Hells did Pandora get enough wild magic to rename the moat monster?

But Pandora wasn't the one trying to call up a demon without naming or binding it. A bound demon could command more power than the most devastating weapon Earth had yet devised. An unbound demon was a mindless god.

The Plain of Elsee—and a good portion of Tambara—would be smoked long before Deryk massed his forces to attack Rupert's court. Reyah smiled grimly. Well, that would take care of what to do about Deryk.

Dammit, it looked like those girls *were* going to have to stop a Demon Witch. But with a little finesse and a whole lot of magic, Reyah might still be able to lay the groundwork for her first Earth franchise.

Reyah rummaged among the possibilities concealed beneath the tables of her booth. Her fingers brushed whisper-soft fur.

"Aha!" Reyah drew a small, blue-gray rabbit with floppy ears and button bright eyes from under the damask-draped table adjacent to her computer stand. Holding the rabbit by the scruff of its neck, She examined it from all angles. "You'll do."

The rabbit twitched its nose with great eloquence. Its left hind paw drummed the air.

"You'll have plenty of time for that later," Reyah told the rabbit. "You've got work to do."

ଈ)ଔ

Morgana stretched until the joints of her shoulders and upper spine released with audible pops. "Sorry. I've been dying to do that all morning," she confided to Doug.

"But getting back to this year's costumes," Morgana continued, "I agree he's not much of a Pinhead, but he's the best Pinhead we've got. Now last year we had four Pinheads, and one of them was... Doug, is something wrong? Hey, if you don't want to spend your break talking costumes, I don't mind."

"It's not that," Doug replied in a strangled voice. "Are you seeing what I can't be seeing?"

Morgana followed Doug's gaze to the booth of the little old tchotchke dealer who called herself Madame Reyah. A half dozen of Madame Reyah's scented, cinnabar-colored fans hovered in mid-air around the old woman, flapping back and forth. There didn't seem to be any wires holding them up, much less operating them.

Madame Reyah nattered at a little blue-gray rabbit in a series of clicks, chitters and small huffs. The old lady sounded like a chipmunk on speed. Then she swung the rabbit straight at the screen of her high-end laptop.

Morgana's throat locked on a scream.

But the rabbit didn't slam into the monitor. Its head and forequarters disappeared into the screen. The rabbit's rear haunches pumped the air a few times, and the rabbit shot forward, vanishing with a loud "pop".

Morgana closed her eyes. "Nuh uh, Doug, didn't see a thing."

ଈ)ଔ

Back at the Keep

The heather gray walls of the Keep stretched for miles on either side of the observation deck on top of the Great Gate. The ramparts were wide enough for two SUVs to drive along side by side and still have room for a passing Volvo. Beneath

Brigid's feet, a large city of stone and slate, gardens and gold domes spread across the landscape.

The vista made her feel giddy and strangely possessive. Brigid shared Kait's and Marisol's concern about the families they left behind. But somehow, some way, she knew she belonged here, in this place, in this world, in a way she'd never belonged in any of the places she'd lived on Earth. She knew it in her blood and in the marrow of her bones. The funny thing was Brigid didn't think Reyah had anything to do with the feeling.

"What is this city and where's the Keep?" Free asked.

A chilly breeze reminded Brigid it was barely spring here. She made a mental note to grab a shawl for the outdoor ceremonies. But she wasn't ready to leave yet.

"I think this is the Keep." Marisol's words echoed Brigid's thoughts. "It's like a city all by itself."

"No way," Free insisted. "The Keep's a castle, not a city. Remember the one they used on the show? I think the wizard guy Ported us to the wrong place."

"This isn't the show, Free," Marisol said. "Heck, the way Jagger looks should've been your first clue. Man, this place is huge. Brigid, look at the spooky black dome over there. And the towers! I wonder which one's ours?"

"But it doesn't look anything like the show!" Free bleated. "This isn't right. It's got to be like the show. Everything's got to be like the show. Stefan's *got* to be like the show!"

"Dios, Free," Marisol snapped. "Get over it!"

"Quit arguing, you two." Brigid turned on her heel and pointed to the zaihn on the stair shed. "The Portal wizard gave us the code to call him. I'll just give him a buzz and ask. Maybe we can talk him into giving us the fifty-cent tour."

Nobody answered. Brigid looked over her shoulder. Free and Marisol crouched next to the parapet. Jesus, now what?

"What the hell are you guys doing?"

"Sssh!" Marisol nodded at a corner of the observation deck. A small rabbit huddled against the parapet. Brigid noted the rabbit's fur almost exactly matched the blue-gray color of the stone.

"Isn't he adorable?" Free cooed.

"I wonder how he got up here," Marisol said. "Do you suppose it had something to do with all the magic Val was tossing at the moat monster?"

"He doesn't seem afraid of us. Do you think he's somebody's pet?" Brigid asked.

Free ran over and grabbed Brigid's sleeve. She started dragging Brigid toward the rabbit. Brigid blinked in surprise. She'd never seen Free so animated.

"We've got to catch him," Free explained. "I heard one of the servants say they'll be selling Rabbit Seshmeel in the stands during the tournament."

Marisol extended her hand. "Here, bunny!"

"Come on, little bunny," Free crooned.

The rabbit darted across the deck.

"Quick, Marisol, you go around that way, and I'll grab him when he comes back," Free said.

"Darn, I missed him! Brigid, which way did he go?"

"He's to your left."

"Don't let him get near the edge."

Brigid quirked an eyebrow. The lowest parts of the parapet were chest high.

"Wait a minute," Marisol said. "Let's call for some guards to help us catch him."

"No!" Free shook her head. "They'd take him away and give him to the cooks."

"What if Brigid stands in front of the door to the stairs, and we spread our skirts and herd him toward her?" Marisol said.

"Good idea." Free fanned her skirts wide.

Brigid hunkered down in front of the door. She wished she had a carrot or something to persuade the little monster to cooperate. Maybe she could use the tangerine-enameled dagger dangling from the end of her belt.

"Ready, Brigid?"

Brigid grinned. She couldn't help herself. "Okay, girls, be vewy, vewy quiet. We're hunting wabbits."

"Cute, Brigid. Real cute."

಄ೞ

"Game, point and…" Hawke leaned down and gave Kait a lingering kiss. "Match." The Vanyr warrior rolled to his feet.

Kait sprawled on her back in the middle of a muddy patch of grass. She lifted a trembling hand to her lips. She was stunned, breathless and more than a little confused. How had she ended up on her back in the dirt? It didn't compute.

Kait stared at the clear blue sky over her head. Earlier, she and Sarah had decked themselves out in their warrior garb to check out the Keep and all the preparations for the festivities. The show had made it plain there were lots of women warriors in Domain. Who'd pay attention to two more?

She'd been barely able to stop herself from squeeing every time they turned a corner. Kait loved that the Keep wasn't just a castle, but an enormous walled city. She loved all the exotic costumes and faces. She even loved the funky smells. She loved everything, right down to the shouting food vendors and snarky knights straight out of *A Knight's Tale*.

They came across a cheering crowd gathered around a roped off ring in front of some big stone building. Conlan stood to one side. The Vanyr spotted them and raised a hand. Sarah didn't need any prodding to go stand next to the uber-hunky Conlan. Another roar from the crowd drew Kait's attention back to the ring. She looked over in time to see a weedy little guy swing and knock a wooden sword from Hawke's hand.

"Point and match," Conlan called. "Prize goes to Willber Sugginsson." The weedy guy shook Hawke's and Conlan's hands and pranced off with a bag of coins.

"Good timing," Conlan told Sarah. "We're done here—why don't we go get some breakfast?"

"No, no, no!" Kait bounced from foot to foot. She was dressed to kick ass. This was the perfect chance to show her stuff. "I want to beat Hawke too!"

Hawke, Conlan and Sarah all turned and looked at her. "What?" Kait asked irritably. "If that little weedy guy could beat Hawke, I can too."

"Kait, maybe you should wait," Sarah said. "You don't know…"

"It'd be my pleasure to go a round in the ring with Kait," Hawke interrupted. "I'm sure you'll go easy on an old man. Right, sweetling?"

Kait laughed. "You wish." She snatched up a wooden sword and waved it at Hawke. "En garde!" she cried in her best *Queen of Swords* imitation.

At first it was all good. She and Hawke bashed their wooden swords together for a few secs. She pulled a Sekhmet sneaky and kicked Hawke's feet out from under him. It was totally satisfying to see the big guy fall flat on his ass. She'd strutted over and stepped astride him to claim her victory. Then *Hawke* pulled an even bigger sneaky. He

171

rolled, and the next thing Kait knew, she was flat on her back, and it was "game, point and match", and she'd lost. She touched her lips again. Sort of.

"Are you all right, Kait?" Sarah asked.

Hawke loomed over her. "Did I hurt you?" He reached down and pulled Kait to her feet. She swayed on unsteady legs. Hawke swatted mud and grass from her butt. She squealed and slapped his arm. Did Hawke have to embarrass her in front of everyone too?

Kait whirled away from the laughing warrior and stomped up to Sarah. "I don't understand how he did it," Kait said. "There's no way he should've beaten me. I'm a Theater major, dammit! I've taken Stage Combat classes! I've attended every panel of the Crossed Swords at Dragon*Con! I even almost dated a guy from Swordplay Alliance!"

"I'll be happy to show you how I did it," Hawke offered. "Later. In my quarters."

"With your magic lance?" Sarah said slyly.

Kait didn't understand why Hawke, Conlan and Sarah nearly busted a gut laughing. It wasn't *that* funny a comeback.

"I want a rematch," Kait demanded. "I was scammed!"

"Not now." Conlan offered Sarah his arm. "We all need to get ready for the presentations."

"I'll wash your back if you wash mine," Sarah purred to Conlan.

Kait rolled her eyes. Puh-leeze. She so didn't have time for this. She retrieved her sword belt and slung it over her shoulder. Hawke slipped the knot on one of the ropes marking off the ring. The end rolled across the grass, drawing Kait's eyes to a stack of battered practice gear. A pair of long blue-gray ears followed by big button eyes and a cute, twitching nose angled around the pile of weapons.

"Sarah, look!"

≈ ∝

The Plain of Elsee

Lydia swore as she lurched down the rutted, narrow track she hoped led to the village. Things were not going well. In fact, the whole day was going right down the toilet. She'd made her escape easily enough. In fact, there hadn't been anyone around to try to stop her. It was insulting. Deryk hadn't brought in a single servant to wait on her hand and foot. Damn the man, did she look like a woman who took care of herself? She was high maintenance and proud of it.

She'd tried to call a demon when she reached the plain, but that hadn't worked either. For a moment, she'd thought she was going to pull it off. Then some stinking squirrel had thrown a nut and distracted her. Lydia shrugged. She'd have to practice, practice, practice once she was safe.

Getting down the steep trail from the tower in Deryk's oversized boots had been a trial, but cutting across the plain was not an option. Deryk's boots kept sinking into mud puddles, and once they pitched her right next to a shingled heap of brown ooze which smelled too ripe to be anything but cow shit. She returned to the trail.

Lydia slipped on a pebble, sailed ass over ears and landed flat on her stomach in a dead bush. The branches dug into her like pins and needles. Her bags of loot fell to the ground with a loud clatter. As she heaved herself off the shrubbery, Deryk's mage robe flapped open and she heard the scritch of a seam in her gown giving way. Damp wind licked a newly naked strip of skin running from thigh to armpit.

Someone sniggered. Lydia whipped her hair out of her eyes. The bush marked the boundary to a tree-shaded clearing dotted with firepits. A green- and brown-painted tent stood near the central fire. Three other, smaller tents camouflaged with branches sat opposite. Heavily armed, verminously dirty, villainously ugly men lolled around the camp. The place smelled like the last direct-to-video sword and sorcery flick she'd acted in. God, but she hated the smell of horse shit.

These were bandits, not barbarians, Lydia realized. There were maybe thirty? Forty? After a moment of stunned silence, the bandits erupted in catcalls and whistles. The flaps on the largest tent bulged, and a man emerged. He took one startled look in Lydia's direction and strolled over.

Lydia gawked at him. She'd never seen anyone who looked like this on the show. She cast her mind back, trying to remember a character who resembled him in any way. She shook her head. Not even an extra. And she would've remembered someone as…*sexy*.

Lydia's eyes narrowed. Her mouth started to water. Yes, that was the word…*sexy*. An intricate tattoo covered one side of the man's narrow, clever face, extending back around his head and disappearing under a long black scalplock. A short moustache and beard rimmed his mouth. Battered leathers and furs studded with metal rings and wicked looking spikes clung to the bandit's rangy frame.

173

"My name is Kaltar," the bandit rumbled, wiping greasy fingers on the front of his stained, leather tunic. "Where did you come from, wench?"

Lydia raised her chin still further. "I am Megeara, Demon Witch and Destroyer of Worlds." Lydia preened a little, proud of that last bit. She'd been trying to add it to Megeara's titles on the show for ages, but as usual, the producers hadn't paid any attention.

"I am allied with Vanyr Deryk, you clod." Lydia snapped her fingers. "I demand an escort to the nearest Portal."

Kaltar snorted. "Megeara, huh? Sure you are." He circled Lydia, examining her like she was a starlet past her prime. "You know, I could swear I've seen your robe before." He prodded one of the pillowcases with the toe of a worn boot.

"I don't know what you're talking about," Lydia huffed. "I am Megeara. Escort me to the Portal now or else…"

"Escort you to a Portal? Hell, Megeara would've called her own. You're nothing but a thief, sweetheart." He patted Lydia's rear. "I'll admit you do look a bit like her. But Alfred and that sanctimonious prick Theron did Megeara in a long time ago. Besides, what would the famous Demon Witch be doing wandering around Tambara looking for a Portal wearing someone else's shoes?"

Lydia sighed. She'd known those damn purple boots were going to be trouble. Kaltar's hands moved up to her breasts. Her nipples went rock hard. She slapped his roaming fingers away. No matter how gorgeous he was, no matter how much she was turned on, no one, no one touched her unless she gave them permission first.

"Come now, sweetheart, let's be friendly." Kaltar ran a finger down the ripped seam of her dress. Lydia shivered at his touch. "You're a little skinnier than I like my women," the bandit said with a leer, "but you'll do until I get tired of you."

The other bandits roared with laughter.

Lydia saw red. They were laughing at her. She stamped her foot. "Listen to me, you cretin. Vanyr Deryk brought me here. You know what *that* means. If you hurt me, Deryk'll eat you for lunch. I'll tell you one last time. I am Megeara, the Demon Witch. One more insult and I'll blast you into little pieces."

One of Kaltar's bandits, a stocky brown-haired man, sneered, "I've seen old chickens with more meat on their bones. Kaltar, are you sure you want a skinny pullet like her?"

"Chickens? I'll show you chickens!" She pointed at the brown-haired bandit.

A green bolt sizzled from her finger. The man vanished in a poof of green smoke. In his place clucked a very unhappy, brown-feathered chicken. The chicken charged Lydia, squawking and pecking at her feet. Lydia smiled and booted the chicken to the center of the camp in a flurry of feathers and outraged squawks.

"Now do you believe I'm Megeara, or do I have to turn the rest of your men into chickens to convince you?"

Kaltar frowned at the brown chicken staggering around the firepit. Lydia held her breath. She hoped she didn't have to make good on her threat. She'd meant to blast the bandit to bits, not turn him into a chicken.

Where are special effects when you need them? Lydia thought irritably.

Her fingers were beginning to twitch when Kaltar smiled. "My lady Megeara." He bowed. "I apologize for doubting you. Times being what they are, it's hard to know whom to trust." Kaltar offered Lydia his arm. His golden brown eyes glinted at her in a most disquieting way.

"Quent, get the lady's bags and take them to my tent," he ordered. Kaltar gave Lydia a heart-stopping smile, revealing a gap where one front tooth was missing. "Please, my lady, allow me escort you to my tent. I think we could profit from getting to know one another."

Lydia nodded regally. As she and Kaltar passed the chicken, he reached down and grabbed it. With a casual flick of his wrist he snapped its neck and tossed it to a nearby bandit. "Wat, fix Lady Megeara and me something to eat."

The bandit caught the chicken and stared at it in horror.

Lydia's heart went pitty-pat. She turned, eyes like shining stars, toward Kaltar.

"Oh goody," Lydia cooed. "I love roast chicken."

෨෬

Back at the Keep

Pandora marched down a long, stone hall, sandwiched between four guards. One of Al's knights, a huge guy decked out in form-fitting blue and silver, led the small group. The knight turned down a hallway that smelled like the soup kitchen where Pandora got her high school public service credits. The cabbage and onion smell faded before they were halfway down the corridor.

Man, this hallway was long. Just how big was the Keep?

Humongous enough Pandora's toes ached at the thought of clomping down yet another hallway. Pandora squinted at her feet. Funny, her boots hadn't looked nearly as pointy-toed when she put them on this morning. She could've sworn they were flats too. Maybe all the magic Val had been flinging around changed them?

Too bad Val couldn't zap her back to normal. Then nobody would be trying to shove her into one of those uncomfortable girly dresses. And a corset. How wrong was that? Pandora didn't even wear a bra if she could help it. Why would she willingly strap on a satin-covered Iron Maiden?

Pandora wished with all her heart someone would come to her rescue. Then she wouldn't have to deal with all the "What were you thinking!" smack Anna was sure to hand her. Pandora would rather face a horde of vampires or demons than a buncha asshat lectures on how to behave like a lady. Because she knew it wouldn't only be Anna flaming her ass. Free and Sarah would be getting their licks in, too.

"Talk about a gang bang," Pandora muttered. "I'm so dead."

The knight looked over his shoulder. "Did you say something, Lady Pandora?"

"Nah. Just bitching to myself. Lead on, McDuff."

The knight paused. "I humbly beg your pardon, Lady, but with all the confusion at the bridge, you may not have heard Lord Alfred's introduction. My name is Tanak." The knight swept Pandora a low bow. "Sir Tanak Sitthinan, of the island of Danung Qinabalu in Paelinor."

"Paelinor, huh? Islands and waves and beaches, right?"

"Yes, Lady."

"Excellent! Think you could teach me how to hang ten?"

Tanak blinked. "Hang ten what?"

Pandora giggled. "Um, never mind. Momentary mind boggle."

Tanak looked confused, but he smiled at Pandora anyway. She decided she liked Tanak. He sort of made her think of the Rock, if the Rock had morphed into Bruce Lee's giant cousin.

Pandora ogled Tanak's chest. Too bad they weren't back home. Tanak could make a fortune on the wrestling circuit. Yeah. She imagined him in electric blue spandex and badass tribal face paint, body slamming Triple H.

"We've not much further to go, Lady," Tanak said. "The Portal mage is only a quad away."

"Thank God," she groaned. "My dogs are barking."

"Dogs? What dogs...oh. Dogs. I think I understand what you're saying. Goddess help me." Tanak rubbed his forehead.

Pleasant images of sweaty men grappling with each other evaporated from Pandora's mind as she followed Tanak down another hall. Too bad. She'd almost had an idea for a great slash story. No prob. The story idea would come back, or there would be one even better. Pandora eyed Tanak's very fine tush. Considering all the studly males littering the Keep, finding inspiration for some great yaoi wasn't going to be hard at all.

"Yo, Tanak! Wassup, man?"

Pandora stopped so fast the heels of her boots left skid marks on the stone floor. Her heart fluttered in her chest. Ohmigawd. It was Donatien.

Chapter Eighteen

Pandora sucked in her breath as her stunned gaze traveled across a tanned, muscled chest liberally swirled with crisp hair, over broad shoulders, past a square jaw, finally meeting Donatien's sapphire blue eyes. Don looked like he'd just come from a shower. He was only wearing tights, knee-high boots and a towel slung around his neck.

Man oh man, but he was hot. From his chiseled chest to the turgid shaft fully visible under the damp tights that fit him like a second skin, everything about him shrieked, *Put me in a slash epic, please!*

Tanak cleared his throat.

Pandora jerked her gaze away from Don's crotch. *Come on, Pandy*, she told herself. *Look at his face or his ears or anything but his huge you-know-what. That's* so *not cool.*

Looking at Don's face didn't stop her southern twitches. Pandora gulped as she got lost in his molten blue lava eyes. Damn, but he was five times better looking than the guy who played him on the show. And wouldn't the Barasheban Horde howl with envy if they only knew how much better looking—Pandora risked another quick peek at his crotch—better *everything* the real Donatien was. Pandora made a mental note to start rewriting all her old stories as soon as she got to a computer. Obviously, two months of screen time hadn't been enough to capture the full effect of Don's hunkiness.

"Donatien," Tanak ground the name through his teeth, "Lord Alfred wants Lady Pandora back in her quarters as quickly as possible. Her sisters are waiting for her. We're cutting it fine on making the rehearsal as it is."

Sisters.

Rehearsal.

Pandora pouted. It sucked rocks she still had to face Anna and climb into some dumb dress. Especially when she'd rather stand and stare for hours at Don. For a nanosecond, Pandora understood Free's obsession with Stefan Warner.

Pandora sent Don an apologetic smile and turned to leave. Before she could take another step, he caught her hand and raised it to his lips.

"Lady Pandora," Don said. "Your beauty rocks my world."

"It does?" she asked.

"Word."

"Isn't this a pretty picture," a sultry female voice said. "Did you strip down to show the new Blue Lady your inestimable charms, Sir Donatien?"

Don straightened. Red tinged his cheeks as he bowed. "Lady Bettyna," he murmured. Tanak and the guards bowed too. Pandora folded her arms across her chest and studied the woman strutting down the hall.

The chick was as short as Free, and had hooters almost as big as Free's, but the resemblance ended there. Pandora sniffed. Bettyna, huh? Well, this Bettyna bimbo sort of looked like Christina Aguilera—before Christina dyed her hair black. Pandora grinned. Christina would give her left arm for a boob job like Bettyna's, though.

Bettyna paused in front of Pandora. "What an…unusual outfit. A new look for the Blue Ladies?" She raised an eyebrow. "Or is the carnival visiting the Keep?"

Pandora frowned. "Blue Ladies?"

Another woman walked briskly down the hall. "Bettyna, don't make a bigger ass of yourself than you already have," the newcomer said.

All the men did the bowing thing again. Pandora's eyes widened. She knew *this* woman. It was Lady Amorian, one of the sneakiest ho's ever to slink across the *Domain* screen. And like Don, the reality of Amorian's beauty was much, much more than that of the actress who played her on the show.

This Amorian's features were so perfect she almost looked like a painted statue. If it weren't for the small mole beside her mouth, she *would* look like a statue. And her clothes—even the costumes Anna had brought to the con looked shabby in comparison. Despite her transformation, Pandora felt small and grubby next to Amorian's polished perfection.

To Pandora's surprise, Amorian swept into a low curtsey. "Most exalted lady, please, allow this humble servant of Seshmeel to welcome you to Domain. It is an honor to be among the first to greet one of Reyah's new daughters."

179

Pandora shifted from foot to foot. Oh crap, was she supposed to curtsey back? Where the hell was Anna or Liz when you needed them?

She glanced at Tanak who winked at her. He inclined his head. Pandora followed Tanak's lead and nodded. One of Amorian's hands shot out and tugged Bettyna's skirt.

"You'll have to forgive Lady Bettyna." Amorian tried to pull Bettyna down into a curtsey. "This morning's announcement of your arrival did not make plain Domain had been blessed with nine female Vanyr."

"What?" Bettyna shrieked. Pandora winced. "What do you mean 'female Vanyr'?"

"Exactly what Amorian said," a familiar, girlish voice replied. Ember peeked out from behind Tanak. "They're true daughters of Reyah, like Hawke and Conlan and Roarke and Jagger are Her true sons. Maybe you'd better curtsey, Lady Bettyna."

Bettyna's smile bared all her teeth and most of her gums. She spread her skirts and sank down. Amorian raised an elegant eyebrow. "What about you, Ember? Shouldn't you honor Reyah's daughter too?"

Pandora held out her hand to Ember. "She doesn't have to. We think of her as one of us."

A shocked look crossed Bettyna's face. Amorian looked thoughtful. Ember tugged on the hem of Pandora's shirt and crooked a finger.

"Tell them they're dismissed," Ember whispered. "Or they'll stick around forever."

"Oh." Pandora visualized Judy Dench as Queen Elizabeth. "You may go."

"Of course, Lady Pandora," Amorian said, a trace of amusement in her voice. "I pray we will meet again." The willowy brunette hauled the fuming Bettyna to her feet.

"Whew." Pandora swiped a hand across her forehead as the two women disappeared around a corner. "Those two give me the heebee jeebees."

Ember nodded. "Me too. Whatever hee bee jee bees are."

Tanak leveled a hard glare at Don. "Why are you still here? You're not even dressed yet, you nodcock. They'll put you on report if you're late to Lord Alfred's office."

Another guard trotted down the hall.

"What is this, Market Day in Salentia?" Tanak muttered. "What is it, Jelamas?"

"Lord Alfred is looking for Sir Donatien," Jelamas said

"Crap!" Don yelped. "I'm so dead." He sketched a bow to Pandora. "Catch you on the flip side." He bolted down the hall. Tanak shook his head.

"I have a message for you and your men, too, Sir Tanak," Jelamas said.

"If you'll excuse me for a moment, ladies." Tanak turned away.

Ember giggled as she watched Don skid around the corner. "Donatien's funny."

"At least he talks normal," Pandora commented. She peered through an open door into a small sitting room. "Oh my God! Look over there!"

"Where?" Ember followed Pandora into the room.

"There's a little bunny under the table."

"There is?"

"He's getting away! Let's catch him."

A golden flash of light caught Tanak's eye. "Lady Pandora? Ember?"

No one answered. Perplexed, Tanak spun in a slow circle. "Which way did they go?"

෨൙ඓ

Anna braced herself against the door to Liz's room and took a deep, shuddering breath. Thea wondered if someone had laced the raven-haired sorceress's corset too tight. The creamy half-moons visible over Anna's jeweled stomacher appeared to be waxing dangerously full.

"Thank the Goddess you're still here." Anna's quavering voice made it sound like Thea and Liz were all that stood between Anna's voluptuous self and unmitigated disaster. Anna raised a hand, stopping short of touching her forehead. Unlike Thea and Liz, Anna was wearing make-up. Thea wondered why since it only disguised Anna's goddess-perfect coloring.

"Where else would we be?" Liz asked.

"Gone. Vanished like the rest of them." Anna collapsed into the nearest chair and began fanning herself with a feathered monstrosity of a hat Thea had refused to wear.

"Well Lawdy, Miss Scarlett, just you have that nice Mr. Yeves call you up a Portal mage and have them Ported ra-aht back here." Abandoning the fake southern accent, Liz added, "What took you so long? Rehearsal's supposed to start in something like... Zaphira, what do you call minutes around here?"

"That's my point!" Anna exploded, before the maid could answer. "Yeves spent the last hour talkin' to every mage in the palace, including Vallenius. No one has seen Kait and Sarah since they left the exhibition ring with Hawke and Conlan."

Damn, Sarah beat me to the punch, Liz swore mentally. *I may have to dance with Hawke after all.*

What you mean "you", kemosabe? Thea shot back. *You're lucky there's a lot of him to share.*

"I saw those looks, and I know what you were thinking," Anna said. "Hawke and Conlan had been prize fighting all morning. They were dirty. They were sweaty."

"Anna," Thea began, "Some women like—"

"But some women find some place to do it, preferably where they don't scare the horses or scar the children. But they didn't. They aren't anywhere inside the Keep or on the grounds. Gareth even checked that big picture of Reyah in Alfred's office—you know, the one with all the jewels. Each of those jewels stands for a Vanyr. They glow blue when Reyah's sons are in the Keep. But the ones for Hawke and Conlan aren't glowin' anymore."

"What about the rest of the girls?" Liz asked.

"You want chapter and verse, or will me telling you they're gone too satisfy you?"

Thea shook her head. She was going to hate herself for asking, but somebody had to. "What about Jagger and Roarke? Do they have any ideas?"

"Don't you remember the show—I mean the 'scrolls' Reyah gave us?" Anna wrung her bejeweled hands. "Nobody less than Reyah Herself summons the Vanyr from their tower unless the Keep is under attack."

"The 'scrolls' haven't exactly been the last word in accuracy, now, have they?" Liz replied.

We're going to have to ask them, Thea sent to Liz. *I have a feeling they're the only ones who'll be able to help. Dammit.*

Liz considered the prospect. The hair on the back of Thea's neck rose. *Uh oh.*

Don't get spooked. I was thinking it might not be a bad thing to confront them. It's not like they'll be lying in wait for us. A visit from us is the last thing those two would expect, even if the place was under attack, Liz told Thea mentally.

Aloud Liz said, "Zaphira, would you mind scaring up a Portal mage and a couple of guards? The Lady Thea and I will need to be Ported to the door of the Vanyr tower. I presume someone will answer if we knock?"

Zaphira bobbed a curtsey. "Oh, absolutely, Lady Elizabeth!"

"Now, why couldn't you have been this agreeable about my hat?" Liz asked.

"But you were trying to wear it all wrong. You don't wear a trevette flat on the crown of your head. It was meant to be pinned to the side with the feathers fingering your hair."

"Grrrrrrr," Thea started to growl.

"Who let that critter in here?" Anna demanded.

"Don't pay any attention to Thea. She has this thing about hats," Liz said.

Thea nodded. Damn straight she did.

Anna grumbled, "If I knew I could use my magic like I wrote it, I'd lock your lips and throw away the key. Not Thea, you hair-brained Yankee—that hare!"

"Where hare?" Liz and Thea chorused.

"You nitwits! We don't have time for this. That critter over there."

A little gray rabbit crouched in the entrance way. Instead of scampering away at Anna's shout, it shivered in place, wriggling its cute button nose.

"Oh, Anna, how could you call this little bunny a 'critter'?" Liz eased herself onto her knees more gracefully than Thea thought possible for a woman wearing three-inch heels, a corset stiffer than a steel breastplate and a hat that had denuded at least three pheasants.

"Do you suppose it's somebody's pet?" Liz said.

"Don't you go all mushy on that furball. It's bad enough Free and Pandora are already threatening to turn this place into a kennel. I will not have any animal adoptions on my floor. I'm allergic," Anna announced.

"Dammit, Anna," Liz said. "Quit braying like a mule, will you? You're scaring the bunny."

"Come on, sweetheart," Liz crooned to the rabbit. "Pay no attention to the loud, black-haired lady in the lilac dress. She's all bark and no bodkin. Come to Liz, sweetheart. I won't hurt you."

"Oh, please! Did you ever think that thing could be someone's familiar sent to spy on us? Have your maid get rid of it."

"Can it, Anna. Nobody's going to bust a little gray rabbit on my watch. For all we know he could be Bugs Bunny in disguise," Liz said.

But the rabbit isn't gray, Thea thought. She squinted against the sunlight burning her eyes. *It's...* "Blue," Thea said aloud. "It's a blue rabbit."

"Shit!" Zaphira yelped. The maid vanished in a pop of ozone.

"Blue gray," Liz agreed. She glanced at the spot where Zaphira had been standing. "And here Anna was worried about Double-Oh-Rabbits."

"Are you thinking what I'm thinking?" Thea asked.

"I think so, Brain. If Bugs isn't Reyah's emissary, somebody's gone to an awful lot of trouble to get our attention."

The rabbit nodded with as much gravity as a rabbit could muster.

"You're from Reyah?" Anna demanded.

The rabbit nodded again. It turned toward the door, cocking its head as if it expected the three women to follow.

"I detested *Alice in Wonderland*, you know," Anna said. "I never understood what that fool blonde was doing tearing around the countryside after a long-eared lettuce-eater that was no better than it should be. What's Lord Alfred going to think if Gareth comes here and finds us all gone?"

Liz got to her feet and shook out her skirts. "He'll rightly assume something happened to us. Write him a note, Anna. There's paper in the desk."

"I'd give my left tit for a ballpoint pen," Anna complained, rattling the veneered drawers.

The rabbit hopped toward the door.

"Hurry, Anna," Liz hissed.

"I'm hurrying! I'm hurrying!"

The rabbit bounded through the doorway. As it cleared the threshold, a rainbow of fractal shapes replaced the opening. For an instant, Thea thought she could detect the shape of bunny ears in the swirling color, but the blue scintilla shifted too quickly for her to be sure.

"After you, White Queen," Liz said politely.

"No, after you, Red Queen," Thea replied. "I positively insist."

The Portal yawed, its tone as wide and deep as the song of a hump-backed whale. The fragrance of roses and magnolia wafted from the glittering colors.

"Together." Thea clasped Liz's hand. They jumped.

"All right, I'm ready," Anna said, turning back to the door.

All the sharply faceted color of the rabbit's Portal ran like a waterfall through the seam between the threshold and the floor, and vanished.

"Yeeeeeeeeeeeeeeeeeeeeeeeeeeeeeeeeeeeeeeeves!"

Chapter Nineteen

A Dark and Scary Place

"Damn it, Hawke, did you have to land on my foot?"

"Sorry, Conlan. I was trying to catch Kait."

"Next time try to catch her some place other than on my foot!"

"Whoa." Kait squirmed out from under Hawke. It was dark. Really dark. The air smelled of loam and Christmas trees. Pine needles rolled under her hands. "Something tells me we're not at the Keep."

Sarah's breath came fast and thready. "Where the fuck are we?" Sarah demanded. "What happened to us? Why can't we see?"

Kait could almost taste Sarah's panic. That was odd. Sarah didn't seem like she'd be afraid of anything, much less the dark.

Conlan grunted. "There's no need to get excited, Sarah. We fell into a Portal. Give Hawke and me a minute and we'll figure out where we are."

"But why is it dark?" Kait wasn't afraid—especially not with Hawke and Conlan sitting next to her. She just couldn't understand where the daylight had gone.

"Probably because we're on the other side of the world," Hawke said.

"No way," Kait protested. "It's like, you know, noon!"

"It's noon at the Keep," Conlan said. "But we're not at the Keep anymore."

"Yeah, Toto," Sarah snarked. "We're not in Kansas anymore."

Kait giggled. She was relieved Sarah seemed to have pulled herself together. It would be awful if Sarah turned out to be one of those people on the show who couldn't handle Porting. How would Sarah be able to explore Domain if she couldn't Port?

Kait heard a soft snick. A match-sized flame erupted from a tube in Conlan's hand. In the instant before the flame died Kait glimpsed lots of huge tree trunks. Dark brown mulch carpeted the ground.

"Kush," Hawke said.

"Looks like," Conlan replied. "Kelan trees don't grow anywhere else. Time's about right too."

Kait hugged herself and grinned with delight. "Oh man, we're in Kush! That rocks." A damp wind sighed through the trees. Kait shivered. Too bad it was cold.

Hawke shifted. From the movement, Kait guessed Hawke was shrugging into his doublet. She remembered seeing it in his hand just before...

"Hey," Kait said. "What happened to the rabbit?"

"What rabbit?" Sarah asked.

"The one I was trying to rescue," Kait answered. "You know, long ears, white fluffy tail, blue-gray fur?"

"Did you say 'blue'?" Conlan said in a strange voice.

"Yeah." Kait moved a little closer to Hawke. He was nice and warm. "It was more blue than gray. You know, like one of those dyed bunnies you get at Easter."

"Easter?" Hawke said.

"I didn't see any rabbit," Sarah said. "Just your dumbass running into a Portal."

"But it was there," Kait said. "I don't see how you could've it missed it!"

"Easy—if you weren't meant to see it," Conlan said.

Sarah growled. "Jesus H. Christ! Will you assholes quit talking fucking nonsense? I don't give a damn about any fucking rabbit. I don't give a damn about fucking Kush. I want to get the fuck back into the fucking Portal and get the fuck out of here."

"Which fucking Portal are you referring to?" Hawke asked.

"The fucking Portal we came through!" Sarah exploded. Kait winced. Obviously, Sarah didn't know Domain canon as well as Kait thought she did.

Conlan said, "There's no Portal here, Sarah. Not anymore. Portals don't wait around for people to change their minds and go back through."

"But...oh bloody hell," Sarah growled. "Why the hell did we end up in Kush?"

Kait waited for one of the guys to explain. She wanted to know too.

"Because Reyah wants us here," Hawke said.

"Reyah?" Kait and Sarah chorused.

Jean Marie Ward and Teri Smith

"Blue rabbit." Conlan sighed. "Has to be Reyah."

"She's up to Her old tricks. Do you remember the time She sent us chasing after the blue pygmy potlyii in the middle of downtown Salentia?" Hawke didn't sound like he was recalling a Kodak moment. Kait wondered uneasily what she'd gotten herself into. And what was a pot-lee-eye?

"You *had* to follow that rabbit, didn't you?" Sarah snapped.

"I'm sorry," Kait said. "But it looked so small and helpless. I was afraid it was going to get trampled. I mean, I remembered when I had a pet rabbit and how it would freeze when people came after it."

"Don't worry about it," Conlan said. "You'll get used to it."

"Not in this lifetime," Sarah said. "Right. Now what? How do we get back to the Keep?"

Kait smacked her forehead. "Oh crap, I bet Anna is having a cow."

"Try a herd," Sarah said.

"We're not going anywhere," Hawke said, "at least not until we figure out why we're here. Conlan, you got any more tinder tubes?"

"What do you mean, 'we're not going anywhere'?" Sarah demanded. "We can't sit here in the dark in the middle of Nowhere, Kush."

"You're absolutely right, Sarah." Hawke agreed in a bland voice. "I hate sitting in the dark. We need to build a fire. May I borrow one of your knives to cut kindling?"

"Take one of mine. C'mon, Sarah, it'll be okay." Kait wished she could see to pat Sarah on the shoulder. Sarah sounded like she'd go postal at any moment.

"Cheer up, girls. When it's this dark you can be pretty sure there aren't any bandits in the area. They like their fires," Conlan said.

"So do I," Hawke said. "Tinder tubes, Conlan. I'm freezing my ass off here. Ladies, when the tube ignites, keep your eyes low. Look for branches the size of your wrist or smaller and memorize the location. There'll be a test afterwards," he added.

Kait slitted her eyes against the sudden glare. She saw a branch a few feet in front of her. If she was lucky, she might be able to grab it before the light went out.

The tinder tube stuttered and died. The light didn't.

Hawke turned the blue air bluer with curses. Kait hadn't heard such creative cussing since the last rap concert she'd attended with her brother. A little bit scared, she followed the direction of Hawke's gaze.

A small, lop-eared, long-haired rabbit sat on an exposed root, grooming its whiskers. Its light blue fur glowed like it was lit from the inside with a 100-watt bulb.

"That's him!" Kait caroled.

"Shit," Conlan grumbled, "I knew I should've brought my sword along this morning."

The rabbit cocked its head at the sound of Conlan's voice. It drummed its hind legs against the root, then took a flying leap into the tree-shaped shadows.

"Move!" Hawke grabbed Kait and Sarah by the arm. "Don't let it out of your sight."

They ran. They ran past the point where Kait got a stitch in her side. They ran until it felt like somebody was stabbing her legs with ice picks.

They ran some more.

Eventually the trees thinned enough for moonlight to start filtering through. About the same time, Kait started to hear what sounded like thunder. The roaring grew in volume as they chased the rabbit to the edge of a large clearing. The rabbit dashed past the last stand of trees and disappeared. Kait and Sarah stumbled to a halt. Kait bent over at the waist, put her hands on her knees and wheezed.

Sarah tugged Kait's arm.

Kait looked up. A burning white moon sailed above the crest of a waterfall the size of Niagara. After the blackness of the forest and her single-minded focus on Reyah's blue bunny, it was like staring straight into a camera flash. Orange spots marched across her vision.

Sarah tugged again. She pointed across the clearing at the spots.

Kate gaped. Those weren't after-images. Those were torches, clutched in the hands of some of the skankiest thugs Kait had ever seen. Every one of them was armed to the teeth, especially the huge, hairy Atilla the Hun clone standing in the center of group.

The big goon's eyes narrowed. An ugly grin spread across his face. Kait couldn't hear what he said to his men, but the intent became clear a moment later. Every last one of his thugs turned in her and Sarah's direction. The thugs drew their weapons.

A cold bead of sweat trickled down Kait's spine. *Oh shit. They were so in trouble.*

Chapter Twenty

In the Great Cauldron of the Shadowlands

After being dumped head over heels in a gloomy, sultry bayou by a wascally Porting wabbit, Brigid led Marisol and Free to a tiny, weed-covered hummock. All around them, snaky wisps of mist rose from murky black waters studded with bulbous, faintly phosphorescent trees. Occasionally the inky water would swirl and bubble. Brigid's first thought on reaching dry ground was to get rid of as much of her wet clothing as possible. Marisol felt the same way. Brigid was glad she'd worn her little dagger.

Some unseen animal rattled the nearby reeds. In the distance, Brigid heard a deep-throated bellow, followed by the loud splash of a heavy, low-slung body hitting the water belly first.

"What was that?" Free gasped.

"You don't want to know," Marisol assured her, sawing even harder on the lacing of her skirt.

"Yes I do!"

"Does anybody have any idea where we are?" Brigid interjected.

"I want to know what it was," Free said mulishly.

"The Shadowlands," Marisol replied, before returning her attention to Free. "Would it make you feel better to know it sounded like the papacito of all alligators?"

"Oh, like you know what alligators sound like."

"Oh, like you've ever spent any time in the Everglades."

"Is that why you think it's the Shadowlands, Marisol? Because it reminds you of the Everglades?" Brigid pulled a length of cord from the wreck of her skirts and tied back her hair.

"Huh?"

"You said we were in the Shadowlands like it was obvious," Brigid said. "Were you making a guess because the Shadowlands sets looked like a cypress swamp?"

Marisol's brow furrowed. "What are you talking about? I said it was the Shadowlands, because..."

"Because...it's the only place in the world where the air would feel like this. How cool! It's so easy! I *am* a weather mage! Man, am I glad I wrote myself as an elemental. I bet I could dry our clothes and change the weather without even thinking about it."

"Nooooooo!" Brigid and Free shouted, startling a flock of bugs the size of sparrows into flight.

Marisol, the Florida native, started. Free, who claimed to have never traveled further than the Iowa border before coming to Atlanta, screamed. And screamed. And screamed.

Every animal in the surrounding underbrush scampered in the opposite direction. Free flapped the mud-plastered silk of her gown at the bugs as hard as she could. "They're swarming me! Quick—get them off me! Get them off!"

Brigid jumped to her feet and grabbed Free's arms. The busty redhead trembled so hard she practically vibrated.

"Ssssh. It's okay, Free. You don't have any bugs on you." Brigid hoped. "Especially since I don't think they can smell you under all the mud."

As if to give Brigid the lie, one of the bugs fluttered onto the side of a nearby tree. It looked like a cross between a gecko and an exceptionally friendly preying mantis. The insect's enormous, neon green eyes swiveled independently of each other, taking in multiple views of each woman in turn.

"Don't get any ideas," Brigid told the insect. "I bet you taste just like chicken, and I'm beginning to work up an appetite."

The insect made a disgusted, chirruping sound and scrabbled around the tree. Free's shoulders hunched and she crossed her arms in front of her breasts. She stared at the point where the insect vanished.

"Maybe it's a magic bug?" Free's question was very close to a whimper.

"Maybe," Brigid said. "If we're in the Shadowlands, it's possible. The Voice has her main temple here somewhere, and the College of Wizardry is in Zakharville."

Free nodded. "So it's probably friendly, and it can come back and help us if it wants?"

Brigid pitched her voice to carry. "Well, if it is a magic bug and if it is friendly, surely it would find some way to let us know."

Silence. Brigid, Marisol and Free waited. Eventually, the local version of cicadas resumed their concerto.

"Maybe leaving you alone counts as friendly around here," Brigid said.

Free took a deep breath. "I was hoping for something a little more positive."

"I think that's about as positive as you're going to get." Marisol jerked the knife through the last cord at her waist and pushed out of her skirt.

Free squinted. "Did you see that?" She pointed to her right. "I think it's a light. Maybe it's a house, and they can help us find a Portal."

Brigid stared in the direction Free was pointing. "I don't see anything, Free. Are you sure you saw a light?"

Free flushed. "I'm scared, but I'm not seeing things. I saw a light, Brig, I'm sure of it."

"Wait," Marisol said, "I think I see it too—yes! It's hard to see, because it's a kind of green-y blue. But Free's right, Brig. There is a light over there."

Once she realized the flash of aqua blue in the distance wasn't a bird or a patch of sky, Brigid finally spotted Free's light. Brigid also had a pretty good idea of how much smelly black water wallowed between the three of them and the light.

"I don't want to get into the muck again," Brigid said. "Especially with Papacito Gator out there."

"Neither do I," Free replied. "But how else are we going to get there?"

"Free, look at all those vines hanging from the trees," Marisol said. "You've got plant magic. Do you think you could do something with them so we could get over to the light?"

Brigid couldn't help but laugh. "Let me guess, we're supposed to yodel like Tarzan and swing from vine to vine."

Free put her muddy hands on her hips. "You are barking up the wrong tree, Brigid, if you think I'm going to do a Tarzan imitation. I might as well wish for the vines to pick me up and carry me over to the light—Eek!"

192

A thick vine snaked around Free's waist, lifting her from the ground. More vines swarmed from the branches of the trees, passing Free along like a redheaded package from leafy vine to leafy vine.

"Oh my God!" Free shrieked. "They've got me! Let me go, let me go!"

"Free!" Marisol yelled. "Calm down! It's only your magic!"

"Help! Killer vines are going to eat me!"

"*Free! I said, Calm down! It's only your magic!*"

"Run, Marisol and Brigid, or they'll get you too! Oh God, oh God, oh God, I don't want to die hanging from a vine!"

୫୦ଋ

In Tambara

In front of a ramshackle hut crouched in the foothills that formed the northern border of the Plain of Elsee, a swineherd tossed swill to six large pigs barely contained by an even more ramshackle pen. One of the pigs emitted a nasal squeal. Obligingly, the wind lifted the earthy aromas of slops and manure away from the enclosure. In the process, the breeze tossed a snatch of conversation the swineherd's way.

"Pandy?" a young girl warbled.

"Yes, Ember?" answered a breathy, high-pitched woman's voice.

"When we catch him, can I name him?"

Wondering who or what they wanted to name, the swineherd extended his senses. Two pairs of feet in city shoes alternately galloped and tumbled along the rock-strewn path cutting across his land. The woman panted as she ran. Her sweat carried an increasingly familiar musk.

"I want to call him George," Ember said.

"I *like* it!" the woman crowed. "Look, he's slowing down. Here, George, come to your new mommies. We'll hug you and squeeze you and love you forever and ever."

Didn't it figure one of Reyah's damned rabbits would lead one of Her daughters straight to him? The swineherd swore several ripe oaths involving Reyah's sexual habits in a language even older than Jagger. The swineherd congratulated himself the woman wasn't one of the brighter ones.

Gareth Weston's daughter crested the small rise at the border of the swineherd's property. Streaks of dirt and grass painted the skirts of Ember's court gown. The remnants of a flowered and beribboned wreath clung precariously to the back of a skullcap of short braids. What happened to the rest of Ember's hair?

The seneschal's daughter must have been attacked by the same demented hairdresser who'd chopped Pandora's curls to within two digits of her lovely head. Nevertheless, the petite demigoddess's glamour was such that despite her close-cropped hair and tawdry clothes, she still seemed more exquisitely female than any court beauty the swineherd could remember.

He shook his head. Why did he know this lot was going to be trouble?

Sure enough, the slight movement proved to be enough to catch Pandora's eye.

"Hellooo!" she hooted, flapping her arms. "Can you tell us where we are?"

"Aye," he drawled, pulling a straw from behind his ear and sticking it in the corner of his mouth. "Reckon I can."

Ember giggled. Pandora huffed. The swineherd could tell she wasn't impressed. She wasn't supposed to be. In his swineherd identity, he looked very ordinary—average height, with shaggy brown hair and a scruffy beard. There were patches on the patches holding his clothes together, and mud crusted his boots.

His eyes were another matter. They were the color of dark gold encircled by a deep blue rim. But if he didn't look people in the eye they didn't always notice. "I'm called Tristan. And who might you be?"

Pandora burst into laughter. "It figures. I should've known by the pigs."

Ember looked as confused as Tristan felt.

"Never mind," Pandora said. "Private medieval lit joke."

Ember held her hand out to Tristan. "Hello, Tristan. I'm Ember Weston, and this is Lady Pandora. She's a Daughter of Reyah, not a Blue Lady, but a real daughter, like a Vanyr only different. We're lost. Where are we? Is there a Portal around here?"

"You're in Tambara," Tristan said when Ember paused to suck in breath. "Howsoever, if you follow the path to the next rise, you'll find it forks. Take the left-hand fork. It will lead you to a road. Go left on the road, and in a little while, you'll come to a village. There's an old Portal wizard in the village. He can help you get back to the Keep."

"Thank you," Pandora said. "You've been very helpful. Come on, Ember, let's get home before we both get into any more trouble."

The pair hurried away. Tristan returned to feeding his pigs.

"You know, girls, I wonder if I should've told them about the mercenaries hiding in the foothills, or the brigands and the wizards across the plain."

The pigs' answering grunts caused him to shake his head.

"Come now, Maisie and Petal, I think you're just being worrisome. None of Deryk's people have bothered the village. I doubt the ladies will take any harm."

Tristan frowned at the pigs' answer.

"Nay, if they keep to the left-hand path, they'll not run into the mercenaries. I've made sure."

Tristan heard Pandora cry, "Look! There's George!"

Tristan glanced up in time to see Pandora and Ember run down the right-hand fork of the path. Two of the pigs grunted with satisfaction. Tristan shook his head as he set down the bucket and ambled into the hut.

"Women," he grumbled. "Always going in the wrong direction."

ℰᏆᏅ

"Do you see him?"

"No...wait! There he is! Look, he's there under the big thorn bush." A gust of wind rattled the thorn canes. Pandora rubbed her arms and tried not to shiver. It wasn't as warm here as it had been at the Keep. Now they weren't running anymore, the cool-looking fuzzy vest she'd thrown over her shirt before heading out to sightsee wasn't enough to keep her from getting cold. "You know, George, I'm beginning to think you're more trouble than you're worth."

Unperturbed by Pandora's censure, the little blue-gray rabbit continued nibbling on a stalk of grass.

Ember, however, gave Pandora an indignant look. "I still can't see him."

"He's there," Pandora assured her. "It's the angle of the light. George is using the bush for cover."

Ember sank to her knees and peered into the bush. The bush's long thorns caught one of her sleeves. Ember tugged. The sleeve parted from Ember's dress with what sounded like a sigh of relief. Ember tossed the grass-stained rag aside.

Not that Pandora's clothing was in any better shape. For about the millionth time since arriving in Domain, she wished she was wearing her favorite Levis and Nikes.

Ember lifted her head and sniffed. "Do you smell that?"

Pandora took a deep breath. "It smells like…"

Ember rose to her feet. "Smells like…"

Their voices chorused, "Chicken!"

Ember looked hopefully at Pandora. "I'm starving, Pandy. Can we go find who's cooking? Please? Maybe they'd share."

"I don't know. I'm not sure it's a good idea."

A vague memory of a show about bandits attacking a wagon train crossing Tambara flitted through Pandora's mind. Or had it been an episode of *Firefly*, and space ships being attacked in outer space?

The wind shifted and the tantalizing aroma grew stronger. Pandora succumbed. She couldn't help grinning when Ember's stomach rumbled in time with hers.

"What the heck. I say we go find that chicken." Pandora brushed off her breeches and took Ember's hand. "After all, I'm a Daughter of Reyah. I'm sure whoever's cooking will be happy to share."

છ૭ભ

The Royal Palace, Salentia

A clock set into the belly of huge green plaster frog chimed the half-hour. The notes rang softly in the large room. Thea realized the clock's time was an hour behind the timepieces in Liz's rooms. If Domain was like Earth, the rabbit's Portal had taken them to a longitude a couple hundred miles west of Keep. The question was, where?

Vivid purple silk swathed the room's walls. Pictures of massively muscled men wearing horned helmets and lots of chain mail hung from twisted silk cords nailed to gilded moldings. None of the colors in the pictures coordinated with the walls, the violet damask sofas, jade silk love seats or leopard-spotted chairs. Overflowing bookshelves lined the walls. More books were piled on ornate rosewood tables and much of the floor.

"Good grief," Thea exclaimed. "This room looks like it was decorated by a crazed Sixties' librarian with a Frazetta fetish."

Liz turned in a slow circle and whistled. "Interesting color scheme." She glanced at Thea. "Sixties?"

"You know—psychedelic. What with the bright colors and all." Thea touched Liz's arm. "Don't look now, but the Portal and the rabbit are gone. And it's an hour earlier than when we left the Keep. Where the heck are we, and how are we going to get back?"

Liz moved a couple stacks of books from the nearest sofa and sat down. "No problemo." She patted the cushion next to her. "Sit. Believe it or not, I have a pretty good idea of where we are."

Thea sat. She removed a tapestry bag stuck between the cushions. A small, leather-bound book fell into her lap as she transferred the bag to the carpet. The book was surprisingly heavy. Thea moved it to the arm of the sofa.

"All right, Wrong-way Devereaux, I'll bite. Where are we?"

Liz stroked the arm of the sofa and grinned. "Episode Fifteen: Chivalry."

The book made a very satisfying swacking noise when Thea slapped it against the upholstery. "Smart-ass. We're in Isabeau's palace in Seshmeel. Here's the $64,000 question—why are we here?"

"Don't look at me. The rabbit was Reyah's idea."

"Great, another brilliant idea," Thea said sarcastically, "just like the one Reyah had about us fighting a Demon Witch."

"Mmmm, yeah, managed to forget about that for a few hours." Liz sounded a little less pleased with herself. "On the other hand, since the rabbit claimed to be from Reyah, our little detour might very well have something to do with the Demon Witch or fighting her or both."

"I bet she sent everybody on a quest." Thea rubbed the back of her neck. *Dammit.* She was getting one of her "funny" feelings again. She wished Liz had them too. It was surprising Liz's bag of mental tricks didn't include something like Thea's on-again-off-again presicient ju-ju. Of course, Liz didn't get spooked by the same things Thea did.

"Liz, I'm getting a weird-on, a bad one. First Reyah makes such a big deal about our presentation, then she Ports everybody—as far as we know, separately—from the Keep. If we don't know jackshit, I'll bet you dollars to donuts none of the rest of the group knows jackshit about what Reyah wants or where they're going either."

197

"Something moved up her time table," Liz said with maddening calm. "Thea, worrying about it isn't going to help. Right now, all we can do is play along until we get the chance to do something useful."

Thea snarled a few choice words about Reyah under her breath.

Liz sighed. "Yes, I agree Reyah's a bitch, and yes, I agree, we're in trouble. But there's nothing we can do about it. For now, anyway."

"So just sit here and let the bad premonitions roll, right?"

"Let me finish. We were Ported here for a reason. The reason can't be too obscure. Otherwise we'd never be able to figure it out—and everything that's happened suggests Reyah wants us to figure it out. Since we're in the middle of what looks like Isabeau's private library, my guess is it has something to do with Isabeau and her books. Sooner or later somebody from the palace is going to show up. When they do, we'll explain what we know and go from there."

"Do you think anybody from the Keep is looking for us?"

"Probably. Let's hope it isn't…" Liz broke off when the handles on the double doors to the room rattled. *Show time.*

Right on cue. Thea nervously tapped the cover of the book.

One of the doors opened. A voluptuous blonde dressed in silver-embroidered, carnation pink satin eased into the room. She looked up and down the corridor before latching the door behind her. With a sigh of relief, the blonde turned around. Her jaw dropped at the sight of the two women on the sofa.

"Assassins!" The woman's voice rose until it had the piercing quality of a train whistle. "Help! They're going to kill the queen!"

The woman yanked back the latch and ran out of the room. Her shrieks echoed down the hallway. "Don't let them near me! Guards! Guards! Assassins!"

"Does this mean we're not famous anymore?" Liz asked.

₧₧

Kala Falls, Kush

Sharks and Jets. Yeah, that was it. This was *West Side Story* and she was a Jet, man. She was going to kick ass. The thugs across the clearing shifted, jostling each other as they jockeyed for position near the head hulk. It was almost showtime.

I'm a Jet, man.

Out of the corner of her eye, Kait saw Conlan speaking to Sarah. Hawke cupped a hand around Kait's ear. Kait had to strain to hear him over the sound of the falls. "Sarah's going to get us weapons. We need you to distract them. Think you can keep them busy for a minute?"

"I've got knives," Kait offered. "I can give you a couple of those." She handed him four throwing knives from secret pockets in her fighting leathers.

"Thanks," Hawke shouted. "Don't get fancy. Just keep them busy."

Kait nodded.

"Don't die if you can help it."

I'm a Jet, man. Who was she kidding? She needed the part of her that was Sekhmet, the Egyptian warrior goddess, the part of her that fought with a lion's courage and savagery. In her fan fiction, Sekhmet took over every time Kait's cyber-character got into a rumble. But Sekhmet hadn't shown during the bout with Hawke. It didn't look like she was going to show now, when Kait needed her the most.

I'm here.

Where the hell have you been? Kait groused to the strange new voice inside her head. *You let Hawke beat me!*

You didn't need me then. You need me now. Are you ready?

I'm a Jet, man. Let's rumble.

Her body tensed, coiled, all her energy compressed into a tight crouch. She was a rocket ready to explode. Her lips spread in a vicious grin.

I'm a Jet, man.

"Wait 'til I give the signal," Hawke said.

Kait's fingers tightened around the hilt of her sword.

Across the clearing, the hulk leered at Kait and Sarah and rubbed his crotch. *Not yet*, the Sekhmet part of her said. *Let them think you're afraid. Makes them easier prey.*

Fugly hulk roared with laughter. So did the rest of his nasty crew. Sarah growled. The lioness inhabiting Kait's body growled along with her battle sister. No way they'd let those scum take them down. Not now. Not ever.

I'm a Jet, man. Bring it on!

The pack rushed toward what Kait knew looked like easy prey. Howling like a banshee, she ran to meet them, her hand still on her sword hilt. *When do I draw?* Kait asked Sekhmet.

When it's time. Sekhmet told her. *Wait for it. Wait for it. NOW!*

Kait's sword flashed from its scabbard. The next thing Kait knew, one of the bad guys was trying to stop his guts from spilling from out. Blood gushed from a second outlaw's sword arm and sprayed from a third's neck. A torch fell to the ground and guttered out in the pooling blood.

I'm a Jet, man. Kait told herself over and over again. *No one's going to take me down!*

Two of the larger thugs pounded toward her, attempting to outflank her. The nearest one, wearing a double-bladed axe slung across his back, swung a torch straight at her head. The supple leather of Sarah's whip wrapped itself around his wrist. Kait heard the bone snap over the thunder of the falls. The thug's yell became a scream. Another torch fell to the ground and went out. The clearing got a little darker.

Hawke appeared, grabbed axe-man's head and twisted. Axe-man convulsed and went limp. Hawke took the axe.

The whirring sound of a knife hurtling through the air warned Kait of another bad guy's attack. Without stopping to think, she pivoted, ducking the knife. She kicked the outlaw in the stomach and smashed the pommel of her sword against the back of his head. He dropped.

The outlaws kept trying to surround the smaller party and cut them off from each other. They didn't seem to understand the agility of the big Vanyr or the reach of Sarah's whip. As a result, the thugs wound up crowding each other, blunting the effectiveness of their attacks.

The bad guys' frustration gave way to frenzy. But the crazier things got, the slower things appeared to move. It was like a scene out of a Quentin Tarantino movie—if Tarantino had made a gangsta' version of *The Lord of the Rings*. Plumes of blood hovered in the air. Butchered limbs took forever to fall. Everything not burning was cast in black and white. Black as blood on dark gray grass, white as flashing steel. Fugly hairy guy shouted and cursed. Hawke took off two thugs' heads in one swing.

Nice. Sekhmet purred. *He is a worthy battle brother.*

He's a Jet, man. Like me!

Bandit after bandit fell, their torches guttering in smoking pools of blood. Blood dripped from Conlan's and Kait's swords and Hawke's axe. Blood gleamed wetly on

Sarah's knife and the coils of her whip. More blood and gore spattered their clothes, and Kait knew, somehow, none of it belonged to them.

She looked around. There was no one but the hulk left to fight.

The hulk drew a knife from his belt. "You sons-of-bitches think you've won, don't you?" he roared. "I may be dead, but one of you is going down with me."

He threw the knife at Kait. Whipping around, he lifted his huge sword over his head and charged at Sarah. Hawke knocked the knife away with his axe.

Sarah hurled her whip in the hulk's face. It distracted him long enough for her to do a back-flip and roll to a pile of dead bodies. She rose to her feet with a sword in her hand. For the first time since the fighting started, Kait got a good look at her friend. Sarah's long Nemesis coat was crusted with bits of flesh and other body matter. A dark smear of blood trailed across her jaw. Her eyes blazed ice blue.

"Come on," Sarah screamed at the hulk. "Come on, come on, come on!"

The outlaw hesitated a fraction of a second. Sarah chopped off his hands. The big man fell to his knees. Blood exploded from his severed wrists. Sarah waded into the fountain of blood and swung her sword. His head rolled a few feet from the body. Sarah licked the outlaw's blood from her lips. Eyes still blazing, she turned to Hawke, Conlan and Kait. She raised her sword and took a step forward.

"Sarah," Conlan barked. "Come out of it."

Sarah took another step. And another.

"*Stand down, battle sister! We won!*" Kait could hear the lioness roar in her voice. Fortunately, so did Sarah. The glow faded from Sarah's eyes.

"Shit," Sarah moaned. "I could've killed you."

"You didn't. Kait stopped you." Conlan clapped a hand on Kait's shoulder. Kait didn't notice. Sekhmet deserted her between one breath and the next. Copper-scented blood burned her face. Bits and pieces of dead bodies piled around her feet. The air smelled of shit and blood and vomit.

"You did well," Hawke shouted to Kait.

"I'm a Jet, man," Kait mumbled. She bent over and puked up her guts.

She was vaguely aware of Conlan picking her up and carrying her to a rock-edged pool on the far side of the clearing. He gently wiped blood and tears from her face. Kait wondered where he'd found the clean handkerchief he'd dipped into the water. She buried her face in his shirt. Conlan rubbed her back and made soothing noises.

"What are you doing?" Sarah yelled behind them.

"Checking to see if any of them had provisions. Here's a canteen," Hawke yelled back.

Kait couldn't make out what Sarah said next, but it made Hawke laugh. "Aren't you the squeamish berserker. See if you can find anything fit to eat or drink. Believe me, you'll be hungry soon, and you can't rely on Reyah to provide—especially when She's got the bit between Her teeth."

Kait told herself robbing the dead couldn't be any worse than killing them in the first place. But it made her feel even squickier. Sarah knelt at the edge of the pool and rinsed out a couple of canteens, muttering to herself the whole time. She didn't like it either.

The air over the center of the clearing shimmered like gold lace. A Portal opened in the heart of the dancing color. "Hey!" Sarah called. "You think those bandits were waiting for this?"

Hawke smiled grimly. "Yeah, I think. I also think we should see where they were going and who sent the Portal to get them."

Sarah gathered up the canteens. "Sounds like a plan to me. Kait, are you okay? Can you travel?"

Conlan wiped one last dribble of tears from Kait's face and pulled her to her feet. "She's fine. Aren't you, sweetling?"

Kait nodded. "I want to get out of here."

"That's the spirit." Conlan handed Kait her sword.

"I'm a Jet, man." Kait walked through the Portal.

80Q3

Back at the Keep

Jagger interrupted Roarke in the middle of Roarke's attempt to analyze the water from the pool in the Daughters' Tower. The partially completed orb of water and magic exploded into nine flashes of color. The colors knotted themselves into a diamond rope. The rope spiraled back into the bottle. *Very pretty*, Roarke thought, but he didn't have a bloody clue what it meant. He turned on Jagger. "What are you doing here?"

"Teaching a young dog a new trick. Did I ever tell you—" Jagger lifted the bottle Roarke had brought from the tower and moistened his fingers "—you showed more natural affinity for magic than any student I ever had, save one?"

Again, the water flared into nine colors. This time, however, the colors faded slowly, like the after-image of the sun on a bright day. The Old One frowned.

"Bravo for me. Well?"

"What? Oh, this." Jagger handed Roarke the bottle. "It's Reyah's magic, of course."

Roarke ground his teeth. He knew that, dammit. But what kind of magic had Reyah used?

"By the way, you might be interested to know Reyah sent Her daughters on a rabbit hunt. Alfred's postponed what's left of the Natal Day celebrations."

"Where did they go?" Roarke asked

"Liz and Thea were sent to Seshmeel; Pandora and Ember, to the Plain of Elsee."

"Ember! How'd she get sucked into it?"

Jagger shrugged. "Followed Pandora into the Portal, as far as anyone can tell. As for the rest, Brigid, Frieda and Marisol went to the Shadowlands. Sarah, Kait, Hawke and Conlan Ported to Kush together."

"This doesn't make sense. Why send them on a quest now? Wait, you didn't mention the sorceress, Anna. What happened to her?"

"Apparently Reyah intended her to go with Liz and Thea to Seshmeel. She was in the room with Liz and Thea when the rabbit opened a Portal, but the Portal closed before Anna could reach it."

"Well, at least one of them is safe."

"As long as she remains in the Keep," Jagger agreed. "I've sent Vallenius after the three in the Shadowlands. My agent in Tambara will see to Pandora and Ember."

"Better him than you?"

Jagger inclined his head.

"What about Thea and Liz? Who's taking care of them? They don't know any more about magic than the rest of their sisters. And their power is a siren call to every magical Thom, Darius or Harold looking for a leg up."

Jagger set the bottle back on the table. "You don't want to spill this."

"Jagger," Roarke growled.

"Who do you think? Which brings us back to your original question. I came to see if you'd like to accompany me to Seshmeel."

Damn straight Roarke would. Isabeau's captain of the guard had the conspirators on Roarke's list in custody. But there had to be more people involved in Deryk's failed plot against the queen, including a wizard or two. Deryk always had at least one tame wizard guarding his back.

In the days leading up to the ambush at the Wayward Bard, it had bothered Roarke he hadn't been able to identify the wizard or trace his movements. A wizard strong enough to hide his tracks from Roarke and Gwyn presented a terrible risk under normal circumstances. The thought of a wizard that powerful that close to Thea turned Roarke's vitals to ice.

Roarke yanked the starched lace collar off his shirt and fastened a battered gold talisman around his neck. The pendant was similar in design to the fob hanging from his belt. "Where's Deryk?"

"Kush. But nowhere near Sarah or Kait. "

"Good. I hope you know where Thea and Liz landed in Seshmeel." Roarke followed Jagger through the Portal.

Chapter Twenty-One

The Royal Palace, Salentia

At the behest of the Council of Wizards and the Most Omnipotent Oligarch (Magic User Deluxe), may Reyah look with favor upon his spells and incantations, I, Adept Wizard Myrgatroid of the Shadowlands Order of Omnifarious Wizards will now unfold the tale of the mighty battle waged by nine of our wizardly brethren against the foul Demon Gnatzon. Let it be known that on the fifth day of the month of Gathering, a heroic band of wizards sallied forth from the Shadowlands, little knowing that they were Domain's last hope in its stand against the demon...

"Geez," Liz muttered. "This guy needs an editor."

He should've needed a translator, Thea reflected. Or at least she and Liz should've needed one. The pages of the book had aged to the color of dried oak leaves. The ink wasn't much darker, and the handwriting was a mess. But whatever magic allowed the Daughters of Reyah to understand and converse with the Vanyr, Chosen and mortals at the Keep seemed to extend to the written word. This was not necessarily a good thing. Myrgatroid's epic pretensions reminded Thea of a bad fan fiction writer on crack.

"God, I hope Val doesn't grow up to write like this. Unfortunately, I think this is what Reyah wanted us to find." Thea pointed halfway down the page. "Look at this:"

And so the wizards stood before the Demon on the Plain of Elsee. Dead and dying warriors lay around them, the stench of the battlefield as noxious and foul as the Demon attacking the beleaguered land. The Wizard Elemer called his weary brethren close and laid before them a most desperate plan. "We must link, my brothers," he intoned solemnly, "and fashion our powers into a mighty weapon to bring yon Demon under control."

"Fie!" Wizard Maximullard exclaimed. "If we link we risk losing our minds!"

"So?" Wizard Vantram retorted. "Since we were the ones who thought we could fight the Demon, I say we've already lost them." Vantram gave Elemer a shrewd look from under his beetling brows. "And if your plan works, my brother, what will you do with the Demon when you have him under control?"

Elemer reached into a capacious pocket and withdrew a large crystal. "We shall imprison the demon in this," he told his fellow wizards. "It will hold the fiend until the end of time."

"I don't know," Maximullard worried. "I don't want to lose my senses."

At that moment the Demon gave a hideous roar as it grabbed an unfortunate soldier and bit off his head.

"It's either that or lose your body parts. Which would you prefer?" Vantram asked Maximullard with great irritation.

"There is a way to link that will not endanger us," Elemer proclaimed, putting a soothing hand on Maximullard's shoulder. "Come close, my brothers, so I may explain." The brave wizard glanced over his shoulder and shuddered as he watched the Demon pick its teeth with a splintered thigh bone. "We haven't much time before yon foul Demon turns his attention to us. Harken to me now…"

"There they are! Arrest them!"

The blonde in pink had returned, dragging a handsome man in a bright scarlet uniform behind her. The man was tall enough and the woman's skirts wide enough to block most of Thea's view of the corridor. Nevertheless, Thea thought she glimpsed several guardsmen in electric purple uniforms clustered behind them.

Eight guardsmen, Liz's mind voice confirmed. *Four for each of us, I think.*

You think we're going to have to fight them? Thea's stomach lurched.

No. Liz's mental voice was startled. *What made you think that? I only meant four each to escort us to the queen.* Liz's gaze wandered back to the tall man in red. *You know, Thea, I think the time has come to separate "Blondie" from that very arresting officer. It's not as if hothouse pink and tomato red could ever have a future together.*

And the peachy thing you're wearing does?

Of course.

Thea bit back a snicker as Liz wafted off the sofa. The hem of Liz's heavy skirts and petticoats fluttered like zephyr-kissed clouds around her ankles. Liz smiled up at the officer's faintly exotic, golden face. The man in red gaped at Liz with the kind of stupefaction usually reserved for movie stars and supermodels. Liz occupied her new body so comfortably, it was easy for Thea to forget she wasn't just Liz or even a younger version of Liz. She was Liz Prime, infused with a goddess-like glamour, yet retaining all of Liz's practiced charms.

Thea figured red uniform and the four burly soldiers who filed in the room after him would start melting about the time the clinging blonde went ballistic. Thea slipped Myrgatroid's *Gnatzenod* under a fold in her skirt and practiced looking harmless.

"Arrest them, I say!" Blondie shouted. "They're assassins!"

"Hello again," Liz addressed the blonde in a light, friendly voice. "I don't believe I caught your name. Or the gentleman's."

The man in red shook his head as if trying to clear it of the last lingering effects of Liz. He looked down at the sharp-faced blonde clutching his elbow. Something akin to horror crossed the officer's face. He pried the lady's fingers off his arm as fast as possible without actually committing violence.

Thea grinned when Liz's mind gave off an almost audible thrum of pleasure.

"Chosen Knight Atlee, Captain of the Queen's Guards at your—" Atlee barely stopped himself from bowing. "This is the Marquisa Bettyna fil Romeral Uthriptenwald, lady-in-waiting to Queen Isabeau of Seshmeel. Who are you, ladies, and what are you doing in Queen Isabeau's private chambers?"

"I'm Liz. And this is my sister, Thea."

Thea smiled and waggled her fingers at Atlee. Damn, he was cute.

Liz continued, "We are two of the nine Daughters of Reyah. Sorry to drop in unannounced, but one of Reyah's creatures transported us here to talk with the queen."

Liz, you don't know that.

It could be true.

"Liar!" the blonde in pink shrieked, shaking her finger from a safe distance behind the captain. "I met the Lady Pandora at the Keep, and you don't look anything like her."

Through the thread of their mental connection, Thea felt the twitch of Liz's annoyance like the flick of a cat's tail. "Of course we don't," Liz said. "Like the Vanyr, we represent the breadth of Reyah's creation. Thea and I are as different from Pandora as Hawke and Conlan are from Roarke."

"Make her prove she's a Daughter of Reyah!" the blonde insisted, grabbing Atlee's arm again.

"Lady Bettyna, let go."

There was steel in the soft command, enough to make Bettyna draw back. Atlee didn't like Bettyna. Thea wondered why.

"What's wrong with you, Atlee?" Bettyna hissed. "Arrest them! They've got no business in the queen's chambers."

"And you do?" Liz asked.

Bettyna paled under her make-up.

"No. She doesn't," Atlee answered for the noblewoman, "But I was working my way there. I know Lady Bettyna. You two, on the other hand, are complete strangers. Can you prove your claims?"

Liz uttered a disgustingly winsome chuckle. "When I stepped through Reyah's Portal, I didn't realize I'd need a passport. Would a demonstration of our powers be sufficient?"

Liz, if you scuff your high-heeled tootsie bashfully on the floor, I swear, I'll bite your foot off.

"We could talk mind to mind." Liz slanted an inviting glance to Atlee from under her lashes. "Or would you prefer me to cast an illusion? Of course, if you'd like something spectacular, Thea could always transform herself into a panther."

Oh God, not spectacular, Liz! Remember Alfred's office. Spectacular is a really, really bad idea.

"Oh my Goddess, it's the cat woman!" Bettyna reached toward Atlee, thought better of it and whirled to face the guards blocking the doorway. "She savaged Sir Donatien last night! Do something quick! She's a demon-beast in human form! Save me and my father will re—"

A monstrous bong interrupted Bettyna's tirade mid-syllable. Clocks all over the palace began chiming the hour with demented enthusiasm. At the same time, a Portal winked open in the middle of the room. Roarke and Jagger emerged from the opening, their magic fizzing around them like turquoise and silver fireworks.

The Vanyr swept into bows that put Anna's deepest curtsey to shame. Thea was relieved to see that Liz showed no inclination to respond in kind. However, Bettyna, the guards, even Atlee were dipping and bowing like they were in the presence of royalty.

"The blessings of Reyah's Natal Day upon you, Lady Elizabeth, Lady Thea," Jagger said.

Liz cocked her head in his direction.

"The blessings of Reyah's Natal Day upon you, Lady Elizabeth, Lady Thea," Jagger repeated a bit louder over the clamoring clocks.

Liz's face remained blank.

What are you up to? Thea asked. *I know you can hear him.*

Liz didn't answer, but Thea could feel Liz's simmering anger.

Liz, I don't think this is a good time to lose your temper.

I'm not getting mad.

"I said, *the blessings of Reyah's Natal Day upon you Lady Elizabeth and Lady Thea!*" Jagger shouted at the top of his lungs as all the clocks fell silent.

"Thank you," Liz said. "I believe Vanyr Jagger answered your question, Captain Atlee."

Atlee's gaze darted between Jagger and Liz. The captain and his men executed another round of bows. "Lady Elizabeth, Lady Thea, I humbly beg your pardon, but there was an assassination attempt on the queen two days ago, and—"

Jagger started to laugh.

"Vanyr Roarke!" Bettyna threw herself into Roarke's arms. The startled Vanyr staggered and fell on a nearby love seat. Bettyna's pink satin gown made a faintly obscene, rustle-y slurping noise as she writhed on top of Roarke. "I swear I didn't know who they were! Don't let them punish me!"

"You know, Atlee, that's a very extreme reaction to two women she never met before today," Liz said. "Never mind our connection to Reyah."

"I don't know, Liz, you terrify me." Jagger's warm, amused voice, the engaging tilt of his head, the crinkles at the corners of his beautiful eyes—if Liz enticed, Jagger captivated. Even knowing what had happened to Liz in the pool last night, Thea felt her crotch twitch and her toes curl in pure, sensual delight.

Yeah, he has that effect doesn't he, Liz's mind voice drawled, *but to paraphrase John Ford, 'tis pity he's a skunk.*

"What is a 'skunk'?" Jagger asked.

"It's a black-coated weasel with a nasty smell," Liz replied. "What are you doing here, Jagger?"

What are you doing in my mind?

Liz hurled the mental question with such force, the aftershock rocked Thea in her seat. So much for Liz not getting mad.

The shock waves of Liz's mind voice seemed to touch Atlee, too. He checked his men. The guards' glances shifted between themselves, but Thea couldn't see any sign of pain. Maybe Liz wasn't as dangerous as they both thought. The notion wasn't as comforting as it should be.

Jagger never flinched. "The power of your mind voice is one reason. The other is Roarke and I thought you might need some help."

"How very considerate of you," Liz said in a voice that could cut steel. "How did you find us?"

Jagger must have beamed something directly to Liz. The redhead's nostrils flared. She clenched her hands tight to her sides as if to keep from hitting him.

Maybe it wouldn't sound like I was shouting if you weren't spying in my brain. Liz's words were eminently reasonable. The tone of her mind voice was anything but. *Get out of my head, Jagger. Now.*

Gladly. As soon as you get out of mine.

Thea gasped at the sound of Jagger's mind voice.

Even Liz pulled back. "What the hell are you talking about?" Liz said aloud.

Roarke yelped and pushed Bettyna's hands away from his groin. "Bettyna, stop it!" He turned to Liz. "Jagger tracked you through the Portals, Liz. Is that what you're asking?"

"Do you know where the others went?" Thea asked.

"Jagger does," Roarke said. It was all the answer he could make with Bettyna squirming over him like a perfumed eel.

"Why am I not surprised?" Liz remarked, rage sizzling under the calm words. Thea was amazed Jagger's doublet didn't catch fire from the heat of Liz's fury. "How long did you plan to withhold that piece of information?"

Roarke grabbed Bettyna's wrists and pushed her hands down on the seat between them. "Bettyna, control yourself. There's no danger here."

"How can you say that when that, that, that red-haired Daughter of Reyah is talking to Vanyr Jagger like he was her lackey and treating Atlee like he was her equal? Atlee's a Chosen, not a Vanyr! What was Reyah thinking of, making a bunch of common sluts Her daughters? The next thing you know they'll be inviting peasants or worse to the high table at the Keep. Then where will we be?"

Eyes blazing an unnatural blue, Liz whipped around to Bettyna. "In a hell of a better place than you are now, you obsequious little *ferret.*"

The air around Bettyna imploded in a shower of blue-white light. A streak of blonde fur fell from the air onto Roarke's chest and scrambled toward the neck of his doublet.

"What in Reyah's Name?" Roarke choked out.

The freaky blue vanished from Liz's eyes. "Oops."

"Well," Thea said philosophically, "you were talking spectacular."

The ferret Bettyna twisted in mid-burrow and squeaked in outrage. Teeth bared in what might have been a fearsome snarl in some larger animal, the ferret thumped down Roarke's leg and charged at Liz. As the ferret raced past her, Thea reached down and caught the enraged beast by the scruff of the neck.

Thea shook her snapping, gnashing captive hard enough to get the ferret's attention. "Tsk, tsk. Bad Bettyna. Haven't you caused enough trouble for one day?" Bettyna growled and tried to bite Thea's hand. Thea shook the ferret a little harder. "Listen, you nasty little beast. If you keep aggravating Liz, she'll never return you to human form. And if you keep aggravating me, I'll turn cat and eat you."

The former lady-in-waiting froze, her dark, liquid gaze rolling toward the outer corridor.

"Captain Atlee," a young woman shouted from the hallway, "Edy says the Daughters of Reyah are here! In my rooms! With Jagger and Roarke! Could you, please, tell your men to stand down so I can see them? Please? You know we've got nothing to fear from them."

"That's what she thinks," Roarke said.

The eyes of the ferret that had been Bettyna rolled upward in a ferret faint.

Chapter Twenty-Two

In the Vanyr Tower

Theron leaned back in his chair. On the desk in front of him were two stacks of those oh-so-perplexing sheets of paper. He took a sip of brandy. It was early in the day for hard spirits, but by Goddess, after what he'd had to face this morning, he deserved it. He read on.

Conlan leaned close and inhaled the intoxicating scent that billowed muskily from his dream woman. His darkly handsome face reflected the ecstasy surging through his hunky bod. He sniffed one last rapturous sniff and sighed longingly.

"Damn, but that stuff smells good," Conlan moaned. "What is it?"

Pandora gave Conlan a friendly grin. "We call it 'cherry cola'," she told him. "Would you like to try some?"

Conlan smiled, a caressing smile that made Pandora's denim-covered knees go weak. "You bet, babe," he said. The warrior put the can to his manly lips and drank deeply.

"Wow." Conlan wiped his mouth with the back of his hand and smiled again. Mental images raced across Pandora's cerebellum as she stared dazedly at the sensual smirk that quirked those delectably full lips. Wow, indeed. She could just see those lips tracing a path toward Alfred's muscular groin. The thought made Pandora incredibly hot.

Theron paused and made a note in the margin. He needed to find a spell to supplement his native translation magic. Something from wherever this paper came from was inhibiting his ability to correctly interpret what he was reading. Instead of "Alfred", the text should read "Pandora"—or some other woman's name—in several key passages. But whatever her faults, Theron had to concede Pandora wrote a good tale.

And her faults were many. Theron growled and took another bracing slug of brandy. He still couldn't believe what had greeted him at the Great Gate this morning. Kalin's balls, how had Pandora managed to *name* the moat monster? Only Reyah and Jagger possessed that much magic. Impossible, *impossible* Reyah allowed a woman to wield that kind of raw power.

Unthinkable She hadn't given it to Her most faithful son instead.

To make matters worse, Theron hadn't been able to vent his fury on that impertinent young puppy, Vallenius. By the time Theron had reached the drawbridge, Alfred had sent the inept bungler back to his rooms for some restoratives, depriving Theron of the pleasure of gnawing off a healthy chunk of the young wizard's ass. Instead, Theron had to bite his tongue and send the moat monster back to its lair.

"Spot." Theron's voice shook with loathing. "She named it Spot."

Theron pressed two fingers over each eye and breathed deeply. He reminded himself he needed Pandora's stories to woo the delectable Frieda. Even if for some unaccountable reason she was called "Freya" in these pages and been written with pointed ears (of all things!) Theron recognized his ladylove when he read about her.

Nothing was more important to Theron than winning the Lady Frieda's affections. With Frieda at his side, he would be a force to reckon with. Even Jagger would have to defer to him, listen to his views and follow his orders.

Pandora's head whirled with all the possibilities that smile presented to her feverish brain. It was all she could do to keep from grabbing Conlan and hauling him off to the Lord of the Keep's chambers. Oh, the things they could do there. One more smile like that, she thought bemusedly, and no matter what, I'll make him do what I want.

Conlan leaned closer, so close Pandora could smell the cola on his breath. A small moan escaped her as his lips parted in the most soul-searing grin she had ever seen. "Sweetling, I have to know," Conlan breathed huskily into Pandora's eager ears, "have you ever thought about a ménage a trois?"

"Yes," Pandora squealed in delight. "Oh yes!"

Despite the odd references to Lord Alfred and the fact Conlan wasn't given to frivolous grins, this passage was most promising. Theron dipped his quill into the crystal inkwell on his desk and added another note. As he recalled, *The Arts of Love* also extolled the virtues of a lover's smiles.

Theron cast his mind back to meeting the women in Alfred's office. Unlike her coarse and brazen sisters, Frieda displayed an entrancing shyness and maidenly reserve. Theron had no doubt his little flower was a virgin maid. Which was good. It was much easier to bridle a virgin's magic. Theron studied the odd typescript in front of him. It would behoove him to take Frieda's untouched nature into account when applying the lessons of Pandora's stories. He scribbled another note to himself and read on.

Vanyr Conlan, paramount warrior of all Domain, strong of thew and bold of heart, sable-braided and walnut-eyed, crafty as a fox and brave as a boar, gentle as a lamb and loyal as a dog, bowed low as he opened the door.

Lady Pandora, clad of denim and shod of Nike, bespectacled and brown-haired, stepped through the door and out to the rain-drenched street beyond. Pandora paused and gasped with dismay. There, barring her return to her trendy and most excellent hostelry was a large and very muddy puddle.

"Disgusting!" Pandora exclaimed, staring in horror at the mud. "That is too gross! How for art am I to cross that?"

"Fear not!" Conlan bellowed. He turned and seized a passing merchant. The mighty Vanyr stepped forward and tossed the fat merchant on top of the muddy pool. Pandora howled with delight. Conlan hadn't cared at all that the merchant's rich velvet cloak and its silk lining were forever ruined. The merchant wailed pitifully and tried to crawl out of the puddle.

Conlan planted a booted foot firmly on the merchant's neck and bowed low again, reaching out with a strong, sure hand to guide Pandora across the icky sludge that kept her and her brand new Nikes from proceeding down the street.

"Oh, Conlan," Pandora sighed, looking soulfully into his nutty brown eyes. "How can I thank you for putting someone else's wardrobe in jeopardy just for little ol' me?"

"Think nothing of it," Conlan said, taking Pandora's hand and fervently pressing a kiss on its ink-stained palm. "Only give me leave to escort you to your destination, my lady, and I will be well repaid."

"I don't know." Pandora eyed the hunk. "Can I trust you to behave as a gentleman?"

Conlan ripped open his shirt and solemnly crossed his heart. "You have my word as a Vanyr warrior and demigod, my beautiful temptress," he proclaimed passionately.

"Damn," Pandora muttered under her breath. "Well, maybe he'll change his mind."

Conlan flexed his muscles again. Pandora gazed transfixed at the smooth brown expanse of muscled chest that had been revealed. Her mouth watered as her eyes fixed on a taut nipple. Wouldn't Alfred love to taste that, she thought. "My hotel is two blocks down," Pandora said absently, still staring longingly at Conlan's chest. "Is it okay if I invite the Lord of the Keep over too?"

"Ahem."

Theron nearly fell out of his chair. Hell and Megeara's demons take it! He was just getting to the good part.

"Damn it, M'volio," Theron swore at his manservant. "You'd better have a good reason for bothering me."

"I have some disturbing news, m'lord."

Theron looked up. "Disturbing how?"

M'volio hesitated. "Reyah's daughters have gone missing."

"What! Who told you this?"

The servant rubbed his hands against his breeches. "I was near Lord Alfred's office, and I overheard Yeves questioning Sir Gareth as to the whereabouts of Vanyr Hawke and Vanyr Conlan. According to Sir Gareth your brothers are no longer at the Keep."

Theron frowned. "Those two jump around like rabbits in heat. What does that have to do with the Daughters of Reyah being missing?"

"It's funny you should mention rabbits, m'lord."

෨෬

The Great Cauldron of the Shadowlands

Theron followed the path he'd conjured through the swamp. All around him, Frieda's magic twined through the trees like a living thing. The magic's tangy-sweet flavor lingered on his tongue like the finest lirian-flower nectar. He breathed through his mouth like a cat, drawing in draft after intoxicating draft of Frieda's distinctive power.

When the path paused, he pulled one of Frieda's small silken undergarments from a pocket and held it to his nose. The scent of her essence was strong on the garment. The path changed course, flowing between two clumps of manyen trees. Back on track again. Good.

A vine reached down and tapped his shoulder. He brushed it aside and smiled. Frieda's magic was strong. So very, very strong, and for a mage such as he, delectable beyond belief. And the lady it belonged to was a virgin, he was sure of it. He licked his lips. Initiating a Talented virgin into Reyah's mysteries was a duty he not only took seriously, but one he quite enjoyed.

Theron had lost count of the Hiawati and Gruendian maidens he'd initiated over the years. The power a pure maiden released at the moment of breaching was quite heady. One might even call it addictive. Theron stroked the front of his robe. To be the first to breach Frieda and to bridle her power, as he couldn't do with a mortal, made his hands tremble.

He wanted Frieda, and he wanted her *now*. He wanted to take her to his bed and feast on her power and beauty. Theron's hand moved faster.

Yes, oh Goddess, yes, he would feast for a week on her magnificent breasts, dine like a king between her soft, white thighs. He'd bring her to the point of orgasm. While she writhed under him and begged him to take her, he'd spread her wide and drive into her womb. She'd scream with completion as he broke her maidenhead, and when she did, he'd plunder her incredible magic as deeply as he did her beautiful body.

"Ahhhhh, Frieda…"

Theron groaned and gave into the painful, demanding lust that wracked his body. A few moments later his seed spilled to the ground. He leaned against a nearby tree and fought to regain his breath.

"What are you doing?" Brigid's voice rang over the swamp. "Don't just hang there, Free. Use your magic to make them put us down."

Theron started as if snapped from a trance. "Wasteful," he hissed as he removed the evidence of his unseemly lust. Not only had he wantonly spilled his seed, but he'd also spilled some of his magic. He shook his head. This lack of control was not like him. His excitement over finding a proper mate had impaired his better judgment. "It won't happen again," he vowed. "I will not give into petty lusts. I can't."

"I've tried, Brig, I really have," Frieda answered. "They won't listen to me!"

"Dammit, Free, try harder. Your vine is nearly squeezing me in two," Marisol whined.

"Stay calm," Brigid said. "Arguing isn't going to get us anywhere."

The women's voices seemed close. Theron peered into the gloom. His eyes widened. A half a quad away, hanging like a delectable fruit over a pool of murky water was Frieda. Dangling next to her were Brigid and Marisol. A disapproving frown settled over Theron's face as he regarded Marisol's and Brigid's abbreviated petticoats and bare legs. Had Frieda's sisters no sense of propriety?

"You're the one who wanted to swing through the trees, Marisol. You got any more brilliant ideas?" Frieda asked

"Maybe I could call up a little thunderstorm and have lightning strike the tree," Marisol offered. "The vines would let go, don't you think?"

"*No way!*" Frieda and Brigid shouted.

Theron straightened his doublet and smoothed his hair. They hadn't seen him. Good. He directed his path toward Frieda. It was time to rescue his little flower.

"Ah, Lady Frieda," Theron said a few moments later, "we meet again. Could I perhaps be of assistance?"

Frieda stared down at him, her eyes wide with surprise. "How did you get here?"

"With a Portal, of course." Theron made a mental note to begin training Frieda in magical basics as soon as possible. Her naiveté was adorable but quite useless to him in the long run.

"She means, how did you know we were here?" Brigid said.

"Lord Alfred sent me," Theron lied.

"How did Alfred know we were here?" Marisol asked.

Theron frowned. He was tired of Brigid's and Marisol's impertinence. If he wasn't sure a display of temper would frighten his little flower he'd free Frieda and leave her two slut sisters hanging like the overripe fruit they were.

"Reyah must've told him," Frieda said in a breathless voice. "I bet she wanted someone to take care of us."

"Yes, that's it." Theron was pleased his ladylove had given him such a convenient excuse. "Now, my lady, why don't I get you down from there? It looks most uncomfortable."

Frieda rewarded him with a shy smile. "Yes, please."

Theron's heart soared. Now things were going the way they should.

"Please, Lady Frieda," Theron instructed as he gathered his magic, "I want you to order the vines to release you once I initiate my spell. Do you understand?"

"She'd have to be deaf not to," Brigid said.

"I understand. Go ahead and cast your spell." Theron didn't fail to notice the irritated look Frieda shot her rude sister.

"Nictu tuat floribunda," Theron chanted. "Thekla laat floribunda…" A blue glow radiated around the vines, startling a bird off a nearby branch.

"Vines, drop us!" Frieda ordered. The vines went slack.

Theron dropped his staff and caught Frieda in his arms as she fell. He ignored the shrieks of outrage from Marisol and Brigid as they plunged into the murky water.

Chapter Twenty-Three

The Royal Palace, Salentia

"You don't have to change her back, Lady Elizabeth," Isabeau said. "I'm sure I'll stop sneezing in a...ah...ah..."

The queen's companion, a young noblewoman named Lady Edytha Fitzwalter, handed Isabeau a lace-edged handkerchief the size of a hand towel.

"...Ah choo!"

Liz jumped. It was the kind of sneeze that rattled windows and knocked picture frames askew. The sixteen-year-old queen of Seshmeel would've been a terror on a high school softball field. She had a sturdy, broad-shouldered frame that strained her heavily flounced, powder blue gown with every breath—not to mention sneeze. Liz could only wonder what they used for Isabeau's corset lacings. Corded steel?

"Bless you, Your Highness," Liz said.

Liz hoisted the ferret Bettyna in one hand, the footstool Bettyna had been using as a daybed in the other and carried both to the only unoccupied spot of carpet in the queen's sitting room. Apparently tired of her queen's stroking and sneezing, Bettyna made only token resistance.

However, Atlee's right hand jerked an inch toward his sword as Liz swept past. Liz reflected she ought to take her late mother's advice and stop scaring all the nice boys.

Especially considering what was left.

Liz, I hate to remind you, but you never reverted a ferret back to human form in your fan fiction.

Thanks for the vote of confidence, Liz answered, her mind voice droll. *Here goes nothing.*

"Un-ferret," she commanded Bettyna.

The breath whooshed out of Liz's lungs. Air streamed through the cracks under the doors and the minute gaps between the windows and their frames. The drapes flapped against the walls. The women's skirts flared and whipped against their legs. The separate gusts of air met with a loud clap over Bettyna's furry head.

The ferret yipped. The noblewoman screeched as the spindle-legged stool collapsed under her reconstituted weight.

Isabeau squealed. She sprang out of her chair and blew across the room like a lily of the valley-scented hurricane, scattering books and the seed pearls from her gown in her wake.

"You did it, you did it! How amazing! To completely transform a person and bring her back without killing or addling her wits… You are still in your right mind, aren't you, Bettyna?"

"I, I think so, your ma—majesty," Bettyna stammered.

"I knew it!" Isabeau crowed. "Lady Elizabeth, does this mean you're a goddess like Reyah?"

"No!"

Liz drove the exclamation point home. Beside her, Thea shook her head emphatically. Liz knew Thea agreed, *no goddess, no way.* "No, your majesty, Thea and I are simply two women blessed by Reyah's grace and favor.

"About Bettyna, Your Highness," Liz continued, determined to change the subject. "She's been through a lot today. Wouldn't it be a good idea to send her to her rooms to rest?"

"It would be a kindness, Your Majesty," Edytha concurred in her soft, musical voice. Edytha's limpid brown eyes exchanged an unspoken message with Atlee. "Between her Portal trip from the Keep this morning and two transmutations, Lady Bettyna must be exhausted."

"With the queen's permission, Guardsman Baxxt—" Atlee indicated the best looking of the purple uniforms still in the room "—will escort Lady Bettyna to her husband's suite and wait with her until the ambassador arrives."

Do you suppose that has something to do with Bettyna being in the queen's rooms when she wasn't supposed to? Thea asked Liz.

Bettyna eyed the young uniformed stud. Surreptitiously, she licked her lips and fluffed the tumbled curls of her coiffure.

Bet on it, Liz replied. *Hope the good spy—er, guardsman likes ferret musk.*

Thea managed not to hoot out loud, but Liz heard her mental giggle, notwithstanding.

Isabeau dismissed the matter with a wave of her hand. "Permission granted." Isabeau said. Bettyna backed out of the room, curtseying unsteadily every third step of the way.

"You'll stay for the banquet won't you, Lady Elizabeth, Lady Thea," Isabeau begged. "It would mean so much to Seshmeel if we could be blessed by your presence."

Danger, Will Robinson, danger. Liz's finely honed political instincts went on red alert.

"Much as we are honored by your gracious invitation, Your Highness, Thea and I are new to Reyah's Domain. We are unfamiliar with your customs. Therefore, we must defer to Jagger in this instance."

Jagger flashed Liz a surprised smile. His approval cut as deeply as his abuse of her memories the night before.

Isabeau heaved an enormous sigh. "And I can tell by the look on Jagger's face he's going to say 'no'." The queen flopped back on her throne-like chair. "Oh well, it was worth a try."

Edytha tapped Isabeau's hand. When she caught the queen's attention, Edytha cocked her head toward the frog clock.

"Oh!" Isabeau started. "It's almost lunchtime! Can you stay for lunch, at least?"

Roarke chortled. "I think even Jagger can fit lunch into his busy schedule."

Thea straightened. Her hand slid under her skirts to where Liz knew she'd hidden *The Gnatzenod.* Liz marked it down to reflex. The interesting part was the way Thea's eyes glittered and her breathing quickened whenever Roarke opened his mouth. Knowing Roarke was scum didn't lessen the impact of his cool, cultured voice on Thea.

A feather of curiosity brushed Liz's inner senses but withdrew too quickly to tempt her to respond. *Him.* There was a conversation she and Jagger needed to have that couldn't be put off any longer. Best to get it out of the way, too.

"Your Highness," Jagger said, "with your indulgence, I'd like a word with Lady Elizabeth."

Roarke and Thea rose from their respective seats as if joined at the hip.

"With her sister, Lady Thea," Jagger said. "Alone."

෧෧෬

The Great Cauldron of the Shadowlands

Only three feet away. But uphill. She'd have to crawl further out of the mire. Brigid inched onto the small hump of land where Theron stood. She coldly estimated how far and what angle she'd need to put her dagger squarely in the center of Theron's throat.

If he can't speak, he can't cast any defensive spells. Then we can take the smug bastard apart bit by bloody bit and feed him to the alligators. Being dropped into the muck had worn out Brigid's last frayed nerve. She intended to take care of the problem of Theron once and for all. It'd be better for Free to find someone else to fixate on, anyway.

Free turned her face into Theron's shoulder. One small hand clutched the front of his robe. Brigid's hand slid down to the dagger clipped to her belt. A tiny bit more to the left...

"You mother-fucking pendejo!" Water sprayed over Brigid as Marisol erupted from the swamp. "You sorry prune-faced bastard, you dropped us in the swamp on purpose!"

Thunder boomed. A hundred yards away a blue bolt of lightning sizzled into the swamp. More thunder boomed. Another bolt of lightning incinerated an unsuspecting alligator, overlaying the rank smell of rotting plants with an aroma similar to fried trout.

Theron spun around. Free's head snapped up, connecting with the underside of his chin.

"Gawrk!" Theron stumbled and fell backwards. Free and Theron rolled in a jumbled heap to the edge of the small island.

Brigid stared at the dagger in her hand as Marisol launched into a tirade that would've made a Miami dockworker blush. Could she put a dagger through Theron's throat? Brigid wondered. Her hand caressed the blade. *Absolutely. And I still can. He's totally defenseless now.*

Ozone filled the air. A bolt of lightning exploded a tree into a flaming inferno not more than six feet away. The rush of hot air snapped Brigid to her senses.

"Marisol, stop your magic!" Brigid shouted. "You're out of control!"

But Marisol kept on shouting at Theron and Free. Free wriggled like a beached fish on Theron. His long robe, now as wet and muddy as Free's gown, pinned them down as surely as a weighted net.

Brigid strode to Marisol and caught her by the shoulders. "Stop it. Put your magic away, right now."

The blue drained from Marisol's chocolate brown eyes. "What have I done?"

"Marisol, how could you?" Free howled. "You nearly killed us!"

"How dare you!" Theron roared, "How dare you waste magic!"

"There you are! Thank the Goddess I found you!"

Brigid and Marisol whirled. Brigid's dagger flew through the air and thwacked solidly into a small boat punting up to the hillock where they stood.

"Ouch," Vallenius cried. "You cut me!"

Val tugged Brigid's knife from the boat, releasing his sleeve. He wiped the blood trickling over his fingers on his robe and scrambled from the boat.

"Sorry, Val" Brigid said as the young wizard handed her back her dagger. "We weren't expecting another rescuer. What brings you to our neck of the swamp?"

"Another rescuer?" Val asked. "I don't understand. Vanyr Jagger and Lord Alfred instructed me to find you ladies and give you whatever assistance you required. They didn't send anyone else."

"You mean Lord Alfred didn't ask Vanyr Theron to come help, too?" Marisol inquired. "How interesting."

Brigid looked over her shoulder. Free and Theron had finally disentangled themselves. Theron picked up his staff, wearing his usual Friday-faced frown. Free wore her usual dogged expression, which Brigid thought looked odd as hell on Free's new face. Free's shoulders hunched together as if waiting for a blow.

"Vanyr Jagger and Lord Alfred sent me, not Vanyr Theron." Val squared his shoulders. "I've been instructed to assist you, and assist you I will." Val met Brigid's eyes. "With your permission, of course."

ഇരു

The Plain of Elsee

"Owooooohhhhhhhooooowwwwwoooohhhhlllll…"

"Ungh! Ungh! Ungh! Ungh!"

Pandora scowled at the battered and burned bandits huddling on the other side of the campfire. She viewed the bandits' sorry appearance with great satisfaction. It had taken the entire band and Megeara working together to subdue and truss Pandora and Ember. Pandora swerved between fan girl glee at meeting the fabled Demon Witch and sheer terror at meeting the fabled Demon Witch.

Something niggled at the back of Pandora's mind. Megeara seemed awfully familiar.

Sure she seems familiar, Pandora told herself. *Don't you have every episode of Domain on DVD? Except for last season, which hasn't been released yet, but you recorded all those. Haven't you watched the Megeara eps about a million times each?*

It's a different kind of familiar, the little niggle insisted. Pandora sighed. She hated it when her inner voice started talking to her. Things tended to get weird.

The noises from the tent rose in volume. Her face flamed crimson. It was one thing to write about hot and steamy sex, even if it was between two guys, but it was quite another to have to hear it while tied to a tree next to a little kid. Talk about embarrassing.

Ember squirmed against the ropes binding her. Pandora hollered, "Somebody tell those two to shut up! There's a little kid out here!"

"Ow! Pandy, you're making my ears hurt! Why are you shouting?"

Pandora frowned and shook her head. Another round of ululations and grunts resonated from the tent.

"Because there's...a coyote and a...a...wild pig chasing each other," Pandora lied.

"What's bad about that? I don't understand."

The howls and grunts reached a fever pitch, then subsided.

Pandora heaved a sigh of relief. "Thank goodness, they're done. I was getting hoarse."

"*You're* getting hoarse! I'm nearly deaf! My ears are numb! Why couldn't I listen to the coyote and pig chase each other?"

"Because it's...it's..." Pandora thought fast "...it's...bad luck."

"To listen to a coyote and pig chase each other?"

"Er, well...yes."

Ember gave Pandora a "Yeah, right" look.

"Is this one of those adult things? You know, like in, 'Not now Ember. I'll tell you all about that tribe of women that worship Roarke naked when you're old enough to understand' adult stuff?"

Pandora did a double take. A world of fan fiction possibilities exploded in her head.

"There's a tribe of women that worship Roarke naked?" Pandora began to breathe faster. "Are there any guys with the women? Like, maybe a tribe of naked guys who worship Roarke too? Is Roarke naked when the guys and the women worship him, or are only the women naked...or...oh my! Are they *all* naked?"

Ember frowned at Pandora. "How would I know? I'm too *young*. Nobody tells me *anything*!"

Eyes crossing at the thought of nude Roarke worship and the stories she could write about it, Pandora began to hyperventilate.

"Pandy, are you all right? Pandy? Can you hear me?" Ember shouted. "The coyote and pig are chasing each other again."

"What!" Pandora fell out of her lust-filled reverie. "That's the sixth time since we were captured! Doesn't that insatiable bitch ever quit?"

"How do you know it's a female coyote? Don't they all sound alike?"

"Trust me I know," Pandora insisted. "At least with this one, I know."

The thought of what Megeara might do when she finished getting jiggy with the bandit chief struck Pandora. She strained against her bonds.

"We've got to get out of here!"

Chapter Twenty-Four

In the Shadowlands

Brigid sweltered beneath the tatters of her mud-crusted finery. She'd been covered in slime so long, she was beginning to think her sense of smell might never recover. She was so tired her eyelids ached, and still, bloody bloody Theron argued on and on.

"I will take care of the Lady Frieda," Theron asserted for the umpteenth time. "You can take the other two wherever you wish."

"I was instructed to assist all three ladies," Val replied for the umpteenth time.

Brigid was impressed by the young man's dogged determination in the face of Theron's intimidating high-handedness. She knew it couldn't be easy for Val to face down what he most likely thought of as a demigod. The wizard had more spunk than she thought.

"Listen to me, you stupid little bastard," Theron roared. "No one, especially not some jumped-up mortal, is going to interfere with my plans for Lady Frieda. Now take those two cows and get out of my sight."

Marisol stiffened.

"No," Brigid said, laying her hand on Marisol's arm. "It's my turn. Val, if you'll permit me?"

White with fury, Val nodded and stepped back. Brigid moved in front of Theron.

"Theron. Shut. The. Fuck. Up." Brigid drew her dagger from its sheath and tapped the hilt against one palm. "Or I will cut your lying tongue out of your head. Frankly, I doubt anyone will miss it."

Theron's jaw dropped. "You, you, you…"

"I believe you called me a cow, but I'm willing to let it pass." Brigid ran a finger along the blade of her dagger. "I'm going to let it pass, because I know in a few minutes you're going to apologize to me. *And* you're going to apologize to Val."

Free stood mute, her gaze fixed on the ground. Val and Marisol ranged themselves on either side of Brigid. Brigid realized she was swinging the dagger between two fingers, a move that would allow her to flick the blade into Theron's face should the need arise.

I'm not going to kill Theron today. Brigid put her dagger away. *Besides I don't need a blade to take Captain Asshat here down a peg or two.* Brigid gave the spluttering Vanyr a moment to take in what she'd said. She moved in for the kill.

"Tsk, tsk, such bad manners from a son of Reyah. Now, Theron, shame on you. Where did you learn such bad words, hmmmm? Whatever will Reyah think when Marisol and I tell her how badly you behaved toward us?"

"I shall, of course, be obliged to write out a full report for Lord Alfred and Vanyr Jagger." Val said it with a straight face too. Brigid nearly kissed him.

There was a long moment of silence. "I'm sorry you fell into the swamp," Theron said through gritted teeth.

"And?" Brigid prompted, raising an eyebrow in Val's direction.

"And I apologize for attempting to preempt Lord Alfred's orders to his wizard."

He hadn't actually apologized to Val, but Brigid figured getting two apologies from Theron in one day was about as good as she—or Val—was going to get.

"Good, let's get the hell out of this god-awful swamp." Brigid shook out the muddy remains of her petticoat.

Val asked, "Have you completed your quest, ladies?"

"Quest?" Brigid whipped around.

"Quest?" Marisol asked. "What are we supposed to be looking for?"

Free looked up. "I bet the light over there is part of it."

Theron snorted. Despite her idol's disapproval—or maybe, Brigid reflected, because of it—Free continued to stare at the blue light glowing in a knothole in a nearby tree.

"I'm going over there and see what that light is," Free announced.

"Wait!" Theron said, but Free had already plunged off the path and was wading through the murky water.

"What the hell is she up to?" Marisol asked.

Brigid waved a hand. "Removing herself from the scene. Exit stage left."

Unlike the deep hole Brigid and Marisol had plunged into, the water between the two embankments was fairly shallow, only reaching at one point to Free's thighs. Hoisting her skirts to her knees, Free clambered onto land and trotted over to the tree.

"Reyah's light," Val whispered. "Her sending brought you here to find this."

Brigid thanked her lucky stars she wasn't the one reaching into the hole. Who knew what could be nesting there? Much to her surprise, the bug-hating Free stuck her hand in without hesitation.

Free turned. "Look what I found! It's a crystal, almost like the Wishstone! Do you think Reyah sent us here for this?" A rock the size of a hen's egg glittered in her hand.

Theron appeared next to Free. Brigid started. How had he gotten over to Free so fast—and without them noticing?

"Oh shit," Val muttered and headed toward Free and Theron.

Brigid sighed. This little production was getting tiresome. She was bracing herself for a vituperative round of "give me the crystal", when Theron did the last thing she would've expected. The Vanyr tugged off his muddy outer robe and spread it over a large puddle near the tree. He extended his hand. "You need not soil your dainty feet, my little flower."

Surprise flashed across Free's face. She tucked the crystal into her bodice and took Theron's hand.

"Oh puh-leeze," Marisol scoffed. "There isn't an inch of her dainty feet, not to mention his robe, that isn't covered in mud."

Brigid agreed. She had to admit, if Theron had hoped to impress Free, he'd succeeded. Free gave Theron a look of blind adoration and stepped on the robe.

With a scream that turned into a gurgle, Free sank into a pool of quicksand. Startled by her scream, Theron let go of Free's hand. Recovering quickly, he managed to grab one of her flailing arms just as her head went under. He heaved and was rewarded by the sight of two shocked green eyes staring at him from a sand-plastered mask.

Brigid did her very best not to bust out laughing. Unfortunately Marisol started snickering, and the jig was up.

Over on the embankment, Val reached the edge of the quicksand. "Here, Lady Frieda," he called. "Take my hand." Val grasped Free's other hand.

"Help! I'm drowning!" Free screamed, in direct contradiction to the facts.

Two seconds later, Theron and Val were splashing in the quicksand next to the hysterical Mistress of Leaf and Vine. Wet sand flew in all directions as Free tried to climb on top of Theron and Val in her frenzy to escape.

Marisol collapsed on her ass and laughed 'til tears ran down her face. Brigid laughed so hard she almost peed.

Blue light glowed in the trees. Two vines curled down and lifted Free out of the quicksand, depositing her beside her friends.

The redhead wiped sand and muck from her face. "Why didn't you guys do something? I could've drowned!"

"But you didn't," Brigid pointed out with a final wheeze of laughter.

"I…can't…swim," Val gasped. He grabbed at the bank, but it crumbled under his fingers.

Val was too cute to let drown. Brigid broke off a branch from a nearby tree and waded to the edge of the pool of quicksand.

"Here Val. Catch hold of the branch."

Val was heavier than Brigid expected. He nearly dragged her into the quicksand too. But she managed to brace her feet and heave. On the third try the wizard came mostly out of the pool, his legs still dangling in the sandy water.

She rubbed her bark-roughened palms against her petticoat. A glitter caught the corner of her eye, and she turned her head. The air shimmered like sapphire and gold lace behind Free. The ripples of wavering air assumed the silhouette of a rabbit's head.

"Hey, Brigid," Marisol called. "Look what showed up."

"Surprise, surprise. Must be our cue to go." Brigid leaned down and patted Val's shoulder. "You'll be fine once you barf up all the sand you've swallowed. Thanks for coming to our rescue."

Val was too busy hurling to answer.

"Well, girls," Brigid said. "Shall we go?"

Free scuttled into the Portal.

"Damn straight," Marisol agreed. "Time to blow this popsicle stand."

An instant before Brigid walked into the Portal, a very red-faced Theron levitated himself out of the quicksand.

Ya know, Brigid thought as the blackness of the Portal swirled around her, *Thea's right. Theron really does need to do something about his blood pressure.*

228

Brigid wondered, *Do they have anger management courses in Domain?*

ഇ

The Royal Palace, Salentia

Thea paced the queen's dressing room like a caged tiger. "How do you know they're all right?" she demanded.

Liz waited in the background, seated on a lady-in-waiting's tuffet. She emptied her mind of everything except the input she was receiving from the other people in the room. It was one of the tricks she'd tried on Reyah—to little effect, unfortunately. Jagger appeared to be another story. Liz's inner senses caught the way Thea's questions ground him down. *Tired. He was so tired.* His bones ached with it, and hers ached in sympathy.

"Thea, I'm not omniscient. Without checking with my agents, I don't know what's happening to your sisters this instant. All I'm saying is Reyah's messenger led them to the Shadowlands, Tambara and Kush. I have sent them the best help I can. Now, please, I must talk to Liz about what happened last night."

Are you satisfied? Thea asked Liz. *Because I'm not satisfied.*

Liz shrugged. In this game, she didn't have any opinions. Thea's hot emotions would serve them both until Jagger revealed himself. Politicians, courtiers, demigods— it didn't matter. They all told her what she needed to know. Eventually. All Liz had to do was listen.

"Liz. I want to apologize for what happened in the pool last night. Through no fault of our own, we shared one of the deepest levels of intimacy between mind mages."

"Is that what you call it?" Thea sneered.

"Yes, I do." Anger flared in Jagger's violet-hued eyes. He felt himself wronged, but Liz sensed she was only part of the problem.

"You stole memories of her dead husband so you could get lucky," Thea said, "and now you think you can make up by saying, 'Oh gee, I'm sorry, but it's all because we got a little too aroused mind-mage style?'"

"Is that how you read this scene?" Jagger's fury rattled the pocket door connecting the dressing room to the queen's bedchamber. He turned to Liz and snarled, "By the Hive, if I didn't have your unshielded mind voice blasting out my

229

inner ears, I'd be tempted to Port you to Tambara and let you try and take out Deryk yourself. Then I'd throw you at Reyah when she came to kill me for it. The only problem is I'd feel every scratch on your skin like it was my own hide peeling away.

"What does it take to get the facts through your thick skull? The magic in the pool yoked us together like a pair of oxen. You were in my memories as deeply as I was in yours, *Mistress*, and I don't want you there either."

Mistress. Liz was on her feet, nose to nose with Jagger, with no notion of how she got there. Last night's memories flooded back—a lavender sky the color of Jagger's eyes, orange grasses smelling of sage, flattened by the relentless beat of giant wings. Their wings. Jagger and the *Mistress* flew. And *She* was not Reyah.

She wasn't Liz either. *Wait a minute. If it wasn't me, and it wasn't Reyah, who was the Mistress? And why were they flying?*

Jagger closed his eyes.

"Oh my God," Thea swore. "I thought you said there was no magic in the pool."

Jagger shook his head. "The original pool was designed to help an impotent king sire an heir for Tambara. It used small, self-repeating cantrips to power the machinery, nothing more. Your pool was," he paused, "tampered with."

Liz palmed Jagger's smooth-shaven jaw as she had last night, tilting his gaze to hers. "By whom, and why?"

A sad smile twitched at the corners of Jagger's lips. "It wasn't my magic."

Whose was it?

Jagger didn't answer. Instead he spread the image of his mind like an endless midnight pool. Concentric ripples picked up a glint of moonlight here and there, but his thoughts slipped through her grasp like cool water through her fingers.

She sighed and lowered her hand. The effervescent thrill of his magic tugged at her as she drew away. She resisted it.

I know this game, Jagger. You're encouraging me to take my assumptions at face value, trusting I will be too blind to see the whole truth. Chances are I won't see all the truth I need, which places Thea, me and all the women who came with us at risk.

"Maybe I'm trusting you to find a better truth," Jagger said.

"But I don't trust you," Liz said.

A ghost of his smile lingered. "Yet."

Liz hated fencing with a master. He knew exactly where to prick her.

Jagger raised his arms in surrender. "I hear you, Liz! I hear you."

230

"Talk to us, Jagger," Liz said. "Help us understand."

"The connection was created by the magic added to the pool. You and I were always in danger of linking accidentally, because our intrinsic magic is very similar. What makes it worse is your lack of training. You don't know how to control your mind voice, except to bury it in the emotions of someone else. It's a hell of a trick for an untrained mage, but it can't be easy for you."

"How do we get out of each other's heads? I had a taste of other people's minds in the Keep, and it's not something I'd wish on anyone I didn't intend to kill."

"That's reassuring. I think," Jagger teased.

Beast. Liz's accusation sounded like a caress. *You're determined to make me like you again.*

Yes.

"We're not in each other's heads, precisely," Jagger said aloud. He hesitated again. Unlike before, Liz sensed the effort he put into choosing his next words. There was more to it than a simple matter of translating magical concepts into a form she and Thea could understand. Where was he trying to lead them? What was he trying to hide? And what had he left unguarded in the process?

"It's as if we're tied together by cables of thought," Jagger said at last. "The words and images in our minds stream down those cables like drops of water down a wire. Only the link between our minds flows two ways at once."

"Link?" Thea asked. "Sounds more like an intranet you can't shut off."

"The connection can be broken by erecting shields at either end. You need to be shielded, Liz. I can teach you."

"How long does it take to learn how to shield?" Liz asked

"It all depends on how quickly I can convey the concepts. If you trusted me enough to link with you and guide your mind, we could erect a temporary barrier within the hour."

"There's that word again, 'link'." Thea shook her head and swore. "We're going to regret this." She pulled *The Gnatzenod* from a pocket in her skirt. She thrust the book at Jagger. "This literally fell in my lap. I think it's what Liz and I were sent here to find."

Jagger riffled through the pages faster than any speed-reader Liz had ever seen. "Myrgatroid's *Gnatzenod*. No wonder Reyah wanted all three mages together."

Jagger sank onto a bench facing Liz. For an instant, all his authority and artifice dropped away, leaving nothing but the weary man beneath. Liz's heart went out to him. She couldn't stop its idiotic, irrational flight any more than she could stop herself from resting a comforting hand on his shoulder.

Another sad smile flickered over Jagger's features. He rubbed a finger along the inside of Liz's wrist, drawing small, static sparks of her energy along the connection.

Thank you, he breathed inside her, and she trembled, trembled like a virgin in her first love's arms. A small part of Liz hated herself for letting any man make her feel that way again. But she wouldn't let herself begrudge Jagger the gift.

Thea planted herself in front of them. "Kiss and make up later. This is more important. Deryk was the rogue sorcerer who resurrected the Demon Witch Megeara, wasn't he? Reyah figured out Megeara is going to summon a demon, and she expects us to deal with it like the nine wizards in that book."

"It looks that way." Jagger opened the book at a point about a third of the way from the end and handed it back.

The Wizard Elemer, that great and noble master of release, raised his arms, his demon-draggled robes unfurling behind him like the wings of a storm. His hoary hair stood on end as the blue-white power of his magic called to Maximullard and Sven.

As the blue-white power grew to the heavens, Vantram gathered his disciples Corard and Kilburn to him, and spun the blue-green thread to shape the force of mind into a weapon. And lo, what a weapon it was! A veritable hammer of the Goddess to strike the demon low and beat it into Her deceptively fragile vessel!

Then my brothers turned to the Adept Wizard Polonius, founder of the noble house of Polunax. Would he be sufficient unto the task of binding the most puissant magic of his fellows around the ovoid embodiment of She Who Is Mother To Us All? In the thick of the battle, Polonius quivered with doubt. Would his name ring heroically in the ears of his line, or would his failure here condemn the fruit of his loins to never being born?

Straining to remember every scrap of his masters' teachings, Polonius chanted. Terannio and Donner raised their lesser voices with his. Forever they chanted as the power whirled upward and ever upward toward the heavens. Eternity was theirs. All possibilities, all futures were theirs to command.

Were Polonius's to command, the demon and his evil master Kalin whispered. But Polonius stood firm against Kalin's sendings, forcing the Demon into Reyah's own egg in accordance with Her will.

ഈരു

In the Shadowlands

Theron sat on the embankment and pondered his options. He picked up his staff and, with a muttered chant, waved it over his clothes. Soon he was as neat as when he had dressed that morning.

He could follow Frieda and endure her bitch sisters, or he could return to the Keep and let whatever fate Reyah had planned for them happen without his interference. He didn't like option number two at all. No, he couldn't, wouldn't go back to the Keep. Conlan was out there somewhere. The Goddess knew he and Hawke had an absolute gift for smelling trouble. Not to mention Reyah usually attached at least one of her warrior sons to her freakish quests.

Behind him, Vallenius retched out more sandy water. Deciding he needed a bit of time before he could activate his spell to find Frieda again, Theron reviewed chapter three of Pandora's romance.

"Well, that didn't work. I certainly hope the next chapter is more helpful."

Vallenius opened one eye after Theron disappeared through a Portal. According to every magical theorem Val had studied or been force-fed since he dandled on his daddy's knee, things couldn't get much worse. Despite his youth, Val knew better. He wasn't the least bit surprised when the heavens opened and rain poured over his face.

"Why didn't I listen to my mother and become a bard?"

ॐ෨

Back at the Keep

Fifteen steps to the right.

Turn.

Fifteen to the left.

Turn.

Anna's head pounded in time with Gareth's restless pacing. Back and forth, back in forth, from Alfred's desk to the door and back again. Anna hoped the Keep had the magical equivalent of aspirin, because she had Excedrin Headache #354.

The clock on Alfred's desk bonged nine times. At the same time, somewhere outside Alfred's office, temple bells rang the hour too. Anna did some mental math. Two o'clock in the afternoon, Earth-wise. She wondered if she'd ever get used to counting the hours from dawn instead of midnight.

Two in the afternoon, however, meant her "sisters" had been gone for more than three hours. What, in the name of little green apples, was going on? Surely Jagger, of all people, had to have some magical means of phoning home.

Surely Lord Alfred wouldn't be sitting in his office twiddling his thumbs if Jagger didn't.

When the last bell finished chiming, Gareth snapped to attention in front of Alfred's desk. "Something's gone wrong," the seneschal said. "Jagger left over two hours ago, and we haven't heard from him or his man in Tambara since. Request permission to take a squad to find my daughter."

Anna's heart went out to Gareth. She ached at the pain and worry etched on his face and laced like barbed wire through his voice. Ember was a taking little thing. She even charmed Anna, who didn't, as a rule, dote on children.

If Pandora's done anything to put that child in danger, I'll strangle that platinum-haired pea brain myself, Anna vowed.

"How do you propose to find Ember?" Willem asked.

Anna jumped. She'd almost forgotten Willem, Tanak and Donatien were sitting at the big table on the other side of the room.

"Jagger said she's in Tambara," Gareth growled. "Goddess, Willem, you know what Tambara is like! She's out there, alone, unprotected…"

Willem joined his brother-in-arms in front of Alfred's desk. "Where in Tambara, Gareth? Near Dragnovostok? Up in the Rual Mountains? Perhaps on the steppes?"

"Can't one of the Vanyr find her?" Donatien asked. "You know, have Theron cast a locator spell."

Alfred shook his head, compassion for his seneschal's plight gentling his pale green eyes. "Theron left the Keep over an hour ago. And, thanks to Deryk and his damned spell, the one wizard who might possibly be of help is in the Healer's Ward with a concussion."

"What about Wizard Deltius?" Tanak said. "Or Wizard Orpant?"

"Deltius is in Kush," Alfred replied. "And Orpant's been working on Keep repairs. He's near exhaustion."

Gareth's face crumpled. He put a hand over his eyes. "I can't lose her. I can't. She's all the family I'll ever have."

Anna looked away. Poor man. Poor, poor man.

"I don't understand." Donatien ran a hand through his hair. "There's tons of wizards here at the Keep. Why not have one of them do it? I thought any wizard could do any spell."

"Actually, no," Willem said.

Anna sat up straighter. Well. This was news to her.

Willem frowned at Donatien. "Haven't you attended Sir Lendag's classes on working with wizards?"

"Uh…"

Gareth slammed his fist on Alfred's desk. "I don't give a Goddess-damn what classes Donatien's taken. I want to know where my daughter is! I want to know why she's not back home where she belongs! Where the hell is a demon-cursed magic user when you need one?"

She might not be an actress like Brigid, but Anna knew a cue when one landed in her lap. She patted her hair and smoothed her skirt.

"Present and accounted for, sugah," she drawled.

The room went totally silent. Five pairs of male eyes blinked at her.

"Close your mouths, boys," Anna chided. "You're gonna catch flies if you don't."

∞℘

The Royal Palace, Salentia

A normal demon has a name. It takes its shape from the sound of the name as much as from the sorcerer's intent. The binding that completes the conjuration fixes the demon's form in the corporeal realm and subjects its power to the sorcerer's will. Kill the sorcerer, and the demon vanishes. Its energies revert to the natural forces from which they were drawn.

Summoned by a sorcerer's death curse and fueled by the inferno of the planet's core, the holocaust shambling out of the wide gap in the Tambaran Hills possessed neither name nor stable form. Its manlike shape was built of clouds of burning gas. Its skin was a scrim of blackened ash that sundered and dissolved even as Jagger watched.

Wherever its limbs touched, fire exploded. The headwaters of the Elsen River had long since boiled away. The heat-blasted forests stretching from the flood plain roared in their death agonies. A sound like thunder rocked the hilltop on which Jagger stood—the pounding of uncounted feet and hooves fleeing downstream to what might or might not be safety.

So vivid were the memories Jagger shared Liz could feel the superheated winds buffeting his face. She smelled the fumes of sulfur and other poisons that would soon begin to attack his eyes and lungs and those of the small, desperate band gathered around him.

In the distant present, Liz heard Thea cough. Jagger broke the connection between the three of them. The act of sealing himself behind his mental barriers registered on Liz's inner senses like the shutting of a door. But she still had to fight to surface through the memories he left behind.

Liz's eyes watered. Her lips and throat burned. Dizzy nausea threatened to overwhelm her. She didn't know how much more of living in Jagger's head she could stand.

"Reyah's sending us up against *that*?" Thea rasped.

"I don't know," Jagger said. "Each demon is different, and I've only dealt with one unbound demon. There were others before my time, but I never met anyone who lived to tell about them. This one time, when there were survivors, people still got the details wrong.

"That was Gnatzon's demon, by the way." Jagger's voice turned dry. "No battle, no banter, and every one of us was scared shitless. Myrgatroid pulled his details from several sources, most of which had nothing to do with Gnatzon."

"What about the triple link?" Liz asked. "The reason we latched on to *The Gnatzenod* in the first place was because of the three pods of three that make up the Daughters of Reyah. If that part's wrong, we might as well go home."

"No, Myrgatroid got the ritual right. Leading you ladies and Anna through it will be another matter."

"We're going to try and link? You've got to be joking," Thea said.

"No. I'm not. There's no telling when you'll have to face one of Megeara's demons." He smiled wryly. "I suspect that's another reason you were led here. The palace has a place where you can practice."

Jagger stood and stretched. The light emanating from the dressing room's magically powered sconces played over the jet-beaded fabric of his black doublet, spotlighting every muscle group in his arms, his shoulders and the strong "V" of his chest. The muscles of his thighs and shapely butt did equally interesting things to his close-fitting breeches.

As distractions went, it was a lulu, but Liz wasn't buying. Especially since she suspected what he was trying to distract her from was more bad news. She crossed her arms over her chest at almost the same instant Thea did. Thea upped the ante with a menacing glare.

Jagger chuckled. The lovely sound of his amusement ruffled nerve endings Liz didn't even know she had. Damn him.

"All right, ladies, since you insist. The magic of release is mind magic. Assuming you can bear the touch of my mind for a little while longer, Liz, I can guide you through the link without any problem."

Thea snorted. Liz prided herself on not rising to Jagger's sally, though she suspected she was smiling.

"Gwynian, Seshmeel's Chosen wizard, is the greatest practitioner of binding magic alive today. She'll guide Anna."

"Why do I know I'm going to hate what's coming?" Thea asked.

"Because you're intuitive as well as beautiful, intelligent and able to change into cats," Jagger replied gallantly. "That's the Magic of the Two. It combines elements of mind magic and binding spells, but it operates very differently from either. There hasn't been a true master of the form since Vantram died at Elsee Gap. I've seen sparks of it in healers and bards, but no wizards. Certainly no one strong enough to channel your power and survive."

Thea worried her lower lip. "What about a Vanyr?"

"Thea, I don't know what Reyah told you, but there aren't that many Vanyr mages. And I would strongly advise against trying this with Theron."

"No. Roarke." Thea spat.

"Roarke? He's never done anything but binding magic. And he's got damn little of that. Your magic would crush him in a heartbeat."

"That's not what he told me in the pool. He was so full of himself. He said he needed me to give him my magic for the good of Domain. Roarke sounded exactly like my ex-husband—right before the sorry son-of-a-bitch took off with his new girlfriend and all our money."

Jagger ogled Thea as if she'd grown a second head. "R-roarke?" he stammered. "The Master of Hide All, Tell None? The Roarke who dogged my footsteps up every damned step in your tower to make sure I didn't have my wicked way with you? *That* Roarke?"

"Well, I only saw one Roarke in the pool," Liz said. "As we were leaving, he was shouting something about a truth spell, but I was rather occupied myself at the time."

If her comment brushed too close to their new truce, Jagger didn't acknowledge it. Whatever kind of super-charged hamster he used on his mental wheel was breaking land speed records left and right. When he came up for air, his lavender eyes held a wild gleam.

He caught both of Thea's hands in his. "Thea, would you permit me the liberty of sharing your memories of the time you spent in the pool with Roarke? I wouldn't ask if I didn't think it was vital." If Thea chewed on her lip any more, Liz suspected she'd gnaw it right off.

"Please, Thea. I won't be alone in there with you. In order to open myself to you, all my barriers to Liz will fall, as well. She'll perceive everything I see and know everything I do."

Thea freed her right hand from Jagger's grasp and clasped Liz's arm. *You watch him.*

It was over quickly. Liz didn't know what she was supposed to watch. Jagger dipped in, watched the short scene between Thea and Roarke about twenty times faster than it had played in real life and backed away. His barriers dropped into place. Then he threw back his head and laughed himself sick. He leaned against a wall, bent over double, clutching his sides.

"I'll be damned," Jagger gasped between howls. "This is rich. Roarke has the Magic of the Two. Reyah will shit bricks."

Chapter Twenty-Five

The Plain of Elsee

Marisol stomped over the rise, rubbing her bare arms and swearing. "I'm covered in mud! And it's cold!"

"Freezing," Brigid agreed. "But there's not much we can do about it."

"It wouldn't have been so bad if he hadn't dropped us in the mud. We might have gotten dry! I could kill Theron!"

"But he didn't mean to," Free objected. "He could only catch one of us."

"He could've let us down without dunking us," Marisol grumbled. "But, oh no, not that pendejo…"

"He is not a pen-day-whatever," Free said. "Stefan's wonderful and kind."

"Theron," Marisol and Brigid said simultaneously.

"His name is Theron," Brigid reiterated. "You might want to start remembering that, because I don't think he'll take kindly to being called by another man's name."

Free blanched. "I meant Theron," she said in a tiny voice.

Brigid cursed under her breath. Looking at Free's stricken expression made Brigid feel like she'd kicked a puppy.

Marisol, bless her soft heart, stepped into the awkward breach. "We know you did. Everything is still so confusing, it's no wonder you keep getting mixed up."

Free brightened.

"Speaking of confusing…" Marisol frowned at the small, ramshackle hut and pigpen nestled in a dense thicket of bushes and trees. "I'm lost. My weather sense is telling me we're in Tambara, but I don't remember anyplace like this on the show. Any ideas, Brig? How about you, Free?"

Free shrugged.

"Dunno." Brigid pointed to the hut. "Maybe the person who lives there could tell us."

Marisol shivered. "Maybe they've got some warm clothes to spare."

"Not if they're peasants," Brigid said. "But they might have a blanket or shawl we could trade for."

"My jewelry?" Free yelped. "I won't trade my jewelry for a blanket. I kept my clothes on. I'm perfectly warm."

Liar, Brigid thought to herself. Free's teeth were chattering so hard she could barely get the words out.

"We should've stayed with Theron and Val," Free continued.

"Then why did you jump into the Portal?" Marisol demanded.

"I was angry," Free said.

"About the Portal—" Brigid began. A small, unaccountably familiar itch scratched at the back of her neck. Spooked, she peered down the path. "Sssssh! Someone's coming!"

"We've got to hide," Free said.

Brigid herded Marisol and Free toward the hut. "Inside, ladies. With a little luck, whoever it is might pass by and not notice us."

"What if there's someone in there?" Free asked.

"Why hide?" Marisol said. "We have our magic."

Brigid pushed Free and Marisol into the hut. "First, Free, if there was someone here, they'd have been out staring at us a long time ago. Secondly, Marisol, are you sure enough of your magic to take out a band of bad guys? Remember what happened in the swamp. Our best bet is to lay low and hope whoever it is keeps going up the trail."

"Okay," Marisol and Free grumbled. They stationed themselves at the dinky window overlooking the path in front of the hut. Brigid scanned the tiny room, looking for another way out. Just in case.

The room was nicer than she would've expected from the outside. A cot stood next to the back wall. Much-patched homespun shirts and breeches hung on pegs. The cracked toes of a pair of battered boots peeped from under the hem of the quilted bedcover. The room was warm too. Smoke drifted from embers in a fireplace, curling around a trivet and a pot of what smelled like coffee. A large table buried under scrolls and books filled most of the rest of the space in the room.

"Charters, Great and Small: A Treatise on the Ramifications of Seshmeelan Representative Politics and Their Effect Domainwide," Brigid read. "Wow. Pretty heavy stuff for a peasant."

"Quiet. They're almost here," Marisol warned.

Brigid dropped the cover of the large tome and moved to Marisol's side. Two male voices were talking. Brigid couldn't quite make out what they were saying. "Damn. I wish I had my staff."

Marisol peered over Brigid's shoulder. "Dear Lord, let them be good people," she prayed. "Santa Maria, let them be good people." A part of Brigid's mind noted Reyah's name hadn't cropped up in Marisol's prayers.

Two familiar women and two equally familiar men strolled over the rise. Marisol pushed her way around Brigid and ran out of the hut. "Sarah! Kait!"

Kait fell into Marisol's arms and burst into tears. "Oh Marisol, we were in a fight! There was blood everywhere. And Sarah did a *Highlander* and chopped off someone's head!"

"He was trying to kill me!" Sarah exclaimed. Sarah, Kait, Marisol and Free all started jabbering at once.

Brigid raised her voice to be heard above the din. "Would somebody, please, explain what happened in words of two syllables or less?"

"One of Reyah's magic rabbits led us to Kala Falls in Kush," Hawke began.

Brigid scowled. "Did you say 'magic rabbit'?"

80CR

Pandora tried to ease the nagging pain between her shoulders. Her wrists were chafed raw from struggling against the ropes that bound her to the tree. Blood dribbled down her hands.

Over by the campfire, the guards passed a large jug back and forth. Pandora swallowed painfully. Her throat felt dry as dust; her lips, parched and cracked.

If this is supposed to be an adventure, it sucks like a Hoover, Pandora thought. *Why in the world did I ever think it would be fun to have one?* Pain throbbed through Pandora's arms, legs and back. She tried to shift into a more comfortable position. She couldn't feel her fingers anymore, and her feet were going numb too.

241

She glanced over at Ember and winced. The girl sagged against her bonds, her face pale under the grime and scratches.

"Pandy, I'm thirsty, and I hurt all over. Can't you use your magic to free us? I want to go home." A tear slid down Ember's face. "I bet my dad is really worried about me."

Pandora struggled not to cry too. *Chin up*, she told herself. *If you start crying, so will Ember, and we don't want the bad guys to see they've got us down.*

She smiled at Ember. "We'll think of something." Pandora hoped she sounded more confident than she felt. "Those louses have to go to sleep sometime. We'll get out of here, you wait and see."

Ember perked up.

Wonderful. Why didn't I tell her I was Wonder Woman while I was at it? I'm not a warrior or even a wizard. Besides, I haven't got a clue how to actually use my magic. Shit, shit, shit.

There was a raucous burst of laughter. One of the bandits gathered around the fire leered at Pandora. "That blonde 'un be much better looking than the skinny wench trysting with Kaltar, even if she don't have any hair to speak of." Pandora shuddered and tried to shrink back against the tree.

"Aye, Brud, that she be," another bandit agreed. The second bandit took a long swig from the jug and wiped his mouth with the back of his hand. "Wonder if Kaltar would say aught if we had a bit of fun with her?"

"Dunno." Brud glanced at the tent. "We wouldn't want to bother him, now would we, Clem? He's having his own fun. And we won't harm the lass." The bandit rose and stretched. "Much."

Pandora started struggling all over again.

Brud's grin grew wider. "Moves right nice, don't she?" he crooned, unbuckling his belt.

"You go ahead and play with the old one," a thin reedy voice said. Smoke swirled away from the fire, revealing a short, balding bandit sitting on the other side. The bald bandit stared at Ember. "Me, I like 'em younger."

Pandora felt something strong unfurl inside her, something that reminded her of how she'd felt in Alfred's office, only wilder.

"Touch her and you will die," she growled.

"You hear that, Arne? I think she just threatened you," Brud said.

Clem howled with laughter.

"We can do what we want to the likes of you," Arne sneered. He staggered to his feet and grabbed the jug from Clem. "What can you do to stop us?" Arne lifted the jug to his mouth.

"*This*," Pandora said.

A gust of wind roared through the camp. Sparks flew out of the fire and peppered Arne's breeches. He dropped the liquor jug. The bottle crashed against the rocks lining the fire pit. The fire soared. Pandora, Mistress of Mayhem, nodded as the flames engulfing Arne burned blue. He screamed and ran wildly around the camp.

Good, let him burn, she thought.

Brud took a step toward his burning comrade. His unbuckled belt slid from his pants, which promptly dropped around his ankles. Feet entangled in his pants, Brud staggered and somersaulted into Clem. Clem fell back against Kaltar's tent, which collapsed.

Pandora felt her magic seeping down her bound hands. They didn't hurt anymore. Out of the corners of her eyes she saw wisps of magic like hyacinth blue smoke rising from behind her. A tight smile played across her lips as chaos erupted in the camp. Bandits chased the burning Arne, who managed to set half the camp on fire as he stumbled around squalling at the top of his lungs.

Enraged shrieks and roars echoed from the tent as Kaltar and Megeara tried to fight their way out of the enveloping folds of canvas. Neat stacks of spears and other weapons fell apart and rolled under the bandits' feet, tripping them. They fell against each other or on top of the tent.

"Nice work," an amused voice said in Pandora's ear. "I especially like what you did to that perverted little bugger."

Pandora started. "What? Who?"

A knife slid between her hands and the rope.

"'Tis me, Tristan."

Pandora sighed in relief.

"Hold still, whilst I free you. And for Reyah's sake, keep your magic going. We need them distracted 'til we can get away."

"Oh. Sorry." How in the name of all that was holy was she supposed to keep her magic going?

A bandit scooped up a spear and aimed it at Ember.

"No way!" Pandora shouted.

The torch that had been Arne fell against the bandit with the spear. The spear-carrying bandit burst into flames. He screamed and tried to run, but Arne locked his arms tight around him. The struggling men toppled on the remains of Kaltar's tent. The tent began to smolder.

Two bandits ran to a small stream at the edge of the camp and filled buckets. Green magic glowed through a section of the tent. A large slit appeared, followed by Megeara's head. Pandora grinned as water from two buckets hit Megeara full in the face.

"There you go lass," Tristan murmured. Pandora rubbed her wrists and stomped her feet while he cut Ember free.

Wrestling his way out of the tent, Kaltar cussed like a sailor. Megeara blasted anything that moved, sending the remaining able-bodied bandits scrambling for cover. Two chickens cackled near Arne's charred body. A toad broke all amphibian speed records hopping toward the stream.

Pandora and Ember crouched with Tristan behind a tree. "Get ready to run when I tell you," Tristan whispered. "Go over the stream and keep running down the hill and across the plain until you get to the village. I'll be right behind you."

Pandora took Ember's hand. After a moment Tristan said, "Go!" Pandora and Ember made it to the creek before their luck ran out.

"They're getting away!" Megeara screamed. "Catch them, you fools!"

The thunder of pursuing feet did not follow Megeara's command. Pandora risked a look over her shoulder. Most of the bandits appeared to have ducked behind rocks or trees. Pandora wondered why Megeara hadn't called a demon to eat them.

ᔕᓍᏏ

Lydia pushed dripping hanks of hair out of her face. "Doesn't it figure? If you want something done right, you have to do it yourself."

She sighted down one long finger, aiming at the middle of the blonde's back. "You I'm going to have for a midnight snack."

"Look, Ember!" the blonde shouted. "It's George! We can't let those bandits catch him. They'll eat him for sure!"

Lydia growled as her quarry veered to the right. The green bolt meant to turn the blonde into a chicken smashed into a small tree. The tree shuddered, cracked and fell over.

"Damn it. They got away."

She turned around. Kaltar kicked the last scraps of his ruined tent into the pyre and starting shouting orders. Lydia smiled at her new hero.

"But they won't stay free for long," she added to herself.

"There's someone under that tree," Kaltar barked. "Check it out."

A couple of bandits pulled at the tree. "Nothing under here but a big rock, Kaltar," one called.

"Look again. I know I saw a man crouching under there."

The bandits shook their heads. *Fine, one less problem to worry about.* As for the two women who got away, Lydia didn't think they'd get far. The blonde's high-heeled boot tracks were easy to follow, even through the dead grass. Lydia's lover, however, had other ideas.

"Clean up this mess and get ready to move," Kaltar directed his men. "I have a feeling the fight we were promised is going to start sooner than we expected."

"What!" Lydia shrieked. "You're not going after them? What if they tell someone we're here?"

Kaltar acted like he didn't care. Lydia stomped out her frustration, shouting and firing off an occasional bolt at any unlucky bandit who caught her eye. The sizzle of fried ozone did nothing to alleviate the acrid tang of scorched canvas and the burnt pork smell of charred human flesh.

"Stop it," Kaltar said. He took Lydia by the shoulders and shook her 'til her teeth rattled. "Those two are going nowhere. Deryk's got men all around the Plain of Elsee. They'll catch 'em soon enough. Especially after I tell him what to look for."

In her rage, Lydia missed an important part of Kaltar's speech. "How can you let those two stinking females get away? What's the good of—"

"No!" Kaltar's hands jerked Lydia's shoulders so hard it felt like she'd been rear-ended on the L.A. Freeway. "Didn't you hear me? Deryk will take care of those two. I have to tell him about them anyway. Especially since I was supposed to meet with him a quarter hour past."

Kaltar's gaze wandered to the burning wreck of his camp. His lips thinned. He mumbled something about coming up with a good excuse.

Meeting with Deryk? Kaltar works for Deryk? *Oh, shit,* Lydia thought. *I'm screwed. Psycho-sorcerer's going to be pissed when he finds out I'm gone.*

Lydia felt her gaze pulled toward Deryk's tower. In her mind's eye, she could see the tower's narrow windows puffing little red clouds of magic smoke, like steam from Deryk's ears.

Kaltar swept Lydia into his arms and bruised her numb, unresisting lips with his kiss. "Be a good girl and stay here, and later on I'll bring you some nice prisoners to torture." He slapped Lydia on her rear in passing. As she feared, he took the path leading to the ruins and Deryk's tower.

She waited until Kaltar was out of sight before she started to shake. "Damn it, damn it, damn it!" Lydia wrapped her arms around herself in a death grip. "Deryk knows I left, or he will soon enough. I'm the Demon Witch. I can handle it. All I have to do is follow the Golden Rule— 'Do unto others before they do unto you'."

Lydia thought for a moment about what it would take to do unto a guy who sucked blood out of people as easily as soda out of a can.

"Tambara's a big country. How hard can it be to hide?"

෨෬

In the Shadowlands

"Wake up!"

Vallenius's eyes snapped open. His fingers spasmed over wet, gritty sand. The gray boles of manyen trees surrounded him. Cold water dripped from his hair down the back of his tunic. "What in Domain?"

"Get your butt up and into my Portal, mister."

A chill raced down Val's spine which had nothing to do with the fetid water soaking his tunic. He rolled over onto his back.

The Voice of Reyah loomed over him—all five-feet-naught of her. The air around the sand spit shimmered with her fury. Her ankle-length corkscrew curls quivered and danced around her plump body like blood red snakes. The Voice pounded her fisted hands against the air over Val's head. The young wizard cringed.

Another voice—masculine and possibly the last voice Val wanted to hear under the circumstances—crooned, "C'mon Vee, let me throw him against a tree a coupla times. Just this once."

Keghan, the Voice's acolyte and personal bodyguard, universally agreed to be the craziest monk ever Chosen in the history of Domain, stood at the Voice's left shoulder, an empty bucket in his hands. Val started to close his eyes, but thought better of it. Even Vanyr Deryk thought twice about turning his back on the Mad Monk of the Shadowlands.

Keghan's shaved head gleamed in the diffused light as he bent over and scooped more water from the rippling swamp. The monk hefted the bucket over his head. A beatific if somewhat wolfish smile sliced Keghan's bearded face.

"But...wait a minute...you don't understand..." Val sputtered. "Theron..."

"I don't care two hoots in Kalin's worst hell about Theron," Reyah's High Priestess snapped. "Good and evil personified are about to start mixing it up on the Plain of Elsee, and where do I find the Keep's and—I might add—*my* Chosen wizard? Rolling in the muck of the Shadowlands like a hog in swill. It's enough to make me wish you unborn!"

Keghan's grin grew wider. The monk began humming the opening bars of one of the wordless spells the Voice had never taught Val. Val wondered if it would help if he died praying to Reyah.

The Voice snapped her fingers. A Portal shimmered in the air to Val's right. The Voice jerked a short, beringed thumb at the shimmering air. "I'm giving you another chance, kiddo. Haul yourself up right now and march your cute little tush through that Portal, or I'll have Keghan throw you through. Either way, you're going to the Plain of Elsee. The Daughters of Reyah are there, and they need you. Not one of them has ever fought in a real battle before."

Val scrambled to his feet. "Yes, my lady." He bowed in the Voice's direction. "Of course, my lady." He wrung out the hem of his tunic as he hurried toward the Portal. "I am more than ready to serve you and Reyah..." Val jerked to a stop, one foot extended, nearly in the Portal. "Did you say 'battle'?"

"I sure as Kalin's dick didn't say 'fancy dress ball'." The Voice cocked her head. "What's the matter, Val? The Lord of the Keep picked you as his wizard. You knew you'd have to follow him in battle one day. You wanted it, you've trained for it.

"But you didn't think it would be today." The Voice's round face softened. Her normally piercing gaze drew inward. "Nobody ever does. It's one of those rules. Damn shitty rule, if you ask me, but no one did, so there you are."

She patted Val's butt. "Keep your focus. You'll do fine."

She shoved the startled Chosen into the Portal. Val had time to squawk once before he and the Portal winked out.

ℬ℧

The Plain of Elsee

"Why is the grass acting freaky?"

Brigid glanced at Free. Unlike the patchy, winter-burned stubble everywhere else in the yard of the hut, the crisp, green blades of grass around Free's feet reached her knees. Free bunched her skirts and took a quick step sideways. The sparse vegetation around her feet immediately turned emerald green.

"It's your magic, Free," Marisol said. She sidestepped a vine slithering like a leaf-covered snake toward Free. "You know, Mistress of Leaf and Vine—stuff goes green and grows."

Free kicked at the vine as it tried to wind around her ankle.

Brigid chuckled. "How sweet—one Free's friends followed her from the swamp."

"It's not a pet!" Free snapped. Before Free could kick at it again, the vine wriggled under her skirt and around her ankle. "Get away from me!" She hoisted her soggy skirts with one hand and tried to grab the vine with the other.

"Need some help?" Conlan offered.

"No!"

"Pity."

"This is wrong." Free tugged on the vine. "My plants never did this in my stories. How do I make it stop?"

"Put a sock in it, Free," Sarah said. "What I want to know is where are the rest of the girls?"

"Let's hope we find out before night falls," Marisol responded. When everyone turned to look at her, she said, "Look at the shadows. It's got to be at least mid-afternoon."

"I bet it gets blacker than the inside of a donkey out here." Sarah shivered. "And not a street lamp in sight."

Brigid couldn't agree more. She didn't relish the thought of wandering around the wilds of Tambara in the dark.

"We'll be in the village long before dark," Hawke said.

"Yes, but what about Liz and Thea?" Kait asked. "And Anna and Pandora. Do you think they followed a bunny too?"

Brigid grinned. "Can you imagine Pandora not following a bunny?"

"Speak of the devil." Marisol pointed to the right. About a quarter of a mile away, on a natural terrace much lower than the hut, two slight figures zigzagged through the scrub.

"Right on cue," Brigid said. "There's Pandora. But who's with her? It's sure not Anna."

"Kalin's balls," Hawke swore. "It's Ember. What the hell happened to Ember's hair?"

"Here, George!" Pandora hooted, her voice carrying clearly to the group by the hut. "Come to Mommy!"

Brigid put a hand to her eyes. Something bobbed through the grass ahead of Pandora. For a brief moment, two long, blue-gray ears lifted over a clump of brown weeds. Brigid could almost hear Lewis Carroll rolling in his grave.

"Pandora, you twit!" Sarah shouted at the top of her lungs. "Get your ass over here!"

Either Pandora didn't hear Sarah's call, or she chose to ignore it. Pandora and Ember ran down the other side of the terrace toward the plain. Brigid shook her head. "I guess we better go and stop them. They'll chase that rabbit forever."

"We might as well." Sarah tucked a few strands of wind-ruffled hair into her plait. "Or we'll have to spend the rest of the week explaining to Anna why we didn't."

At least the mud pack saved Brigid from worrying about hair in her eyes. Brigid groaned at the prospect of chasing Pandora across the plain. It was like the con, only worse.

"Wait," Conlan said. "Why don't Hawke and I go after Pandora? You ladies can stay here 'til we bring her back."

"I'm not sure Pandora would agree to come back with you," Brigid said. "She can be as stubborn as a mule about some things, and animals qualify as one of those things."

"And tossing her over my shoulder would not be a good idea." Hawke rubbed the base of his spine. "My luck, she'd throw *me* over *her* shoulder, and I'd land face-first at the foot of Mount Tuumb."

"Forget Pandora. Ember—she's used to obeying us," Conlan said. "If we herded her back here, wouldn't Pandora follow?"

"No," the women said as one.

"Oh." Conlan glanced at Hawke, who shrugged.

Brigid's eyes narrowed. "Enough of the enigmatic looks. Why don't you want us going after Pandora?"

Hawke grimaced. "There've been reports of bandit activity in these foothills. According to...someone I know, there's at least three bands of outlaws hiding out around the Plain of Elsee."

"Bandits?" Kait gulped. "There are bandits around here too? We've got to protect Pandora and Ember!" Kait pelted down the hill.

"Oh my God!" Marisol exclaimed. "We can't let bandits hurt Ember!" Marisol sprinted after Kait.

"Marisol! Kait! Wait! You could get hurt!" Free cried, hefting her skirts and joining the parade. The vine dropped to the ground and followed the green footprints Free left in her wake.

"This is stupid," Sarah snarled. "The three of them are running around like chickens with their heads cut off."

"Five chickens," Brigid corrected. "Don't forget Pandora and Ember."

"As if I could. Let's go, Brig. Someone has to keep them out of trouble."

"I'm right behind you."

Sarah checked the holstering of her knives and whip. "Where are our damn magic users when you need them?"

"Who knows?" Brigid said. "But I hope they get here soon." *Because I have a feeling we're going to be in even worse straits than we are now.*

"Do you think they do this all the time?" Conlan asked his brother.

Hawke closed his gaping mouth. "Somehow I get the feeling they do." Hawke shifted his grip on his ax and motioned toward the plain. "Let's get moving. Reyah only knows what they're running into."

"That's the problem," Conlan said. "I've got this sinking feeling She probably does know."

Chapter Twenty-Six

With a whoosh of displaced air and a loud hum, a Portal appeared. Exhibiting as much aplomb as if he were strolling into the throne room in Seshmeel, Theron stepped through. The mage paused, an expression of mild surprise on his face. The vista was not one he had expected to see.

A hundred feet beneath the rocky hilltop on which Theron stood, the enormous cow pasture known as the Great Plain of Elsee stretched to the foot of Mount Tuumb. To his left a dense copse of trees and brambles partially sheltered an empty pen and tumbledown shack. A nervous squeal echoed from the bushes behind the pen.

A worn goat track crossed in front of the hut, straggling over the foothills and terraces bordering most of the plain. Theron rubbed his chin with the tip of his staff. Somewhere, not too far away if he didn't miss his guess, was Lady Frieda. Theron smiled.

He could feel her presence vibrating through his very bones. Theron ran his hand down the front of his tunic. He snatched it away. Oh no. He wasn't going to lose control again.

He considered the unappetizing hut. No, his lady would never enter such a hovel. Regarding the landscape to either side of the hill, Theron sighed. If he remembered correctly there was a small village toward the western end of the plain overlooking the Elsee Gap. From the position of Mount Tuumb, it couldn't be more than an hour's easy walk through the hills. If she'd followed the path to the west, that's where Frieda was probably headed.

And if Frieda didn't follow the easy trail to the west? Theron thought of Frieda in the Shadowlands, dangling helplessly from a vine and laughed. His sweet, innocent little flower was bound to get lost again or something. Females were always getting themselves into difficulties they needed a man to extricate them from. After all, everyone knew women lacked the mental capacity of men.

A woman needed a man to guide her. Theron firmly believed this. Especially a woman of Lady Frieda's abundant...talents. Look at all the trouble she'd gotten into back at the swamp. Theron knew in his heart Frieda needed him to help her control her magic.

He blithely ignored the fact Vallenius would've found and helped the women in a relatively short time. Instead Theron congratulated himself that without his help, Frieda and her two bitch sisters would never have gotten out of the tree. Frieda certainly had no idea how to use her magic to undo what she'd done. It was as plain as the nose on Roarke's face, Frieda needed a strong hand.

And that hand will be mine, Theron promised himself. *Now to find my lady before she or one of the others find a Portal to get back to the Keep.* This time, he'd make sure he held his temper. This time, there wouldn't be a dimwit wizardling to foul things up.

With a little luck and a bit of Vanyr magic, Theron would find a way to impress Frieda and win her everlasting gratitude. It didn't matter how much magic it took. Whether Frieda followed the path east or west, it was a win-win situation. Theron would come out on top.

"In more ways than one," Theron murmured, images of Frieda's lush body and full red lips sizzling through his mind.

Theron combed his fingers through his hair and straightened his tunic. Something heavy crashed into him, leaving him eating dirt. Over the ringing in his ears, he heard the hum of a fading Portal. Spitting out a mouthful of grass, Theron groaned. It felt as if a Gruendian behemoth had landed on his back.

"Oh, it's you, Vanyr Theron," Vallenius mumbled. "Thanks for breaking my fall."

The crushing weight lifted from Theron's back.

"Pardon me, but I've got to hurry. Reyah bless me, but I'm late and the Voice will have my head if I don't get there in time. Reyah's daughters are in grave danger. I have to be there to help."

Theron lifted his head. Vallenius struggled to his feet, his clothing in mud-stained disarray. The reek of the Shadowland's swamps hung about the young wizard like an almost visible fog.

"What in the name of Kalin's Seven Hells do you think you're doing?" Theron snarled.

With nary a look in Theron's direction, Vallenius staggered down the steeper path running east—away from the village. Theron blinked. Vallenius had ignored him! That incompetent, inconsequential, inept young whelp had ignored...

Theron opened his mouth to blast Vallenius insensible with a spell. Yet even as the first cantrips of the spell were leaving Theron's lips, Vallenius's words sank in. Theron choked, dismissing the spell.

"Who's in danger, you young fool?" he roared. "Get back here and tell me what you know!"

Vallenius didn't break stride. "The Daughters of Reyah," he shouted as he disappeared around a bend in the path. "I'm late, and I have to help them..."

Theron rolled over on his back. Could the nitwit be right? The Daughters of Reyah—his Frieda was in danger?

Theron frowned. Danger from what?

He ran what he remembered of Tambaran flora and fauna through his mind. A slow smile crossed his face. There shouldn't be anything more dangerous than a large pile of cattle droppings. This was even better. Here was Theron's chance to impress Frieda, to sweep her off her feet and into his arms. Whatever it was the young wizard thought was a danger, only one man was going to effect a rescue.

"Me," Theron vowed. He rose to his feet in one fluid motion and snapped his fingers. His staff levitated into his hand.

"It's probably nothing worse than a stray bull or a wild pig," Theron decided. "The way Vallenius is rushing around, you'd think the idiot was going to save Reyah's daughters from a demon."

ฃଔ

I'm going to kill her, Brigid thought, her breath coming hard and fast as she ran across the wide, stubble-covered plain. *I'm going to flay every inch of hide from Pandora's skinny body. I'm going to chop her into little bitty pieces and feed her to those pigs on the other side of the hill. And once I'm through with her, I'm going to kill Free and Kait and Marisol.*

"Damn it to hell!" Sarah wheezed at Brigid's side. "Wait 'til I get my hands on those fools!"

"Get in line," Brigid panted. "I get to kill them first."

Ahead, a little more than half the way to the southern border of the plain, the rabbit flicked a glance at Pandora. Brigid could swear she saw the little beggar wink at the demented blonde. Brigid put a hand to her side and grimaced at the stitch burning there. What in the world was she doing? Pandora was capable of running after that damned rabbit all day.

"Wait a minute," Brigid gasped, clutching Sarah's arm. "Let's stop and think about this."

Hawke slid to a stop next to Brigid. "Giving up?"

Brigid shook her head. "No, looking for a better way to stop Pandora," she said, struggling to control her breath.

Conlan wiped his forehead. "She has a point, Hawke," he puffed. "The way we're going, we'll be chasing them right into the Tambaran Barrier."

"Pandora doesn't listen to anyone, and it's totally pissing me off," Sarah growled.

"Wait a minute." Hawke grinned. "I know someone who'll listen to *me*."

"*Ember Weston!*" Hawke roared. "*Stop running from me this instant!*"

Brigid grinned. Talk about a parade ground voice. Ahead on the plain, Ember looked over her shoulder. Her eyes widened. Brigid could almost hear Ember's mental "uh oh".

In front of Ember, Pandora bent down to grab the bunny. "I've got you now!" she crowed.

The bunny bolted down a nearby rabbit hole. As he did a vine twisted out of the grass and twined around Pandora's ankles. Brigid wondered if Free was directing the vine. Under Free's direction or not, the vine wrapped another few loops around Pandora's legs. The Mistress of Mayhem's arms flailed as she fought to retain her balance. Ember kept running, still looking at the adults behind her.

"Oh shit," Brigid said.

It was like watching a train wreck. You didn't want to see what was going to happen but you couldn't look away. Ember ran smack into Pandora. Pandora and Ember wobbled back and forth while the vine tried to shimmy up Pandora's leg.

The other train came swooping down the track.

Free wailed as she ran toward Pandora and Ember. "I can't stoooooop…"

Pandora and Ember had time for one horrified gasp before Free slammed into them. Pandora grunted and dug in her heels trying to keep from falling over backwards. Ember was sandwiched between Pandora and Free, her face lost somewhere in Free's ample bosom.

Marisol and Kait, hot on Free's heels, shrieked in unison as they plowed into Pandora, Ember and Free. The five of them tumbled to the ground.

Kait glared at Brigid from under Marisol's knee. The grass where Free landed turned lush and green. Sarah shook her head and turned away, muttering under her breath about stupid elementals.

"You were right," Hawke chuckled. "They are dangerous."

"If only to their dignity and everyone else's around them," Brigid agreed.

Conlan ambled over to the pile of women. "Pardon me. Do you ladies need any help?"

Three muffled groans and two fervent yeses answered his question. Conlan reached into the heap and extracted Marisol.

"Thanks," Marisol burbled. "Someone's foot was in my ear."

"My pleasure," Conlan assured her. Marisol gave Conlan a melting smile and trotted over to stand by Hawke. Conlan raised an eyebrow as he lifted Ember to her feet. Ember's face glowed bright red. "Are you all right?"

"I thought I was going to suffocate!" Ember huffed. "Lady Frieda's...um, bosom was smothering me!" Ember shook off Conlan's hands and straightened the bodice of her dress. "I don't think it's a bit funny," Ember told the snickering Hawke.

Conlan reached down to help Kait, who gave him a rueful smile as she got to her feet. Kait ducked behind Marisol, trying to look nonchalant when she passed Brigid and Sarah.

Conlan bent down once more, lifting Pandora and Free to their feet.

Pandora said, "Thanks! These things always seem to happen to me."

Free peered at Conlan from under a curtain of tangled, mud daubed, red hair. "Thank you." Free swiped at her snarled tresses. She batted at the vine, which had slithered back from Pandora to its favorite spot around Free's ankle. "You didn't have to help me."

"No, I didn't." Conlan turned on his heel and walked back to Hawke. Free's jaw dropped.

It's a good thing Theron wants Free as bad as she wants him, Brigid thought. *It looks like she's totally fucked up any chance of getting with Conlan.*

"How rude," Free groused. "I said thank you, didn't I?"

"Christ on a crutch, shut up, Free," Sarah growled. "We've wasted enough time chasing rabbits and Pandora. Now that we're all together we need to get to the village and back to the Keep."

"Conlan started it!" Free exclaimed.

Brigid's stomach suddenly rolled. Goosebumps marched up and down her arms, and chills spilled down her spine.

Oh shit. Brigid shuddered. *What's happening? Am I getting sick?*

Without conscious thought, Brigid turned to the north. Her eyes widened. Another wave of chills and goosebumps coincided with her body swinging around to the southwest. *Oh. My. God.*

"Shut up, both of you," Brigid ordered.

"What did you say?" Sarah erupted.

"I said shut up. We've got a bigger problem than your squabbling."

"Squabbling?" Free squawked. "Squabbling? Me?"

"What problem?" Sarah demanded.

Brigid turned Sarah to face due north, where the foothills thinned and a broad swale sloped down to the plain. Silhouetted against the steel gray sky at the top of this natural ramp was a troop of horsemen. The riders bristled with weapons. Brigid spun Sarah around to face the tower and ruined castle to the southwest. Poised on the rubble-strewn terrace in front of the ruins stood another troop of men. This bunch was on foot, but no less armed than the ones on horseback.

"That problem," Brigid said.

"Oh shit," Sarah said.

"Oh shit," Free, Kait and Marisol squeaked.

"You got that right," Brigid said.

"Ladies, I think we're in trouble," Conlan said. The two men stepped in front of the women and assumed a defensive posture while pasting menacing looks on their faces. Laughter rang from both sides of the plain. Hawke and Conlan looked at each other and shrugged. "I was wrong. We are definitely in trouble."

"The terrace in front of the hut would be defensible, if we could get to it," Hawke said. "There are some caves near the tree line. We might be able to hide the women there."

From somewhere behind them, a voice sang out, "Don't worry, Daughters of Reyah! I'm here!"

Val ran down the hill. About twenty feet away, he tripped and, after several spectacular somersaults, rolled the rest of the way to the girls. The volume of the soldiers' hoots and catcalls increased to the point where Brigid could pick out individual insults to Val's manhood.

"Our hero," Sarah said. "Girls, the cavalry has arrived."

"Oh great," Kait snorted, putting out a foot to stop Val before he rolled into her. "But who's going to save him?"

ᔓᘉ

Back at the Keep

Doomed.

The word tolled through Alfred's mind like the Bell of Judgment.

Twelve hundred years in the service of the Goddess, fighting Her battles, facing down demons—at times, Her own immortal sons—clawing his way back from the clutches of Death itself, all for the glory of Her Holy Name. None of it mattered. Alfred was doomed.

He recognized his fate the moment Anna joined the squad of thirty men Willem had assembled in the Terminus. In the scant half hour since she left his office, Anna had washed off the elaborate make-up which only served to dull the perfection of her features. Gone were the jewels and brocade which would've made a flint-hearted social climber like Amorian weep for envy.

In their place were a jerkin and breeches of black leather, pieced and riveted for protection and ease of motion. A gray silk shirt covered her arms and throat. Beneath the silver circlet she'd worn last night, the wonder of her raven black hair was drawn back in a single braid hanging past her shapely hips. All that remained of the pampered aristocrat was the bewitching fragrance of her perfume, and the jeweled chatelaine and fan Alfred now recognized as the instruments of her power.

Oh, that he could be the jeweled belt wound around Anna's slender waist. Oh, that he could feel those leather-covered legs wound around *him*.

Doomed. Doomed. Doomed.

But Anna wasn't for the likes of him. Reyah intended her as a bride to bring one of Her Vanyr sons to heel. Alfred was too schooled in Reyah's ways not to know the

257

truth when Reyah skewered him with it. Alfred had been content. It wasn't a man's place—even a Chosen's—to question the will of the One True Goddess.

It didn't matter Anna showed as much poise carrying Brigid's staff, Sarah's bandoleer and miniature crossbows as a monarch carrying her scepter. The fact she had the spirit of a battle mage went without saying. Why else would Reyah have named her "daughter"?

Anna turned to Gareth. "We'll find your daughter, Gareth honey. You have my word, and I *never* go back on my word."

The absolute commitment in Anna's blue-violet eyes as she made her promise felled Alfred as surely as a saber stroke.

Reyah had never blessed Her servants with such a promise. Nor the Vanyr either. Alfred counted himself lucky he had known such a gift—given freely without regard to name or station—once in his life. His long-dead wife had given it to him on their wedding day, and she had died fulfilling her vows.

"Are you all right, Lord Alfred?" Anna asked. Her concern was another wound to his much-abused heart.

Alfred scrounged a reassuring smile from somewhere. "I'm fine, Lady Anna. I always spend a little time clearing my thoughts before a hunt or a battle. Ideally, a warrior's thoughts should be as sharp as his sword."

Ideally, Willem wouldn't call him on that mound of bullshit until after they rescued Ember and Pandora. Anna eyed Alfred and the soldiers with him skeptically.

"Are those itty bitty pieces of armor up to a battle if we get attacked?"

Since the "itty bitty pieces" in question consisted of a stout helmet, cuirass and a full kit of light armor in Reyah-blue steel, Alfred nodded. "Have no fears for us, Lady Anna. My men and I are well armed. Besides, with luck, we'll simply Port to wherever Pandora and Ember are, and jump back to the Keep again. An easy reconnoiter and rescue."

Anna heaved a deep sigh. Alfred's gaze never strayed from her troubled face. He truly was doomed, he decided.

Anna scanned each of the room's eight doorways to nothingness in turn. Absently, she thrust the weapons she carried at Alfred. "Do you mind, sugah? I need my hands free for this."

Anna cracked her knuckles. "Okay, boys, step back, and give a gal space to work."

Alfred couldn't help but smile at how quickly the troop—still keeping in formation—complied with the lady's request. In the closed space of the Terminus, the sound of sixty scuttling feet resounded like thunder. Alfred remained at Anna's side. Dying by her magic (if such a thing were possible) was a pleasure even Reyah couldn't deny him.

"Chickens," Anna snickered, voicing Alfred's secret thoughts. She closed her eyes, lifted her arms and began to chant.

Three by three,

Two by two,

In and out,

Going through.

Blue whorls of magic swirled from Anna's hands, circled her lush curves.

Portal by Portal,

Out and in,

Show me where

We should begin!

The smoke-like tendrils of Anna's magic drifted toward the Portals leading to Kush, Tambara, the Shadowlands and Seshmeel. But the magical haze faded quickly. By the time Anna opened her eyes, the traces of Goddess Blue had all but vanished from the room.

But the color of Reyah's magic still flashed in Anna's eyes. "This is the outside of enough." She raised her fan as if to hurl her magic at one of the voids before her. "The Wishstone gave me the power to find that blonde-haired dingbat, and I'll be damned if I let the wording of some stinking rhyme keep me from doing what I promised.

"You there." She pointed her fan at the Portal to Tambara. "You've got precisely three seconds to show me where I want to be or else I'll, I'll…what the hell?"

Alfred frowned. Why had she stopped her magic? What in Domain was she looking at?

Anna dropped her fan with an angry flick of her wrist. "Why am I not surprised to see your furry behind standing there all of a sudden?" Anna asked the Tambaran Portal. "All right, you worthless fuzzball, this time you'd better wait for me and everybody with me, or I swear there'll be rabbit stew on the menu tonight."

The rabbit was back? Alfred wondered if he had time to call for more troops.

As if in answer, the Portal void began to glow blue and gold.

"Gentlemen." Anna retrieved the weapons from Alfred. "I suggest you follow me."

ଛଠ

The Plain of Elsee

A mounted troop of mercenary cavalry was gathered to Theron's right. Another contingent of brigands ranged in front of the old Tuumb castle. Hawke and Conlan postured at the cavalry. Kait seemed frozen in place, her hands fixed on the hilt of her sword. Sarah pivoted slowly on her heel as if to assess the threat from all sides. Clustered behind the warriors were Vallenius and the rest of the women.

Theron noted Marisol and the crazy blonde were arguing with Vallenius. Vallenius seemed to be trying to get them to stand behind him, while they seemed equally determined to stand with the warriors. Frieda stood next to them. Theron frowned. It looked as if those idiot women planned to put his precious Frieda in danger.

The cavalry shifted in place, a sure sign of an impending charge. Theron gritted his teeth and gathered his magic. Why did Vallenius, for once in his useless life, have to be right? The Daughters of Reyah were indeed in danger, and it was going to take a considerable amount of magic to get them out of their predicament.

"Maybe more than I have," Theron muttered.

A low hum buzzed in his ears. Theron spun around. A large Portal shimmered in the air. Anna marched through, carrying Reyah's staff, a belt of dart-sized arrows and two small crossbows. Gareth emerged behind her, followed by Willem, two Chosen knights and about thirty Blue Guards. Last of all, Alfred stepped from the Portal.

Theron heaved a sigh of relief. He didn't have much use for soldiers, but in a situation like this they could be invaluable. At least he would be able to stand back and work his magic without having to become physically involved in the fighting. It wasn't that Theron couldn't fight. He simply preferred not to.

"What are you doing here?" Anna demanded. "Where are my sisters?"

"They're down there." Theron pointed at the plain. "I was about to descend and give them aid." He stared at the staff in Anna's hand. Reyah's staff. It should be his staff, damn it. Wasn't he Her most faithful son? How could Reyah waste a staff of such obvious power on a mere warrior?

Theron knew better than to try and take it, though. At least, for now.

"What are we waiting for?" Anna glanced at Alfred. "Well? Are you going to help them or are you going to wait for an engraved invitation like Theron here?"

Anna trotted down the hill.

Alfred was so used to people waiting for his orders that for a critical instant he didn't react. By then it was too late—not only to stop the woman he'd give his last drop of blood to protect from rushing into danger, but to prevent Gareth from unsheathing his sword and marching right after her.

It was a good thing Alfred was wearing a helmet, because he was ready to pull his hair out by the roots. "Damn and blast! What the hell is wrong with them? Why didn't Gareth stop her? Until Anna headed down the hill, those brigands didn't know we were here."

"Well they know it now," Willem said. "Orders?"

"Theron, Port those fools back up here. They're sitting ducks down there."

"Can't. They've got wizards in the hills above us. If I try to Port anyone but myself I'll need Vallenius to shield me." Theron's smile was thin as a razor. "And he's down on the plain."

"Port Vallenius up here," Willem said. "Quit wasting time talking about what you can't do and do what you can."

"Dammit, I'm not Jagger," Theron said. "The minute I open a Portal I'm vulnerable. As is your Chosen. Call Vallenius to heel, Alfred. Then I might be able to help you."

"That's not going to work either. If any of them start running for the hilltops, the cavalry will charge." Willem spit on the ground. "It looks like we're going to have to go down there and fight."

"What else is new?" Alfred said.

Chapter Twenty-Seven

Back at Dragon*Con

"So I sez to him, I sez, 'I don't care if you played the President of the Universe's hot-shot son, get your hand off my tit.' And then he sez, 'Don't you want to do it with a famous star?' And I sez, 'Yeah. You know any?'"

Reyah glared at the inside door of the bathroom stall. Outside the stall, female con-goers bragged or complained about their brushes with the famous and once-famous. Inside, images of the Plain of Elsee marched across a small section of the gray metal. Didn't it figure the minute things started looking up on Earth, things started going to hell in Domain?

The Elder Goddess sighed. She was *this close* to closing the deal on an Earth franchise, and everyone and their cat in Domain knew Deryk was attempting a coup in Tambara. Not only was the little bastard pulling a major stunt on Her birthday, but he wasn't even trying to hide his tracks! How in the world was She supposed to get him out of this mess?

"So he jumps on the table to show everyone how he used to activate his magic baton on the show. Next thing you know, he's fallen on top of some goth chick. When they pull his head out from between her legs he keeps insisting, 'I meant to do that.'"

I meant to do that.

Reyah brightened. Well, now, that was one way to save Deryk's hide.

She waved a hand at the door. One last check. Alfred and his men marched after Anna. Theron, naturally, stood like a stick on top of the hill. Lydia, thank the stars, seemed to be running for the Barrier. Reyah flushed the toilet and patted her robe back in place.

262

Things weren't as bad as she thought. Jagger should arrive any minute with reinforcements for Alfred. Deryk would run as soon as he saw Jagger. He always did. Still, it wouldn't hurt to check back a bit later. The main thing was She still had time to hook those worshippers. Yes! She hummed a little tune as she washed her hands.

An Earth franchise—just what she'd always wanted and on Her birthday too! Come to think of it, it was all because of her naughty boy's pranks. She *had* to save Deryk.

After all, She owed it to him.

ℰℛ

Deryk's Tower, Mount Tuumb

Deryk couldn't believe the gift fortune had tossed in his lap. He refocused the spyglass. Yes, next to Theron stood Alfred and his captain of the guard. Alfred's seneschal marched double-time down the slope, chasing yet another headstrong woman with more power than sense.

Where in the name of every unclean thing were all these women coming from?

Deryk decided he didn't care. The world, the entire fucking world was suddenly his to grab. Like a bundle of Winter Solstice gifts, the Lord of the Keep, five of the Keep's Chosen, three of Deryk's hated brothers and seven women with more power than he'd ever seen before waited for him to break and burn.

His hands trembled on his spyglass. The Great Serpent had smiled upon him. With Alfred dead, Deryk could take over Domain much quicker. With the women's power at his command, he would be much harder to defeat. He wiped his mouth. This was perfect. At a signal from Willem, Alfred's troop marched to the center of the Plain—where Deryk's cavalry could run them down and his archers could pick them off one by one. Talk about shooting fish in a barrel.

Brushing his fingers over the smooth head of his snake, he considered his chances. There were only two mages protecting the small group. Theron was only half of a Vanyr mage—like Deryk used to be. As for Vallenius… Deryk smiled. Vallenius would provide him with some much needed energy by the end of the battle. He couldn't wait to suck the puppy dry.

Deryk was glad Theron or Vallenius hadn't tried to Port. Sure, his hedge wizards would've taken Vallenius and Theron down, but watching them drain his brother would be much more enjoyable. He figured he'd lose about half of his hirelings in the process. But what the hell, he hadn't intended on keeping any of the turds around anyway. Afterwards, he'd personally chop Theron to bits and have his men scatter the pieces to the four winds.

The warriors—at least the Chosen ones—would be overrun, dismembered and burned. He'd already given Kaltar explicit instructions for the complete destruction of the Chosen. Deryk giggled. As for Hawke and Conlan, it would be interesting to see if Reyah would try to resurrect his bastard brothers. The women…

Deryk planned to spend a long time with those women. He wanted to break them slowly. Very slowly. He would kill them only when he'd sucked the last precious drop of power from their fresh-cracked bones. With Hawke, Conlan and Theron gone, there'd only be that drunken pretty boy Fynn—and Aleks, who was nothing but a silly, unbridled brat. Neither had ties to Roarke or Jagger.

Ah, Jagger and Roarke. Deryk planned to capitalize on Roarke's hatred of the Old One. He knew how to use his brothers' and the women's deaths to set the two against each other.

With most of Her sons gone, Deryk could easily take down Reyah.

He wondered what *Her* power would taste like.

Chapter Twenty-Eight

The Grounds of the Royal Palace, Salentia

After a brief discussion with the queen's Chosen wizards, Jagger Ported Liz, Thea and Roarke to a building he called the "Sorcellarium". Liz couldn't help but wonder what the building looked like from the outside. The inside looked like a medieval missile silo with lead-shuttered windows. Twelve wooden posts, each about a foot wide, supported the structure's heavily braced conical roof. The depth of the concrete-faced window openings suggested the walls were at least as thick as the posts were wide.

According to Jagger, the whole point of the building was to provide a secure place to conduct high-powered, collaborative rituals within the palace complex. The fact the only structures within a hundred yards were the hay bales of the archery range was a bonus. The shutters were probably a precaution against magic-fired shrapnel.

A round table of some dense hardwood occupied the center of the room. Jagger sat at one of four, straight-backed wooden chairs drawn around the table. His elegant, long-fingered hands rested palms up on the tabletop, forming the base of a triangle of shimmering air.

Liz recognized the disturbed air functioned as some kind of screen. Jagger's eyes were hazed over with blue. His turbo-charged, mental hamster was doing its thing again, and the mind mage was blinking rapidly.

Thea sat in the chair to Jagger's immediate left. *He's been doing that an awfully long time*, she fretted.

I wonder who he's talking to, Liz mused.

Roarke stood to Liz's right. His arms were braced against the top of the chair facing Jagger. His expressive mouth was stretched in a thin, inflexible line. Roarke looked as tense as Thea's mind voice sounded. Liz itched to wriggle her mental mojo in Roarke's direction to see if the Vanyr swordmaster would let her in. By now, she was pretty sure they couldn't hurt each other magically, Liz wanted—no, she needed a more informed perspective on what was happening. But Roarke didn't look like he would be an easy sell on the idea, and Liz didn't want to distract Jagger.

In contrast to Roarke's skittish glamour, the well-padded, middle-aged wizards Gwynian and Sejanus projected a sense of stability and homeyness Liz found very comforting. They waited side by side on the row of chairs ranged against the wall. Gwyn settled her head against Sejanus's springy curls. Sejanus closed his hand over hers.

Afraid of drowning in Devereaux-might-have-beens, Liz turned back to Jagger. Every muscle in his perfectly drawn face went rigid. His blue-blinded eyes stilled their restless searching, fixing on a vision only he, literally, could see.

That looks so not good, Thea said.

As if he heard her, Jagger's obscenely thick lashes fluttered, lowered and came to rest like sable fans. He turned his hands over, shutting off whatever spell he'd been using. When Jagger opened his eyes again, they had returned to their normally abnormal purple color. "Anna won't be joining us. She's with the rest of your sisters, Alfred and a squad of soldiers on the Plain of Elsee in Tambara. They're facing a double company of mercenaries and assorted brigands."

Gwyn jumped to her feet. "Deryk's men." A wisp of light blonde hair settled at an angle over Gwyn's square-jawed face. The hand of Sejanus's magic brushed it back into place before Gwyn had a chance to. "Well, what are you waiting for? Port us. Unless Alfred's hiding a regiment in a pocket Portal, they're going to need our help. Demon containment rituals can wait."

"I don't think so," Jagger replied, his voice terrifyingly calm. "The spell Deryk cast the other night summoned the Demon Witch Megeara from the void. Megeara's skulking in the Elsee hills, within shouting distance of Deryk's tower on Mount Tuumb.

"According to Tristan, she's not acting like herself, which isn't too surprising. After all this time, there's no telling who she is or what she knows about her gifts," Jagger added.

The blood drained from Gwyn's face. She dropped back onto her chair with a thump. "Mercy. If Megeara accidentally calls a demon without restraints it could be Gnatzon's hellspawn all over again."

Sejanus retrieved her hand and began chafing it. "There, there, love. We must have faith."

Gwyn shot her husband a look that would've pierced Kevlar.

"Not in Reyah." Sejanus chuckled even more softly than he spoke. "But in the fortune that brought Thea and Liz and all their Talented sisters together at this time."

"Wonderful. You hold onto that faith, Sejanus." Gwyn smacked her free hand against the chair beside her. "Without Anna, you're going to be the one trying to close this link with me, and it isn't going to be easy."

"Look, folks," Liz said, "Thea and I need to know two things. First—how does the link work? Second—and this is very important since there appear to be people who aren't Vanyr, Chosen or Daughters of Reyah out there in Tambara—how dangerous is this link to regular people?"

"Not half as dangerous as an unbound demon," Gwyn retorted. "The problem with the wizards facing Gnatzon's demon was the mortal Adepts weren't strong enough to contain the magic of the link. Most of the people with them were killed by the power leaks from the link itself."

"And the rest?" Thea asked.

"They got caught in the backwash from the Adepts' death," Gwyn said.

Us, contain our magic? They've got to be kidding. Thea sounded like she was ready to let loose a full mental howl. But crying on each other's shoulders wasn't as simple as it used to be.

Jagger's power reached out to Liz like the banked heat of a furnace. He plainly meant it as a gift to warm away Liz's apprehensive chill. But Liz was so rattled, every kindness he offered only made things worse. She almost wished Jagger would do something to piss her off again. Fighting things she could touch and trick and intimidate by sheer ferocity of will—Liz excelled at that.

"Aren't you going to join us at the table?" Thea asked Gwyn and Sejanus.

"No. If your powers are equal to the Vanyrs', it would be too easy for us to lose ourselves in the link. We would be unable to close it at the appropriate time," Sejanus replied.

"The rite is divided into three parts, each of which entails its own danger," Jagger explained. "Mind mages open the link by breaching the mental barriers between the participants. The various personalities pour through each other. If the participants do not have a strong sense of who they are, they risk forgetting their separate identities in a group whole. Not that I think it will be a problem in this case."

Jagger slanted a smile in Liz's direction.

He thinks I'm stubborn. Talk about the pot dissing the kettle. Maybe I can work up a good mad-on after all. Liz bit back a grin.

Thea asked, "What do you mean? Doesn't everybody need to think together for the link to work?"

"Yes, and a group mind has many advantages within the link. Everyone's memories and ideas become one, making it easy for the group to use its shared power," Jagger said. "But when the link is broken, the participants either die or go mad. Humans can't share a single mind, no matter how you distribute the pieces."

Thea made an unhappy noise in the back of her throat.

Gwyn said, "You're not some weak-willed lady-in-waiting, are you?"

"I do believe Edytha would consider that an insult," Liz noted.

"Oh, Edy!" Gwyn laughed. "She doesn't count. She's as much of a politician as any of Isabeau's ministers. Edy doesn't rank a decent title. I was thinking of someone like Lady Bettyna."

Liz snickered. "You've obviously never gotten between Bettyna and a good-looking guardsman."

"After the link is joined," Jagger continued, "the energies released by the link must be harnessed and directed. The magicians who perform this part of the ceremony must be as strong and determined as the mind mages in order to shape the group's power into an effective weapon. Otherwise, the backlash of mind magic will destroy them. Again, I don't see that happening."

Roarke developed a sudden fascination for the heat rings burned into the table. It was almost as if he suspected a problem would arise with his portion of the link. *Just what we need*, Liz thought, *more complications*.

"Finally, the spell-casters must bind the others' magic to its purpose and break the link. Once the group accomplishes its goal, binding the magic to an object or a place is relatively simple. Breaking the link is another matter.

"You and your sisters were transmogrified by the Wishstone as a triple trine. From everything you've told me and everything I've sensed on my own, your powers are well balanced. You won't kill each other by linking. Likewise, you won't endanger the mortals around you by entering the link. The sticking point for you will come when you complete the ritual and achieve your goal.

"The power released by the link is very seductive. Watching the energies multiply and reach out to accomplish their goal is like watching a rose unfurl its petals in front of you. The power hums like music. It's as if the magic itself is trying to make you forget how fragile the separate parts of the link truly are.

"Pump a wineskin too full of wine, and it bursts," Jagger said. "Keep pumping power into the link, and it will explode, devastating everything within a four-day's ride."

"A true Adept would never lose sight of that," Sejanus demurred. "It would be suicide. There would be nothing left except ash and air."

Thea's face looked as grim as Liz felt. Their minds met, Thea voicing what they both knew. *Suicide or not, none of us are true Adepts, even in our dreams.*

At least we were warned. Liz tried to put a better spin on it for both their sakes. At the same time, another part of Liz's mind began constructing the vision of total destruction she would use to convince Anna, Pandora and Brigid of the importance of their role. For someone who had been standing in the Pentagon parking lot when Flight 77 exploded, the necessary images sprang all too readily to mind.

⁎⁎⁎

The Plain of Elsee

"Welcome to the party," Brigid said to Anna. "Where are Thea and Liz?"

Anna frowned. "Off chasing some damned rabbit."

Brigid suspected as much. You had to hand it to Reyah—when the old girl did something, she did it all the way.

"It's about damn time you got here," Sarah said. "Pandora's been a major pain in the ass."

"It's not my day to be her keeper," Anna replied.

"She's your damned elemental," Sarah shot back. Brigid hoped Sarah wouldn't lose her temper like she did at the con. Things were dicey enough.

"Look," Anna said, "do you want your popguns, or would you prefer to abuse me 'til those hooligans up there decide to come down and play?"

Instead of flaying Anna alive, Sarah laughed. "I'll take Choice A." Brigid mentally wiped her forehead. Whew, another bullet dodged.

"Wise decision." Anna handed Brigid her staff. "What happened to ya'll? You look like you were dropped in a swamp."

"We were, dammit." Brigid regarded Anna's leathers with envy. What she'd give to be out of her mud-encrusted rags and wearing something with proper protection. Like two or three inch thick leather and maybe some nice bits of steel protecting strategic areas of the body.

"Brig? You okay?"

"It's been a helluva day, Anna."

"You'll have to tell me all about it after we get back to the Keep."

"Deal. By the way, thanks for remembering my staff."

Anna nodded, her attention straying to Alfred as he led his men across the plain.

"There's not a lot of them, are there?" Brigid remarked. "Too bad. From the looks of it, we could use a whole army."

"Tell me about it." Anna sighed. "Unfortunately, we thought we were going on a rescue mission. Alfred didn't realize we'd be Porting into the middle of a war zone."

Brigid grinned. "He don't know us very well, do he?"

Anna grinned back. To Brigid's right, Marisol uttered what sounded like a whimper. Brigid followed Marisol's gaze. Gareth caught Ember in a fierce hug. Something like longing moved across Marisol's face.

Gareth pressed his cheek to the top of Ember's head. Desperate worry and fury struggled for mastery on his face. Ember sniffled and wiped her nose with the back of her hand. "It's all my fault we're in danger, isn't it?"

The hard line of Gareth's mouth softened. He kissed Ember's forehead. Brigid felt her own heart lurch. "No, honey. It's not your fault."

"Are those men…going to hurt us?"

Gareth's face set in implacable lines. "No, Ember, no one is going to hurt you. I promise."

Brigid made a similar silent promise to herself. No way she was going to let Ember get hurt.

All business now, Hawke said, "Gareth, your family reunion is very nice, but you need to have Ember get back by Anna and the other mages. We need your sword. Alfred, by your leave, Conlan and I need to borrow your wizard."

Alfred nodded and began barking orders to his men. Hawke and Conlan handed off the weapons they'd been carrying for distribution to the troop. Brigid's eyes widened. Didn't anybody else think it was weird the big guys were getting rid of their weapons? Did they plan to strip and go berserker? Yet another thing the show never mentioned.

Each of the Vanyr warriors reached under his shirt and pulled out a large medallion on a heavy silver chain. The medallions reminded Brigid of those old Chinese coins with square holes in the center, only much larger. Black enamel threaded with silver circles and triangles covered one side of Hawke's medallion.

As if sensing her interest, Conlan tilted his medallion. The front was enameled in purple and covered with silver squiggles. The back, oddly enough, looked like an engraving of a circuit board, only more complex than anything Brigid had ever pulled from the inside of her computer.

"Jagger's armor talismans," Conlan explained. "The best of the best—everything from toe guards to helmet points and all the necessaries in between. And it takes very little magic to activate. Somebody like Val could do it in his sleep."

From the way Val started, it was news to him. But he gamely traced a pair of small symbols in the air. The holes in the medallions seemed to inhale the blue lines of his magic. The noise they made sounded like a vacuum cleaner. The medallions buzzed and spat colored light. Val, Brigid and the other women jumped back. Blue-white sparks wrapped themselves around Hawke like the mapping lines for a three-dimensional CGI. The purple static playing around Conlan seemed to grow in rows, almost like knitting, working its way outward from his chest.

The various lines around each man connected with an explosive flare. By the time Brigid's eyes began to clear, Hawke was covered head to toe in blue steel plate armor which looked like it owed as much to SWAT gear as it did to the Middle Ages. The short, black tunic covering his breastplate was emblazoned with a silver hawk. Each polished steel blade of the double-headed ax in his right hand was big enough to reflect Brigid's astonished face.

Conlan's oval helmet and visor were similar to Hawke's but the black warrior's braids had been neatly gathered under a mesh coif which served to pad and protect the back of his neck. The spaces between the plates of his armor were covered in chain mail so dense it looked like mesh, but so supple it moved like fabric when he drew his giant, two-handed sword.

Brigid sucked in her breath. Sweet Mother of God, Conlan's sword was longer than she was tall.

Hawke popped his visor open and grinned at her. "And he knows how to use it too." Hawke glanced at Val. "Val, get back to your troop. If those bastards have wizards, which I'm pretty sure they do, we're going to need shielding. And make sure you look after Ember."

Hawke frowned at Brigid. "You need armor, but I'm not sure Val…" Hawke's head whipped around. "I'll be damned, Theron's here. Theron! Stop skulking in the heights. We need help down here!"

ॐ

Theron stared to the west. Somewhere, near the Elsee Gap, he felt Deryk's presence. A group of archers had moved into position at the foot of Mount Tuumb. One of them glanced back toward the castle's ruined Hall. A stray sunbeam sparked along a narrow metal pipe and a lock of pale gold hair. Deryk raised his head from the spyglass. Across the distance separating their respective positions, Theron could have sworn he saw his brother smile.

"Reyah blast you, Deryk. What do you think you're doing? Not even our doting Mother will ignore an offense of this magnitude."

"Theron, damn it to Kalin's Seven Hells, are you going to help or not?" Hawke bellowed.

Frieda turned in Theron's direction. Theron couldn't see her expression, but he could feel the intensity of her gaze.

Damn Deryk anyway, Theron thought. *This is one battle I won't walk away from.* Theron looked again at Frieda. *I need this woman, and I refuse to let you get your greedy hands on her or her magic.*

"Theron!"

ॐ

One second Theron stood on the hilltop, the next he stood by Conlan. Frieda gasped in delight. Her breathing grew ragged. Oh yeah, Brigid thought, Free was definitely getting off on Theron doing magic. Brigid, on the other hand, could feel her upper lip lifting in a snarl almost as eloquent as Hawke's. Theron, the bloody bastard, took his time.

Conlan gave Theron a sardonic look. "Didn't think you were going to join us there for a moment." Theron's cheeks flushed, but the mage said nothing.

Free shot Conlan an icy glare. "Of course he wouldn't leave us. Theron *always* helps the good guys."

"Armor them," Conlan ordered and strode over to Hawke's side.

"Where does Conlan get off doing stuff like that?" Free fumed.

"Can it, Free," Brigid said. "We've got bigger things to worry about."

Theron slanted a look at Free. He started chanting under his breath.

"Hey!" Free shouted. The accumulated muck of their adventures in the Shadowlands vanished from her person. A wide-brimmed helmet landed softly on her hair, and a breastplate wrapped itself around her torso. "What is this?"

"Protection," Theron said. "It will keep you from being harmed."

"What about us?" Marisol demanded. "Don't we get to be protected too?"

"Thanks but no thanks," Sarah said.

"I don't want it either," Kait retorted. "I've got my leathers."

"You'll take some," Brigid said. "And so will I. No arguments." Sarah swore under her breath. Brigid ignored her.

"I'm good," Anna told Brigid. "Anything iron would interfere with me doing magic."

"I want some armor," Pandora said eagerly. "This is going to be so cool!"

Theron chanted another phrase, repeated it. Steel-reinforced leather gauntlets snapped over Free's forearms while heavy socks and a sturdy pair of steel-toed leather boots replaced the stockings and shoes she'd lost in the swamp. With a final glance at Free, Theron pointedly turned his back on the rest of the women and stared across the plain.

"Yo!" Pandora hollered. "I thought you were going to armor all of us? What gives?"

Brigid fought the urge to bash Theron over the head with her staff. Or better still, shove it up his sorry ass.

"If my sisters don't get cleaned up and armored, I won't wear this," Free declared. She tugged at the breastplate. "Whatever happens to them happens to me."

Theron turned. "It stays on until you're safely back at the Keep.

Free's cheeks flamed red. She made a soft sound, like a baby kitten cuffed by its mother.

In two strides Theron was at Free's side. Taking one of her hands in his, Theron gazed into her eyes. "Please, Little Flower. Wear this for me. I don't wish for you to be injured in any way." Theron raised Free's hand to his lips and brushed a kiss across her knuckles. "Please."

Oh shit, Brigid cursed, *the bastard's going to schmooze Free, and the rest of us are going to be left high and dry.*

Free bit her lip. She stared at the ground and pulled her hand away. "No. Armor my sisters, or I take it off."

"What?" Theron obviously couldn't believe his ears.

Brigid felt like cheering. Free had actually stood up to Theron. Outstanding!

"You must obey me," Theron commanded. "I told you…"

"You've told me nothing but crap! Armor my friends or go away and leave me alone." Free yanked the helmet from her head and threw it to the ground. "You're not acting like the man I know you are."

"The hell with him, Free," Sarah said. "We'll be all right."

Hawke, Conlan, Alfred and Willem watched the farce impassively. Brigid wondered when—or if—one of them planned to step in and make Theron do the right thing. At least, she hoped they'd step in. She hated to think of facing the thugs up on the hills wearing nothing but rags.

Free and Theron glared at each other.

"As you wish, my lady," Theron said. "But you realize this could severely impair my ability to defend you."

"I don't care. Clean them up and give them armor."

Theron resumed chanting. Brigid could tell he hated every minute of it.

Brigid tugged at a flimsy chain mail top that didn't reach to the point of her corset. A pair of gleaves braced her arms and a steel helmet covered her head. She still wore the tatters of her skirt, but at least it was clean and dry. A sturdy pair of boots gave her lower legs and feet some protection. She shrugged. It was better than nothing.

"Satisfied, my lady?" Theron asked Free.

"No," Free said. Theron's jaw dropped. "Give them good stuff like Conlan and Hawke."

Theron breathed loudly through his nose "You don't understand."

Free undid one of the buckles of her breastplate. "Yes, I'm afraid I do. And I wish I didn't." Tears sparkled in her eyes as she worked the next buckle.

A couple minutes later, Brigid, Kait, and Sarah all wore suits of armor similar to Alfred's soldiers. Their armor didn't afford them as much protection as Hawke's or Conlan's, but Brigid suspected it was a lot easier to maneuver. Marisol and Pandora sported the same breastplate, helmet, boots and gleaves as Free. A pair of loose pants replaced Marisol's petticoat.

Free nodded. She walked over to Pandora and Anna. Theron pressed his lips together and marched over to Alfred. Conlan stared at Free, a strange look on his face.

"I never thought she'd stand up to him," Marisol whispered to Brigid.

"Neither did I." Brigid took a deep breath, trying to adjust to the weight of the armor. "Ladies, listen up. We've got some important things to discuss and not a lot of time to do it."

"Like what?" Sarah asked as she wrestled her stained and ripped coat over her armor.

"Like that." Brigid pointed to the north. The cavalry walked their horses down the swale in long, even lines.

"Oh shit." Kait's voice quavered. "This is not good."

"You're right, it isn't," Brigid said. "That's why we need to talk about what we're going to do."

"What do you mean 'do'?" Anna asked. "We get out there and use our magic to kick their butts."

"Yeah?" Brigid drawled. "What spells you're going to use, Ms. Battle Mage."

"Oh, shit." Anna glowered at Brigid. "Sometimes you're too damn smart."

"No, I'm not," Brigid said. "If I was, I'd have a plan. We have no idea how to do this for real. We *need* a plan."

"I can understand why you want to set things up with the magic pushers, but why do you need to talk to Kait and me?" Sarah complained. "After all, we kicked major ass in Kush."

Kait sucked in her breath. Her face was sheet white.

Brigid crossed her arms. "You might've kicked ass in Kush, but do you know what you're going to do here? Are you going to stick by Ember, Val and your sisters, and protect them? Or are you going to rush out there and try to slaughter as many bad guys as possible?"

Sarah flinched.

"She has a point, Sarah," Kait said. Brigid could smell Kait's fear. Her terror had the potential to bring one or more of them down. But Kait, bless her, tamped back her dread. "The horses are picking up speed. You've got the floor, Brig. What do we do?"

Brigid looked down at her hands. *Damn it, why aren't Thea and Liz here?*

A little voice whispered, *Because they're not. No one else is going to think of this stuff. Get to work, girl, or you'll be trying to direct this show while fending off nasties.*

Brigid straightened her shoulders. Show time. "Listen up. Anna, I want you to hit the front line with every nasty spell you can think of. I don't care if you're chanting nursery rhymes, get some mojo working on those bad guys."

Anna fingered her chatelaine and nodded. "I'm your girl."

"Fantastic. Pandy, those guys want to hurt you, hurt Ember, hurt all of us. You don't want that to happen, do you?"

Pandora's eyes sparked blue fire. "No way." The ground trembled.

Out of the corner of her eye, Brigid saw Hawke and Conlan edge closer, as if curious about her tactics or her friends' powers. "Anna, can you use that?" Brigid asked.

"I can sure try."

"Good enough. Free, I want you to get something growing out there. Push up some thorn bushes, grow a couple of trees, hell, throw daisies at 'em if you have to. Slow those bastards down. Got it?"

Free nodded.

"What about me?" Marisol asked. "I could whip up a storm."

"A storm would hurt us too. No, too risky," Brigid said.

"Lightning, maybe? One of Liz's stories had me picking a guy out of a tree with lightning. The tree burst into flames too."

"Christ. Okay, but I don't want you throwing it anywhere near us. Pick off the guys at the rear. It'll cut down on their back-up.

"Sarah and Kait," Brigid continued, "we have no idea what's going to happen. Let's stick together as close as possible. I don't know how the Vanyr and Alfred's guys work in real life, so I don't know what our protection will be. For now, let's say protecting each other is our job. Okay?"

"Okay."

Brigid shifted the staff from one hand to the other. "Ladies, remember one thing."

"What?" Sarah asked.

"We're the Daughters of Reyah. No one takes us down."

Chapter Twenty-Nine

The Sorcellarium, Salentia

Thea raised her hands to forestall more instructions from Gwyn. "Once we harness the mind mage power burst, Roarke and I are going to direct it at some old stables. Gotcha. Now, here's the main thing I want to know—what's to stop Roarke from stealing my magic while we're doing it?"

Liz caught her breath. Talk about shrapnel. Thea's little verbal grenade blew Roarke half-way out of his chair. He might not have much magic compared to Jagger or Gwyn, but what he did have crackled like static electricity against Liz's magical awareness.

Roarke loomed over the table, threat in every line of his lean frame. "Lady Thea, I'm sorry for everything I said in the pool last night. I'm even sorrier Reyah's Goddess-damned magic made me say it. But I am sick and tired of having everything I say or do twisted inside out." Roarke pointed at Thea. "For the record, I cannot *take* your magic. The most I could do is borrow it, and only if you were willing."

Thea folded her arms across her chest, her lips curling in a snarl.

"Remember your sisters," Jagger said.

"I'm trying," Thea said. Her gaze locked with Roarke's. "Believe me, I'm trying."

"And anything Roarke might do to Thea, you'd help me undo, right?" Liz purred.

"Trust me, ladies, Roarke doesn't have a bad bone in his body," Gwyn assured them, "much as he'd like people to believe otherwise. And if he did, I'd break it for him myself."

278

Roarke subsided into his chair, somehow managing to sprawl indolently over the narrow wood frame. He didn't deign to express his displeasure at Gwyn, who despite her apparent age was probably several centuries his junior. But you could tell it bit, and bit hard, to be dismissed as nothing more worrisome than an errant schoolboy.

From her still smoldering expression, Thea didn't give a damn.

"Right, Jagger?" Liz prompted.

"Well?" Thea said. "We can't stop a demon if we're magically impaired."

"You have my word. I promise to undo whatever damage you might sustain in the link." Jagger's voice resonated inside and outside of Liz's head, tickling her nerve endings with his amusement. He extended his hands to Liz and Thea. "Now, shall we begin? For your sisters and Domain."

"For your sisters and Domain," Roarke echoed.

With a last suspicious glance in Roarke's direction, Thea clasped the Vanyrs' hands.

Liz rested her palm against Roarke's. More magic than Liz expected throbbed beneath Roarke's cool flesh. But there wasn't enough to master, or even threaten, the well of personal power she struggled to control.

Liz reached her left hand toward Jagger's right. A spurt of power grabbed her, flashing heat, then warmth as her hand settled into Jagger's touch. Jagger's magic was the ocean. He could swamp her if he chose. Bright pulses of energy raced outward from the nerves in Liz's left hand. The left side of her body felt like it was lit like a Christmas tree. She didn't know if her skin could contain the effervescent power or prevent it from overwhelming Roarke.

"You were right, you know," Jagger murmured, the dark resonance of his voice as tactile as his lips would have been had they brushed against her ear.

"About what?" Liz whispered, certain he would hear.

"It would be a better world if mortals treated Vanyr as equals."

Liz didn't trust herself to speak. *How?*

It would be a lot easier to pick up girls.

Jagger slid into Liz's mind on the squall of her outraged delight. He poured information straight into her memory faster than a computer tutorial on speed. Liz accepted the knowledge and tuned out, focusing instead on finding common ground with Roarke. What did she know of him from the show? What had she learned about him here?

Everyone said Roarke was a good—or possibly still bad—man trying to redeem himself from crimes too horrible to contemplate. Without death, where does guilt end? Where's the justice in outliving the last descendant of those you wronged? How can you expiate your sin without hope of absolution?

Roarke's level gaze was bleak. With a shock, Liz realized he expected her to hurt him. Like an abused animal, he waited for the blow.

You can't reach out and grab a wounded animal. You can only allow them to reach you. Little by little, like working the crank on a vintage car, Liz rolled down the window of her mind.

Roarke's essence met hers in the breach. Liz touched him with senses far more refined than those of the flesh, tasted him, drawing from the very marrow of his being. Roarke cringed.

An old wound, yet still raw with grief.

Oh, Liz knew grief, and Roarke's called to her, a siren's song Liz met with compassion and every shred of comfort she could find. But Roarke's wound was too deep, too old, scarred with bitter hatred and anger such as even Liz couldn't fathom. Still Liz poured forth her balm—the hand of friendship to replace the shattered bond of family, realms of fantasy to redirect the brooding.

But Liz's fantasies were Roarke's realities, and her soul slid over his scars, out to the other side.

Counterclockwise around the table Liz's mental energy sped. Jagger's essence moved clockwise, ensuring they would meet twice as often as they "touched" anyone else. Their magic met for the first time after Liz moved past Roarke, and Jagger opened his side of the link with Thea. Liz flowed through Jagger like water through a veil. No force. No constraint. Merely the faintest iridescence of sorrow, bleeding like dye in the rain.

Liz raced into Thea. Their souls embraced. Back again to Jagger. His essence seemed to have gathered more substance. The taste of him was stronger, the sorrow within him more palpable and threaded with resignation. Liz returned to Roarke, showering him with comfort as she passed. Back to Jagger. Always back to Jagger. Liz and Jagger spiraled through and around the others, flowing through each other, giving and taking more every time they met. Jagger knew all her paltry secrets now, as emotions if not words, just as she knew his regret and sorrow—pools as deep as Roarke's burning hate. Liz grasped the inexplicable despair at the root of Jagger's power and wondered at its cause.

Jagger tried to pull away, but they couldn't escape each other. Like an octopus jetting ink to distract pursuit, Jagger's mind poured his knowledge into hers. Confused by the flood, Liz foundered, grabbing facts at random. The arts of illusion and mental manipulation sieved through her, too subtle for her insubstantial grasp.

Telekinesis is accomplished by moving large with small. Small, willful manipulations of naturally caused, directed motion—like air currents or rippling water—combined with subtle alterations of weight and mass acted on the world like the proverbial butterfly sneeze. Jagger almost reduced the process of a miracle to a formula.

Magic as science? Liz wondered. The mathematics of Jagger's magic were everywhere—integers, tables, whole equations, simultaneously familiar and alien. Chemistry too. *The only difference between lead and gold lay in the arrangement of their subatomic particles. The only difference between water and steam lay in the speed of their molecules.* Jagger's recipes for the transmutation of matter, Liz realized. The secrets of the universe spiraled from his calculations. Jagger spilled them at Liz's feet, an infinite number of stars thrown against the blanket of night, each blindingly clear, each achingly familiar.

More! Liz wanted so much more as they chased each other around the link. The power shared between them grew in their pursuit and flared like the sun each time they met.

ಬಿ∞ಆ

The calm acceptance of Liz's mind-touch shocked Roarke to his core. Where Roarke expected loathing, Liz poured empathy. She gave understanding where others rendered quick, brutal judgment.

Thea rode her sister's emotions, accepting the touch of Roarke's mind despite an abiding fear he grasped only in snatches. Strangely enough, he sensed it wasn't a fear of him. Who, then? Not for the first time, he envied Jagger's vivid, immediate magic and the way it granted access to complete memories. Roarke now shared Liz's memories, little though he understood most of them. But that was her gift. He could see into Thea only as far Thea allowed—barely deeper than a cat's scratch.

Deep enough for Roarke to sense the fathomless well of Thea's untrained magic. Thea's power called to him. Her power tempted him to bind her to him even as he understood he could never hope to constrain such force. Thea the woman called to him in ways Roarke didn't understand, yet she ran from him.

Who had hurt her? He longed to put his hands around the bastard's neck and squeeze 'til he couldn't hurt anyone, especially Thea, ever again.

Beneath their joined hands, the table—kelan heartwood, eight inches thick, cured by tar and fire—groaned and imploded in a puff of dust. Roarke's eyes popped open as the Sorcellarium's heavy roof tore free from posts and rafters, whirling straight up on twined ropes of blinding, blue-white power.

A reverse double helix, Thea's mind spoke. The phrase baffled Roarke, but Jagger and Liz seemed to understand, in so far as their absorption in each other permitted. The power of the mind mages expanded each time they touched. Like courting hawks, they touched more and more often. Their twined magic thundered in Roarke's ears. Soon there would be no containing it.

Now! Roarke told Thea, and to his utter amazement, she understood. Her magic fused with Roarke's as he began to spin a turquoise web up the double column. Thea caught his purpose quickly, and they whirled around the mind mages' energies, their magical web growing faster and stronger whenever they touched each other or the burning power of their siblings' minds. Roarke felt Thea's power blossom, the net she wove more than a match for her sister's bright force. Ever upward Thea and Roarke raced, thread by thread, branch by glowing branch of blended magic. Power Roarke never imagined fountained from some unknown wellspring.

Roarke could do this. He could do anything.

He could do nothing.

The turquoise jet of power slammed back against Roarke like a crashing wave, dragging him under. Red blazed across his inner eyes as Roarke gagged and choked beneath the force of the mind mages' power. The once elegant tracery of Thea's magic rained down upon him like the limbs of a falling kelan tree, battering him, hurling him away from Jagger and Liz's lethal energies.

"Sweet Reyah's mercy!" someone shouted. Roarke's last conscious thought was the voice sounded too loud to be Sejanus's.

Chapter Thirty

Dammit where was Terba? Deryk swore as he peered through his spyglass. Why wasn't the fat bastard answering his call? Sweat rolled down Deryk's forehead. A plum opportunity had dropped into his lap but his demon-damned hirelings were doing their best to keep him from capitalizing on it. Nothing was going right. Half of Kaltar's troops were out of commission. Sentenor's cavalry was ready to charge, but Sentenor's idiot brother Septor didn't have his archers in position yet. The fools were letting Alfred dig in and Kalin only knew how hard it'd be to pry him loose.

Pain lanced up Deryk's right arm. The torque around his neck tightened. His heart tried to leap from his chest. Deryk doubled over and scrabbled at the snake around his neck. He couldn't breathe. Fire, not blood, coursed through his veins. His fingers fumbled over the red-hot skin of the snake. More pain surged through his arms, his legs, his head. He felt as if he were being torn to pieces by his own magic.

No. Not *his* magic.

Deryk sank to his knees. He could feel all his borrowed power seeping away. He blinked to clear his vision. Blue light spun toward the sky and coalesced into a turquoise ribbon of pure magical energy. It was coming from the mouth of his snake. He finally managed to crush the snake's head in one hand and grabbed the greenish blue energy with the other.

Sweat poured down his face. The spell nearly jerked out of Deryk's grasp. *Damn them!* He redoubled his efforts. Crimson energies finally, finally began to cobweb around the blue. It wasn't enough. There was only one thing left to do. He forced a finger into the snake's mouth. Its fangs sank into his flesh. Blood seeped through his fingers.

Deryk spoke a *Word*. He released his death grip on the snake. Handful by bloody handful, Deryk clawed the spell toward him. With a final ruddy flare, the snake reared and swallowed the last surge of magic. Deryk bent his head and whispered a spell not meant for human tongues. The snake blazed like a miniature sun, then dulled. For a few moments the only sound in the roofless Hall was Deryk's labored breathing.

He glanced over at the wide-eyed wizard who'd been working the battlefield scrying spells. The man trembled uncontrollably. Deryk was feeling more than a little shaky himself. He'd die before he showed it to vermin, though. Besides, he had no intention of allowing the man to live past the battle. It was cliché but true—dead men tell no tales.

"Call Septor," Deryk rasped as he snatched up his spyglass. "If his archers aren't ready to fire on my command, I'll feed him to my snake."

ഇര

Holy Mary, Mother of God. Brigid gulped. *The horses are trotting now—and there's no place to hide.* A hawk screamed overhead, and three puffs of red smoke flowered over the lines of horsemen trotting down the broad hill. Sunlight peeked through the scudding clouds long enough to shimmer along the blades of wickedly long swords hanging at the waists of the horsemen riding toward the small group of men and women standing on the Plain of Elsee.

The horses' strides lengthened. The jangle of bit and harness and armor tolled in Brigid's ears. A wisp of breeze blew the acrid scent of horse and human sweat past her nose. Throbbing like a hundred heartbeats, the sound of the horses' hooves reverberated in an ominous thrum that seemed to shake the very ground.

"Theron, break the charge!" Alfred barked. The horses' hooves struck the ground like a thousand hammers, gouging clumps of black sod from the earth and sending them flying. "Theron, do you hear me? Take out those horses!"

Theron's staff glowed like a beacon. Crackles of red and blue fire and noxious smoke attested to the fact Theron was engaged on another front. Brigid followed Theron's gaze. Four dark-robed men on an eastern crag raised their staffs in unison. A moment later red fire splattered on a shield composed of iridescent air.

"No help there," Brigid muttered to Kait. "Those other wizards have Theron tied in knots."

Arriving at the same conclusion, Alfred turned to his soldiers. "Halberds at the ready. Vallenius, bind strength to the wood and brace them firm."

Val nodded. He looked green as he raised his hands and began to chant.

The cavalry troop thundered into a gallop.

"I've got it!" Brigid shouted. "I know how to slow them down!"

"How?" Anna demanded.

"Free, get your pet vine. Throw it two hundred yards ahead of us. Make it longer than the front line of horses."

"Ahhh, I think I see where your beady little brain is headed," Anna said.

Free gulped.

"Go on, Free," Anna urged. "I'm pretty sure I can do something downright nasty with your little pet vine."

Free nodded. She unwrapped the vine curled around her ankle. "Get over there and make yourself useful." She threw the vine.

Brigid thought it was a pitiful excuse for a throw, but it didn't matter. A turquoise glow spread along the vine in either direction. Upward and outward it sailed, growing longer and longer.

"My God, it's actually working," Free gasped. "My magic is working!"

"Here's hopin' mine does, too." Anna raised her fan, a blue glow outlining her fingers. She pointed to the horsemen and sang to the tune of "Yankee Doodle",

Bunch a' gangsta's 'tacked Domain,

Riding on some ponies,

Sister Frieda used her vine,

And broke their nasty bonies.

Brigid crossed her fingers. The horses' hooves pounded closer and closer. The vine twisted in the air. The magical glow wrapped about it grew brighter. It dropped to the ground directly in the path of the running horses.

"Shit, it's not going to work," Kait moaned.

"Of course it's going to work." Anna's voice, however, held a note of uncertainty.

"Anna and Free, get back," Brigid ordered. "They're going to hit us hard."

"Stand your ground, men!" Alfred shouted.

Willem, Donatien and Tanak moved to stand with the second row of pikemen. Theron held his staff over his head. The air around him pulsed.

"Do something!" Free screamed.

The vine rose in the air and stretched taut. The horses' feet were swept from under them. Flesh and metal thudded to the ground. Clods of grass flew into the air. Bones broke with the stutter and snap of machinegun fire. Horses shrieked. Brigid flinched as the second line slammed into the wreckage of the first. More blood. More pain. More death. Behind the carnage, horses reared and twisted, turning on their riders and each other in a frenzy to escape.

"It…worked," Anna said.

"You call that a spell?" Theron demanded.

"Hush up and tend to your own spells," Anna snapped. "At least mine took out some bad guys."

Pandora gagged. "It's horrible. Look at all the horses we hurt."

Anna put a hand on Pandora's shoulder. "Can't be helped, honey. They'd have killed us if they could."

An angry growl welled from Pandora's throat. The riders who'd succeeded in leaping clear rushed to get the horses back on their feet, whipping them with their reins and the flats of their drawn swords.

"I don't like that." The Mistress of Mayhem's sparked blue fire. "They're hurting the horses more!"

Saddles slid off horses' backs. Swords turned in their wielders' hands and bit deep. Reins wrapped around ankles and spurs, tripping mercenaries into each other and onto the ground.

"Hold that thought, sugah." Anna chanted,

Here a horse, there a horse,

Everywhere a horse, horse.

Pandora wants to see them safe,

So hurry them home, of course, course.

Every horse that hadn't broken bones in the fall surged to their feet. Horses still on their feet bucked like range ponies. The few riders still mounted were thrown by their spell-crazed horses.

"We did it!" Kait cheered. "We stopped them!"

"We slowed them down," Willem snapped.

"Vallenius! Shields up!" Alfred shouted. "From the south and west. Men, ready yourselves!"

An arrow thudded into the ground inches from Brigid's foot. More arrows rained down, some sizzling against Val's magical shields, others finding marks in the beleaguered group.

"Damn," Willem swore, pulling an arrow from the narrow gap between his shoulder guard and the curved plates covering his upper arm. "I hate it when that happens."

Blood flowed from a ragged hole in the band of sleeve visible between the metal plates. Brigid drew in her breath as the flow oozed to a stop before her eyes.

Willem grimaced. "Heals quick, but hurts like hell."

Brigid nodded, too shaken by the obvious evidence of Willem's immortality to reply.

๙ଔ

The Sorcellarium, Salentia

From afar Roarke heard chanting. The chanting rose to a scream. A tremendous crash shook the numbed husk of his body. Eventually the trembling ceased. He blinked away the grit clouding his eyes.

How interesting—the roof was back, if a little off center. Two damaged posts crunched and splintered. The roof tipped onto the lawn surrounding the Sorcellarium with an anticlimactic thump.

Roarke closed his eyes against another cloud of dust, this one rising from below instead of sifting from above. Trying not to inhale, since sneezing was beyond him, Roarke squinted in the direction of the puff. Liz foundered in the debris of what used to be the table. Her little feathered hat had vanished, and her unbound hair streamed like molten bronze down her back. Liz scrambled to Thea's chair and ran her hands over Thea's forehead and pulse points.

"I'm fine," Thea protested, opening her eyes. "It was just…sudden. What happened?"

"I'm sorry," Roarke muttered. The words echoed over and over in his aching head. *Sorry, by heaven and hell, sorry, sorry…*

Satisfied with Thea's condition, Liz scuttled to Roarke. "Forget sorry. Are you all right? It felt like your magic tore in two."

"You felt..." Sejanus stopped to cough. "You felt the collapse of Roarke's magic?"

"I think so." Liz sneezed.

Thea reached a hand out to Roarke. "I didn't hurt you, did I?"

Roarke shook his head. "My magic choked. Compared to my brothers', it's not very strong. The fault was mine for attempting to link with you, Thea. I humbly beg your pardon."

"You didn't exactly beg her to let you link, now did you?" Gwyn answered for Thea. "As far as I can see, no harm was done."

Sejanus snorted, but Gwyn ignored him. She pushed herself to her feet and padded to the center of the room. "Sejanus and I are surprised you could sense anything in your link, Liz. The smell of snow and mountain winds ran down the column of your magic. The last time that happened, the mages succumbed to group mind."

Liz grinned at Jagger. "Not a chance. Jagger doesn't play fair. He scooped up all my secrets and refused to show me all of his. Hard to lose yourself in a man who's playing games with your head."

"Entirely for your own good," Jagger demurred in a teasing tone of voice. "It would never do for you to surrender to me too quickly."

"It would never do, period," Liz said. "But would you answer me one question?"

"Anything, lady."

"When the link broke, it knocked the rest of us flat. Where did you find the strength to get up and walk?"

"I held something back."

"But doesn't that defeat the purpose of the link?"

Jagger stroked the side of Thea's neck and shoulder. Roarke's muscles clenched as he imagined running his own hand over the silk of Thea's throat.

"The purpose of the link is to survive a demon," Jagger said at last. "The link itself is nothing more than a tool. Try to remember that when you open the link with your sisters. Always save something for yourself."

Thea craned her neck to look Jagger in the eye. "You sound as though you expect us to do this on our own."

Jagger yanked his hand away. "My apologies, Thea, I forgot myself."

"No problem, it felt good. But I don't like what I think I'm hearing. Do you actually expect the nine of us to try this on our own against a demon?"

"We have no choice. You heard Jagger. The components of the link must be perfectly balanced or the structure will collapse of its own weight. In a fight, the result would be fatal. The mind mages would be spinning toward the stars, while—" Roarke fought back a vision of Thea, blind-eyed and helpless, amid an inferno of charred earth and smoking rivulets of blood.

Jagger clapped his hands against Thea's arms, raising another cloud of dust. "Wouldn't you rather have Roarke and me guarding your backs? You both know what must be done, and I believe you can imprint the knowledge on Anna easily enough. She's not a stupid woman, despite her burning passion to marry Alfred and become Lady of the Keep."

"Damn it, Jagger," Liz cursed, "are any of us safe from your prying mind?"

"Prying mind?" Jagger sputtered. "By the Goddess, woman, you saw the lady when she introduced herself to Alfred. She all but offered him her breasts on a silver salver."

Liz covered her mouth with her hands in time to catch an escaping giggle.

"He's got you there," Thea chuckled. "Anna is kind of obvious."

"Obvious! Anna would die if she thought you knew." Liz wobbled to her feet. "Please, don't let her know you—" She lurched to her right, eyes wide and blank. Her left hand slapped her right shoulder. Glistening pink fluid oozed from a rent in her jacket beneath her collarbone.

"Oh God. Sarah's been shot."

§⊘℞

The Plain of Elsee

Brigid hunkered down next to Sarah. The feathered haft of an arrow protruded through a tear in the shoulder of Sarah's coat. Free, Marisol and Kait crowded close.

"Is she...she...dead?" Free blubbered.

"Hell no, she's not dead," Sarah croaked. "But she is going to kick some major butt as soon as she can get to her feet." Sarah tried to sit up.

"Will you lie still!" Brigid unbuckled Sarah's helmet and shoulder guard. "You're losing blood fast. The arrow may have hit an artery. We've got to figure out some way to stop the bleeding."

"Dios, Sarah," Marisol wailed, grabbing Sarah around the ribs. Sarah landed hard against Marisol's breastplate. From the way Sarah's eyes rolled back, Brigid guessed she almost passed out.

"There aren't any hospitals. What will we do?" Marisol cried.

"Marisol, pull yourself together," Brigid said. "We need your magic. See if you and Val can get a cross wind going to screw up those damned arrows."

"Sarah needs me. Don't you, Sarah?" Marisol said.

Sarah's protest ended in a sharp intake of breath as Brigid scooped an arm under Sarah's shoulders and edged her off Marisol's lap. "Go on, Marisol," Brigid ordered. "You'll help her more if you keep those arrows away." Marisol reluctantly nodded.

"Kait, Free, go with her. Free, I need those bushes you promised me."

"I'll try." Free sobbed as Kait dragged her away.

"Keep them away from me," Sarah snarled.

"They're gone," Brigid soothed. "Lie still."

"You need to get the arrow out so the wound can heal," Hawke said from behind Brigid. Brigid sighed with relief. Hadn't the show shown Hawke and Conlan doing battlefield surgery? It took a minute for Hawke's words to register.

"What do you mean, so the wound can heal?" Brigid demanded. "Who do you think we are?"

"The Wishstone translated you, right?" Hawke reminded her. "I can't imagine it not blessing you with immortality too."

"Hawke, hurry up," Conlan urged from the front line. "They're starting to pull back the archers. We're going to have foot soldiers down here before long."

Sarah fingered the shaft in her shoulder. Brigid didn't like the intensity of her gaze as it rested on the hills to the south. "If I pull this out," Sarah said, "I'll heal like you or a Chosen?"

"Yes," Hawke said. "The pain will knock you flat, but the wound should heal pretty quick."

Sarah stayed focused on the hills. "And I'll be able to start fighting again, right?"

"Almost immediately."

Brigid wondered if the copper smell of blood filling the air was what put the hungry smile on Sarah's face.

Sarah licked her lips. "Good. I want to return a favor."

The hungry smile and the hatred in Sarah's unnaturally glowing eyes frightened Brigid more than all the arrows aimed in their direction. Pain and rage twisted Sarah's face. For one insane moment, Brigid expected Sarah to morph into a werewolf. Or worse.

"Could you help me to my feet?" Sarah purred. "I'd rather take this standing."

"Are you sure?" Hawke shot Brigid an uncertain glance.

Brigid felt pretty uncertain herself. But what else could they do? Together they helped Sarah to her feet.

Sarah pushed herself out of their arms. Swaying only a little, she grabbed the protruding arrow shaft with both hands and pulled.

"No!" Brigid shouted as fresh blood spurted from the entry wound. "Wait! You'll make it worse!" Blood slowed and stopped as the shredded flesh of the arrow wound smoothed itself into an angry pink scar. Sarah flung the bloody arrow away.

"I want it worse. Much worse." Sarah raised a fist toward the hills and roared, "Do you hear me, you scum? The Mistress of Retribution is coming to exact punishment! Your ass is grass and I'm the lawnmower coming to whack you down!"

With a wild ululation, she rushed forward, vaulting over the guardsmen's line. She whipped her knives from her belt and ran toward the southern hills.

"There she goes." Brigid retrieved her staff. As she turned, her boot grazed Sarah's bandoleer of small arrows. Not far from the bandoleer, the Mistress of Retribution's crossbows—the magical crossbows Liz's fanfic used to such lethal effect—slid deeper into a shallow trench of muddy water.

Hawke shook his head. "This battle is going to hell in a hand basket, and it's only started."

∞⌘

The Sorcellarium, Salentia

Liz twitched like a puppet on strings. Thea felt her own muscles spasm in sympathy. Her eyes glowing like bad special effects, Liz seemed to be seeing a scene far away from the confines of the Sorcellarium.

"God damn it, Sarah, for once in your life do something smart. Listen to me! I said…Don't!" Liz screamed as her right shoulder jerked forward, the skin beneath her collarbone tearing outward, spraying her companions with blood.

Jagger gathered Liz in his arms, smoothing torn muscle and skin together as he crooned something Thea suspected Liz couldn't hear. Thea felt as much as saw Roarke's mouth twist in a cynical smile.

"Right where he wants her," Roarke murmured.

Thea didn't think so. Jagger's eyes began to pale and glow in a silver blue haze much like Liz's. "Where are you?" Jagger whispered.

Liz's eyelids fluttered. "Green bowl?" She pushed as far away from Jagger as his hold allowed. Not to escape, Thea realized, but to get a better view. "No…a plain…wilted stubble. Hills all around except to the west. There's a wide cut with a ruined castle guarding the opening. Red magic in the Hall. Deryk. Corruption—he's foul!"

Liz hissed like an angry cat.

"Back to the plain," Jagger said. "Where are they?"

"Wouldn't it be better if you told me?" Liz said. The blaze of uncontrolled magic faded from their eyes. "Unless there's a street sign at the corner, I'm lost."

And usually, even then, Thea couldn't help adding to herself. Liz was going to be all right. Relief left Thea shaky.

A wide-angled, aerial view of a bowl-shaped crater opened in the air in front of Thea and the Vanyr. *The Plain of Elsee,* Jagger's thoughts informed Thea. Thea's gaze swept from the ruined castle guarding the main entrance to the valley over a small, tightly shuttered village to a long ramp of grass, which seemed to be the goal of a handful of scrambling, ant-sized soldiers.

Behind the soldiers spread a jumble of horses and men splashed with red. Their pain and terror vibrated along Thea's nerves. Horses gouged the earth with shattered legs in a desperate struggle to follow the riderless column streaming toward the plain's western gap.

Kait! Free! Their spirits cried out from the center of the plain. Arrows rained over them, losing momentum in some kind of force field. Kait clutched her sides in a death grip. Brigid, Hawke and Alfred tried to hold the center.

Sarah raced toward the castle and the archers seeding the air with death. Marisol raised her arms. Blue sparks shot from her hands.

"*No!*" Liz and Jagger roared together. The lightning bolts arced high, striking the rock-strewn hills above the brigands, loosing a handful of boulders. Down the slopes the boulders rolled and bounced, gathering smaller stones and saplings in their wake. The brigands closest to the strike shouted at their neighbors. Men ran left and right to escape the rockfall.

"Shit," Jagger said. "She thinks she did something right."

"East southeast," Roarke interrupted, redirecting the group's focus. "Look to the clearing near the stream. Forty, maybe fifty more outlaws. Their weapons carry Deryk's sigils."

"Led by one of Deryk's Chosen," Jagger said. "Which one?"

Roarke shrugged. "Can't say for certain. Probably Kaltar. Demon Witch too. By the stream. Follow the water and you'll see her. Look about a stadian downstream from the clearing. Unless my eyes deceive me, the crimson smear behind the longthorn bushes is Megeara."

"We've got to get there," Thea said. "We've got to help them."

"Us and whose army?" Liz asked. "Deryk has hundreds of men deployed around the plain, and there's a bunch of cavalry waiting outside the gap. His wizards are bleeding Theron dry."

"Seshmeel's army, of course," Sejanus replied. "We'll inform the queen."

"But it's going to take a while to get them there," Gwyn apologized. "Jagger, do you and Roarke think you could hold off Deryk's men until Isabeau's forces can Port in?"

"We don't have much choice," Liz and Roarke said together.

"We'll bring reinforcements as soon as we can," Gwyn promised.

"Notify Rupert first. I know it's a losing battle, but try to keep Isabeau...home," Jagger's voice trailed off as Sejanus and Gwyn disappeared in a Portal blink. "Damn."

Do you have any idea how gratifying it is to see you stumbling and fumbling like the rest of us, brother mine?

Thea wondered why she could still hear Roarke's thoughts. His hatred burned in Thea's gut, but Jagger ignored it.

Jagger fingered a strand of damp hair away from the corner of Liz's mouth. "Don't close your eyes when we get there. Men will be making monsters of themselves all around you, but what you don't see can kill you. Gather your sisters together in the middle of Alfred's defensive formation. Pull the warriors back too. Since they have less magic than the rest of you, they'll be the easiest marks in the link."

"Megeara hasn't called any demons. She's running for her life." Liz spoke her opinion like it was fact.

"You can't take the chance she won't. Can you stand?" Jagger asked. Liz nodded.

Jagger stepped back and swept his open hands from the ground to a level just above Liz's shoulders. As the mage moved his hands, Liz's shoes and grit-covered gown transformed into overlapping plates of armor. It reminded Thea of the way Major West had suited up in *the Lost in Space* movie, except the scales on this armor were white. A flexible gorge of white mesh slithered under Liz's hair and locked itself in place over the hollow of her throat.

A light fragrance teased Thea's nose—vaguely green like grass or rose leaves, but not really like either. Liz's eyes narrowed. Thea could tell Liz was also trying to place the unusual scent.

"Thank you." Liz tapped a gauntleted finger against the oddly jointed breastplate. "What is this stuff? It feels like plastic."

Jagger didn't answer. Instead he handed Liz a white mask and a skirted helmet resembling a samurai bonnet. With a little help from Jagger's magic, Liz's dust-streaked, medusa tangle of hair arranged itself into a neat French braid.

"Do I need the mask?" Liz asked in a constricted voice.

"It helps secure the helmet, and you do need the helmet. Most death blows go through the nose."

Liz settled the mask over her face. Jagger adjusted the white helmet to his satisfaction. Meanwhile, his own clothes changed into a black, masculine version of Liz's outfit.

Roarke's gold earring, medallion and the fob on his jeweled belt seemed to ignite. A peaked sallet grew over his head, its leather ties snaking under his chin. A stream of gold-chased steel flowed from the medallion and resolved itself a cuirass with a thigh-length "skirt" of overlapping steel plates. Stout boots replaced his shoes, greaves covered his shins.

The fob quivered and exploded into a metal-scabbarded broad sword with a small, round shield balanced precariously over the hilt. Thick, leather gauntlets with dark metal rings sewn over their backs covered Roarke's hands. Roarke glanced at

Thea as Jagger pulled a black helmet, mask and what looked like a spike-topped hammer with a thirty-inch handle from the air.

"Why aren't you armoring Thea?" Roarke demanded. Thea gulped. She'd been wondering about that herself.

"I can, but it would be better for her to transform herself into a large cat as soon as we arrive. The archers should be shooting their last volley about now. In hand-to-hand, her best defense would be to scare anyone from coming close."

"I could use my magic." The memory of her first, uncontrolled metamorphosis brought a sick chill to Thea's stomach. Remembering it brought another memory— the terror linking her to Kait's personal struggle so many miles away.

"Do you know how to use your magic, Thea?" Jagger's damnable, reasonable voice sliced into Thea's fears.

Liz extended her hand to Thea. "Armor her, please. We work better together."

A thought later, the deed was done. Jagger found no excuses to touch her, Thea noted with amusement. A coffin-shaped void, black as death, opened in the air behind Jagger. He captured Liz's gloved hands in his own.

"It's customary in Reyah's Domain for a lady to grant her defender a favor before he engages the enemy on her behalf."

Liz's panicked glance darted to Thea. Liz might have set aside her anger about what had happened in the pool, but Thea suspected her friend didn't trust the Vanyr any more than Thea did. Thea wouldn't have granted a request to either of them without knowing, in advance, what it was. And why. And Liz was even more paranoid about favors than Thea was.

"It used to be the custom in my world, too," Liz stalled.

"Kalin's balls, let's get on with it." Roarke grabbed Liz's arm and strode toward the Portal. The normally graceful Liz nearly tripped over her armored boots scrambling after him. She didn't look back.

With a shrug and wry smile, Jagger offered Thea his hand.

Thea glanced down at the armor encasing her body. "Mutant Ninja Turtle Women to the rescue," she joked before the Portal closed around her.

"Who?"

Chapter Thirty-One

Deryk's Tower, Mount Tuumb

Deryk watched lightning erupt from the upraised hands of one of the taller women—a standard weather witch ploy and a badly aimed one too. But powerful. Incredibly powerful. The bolt lanced straight from her fingertips to the front line of Septor's men. She might be powerful, but her attacks were downright childish. Any one of the sorry assholes he'd hired could take her down. At best, all she would take out was one or two men.

Halfway to its target the bolt jerked upward, tracing a steep, narrow arc. All its power crashed on the hillside behind Septor's position. Boulders, stones, clotted earth and scrub burst into the air and slammed into the rear of Septor's troop.

Impossible! Deryk thought. *You can't change the path of lightning!* Everything in Deryk's training and experience insisted it couldn't be done, even as Septor's men scattered or died in the wake of shifting earth and hammering stone.

In his outrage, Deryk almost missed the implication of the greening field around Alfred's men. "Theron can't do that!" Deryk shouted as the vegetation reached knee height, darkening to the color of thornberry canes.

Nor Vallenius. No spell at all! Deryk gagged as the taste and sensation of fresh herbs prickled his mouth. Pure, elemental power flowed from a small, half-armored figure wearing a green skirt. The woman shook as she coaxed the thorn bushes to grow around the women and Alfred's men. Need and greed roared in Deryk's ears. He wanted that woman—he wanted the weather mage. Hell, he wanted all the women.

He had to stop them first.

"Get Septor and Sentenor," Deryk commanded the scry wizard.

Out on the field, the bushes shot up past the height of a man's waist, growing wider and denser as they gained in height. Deryk's troops faltered in the face of the intimidating thorns.

"I'm going to burn those bushes," Deryk told the wizard. "Tell the men to charge as soon as Septor regroups and the greenery starts to smoke."

"Bushes?" the wizard squeaked.

"Yes, bushes, you cretin! Do what I say! Ready yourself to Port. Your brethren need your help with Theron."

The wizard shuddered. Deryk turned back to his spyglass. Now to burn those bushes.

ᔓᲝᲒᎡ

Red flashed in back of Kait's eyes an instant before red magefire attacked their position. Kait yanked Free away from the burning thorns. Val followed Kait's lead, hustling Free from the other side. The three of them barely escaped getting scorched. The orange red flames whooshed upward. The heat seemed to suck the air from Kait's lungs. To their right, Marisol found the breath to scream. The sky above them opened, and water hosed fire and people with equal fury, hammering Kait, Val and Free into the ground.

Brigid and Alfred shouted something, and the rain stopped.

"What's happening?" Free sobbed.

Kait wanted to say something smartass, like one of her favorite heroines. But she couldn't get her scrambled wits to come up with something suitably snarky. Kait realized Free was staring where the bushes and the fire used to be. Green shoots continued to push upward from the smoking skeletons of the bushes, but as soon as the shoots branched, they sparked into foul-smelling, red fire.

"Stop it, Free! Stop growing the bushes!"

Free scooted backwards over the mud, green grass trailing every movement. "I can't. I can't. It's like the vine and the grass."

"Vallenius," Willem shouted, "we need some shields, and we need them yesterday!"

"Marisol, Anna," Kait yelled. "The bushes are burning on their own. Do something! Without the bushes, we're dead!"

"Vallenius," Alfred barked, "we need your magic now, not by Harvest Moon!"

"Vallenius, you imbecile," Theron forced through gritted teeth, "what have you done?"

"It wasn't me!" Val pointed at the wizards on the eastern ridge. "Someone's Ported in up there. Oh shit. I know those gestures. He's the guy who torched the Chancellor's house at the College of Wizards. He's the real thing."

"And you're not?" Kait demanded.

"Yes, of course I am. I'm not—" Val flinched when more people yelled his name. "I'm not Theron, damn it."

"Stop trying to be." Kait clenched her fist on the hilt of her sword. She was thankful Val had spoken up. If she concentrated on Val, on his problems, she wouldn't have to think about the battle raging around her. The battle she knew she was going to have to join very, very soon.

"You don't see me trying to be Sarah, do you? Look, on the show you—er, I mean, I once knew a guy like you. This guy didn't care what people thought about his magic. He just did whatever he could to get the job done, no matter how weird it looked."

"Sounds like Sejanus's and Gargyl's magic. Vanyr Theron *hates* the way they work."

"Theron hates everything and everyone. Except himself." Kait tilted her head toward the smoldering bushes and the rocky slopes beyond. "The bad guys are marching down the hills. Both bands. It's live or die time, Val." Kait shuddered. She put a hand on Val's shoulder. *Oh God.* She could feel the fear pouring off him. He was as scared as she was.

Kait shook her head. No time for fear. "Well? What are you going to do? Live? Or die?"

Damn good question. Vallenius drew his lower lip between his teeth. Technically, he answered only to the Voice and to Alfred, and both of them had charged him to keep the women safe.

Goddess, I'm not ready for this.

No one ever is, the voice of Reyah's chief priestess whispered in his head. *You just do the best you can anyway.*

But what do you do when your best isn't working?

"Anna!" Kait yelled. "Didn't you hear me? Free needs help!"

"I heard you, I heard you!" Anna shouted. "Free! Tell me what kind of orders you're giving those poor bushes so I can make up a spell to counteract them!"

Make up a spell? Val thought about the success of Anna's odd spells. Maybe he…

"Vallenius."

Val froze at the sound of Theron's voice. Great droplets of sweat rolled down the Vanyr's face. The tip of Theron's staff smoked.

"The last outlaw to join the wolf pack on the hill—Deryk's working through him. I've got him now, but I can't hold him. Take him out. Please."

"Deryk?" the women beside Val gasped. He heard only the "please".

Yanus, Val remembered as he pushed himself to his feet. *That's the bastard's name. My father used to hold Yanus's successes over me every chance he got until Yanus finally got caught with the Chancellor's goat. I owe both those assholes a favor.* Focusing his energies, he raised his hands over his head and began chanting,

Sweet and sour,

Fire and rain,

Sugar gets you more

Than beating with a cane.

Theron's head whipped around. "What are you doing?" the Vanyr demanded. "That's not the proper spell to take down a wizard!"

"Oh, shut up, prune-face," Anna snapped. "It's not like you're doin' any better."

"Anna, don't call Stefan that!" Frieda yelped.

Val blotted out the women's voices, blotted out every sound in the world except his own voice and the power he wove there.

Spin and turn,

Cold then hot,

Here's a little something

To hit the spot.

"Hot damn!" Kait whooped, jumping up to punch the air above her head. "Look at what Val's doing!"

At the top of the hill a dark fog congealed over the heads of Deryk's wizards. The fog spun faster and faster, shrinking until it looked as if a large barrel whirled over the heads of the renegades.

"He's going to drop a barrel on one of them? That's not real magic. If he wasn't fighting those bad guys on the hill, Stefan, I mean Theron, would blast them with magefire," Frieda huffed far too close to Val's ear.

Val narrowed his concentration until he barely heard Anna's answering snort.

The barrel began to contract and expand like a bellows. In and out, larger, smaller, larger still, then even smaller until the barrel exploded in a clap of thunder. Viscous syrup rolled over the hedge wizards' heads. The shields they raised in front of themselves to ward off Vanyr magic did nothing to hold back fifty gallons of hot treacle raining from the sky.

The wizards broke ranks, flapping staffs and robes, nearly falling over the edge of the rise in their haste to get out of the spray of syrup. Theron sagged over his staff, breathing hard. Shrieks rang down the hill as the wizards who caught the most treacle—Yanus and the wizard in charge of the attack, unless Val missed his guess—dropped to the ground to roll in the dirt and grass.

"Hot damn!" Kait exclaimed. "Val tarred and feathered—er, grassed them!"

Val grinned at his partisan. He was about to tell her how much she was responsible for his success when he caught sight of the bushes. The damned things were still growing, sparking into tiny red flames that died under the weeping sky. The red smoke didn't die. It threaded upward, growing denser as Val watched.

Theron's eyes narrowed to slits. His staff glowed like a lantern from within, the power growing whiter, hotter as it shot up the ensorcelled wood.

"*Nichtu kanetka marpetha barantuu tuat! Barantha muat! Nichtu laat!*"

"Good job, Theron, blow the smoke in those bastards' faces," Alfred yelled in passing. "Halberds, there, there and there! Vallenius!"

"Shouldn't I…" Val began.

"Make some pikes from the splinters of broken halberds." Willem grabbed Vallenius's arm. "Now!"

"Go on." Kait gave Val a shaky smile. "Theron's got us covered."

Val cast a single harried glance at the smoke, now overlaid with a sheen of blue fog. But Willem's hold on his arm would not be denied.

෨෬

Theron kept shouting what Kait hoped were his best spells, his face growing redder by the second. *Jesus, Mary and Joseph*, Kait swore. *Things didn't look good.*

Next to her, Free wrung her hands. "Free," Kait barked, "can't you help Theron out?"

"I'm trying. But, but the bushes aren't listening to me."

"Dammit, Free, now is not the time to talk your plants."

"Well, what else is she supposed to do?" Anna bustled over. "That's what her magic is about, after all." Anna frowned at Theron. "Speaking of magic, I thought Theron was a lot more powerful than this."

"Everyone move back! I want those bastards to hit the smoke before they hit us!" Alfred bellowed.

Anna yodeled, "Theron, what we need is weed killer, not more smoke. Theron! Are you listenin' to me?"

Anna took two steps in Theron's direction, and Kait had to strain to see her through the puffs of blue and red smoke. Kait's eyes watered. A nasty smell like burning trash scoured the inside of her nostrils and the top of her throat.

Tears poured down Free's face, but Kait suspected it had more to do with fear than the acrid smoke.

"I'm trying, I'm trying, and nothing's working," Free cried.

"You've got to try harder," Kait urged. "The rest of those bandits are coming."

"I don't know what to do! How about cactuses? What if I grow something with thorns?"

Kait nodded. Blood roared in her ears. No, not blood—shouting and heavy, running feet. Swords hammered on shields, and the men wielding them howled like wolves.

"Get back! They're here!" Kait shouted.

As if from a thousand miles away she heard Anna trill,

Rid the grass of burning kudzu

Fa la la la la la la la la la

Kill the roots and all the buds too

Fa la la —

Hundreds of voices screamed. Kait screamed with them, the war cry bursting from her chest as the first rows of armored men charged into the remains of Free's living wall, straight into the smoke. The evil-smelling fumes closed around them, blinding them to the swift maneuvers of Alfred's guards.

Free screamed too. She ran.

"No!" Kait shrieked. She tried to catch Free as she darted past. "You're running straight for them!" But Free kept on running.

Kait drew her sword and chased after Free. A heavy-set bad guy plowed through the unnatural fog, oblivious to the guardsman's halberd braced at the level of the bad guy's unprotected belly. The baddie grunted in surprise when he impaled himself on the sharp blade.

The guardsman jerked his weapon free in a spray of blood and waste, and thrust it at something else hidden in the smoke. The bad guy reached a hand toward Free and fell dead at her feet.

Free plowed to a halt. Her mouth formed a horrified "O". Kait pounded toward Free. She intended to drag Free back behind Alfred's men. Kait wanted to put as much distance as she could between herself and the fighting.

But something inside Kait didn't want to go. *Sekhmet* yearned for combat. She strained toward the warm metallic scent of blood, the sweet corruption of burst entrails. *Sweet?* Kait almost choked. From some distant memory of a nature show, a factoid surfaced. Lions ate the intestines first. And the Egyptian goddess on whom Kait based her character wore a lion's face.

"I will not be a cold-blooded killer," she muttered under her breath. "I won't do it. I won't."

Brigid's voice echoed eerily through the smoke. "Free! Try and get more bushes to the east! Or even some trees! Free, can you hear me?"

Free sobbed. "This isn't the way it's supposed to be. This isn't right. I'm not supposed to do stuff like this. They can't make me do stuff like this, see stuff like this. I want to go home!"

One of Alfred's pikemen, a flail buried in the side of his head, fell through the smoke in front of Kait. Free shrieked and turned to run. But her feet slipped in the blood and guts. She fell. Kait marveled at the visible crack in the pikeman's skull and the way the curds of brain seeped through the bright, gushing blood of his scalp. *I can't be enjoying this*, Kait moaned inside her head. *I can't!*

A bandit stepped through the smoke and jerked the flail from the pikeman's head. The bandit's eyes locked on Free. Another bandit appeared. And another. And another.

"Shit," Kait said. The mercenary took a step forward, swinging the ball of the brain-spattered flail. Free tried to scoot away from him. She couldn't put it off anymore. Kait opened her mind and let Sekhmet in. *'Bout time,* Sekhmet whispered in Kait's head. *I've been missing out on a lot of fun.*

Kait moved between Free and the men. "Get up and run," she told Free. "Get to Anna or Brigid."

"I can't! They'll hurt me!"

"Do it. Now."

Free curled into a ball and shook like a bowl of Jell-O. Dammit, dammit, dammit. Why did Free have to choose now to fall apart? The bandits behind the man with the flail appeared to be two swordsmen and a short man with a mace.

My God, can I handle four guys at once?

Piece of cake, Sekhmet purred. *Watch us take them out.*

Kait danced forward, surreptitiously loosening one of her throwing knives with her left hand. The men moved back, spreading farther apart.

"Come on, boys," Kait chided. "Don't you want to play?"

One of the swordsmen charged. Kait knocked the swordsman's blade aside. A knife hilt bloomed in his throat. She laughed, leaping back as he dropped like a butchered ox. She drew the knife strapped to her right hip and placed herself in front of Free.

And stopped. Instead of three men, Kait faced seven. The men circled the two women. Suddenly she was fighting for her life. Blood from numerous cuts streamed from the gaps between her armor. The cuts healed, only to be reopened again and again. Every time she cut down one bandit, two more took his place.

I'm in trouble, Kait thought. *I am really, really, really in trouble.*

"Oh God, oh God, leave us alone!" Eyes tightly closed, Free pounded the ground with her fists. "Go away, you're just a bad dream! Go away!"

"Dammit Free, get up!" Kait shouted. "You've got to help me fight them! I can't protect you and fight them too!"

A bandit reached down and jerked Free from the ground. He backhanded Free's helmet off her head. Her eyes rolled, exposing the whites. The bandit grabbed Free's hair with one hand and exposed her throat for a death blow.

Chapter Thirty-Two

"My God, we've Portaled into hell," Thea whispered.

A man in chain mail ran toward one of the soldiers from the Keep. The soldier stabbed the outlaw with his halberd. Blood spewed from the outlaw's mouth as the soldier kicked his body off the blade.

Thea gagged. *I think I'm going to throw up.*

"You'll see worse," Jagger warned.

Thea fought back nausea. "I know. I'll be fine. I have to be. My friends are out there somewhere. They need me."

"Good girl." Jagger lifted Thea's hand to his lips.

"Far be it from me to break up this touching scene, but we're standing in the middle of a battle." Cold fury hardened the portion of Roarke's face visible beneath his helmet.

Jagger gave Thea's hand a final squeeze and disappeared into the smoke.

What did I do? Thea thought to Liz. *Is it because I almost got sick?*

It wasn't you he was staring at. Liz's voice whispered in her mind. *It was Jagger.*

This is crazy. Why does he hate Jagger?

Worry about that later. Now we need to find the girls. They're somewhere to the left.

I'm right behind you.

Steel scraped and shrilled. Men grunted, shouted and screamed. The sounds overwhelmed Thea's hearing even as the unnatural smoke ate away at her sight. Some instinct new to Thea warned her against shifting into cat, no matter how the prospect tempted her. Instead Thea surrendered to Liz's tug on her arm and tried not to think about how abandoned she'd felt when Jagger and Roarke vanished into the smoke.

Liz glanced over her shoulder. Her eyes glowed as blue as they had in the Sorcellarium. *We'll be okay.* She resumed picking her way over the slippery grass. Thea wondered how Liz could see anything useful through the dirty blue and red clouds overlaying the carnage. Thea couldn't see past her own outstretched hand.

I'm reading heat signatures, I think, Liz replied to Thea's half-formed question. *It's something I got from the link with Jagger. Jesus, but I wish I had goggles and an air tank. I'm on fire from my nose to my lungs.*

Liz yanked Thea off her feet. They fell to the ground. A broadsword whistled through the air where Thea's head would've been. Thea and Liz huddled on the ground for a minute like a pair of scared rabbits. Footsteps pounded past them. Thea prayed they belonged to the guy who'd swung the sword.

"Thanks." Thea couldn't tell whose hands were trembling hardest, hers or Liz's.

"You're welcome," Liz whispered back. "Now what?"

"We get up and hope your magic keeps working."

They straightened. The smoke thinned. Not more than forty feet away, Marisol raised her arms. Another monster bolt of lightning ripped through the sky.

NO!

The word shrieked simultaneously from both women's minds. Thea's hand shot forward at the same time as Liz's. Thea felt something flow through her arm and out her hand. The lightning bolt exploded far above the battle with the boom of a jet breaking the sound barrier. Blue white sparks flared and winked over Marisol's head.

Roarke raced in front of Marisol, his sword drawn but resting on his shoulder. He leapt into a bank of smoke, wailing like the damned. Something squealed high and sharp. A heavy body struck the earth so hard, the concussion vibrated through the soles of Thea's boots.

Marisol, are you trying to get us killed? Liz's magic grabbed the front of Marisol's cuirass and dragged her out of the path of two muddy fighters wrestling over a single pike.

Marisol tried to buck free from the psychic hold. *Damn it, Liz, let me go. They're killing us. I was doing what we did in our fanfic.*

In our fanfic, the bad guy was in a tree. You know, "tree", as in wood. We're standing in a muddy field with puddles of water all around us. Electricity, water and metal do not mix.

Dios. I'm an idiot. Marisol scrambled to the relative calm of Liz's and Thea's position.

"Where did you last see Sarah?" Liz's voice startled Thea.

Marisol gestured in the direction of the heights. The glow in Liz's eyes dimmed. An image of Sarah racing toward a clump of archers flickered through Thea's mind.

"Jesus," Liz rasped. "What about the rest of them?"

"Where's Kait?" Thea demanded. "And Free?"

"Where Roarke was headed," Marisol said.

"Wherever that was," Liz muttered. "First things first. We need to see what we're doing. Marisol, I want you to call up a breeze to suck this smoke into the Gap. Something gentle, but constant."

"What gap?" Marisol forced through clattering teeth. Her face was ashen, her eyes wild.

Liz clasped Marisol's wrists. "Don't. You're safe now." Thea doubted it, but the truth would only scare Marisol more.

"Ssssh. Look at me. Look at me," Liz said. Marisol stared into Liz's eyes. Thea felt Liz mentally stroke Marisol's jangled nerves. "That's good, sweetie. Stay with me now. We need you. The girls need you." The blue fire in Liz's eyes blazed as she released one of Marisol's arms and gestured to a point somewhat to Marisol's left. "There. That's Elsee Gap. Send the smoke there."

Blue hazed over Marisol's eyes. "I see it."

"Keep it in your mind, and the wind will find it," Liz said. "Can you do it?"

"Try and stop me," Marisol replied.

Fear knifed through Thea's head, through her heart. She staggered and would've fallen if Marisol and Liz hadn't caught her.

Free. Kait. They're in trouble.

"What's wrong with Thea?" Marisol asked. "Did she get hit?"

"Thea!" Kait's voice screamed through the smoke. "We need you!"

Liz started. A smoke-blurred vision of Kait and the internal echo of Roarke howling another banshee battle cry nearly knocked her down. Liz felt Thea's muscles tense. Thea's power exploded over Liz's senses, a force almost too primal to be called magic. Liz yanked Marisol's hands away from Thea.

Thea cried Kait's name. Her call ended in a roar. A tawny cat, as large as a Shetland pony stood in Thea's place. Two twelve-inch fangs curved over the cat's front lip. The saber-toothed tiger roared again and leapt through the smoke.

Marisol moaned. "What was that thing?"

Marisol's panic felt like acid rising in Liz's throat. She fought Marisol's terror like it was her own, because linked mind and body as they were, it would be Liz's panic if Liz didn't stop it now. *Thea went to help Kait and Free*, Liz's mind voice plowed over Marisol's fear. *Thea's a shifter. Remember Al's office? She's safer fighting as a killer cat.*

"I, I guess," Marisol said aloud. "Shouldn't we go help her?"

"No," Liz said. "We can do more good here by getting rid of the smoke."

Marisol acquiesced to Liz's will. But her fear continued to bubble under the heavy lid of Liz's pragmatism. Marisol needed to be distracted, forced into action. Otherwise, she'd collapse. Liz scanned the vicinity as she pulled Marisol back from the closest scuffle.

Scuffle? Yeah, right. Liz's mind flinched as a tall man not far from her position sliced two brigands practically in half with one blow of his sword. The silhouette and heat signature of his armor matched those of the pikemen wearing Alfred's emblem. A smaller, girlish figure huddled at the man's back was oblivious to a second pair of men sneaking up behind her.

Ember. Gareth. And they were in trouble.

Liz opened her mouth to shout a warning when a thought ran through her mind. *The only difference between water and steam lay in the speed of their molecules.* Liz raised a hand.

One of the would-be attackers managed to scream before his sweat and blood boiled him where he stood. The other simply died, a froth of blood fizzing from his eyes and bubbling through the joints of his armor. Gareth hauled Ember away before she had time to see what happened. Liz and Marisol caught up with them in one of the erratic patches of clear air.

"Gareth, stop! It's me, Liz. And Marisol."

Despite the shadow of beard and helmet, Gareth's lips looked white and thin. What Liz could see of his eyes looked a little crazed.

"Thank you, Lady. If it hadn't been for you…" Gareth clutched Ember tight to his side.

"You're welcome" Liz said. "Gareth, Marisol and I want to clear the smoke. It'll give the defenders some breathing room while Jagger and Roarke get to work. Will you protect us while we raise the wind?"

"Of course he will," Ember said. "My dad's the best knight in all of Domain."

Gareth winced. He knelt and took his daughter's face between both hands. "You have to stay right next to Liz and Marisol, Ember. Promise me you won't leave them."

"I promise." Ember kissed her father's bearded cheek.

Marisol straightened her shoulders. "I give you my word we'll keep your daughter safe. With our lives, if need be."

Wonder dawned in Gareth's eyes. He nodded.

Thank God, Liz thought. *Focusing on keeping Ember safe is exactly what Marisol needs.*

Liz pulled off one of her gloves and handed it to Ember. "There's a chance we'll get lost in the spell. If it looks like we're losing control of what we're doing, hit me hard in the face. It's the only way to break the spell."

"I understand." Ember clutched Liz's glove to her chest. "I won't let you down, Liz." Gareth patted Ember's back and took up a defensive position.

Losing ourselves in the spell? Liz, what are you talking about?

Consider it a dress rehearsal for taking down a demon, Liz murmured in Marisol's mind.

What!

Liz grabbed Marisol's hands and poured the memory of the link she'd formed with Thea, Roarke and Jagger straight into Marisol's brain. Surprisingly enough, Marisol didn't freak out.

Now, Liz urged. *Use your magic.*

Liz felt Marisol's power grow from something as small and as simple to shape as a puff of breath. The soft breath teased their faces and flowed around their heads. The circle of breeze widened in a clockwise spiral. Liz smiled. She almost didn't believe how easy it could be to work with her pod mate. Marisol's power was movement in its most basic form, and Liz drove it as easily as a car. Outward the breezes spiraled. The poisonous smoke retreated before them.

Marisol's confidence swelled with the wind. When Liz was sure Marisol had matters well in hand, she detached her mind from their link.

Time to gather the flock. Liz searched for the rest of her friends.

About fifteen yards away, Anna and Pandora clutched each other's hands. They seemed to be chanting something useful, because people dropped like swatted flies as soon as they got too close. Unfortunately, not all of the people were bad guys. Some of the Keep's soldiers lay in the pile too. Whatever Anna and Pandora were up to, it didn't affect either Brigid or Donatien. Brigid fought in front of her sisters, wielding her staff with lethal precision. Brigid was fighting well, but Liz could tell she was tiring.

Brigid, I need you to bring Anna and Pandora to me.

Liz! Thank God you're here. Give me your position and we'll be there as soon as I can get Anna's attention. Don will cover our backs.

Liz's mental gaze shifted to Donatien. The tall knight circled Brigid, Anna and Pandora like an armored angel of death. He hacked, slashed, stabbed and clubbed brigands with the unnatural gusto of a character in a martial arts movie. Liz blinked. Real people couldn't move that fast, that precisely, without fast-action camerawork

Brigid grabbed the Chosen's arm and pointed in Liz's direction. Donatien nodded.

Three down. Liz remembered Kait's desperate call. Her view moved to the south. There, where the mud of the defenders' position met a carpet of burnt thorns, Kait held the shoulders of a visibly frightened Free. The imprint of a hand slowly faded from Free's face. Free touched her cheek, her eyes wide and staring. Kait shook her until Free's head rocked on her shoulders.

Kait's shock tactics worked. Free shuddered and her magic shimmered downward to the thorns. Liz got the impression of busy little fingers trying to unknot something. Liz reached for Free to lend her magic, but her offer bounced off Free's terror.

What else was new? Liz redirected her thoughts to Kait. *Are you all right?*

Liz? Where are you?

About fifty yards north of you. I need you to get Free to me. Can you do that?

I can try. Kait's mind voice was dubious. *Free's freaking out. She nearly got us killed.*

I know, sweetie. Drag her if you have to, but get yourselves back here.

Gotcha.

Slightly forward of Kait and Free, Roarke and a dozen saber-toothed tigers savaged anything that came close. No, one tiger Thea and maybe a dozen copy cats. Liz recognized the signature of Jagger's magic. The extra cats behaved like computer-generated holograms, mimicking Thea's movements in a random pattern. But that didn't make any sense in the quasi-medieval world of Domain. Liz turned to Jagger as if she'd known where he was all along.

The black-armored mage fought at Al's side. Jagger's war hammer and Al's sword rose and fell in practiced rhythm. Jagger's magic coated the guards closest to him, projecting the protection of their armor outward. The extra shielding didn't hamper the soldiers' movements, but enemy weapons skittered away from them without ever striking home. Jagger's group appeared to be gaining ground, moving into an attack formation.

Jagger.

Yes, lady?

I need Thea.

Done.

Liz took a deep breath and closed down her mental "camera". Now to see if Marisol's wind had helped. Breathing was easier, and everyone was seeing better—including the bad guys. The group of two women, one girl and one tired man was a highly visible target. Liz tightened her hand- and mind-hold on Marisol to keep them both calm.

Hawke and Conlan have to be around here somewhere.

ဆာလ

"Kaltar, appear!"

Kaltar's sweating face appeared in Deryk's scrying bowl. Deryk hated wasting his magic on communicating with lackeys, but since he'd sent the scry wizard away, it was necessary.

"Bring your men in from the east," Deryk ordered. "Front them with a dozen of your best marksmen. Close to within sixty feet of where the bushes were and have the marksmen shoot fire arrows at Alfred's troops. Capture the women I'm about to show you. Afterward, kill anything still moving."

Kaltar saluted.

Deryk broke the scry spell as soon as the final images of a black-haired woman in leathers and a short-haired blonde in breeches crossed the scrying bowl. Chest heaving with the exertion of fighting on too many magical fronts at once, Deryk rolled away from the window. His golden snake lay hot as a slaver's brand over his throat.

His situation had not improved. Theron's and the sorceress's frantic picking at Deryk's burn spell itched like the bite of a thousand ants. Vallenius's spell had effectively doused Deryk's hedge wizards like water on a candle. A tall female berserker chopped large swaths of his archers into bloody bits. Another female warrior effectively kept his hired killers away from the sorceress and the blonde. And now Jagger had landed like a giant Thrallish hill vulture on fresh carrion.

But with two more women. Powerful, powerful women.

Roarke had landed too. Deryk smiled as he stroked his golden snake and welcomed the heat burning his palm.

"More power," Deryk whispered. "More power, and it's all for me."

Chapter Thirty-Three

The edge of Gareth's sword caught in the jawbone of his foe. It took him a heartbeat too long to yank it—and most of the man's face—free. The delay allowed a second brigand to charge Liz, Marisol and Ember. Liz shaped the word "ferret" in her mind. But Ember's grab at her waist and Marisol's terrified shriek in her mind stole Liz's breath. The brigand's sword plummeted toward Liz's helmet.

The brigand's arms and head disappeared. Steaming blood erupted from the standing corpse drenching the three females. Ember howled. Marisol was working up to another good mental scream when Liz forcibly broke the link between them. An ax-wielding giant wearing what looked like fifty pounds of blood-washed steel plate knocked the mercenary's corpse aside. Magic pulsed through Liz's hand. She readied herself to burn the giant from the inside out.

"Liz, don't!" the giant roared, throwing back his visor. "It's Hawke. You called me!"

Restrained power sizzled over Liz's ungloved hand as a small group of fighters in dented blue and silver armor surrounded Liz and her companions.

"Thank Reyah," Gareth said fervently. He turned to his daughter. "Are you all right?"

Ember grimaced as she rubbed blood from her face. "I think so." She looked at her red-tipped fingers and started to retch. When she finished, Marisol gathered the young girl in her arms and wiped away her tears.

"Looks like I arrived just in time," Hawke said.

"Thanks. Sorry I didn't recognize the packaging—the armor," Liz explained.

"Nice job in stopping your magic."

Liz scratched under the mesh covering her neck. God, but she couldn't wait to take her armor off. "Hawke, could you help me retrieve Sarah?"

"Sure. I have a feeling—Shit!"

Hawke's left hand shot toward the heavens as if he expected to raise a magic shield. Liz whirled and aimed her power where Hawke pointed. Volley after volley of flaming arrows slammed into something akin to a force field. The arrows popped like camera flashes and crumbled into ash.

"Damn, you're good," Hawke said. "Think you could do something to those guys over there?"

Liz's magical senses, the ones which allowed her to perceive heat and movement beyond her normal vision, detected a press of bodies rushing down the hills from the east. "The guys running toward us hell bent for leather? I could boil them."

Hawke squinted at another group of armored men moving on an interception course. "Never mind. Conlan can handle them. Let's get Sarah."

ℰℛ

From her hilltop vantage point, Lydia surveyed the plain. She drew in a ragged breath. Kaltar, her Kaltar, was fighting Hamilton Fane. *No*, Lydia corrected herself, *Kaltar's fighting the real Conlan. But I bet the muscleman down there is just like that lamebrain Fane.* Kaltar's men circled the combatants.

Lydia frowned. A gust of wind roared across the plain. The red and blue smoky haze blew away. The flames trying to consume the brambles flickered, turned blue and died.

"What the hell?" Lydia asked.

Shouts rang out as the charred brambles suddenly turned green. Branches zoomed upward and wound around two of Kaltar's men. Another killer branch shot out from one of the bushes. It wrapped around a third outlaw's throat, thorns cutting deep into his neck. Blood gushed from the wounds. The rest of Kaltar's men ran.

"Get back there and help him, you sorry bastards!" Lydia shouted. The wind blew her voice away.

Meanwhile, Kaltar pressed Conlan hard, trying to pummel the Vanyr into submission. Much to Lydia's annoyance, instead of falling down and letting Kaltar chop him into mincemeat, Conlan parried Kaltar's blows and stayed on his feet. Lydia flexed her fingers. *I wonder if I can turn Conlan into a chicken from here.* Lydia licked her lips. *I bet he'd taste great fricasseed.*

313

Kaltar and Conlan met in brief, vicious flurries of swordplay. They played hide and seek between mounds of brambles and jabbed at each other through the breaks in the thorns. Lydia jigged from foot to foot. How could she get a straight shot at Conlan if the dolt refused to stand still?

Kaltar sidled to Conlan's left, trying catch Conlan on what should've been the right-handed Vanyr's weaker side. But Kaltar tripped over one of the bodies littering the field and landed flat on his back. Conlan's blade speared Kaltar's heart.

හ්ශ

An enraged screech pierced Val's eardrums. A crimson shape rose from one of the hilltops to the southeast and soared toward the battlefield, wings flapping mightily. The shrieks of the strange bird grew louder as it closed in on the defenders' position. Val shaded his eyes with one hand, trying to figure out what flew toward him.

Was it a bird? Was it something magical? Had Deryk called a giant Thropter from the deserts of Hiawat to wreak havoc? The weird avian drew nearer.

Val couldn't believe what he saw.

The flying woman's shrieks modulated into words. "You're going to pay for killing Kaltar, you sorry bastards! Do you hear me? I'm going to rip out your guts and your hearts and your lungs and your livers and…"

It was Megeara. The Demon Witch soared over the field, skinny arms beating the air and feet pedaling even faster behind. A muddy purple boot sailed through the air, narrowly missing Val's head. She reminded the stunned wizard of a tattered crimson and black pennant swept by a gale force wind.

"I've never seen anyone fly before. I didn't think it could be done."

At the edge of Val's line of sight, Jagger cursed and pointed toward Megeara. A few yards away, one of Alfred's guards raised his hand in concert with Jagger. Power flowed outwards from the two men, power so impossibly strong the surge nearly knocked Val off his feet. A dome, clearly visible to Val's magical senses, stretched thirty feet high and another ten feet beyond Frieda's thorn bush barrier.

Megeara slammed into the top of the dome, spun around once on her red-robed butt and slid down the side of the shield, shrieking curses all the way. A thud at the western edge of the dome announced her landing. The soldier removed his sallet, pushed a handful of reddish curls off his forehead and snickered.

Val's mouth hung open in amazement and envy. Who was this man who wielded so much power so easily?

"Can you hold it?" Jagger asked the soldier.

"Piece of cake," the soldier answered. "Especially since your girlfriend's rounded up most of the women. I've got them penned behind a protective barrier inside the big dome. Why don't you go get Cat Girl? I'll take care of things in here."

Jagger nodded and Ported.

Val took a step toward the soldier. "Who? How?" The soldier turned his head.

"Kalin's balls," Val gasped, staring into a mirror image of his own face. *No wait,* Val thought in confusion. *My eyes are plain old blue, not gold ringed in blue.*

The world exploded into a million razor sharp lights. Val tumbled to the ground. Blood from a deep cut at his hairline poured down his face. Above him, a brigand grinned. The brigand raised his club for another blow to Val's head. Violet blue light flashed. The brigand blinked and touched one trembling finger to a fist-sized hole in the middle of his chest. Wisps of smoke trickled from the hole. The outlaw toppled over.

Val's eyelids fluttered as the mercenary's body thumped to the ground next to his. Through a whirling kaleidoscope of pain and light Val heard a voice say, "Take a break, youngling, I need to borrow your shape for a while."

I hope he does better as me than I did, Val thought as he fell into the comforting black hole of unconsciousness.

ॐ

A bandit staggered through one of Jagger's imaginary cats, all but shredded by the real Thea's claws. He swung his sword with all his dying strength in one final arc. The notched blade slashed through the illusion and buried itself in Thea's shoulder. Her roar tore the heavens as she crumpled over her right foreleg.

Roarke's sense of self-preservation and the fading link with Thea snapped at the same instant. In the next, Roarke found himself standing in front of her, determined to kill as many of her enemies as possible before they were overrun.

The cold ocean of Jagger's magic washed over Roarke and poured over the numberless enemies facing the Vanyr swordmaster. Wherever Jagger's magic touched Deryk's bandits, their armor groaned like winches in a blizzard. Ice rimed the outlaws' faces and salted their armor, freezing them where they stood. Alfred and some of his men fell into position around Roarke and the wounded Thea.

"She's hurt," Roarke yelled to Jagger. "Do something!"

Jagger nodded and swept the giant, long-toothed cat—a cat fully as big as a pony and much more solidly built—into his arms like she weighed no more than a kitten. Mind mage and cat vanished into a Portal.

Roarke's mouth went dry with envy. Was there no end to the bastard's magic?

Alfred punched Roarke on the shoulder. "Look alive, Vanyr!"

Roarke raised his sword as another group of bandits ran toward him. One of these days, he promised himself, he was going to kill Alfred, too.

⁗

Just my luck, Thea thought, *I don't get to see the white light when I die. I get the heart of darkness.*

Actually, it's the inside of a Portal, and you're far from dead, Jagger's mind voice assured her.

Thea realized she didn't feel too bad. She rubbed her arm and found it smooth and whole, if a little sticky. That was wrong somehow. Thea's thoughts puzzled over images of hardened plastic armor and stiff fur.

Armor immediately formed under her fingers. *You needed to heal,* Jagger told her. *Easier done without armor.*

Oh. Um, thanks.

With measured slowness, more images surfaced in Thea's mind: distant pictures of a battle—her battle, her friends' battle. Thea's sense of well-being and pleasure faded, but slowly enough for Thea to accept the loss. Jagger pressed her head into the hollow of his shoulder like a parent comforting a child. The smooth, sculpted plates of his armor shifted and realigned themselves to accommodate her head. An unlikely fragrance somewhere between the scent of crushed rose leaves and freshly cut hay perfumed the closed space.

Megeara has taken the field. Jagger fed the vision to Thea's mind. *Liz and Hawke are retrieving Sarah. You need to prepare the rest of your sisters to link.*

Has Megeara called a demon? Thea's mind shaped the question as Jagger set her feet on whatever passed for the floor on the inside of a Portal.

Not yet.

What about the rest of the girls? Have they got protection?

An abundance of it. A shade of Jagger's earlier humor returned. *They're behind a magical shield inside a protective dome. They're safe—as long as they stay inside the barriers.*

An instant later Thea, back in full Mutant Turtle gear, stood behind Kait and Marisol in a small area of the plain clear of both smoke and brigands. Both women pounded the iridescent air in front of them.

"Let me out of here! I've got to get to Liz," Marisol hollered. "She *needs* me!"

"Val, how could you do this to me after all I did to help you?" Kait shrieked. "You...you...you Theron clone!"

A few feet beyond Kait and Marisol, Val paused in mid-stride. One ruddy gold eyebrow lifted over a pair of startling gold-flecked, brandy-colored eyes rimmed in blue.

Wait a minute, Thea thought, *aren't Val's eyes plain old ordinary blue? Come to think of it, Val doesn't walk like that either.*

"Marisol and Kait, will you please shut the hell up?" Brigid's demand broke Thea's train of thought. Brigid prodded the shimmering barrier with her staff. "Hawke's with Liz. She'll be fine, and he doesn't need any more people to worry about."

"Damn straight," Anna chimed in. "Hey! Thea's here!"

"Thea!" Kait squealed. Thea's breath whooshed out as Kait's arms locked around her chest.

Jagger appeared at Val's side. "It's about time you got your lazy ass back here," Val said. He cocked his head at the magical cage. "Do you have any idea how loud they are? Where's the other two?"

No, no, Thea thought as Anna charged up and hugged her too. *That's wrong. Val's talking to Jagger like an equal. That's not the Val I met back at the Keep.*

"Thea!" Marisol cried in time with Anna.

"You're okay!" Pandora announced, her blonde head bouncing in and out of Thea's field of vision. "Oh man, where'd you get the cool armor? The junk Theron stuck on us ain't nowhere as rocking as your stuff."

Thea looked at Pandora bouncing up and down like a jumping bean and waited for it. It didn't take long. Pandora stumbled, falling backwards into a wide-eyed, blood-covered Ember. Brigid righted them both. She gave Thea a crooked smile.

"With the exception of Liz and Sarah, the gang's all here. Do you know why Liz wanted us all together?" Brigid asked.

"Unfortunately, I do."

℘℃

Marisol's controlled whirlwind hadn't yet reached the mound of raw earth and tumbled boulders where Liz had glimpsed Sarah's dark silhouette. Liz jumped when Sarah suddenly cawed a ragged imitation of a television Amazon's battle cry. Sarah leapt into a nest of four smoke-shadowed archers. The doomed archers shot Sarah at point blank range. Sarah stabbed or strangled every one of them. She didn't seem to care about the feathered shafts protruding from the gaps in her armor.

Sarah cawed again as she rose, phoenix-like, from the carnage of her own making. She was *laughing*.

"Sarah!" Liz shouted, sending forth a mental call at the same time.

A foot-long knife shot from Sarah's right hand, pinwheeling into the place where Hawke's head would have been if Hawke hadn't moved faster. A second, smaller blade struck Liz over the heart, knocking her flat and breathless. Liz might have been knocked unconscious, too, if it hadn't been for the shock-absorbing properties of her helmet. The fall left Liz dazed. Everything hurt, especially inhaling.

Hawke caught Sarah in a flying tackle before she could attack Liz. They tumbled to the ground. Sarah kicked and gouged and stabbed the joints between the metal plates covering Hawke's left shoulder with a short, wide-bladed knife.

"I'll kill you. I'll kill you. I'll kill you," Sarah panted in time with her knife work.

"For Reyah's sake, Liz, do something! Get into her mind!" Hawke tried to wrestle the knife out of Sarah's hands. The realization Sarah was only a few inches shorter than he was struck Liz like another knife.

Get into her mind? Ha! The madwoman doesn't have one. Nothing I can reach, at any rate. Liz scrambled for a suitable rock. No, she didn't know how hard to hit. Liz focused on the hilt of the knife.

Sarah yelped. Her fingers jerked away from the knife's smoldering leather grip. The knife dangled between two overlapping plates of Hawke's armor like a parody of a lady's favor. It fell to the ground on a stream of blood. Hawke grabbed her arms and held them above her head. His weight augmented by all his armor should've been enough to immobilize her. It didn't. Sarah writhed beneath the armored giant.

"Liz, I can't hold her much longer."

Liz knelt beside Sarah's head. Sarah tried to bite her. Liz backhanded Sarah with her armored hand. She reached between the pieces of Sarah's armor to find the large artery in the crazed woman's neck. Liz pressed down hard. After what seemed like a very long time, Sarah went limp.

Hawke raised himself from Sarah's inert form. "You can take your hand away from her neck now."

He pried off his helmet and shook his head. Sweat flicked off the ends of his hair and pattered against Sarah's armor. "She'll revive in a few minutes, if none of Deryk's bastards find us first. Is there any way you can reach her now? At the Keep, they said you were a mind mage like Jagger."

"But untrained." Liz brushed the damp tangle of Sarah's hair away from her face. "Normally, I can talk to my friends mind to mind, but I couldn't reach her. I tried. I'm trying now."

"Can you Port?"

"No. About the only things I can do reliably are boil men alive, aim Marisol's weather blasts and turn people into small mammals called ferrets."

Hawke snickered. "An embarrassment of riches." With surprising ease for someone encumbered by steel-encased fingers, he frisked Sarah for hidden weapons and bundled what he found with the tail of her whip.

"Funny, I thought she'd have more. Here." Hawke handed the bundle to Liz. He reseated his helmet. "We should get those arrows out of her before she wakes up. Sarah doesn't handle pain well."

ഇരുജ

"Let me in, dammit!" Lydia pounded the translucent blue wall that kept her from incinerating the goody-goodies who'd killed Kaltar. She wanted to destroy them all. Not only Conlan but the whole stinking lot of them. It didn't matter that Lydia wasn't sure who "they" were. All she knew was Kaltar was dead and someone was going to pay. Preferably with buckets of blood and every inch of skin she could scratch off their miserable hides. Lydia ran a few feet further along the wall and beat her fists against the barrier. "I said let me in!"

The harder she hit, the tighter she clenched her fists, digging her nails into her palms until they bled. The cuts didn't register until Lydia saw her bloody fist prints hanging in blue air. "Ow!"

Lydia leaned against the barrier, wincing and huffing and ready to drop from sheer exhaustion. *I'll find a hole. Somewhere.* When her breath finally caught up with her, Lydia yanked off her remaining boot, hoisted her tattered skirts and started jogging.

Dodging arrows, dead bodies and crazed men intent on chopping each other to bits wasn't easy, but Lydia was determined to find a way in. Every so often she stopped and clawed the almost transparent wall with her blood-tipped nails or kicked it with her bare feet. An unpleasant fact began to filter through Lydia's enflamed little brain. There was no way in.

As she closed in on her starting point, Lydia caught sight of Kevin Shertz—or rather, Alfred's magical brat Vallenius—talking to a group of women.

I wonder if this little twerp plays with himself like Kevvy Wevvy does?

A hand grasped Lydia's ankle. Without thinking, she pointed her finger. The mercenary's groan ended in a sizzle as a bolt of green lightning reduced him to a puff of bacon-scented smoke. Lydia's eyes narrowed. *Cool. Something new.* She stared at her hand. Maybe she could blast her way through the barrier. Flexing her fingers, she took a deep breath and gave it all she had.

Green lightning shot toward the wall. The brat wizard raised an eyebrow. Lydia's bolt splattered like a rotten egg and fizzled out.

"Well shit," Lydia growled. The curly-haired bastard grinned and blew her a kiss.

"That does it. No more Ms. Nice Guy." Lydia straightened her gown and cleared her throat. Lifting her arms into the air, she bellowed,

Cauldron bubble

And plot thicken

Upon their heads

…a plague of chickens!

Power crackled from Lydia's hands into the sky. Thunder rumbled once, twice. Lydia realized it wasn't thunder but the sound of a thousand chickens cackling at the top of their lungs as they dropped from the sky onto the plain. Feathers and chicken shit filled the air, along with hundreds upon hundreds of distraught fowls attacking anything that moved.

Lydia kicked a chicken from under her foot.

"Okay—it wasn't Shakespeare. At least it rhymed."

ഇരുള

"What the hell?" Liz and Hawke swore as a storm of chickens rained over the beleaguered fighters surrounding the blue dome.

Sarah, flopped over Hawke's shoulder like the proverbial sack of potatoes, kicked her boot against his armored thigh. "Put me down already. I'm not going to kill anything else today. Promise."

Liz pursed her lips in a silent whistle. "Man. This sucks. What I wouldn't give to have a mass ferret happen right about now."

The heavens squeaked.

Air bubbles burst with audible pops throughout the fowl swarm. Chickens screamed and tried to take flight. Some of the chickens succeeded in hopping on the nearest human shoulder or arm before the ferrets attacked. Wedge-shaped jaws closed over chicken necks and legs and wing joints, and more than a few human appendages too. Lithe, furred bodies began thrashing.

Fighters jumped and squawked. Fur, feathers, blood and waste rose heavenward, thicker than the smoke Marisol had worked so hard to dispel.

"Got any more bright ideas?" Hawke asked.

ഇരുള

Lydia sneezed. And sneezed. And sneezed again. Batting a feathered hank of hair from her face, she glared around the battlefield. Someone had called up an army of ferrets against her chickens. Someone directly, personally had interfered with her magic. A corner of Lydia's mouth lifted in a silent snarl. The whole damn day had been nothing but one stinking disaster after another.

"And I thought producers were a pain in the ass."

There had to be a way to salvage the situation. Lydia studied the barrier. No magic was getting in, but nothing seemed to be coming out either. A ferret attached itself to a trailing end of her gown, growling and worrying at the tattered spandex.

Lydia picked up the disgusting creature by the back of its neck and flung it against the barrier. The ferret landed with an outraged yip and a frantic clack of claws.

If no magic was coming out, whoever created the ferrets must be somewhere outside. She tried to spot someone using magic. The stinking fur and feather blizzard made it hard for her to see two feet in front of her nose, much less pick out one specific magic user on a battlefield littered with freaks.

Lydia closed her eyes. "Dammit, I wish I could see over the top of this mess!"

A cool breeze brushed Lydia's face. She opened her eyes and bent her head. Her bare feet dangled a good twenty feet from the ground. She grinned. "I'm getting better at this levitation stuff."

Her view unimpeded by fur, feathers or briar, Lydia took a gulp of clean air. She stole a glance at her dead lover's final resting place. Kaltar's body no longer sprawled amid the corpses and thorns. Had someone taken Kaltar's corpse as a trophy? Lydia would kill them. She would pound their mangy hides to silly putty with her high-heeled boots. Whenever she found her shoes again.

She searched the plain. Who'd stolen her lover's body? She glanced inside the barrier. The brat wizard and the seven women didn't have Kaltar. Neither did Conlan or the guy in black armor directing a dozen soldiers wearing blue and silver armor.

Lydia drifted closer to the welter of feathers and fur. She squinted through the mayhem for Kaltar's distinctive leather and studs. She couldn't find any trace of him. Someone had to have destroyed Kaltar's body! There was no other explanation. Lydia looked for someone on whom she could vent her all-consuming rage.

A glint of light caught Lydia's eye. A tall blood-splashed suit of armor with a warrior bitch slung over one shoulder marched double-time toward the barrier. A second person, short and dressed like some kind of sci-fi Stormtrooper, trotted to keep up with the knight's long strides. Every so often, the short one turned her head as if checking the trail behind them. Yes, Lydia realized, the Stormtrooper was definitely a "her". The short person moved like a girl.

"Come to mama, bitch," Lydia said.

౫)◑

"Wait a minute," Liz said. "I feel something."

"Dammit, Liz," Hawke wheezed, "you and Sarah need to get behind the barrier."

Liz shook her head, stilling Hawke with one raised hand. A presence, quite clear and naggingly familiar buzzed in her brain. Somewhere, someone...she lifted her eyes toward the red-robed scarecrow hovering over the miasma of feathers, fur and lingering smoke.

"Oh crap!" Hawke exclaimed. "There's Megeara. Come on, Liz. You've got to get behind the shields."

So that's Megeara. She looks exactly like Lydia. Liz blinked. *Wait a minute. She feels exactly like Lydia…oh shit.*

"The Hambone got translated too!"

₧ʘ

Lydia watched the knight point in her direction. He grabbed the short Stormtrooper's arm. A blue glow lit the Stormtrooper's mask.

"Blue magic, eh? You must be one of Reyah's goody-goodies. You'll do." Raising her hands, Lydia called upon her power. While her magic might not be very good against barriers, it worked wonderfully well on humans. Look at the asshole she'd obliterated moments before. "It's about time I get to kick some good guy ass."

Again the unearthly blue glow lit the eye slots of the Stormtrooper's mask. The short woman raised one small, bare hand. Lydia's green fire slammed into a wall of blue fireworks and ricocheted back to its source.

"Well, shit," Lydia griped. Green flames engulfed her.

Pain, more pain than she'd ever felt in her life clawed her inside out. Lydia dropped to the ground screaming. Every part of her body felt as if it were covered in burning oil. She writhed on the ground and howled. Finally, the fiery agony receded. She shuddered through the last few tremors of remembered pain and fear.

"She hurt me. She used my own power to burn me." Gathering the remnants of her strength, Lydia rolled to her knees.

Ten thin wisps of smoke caressed her face. Lydia looked at her hands. Ten fingers, once tipped with bright crimson nails, splayed in the mud of the plain. Ten lovely long fingernails, once razor sharp and ready to do damage now wept smoke from their charred and melted ends. Lydia surged to her feet, all pain forgotten.

"You bloody, rotten, ugly *bitch*! You melted my fingernails!"

₧ʘ

Liz fought Hawke's grip on her arm. "Don't you understand, she's not Megeara! She's an actress! If we take her now she won't be able to call a demon!"

"It's Lydia?" Sarah shouted. "Put me down, you oversized jerk! I can take her!"

"You can *not*!" Hawke used his body to press Liz into the side of the sparkling blue dome, squeezing the breath out of her lungs. "If you and Sarah link now, you'll get caught in Megeara's magic!"

"What are you talking about?" Sarah shrieked, straining and wriggling like a hooked shark. Hawke had her legs trapped against the barrier. But her arms were free, and she hit everything within reach. "I don't need magic to kick Lydia's ass!"

Liz didn't have enough air to speak, much less use her command voice. She tried mind shouting at Hawke. *Put me down!* But the words had no effect. She tried kneeing him in his armored groin.

"Now, Jagger!" Hawke roared. "I need that opening now!"

The wall behind her melted, sucking Liz and Sarah through. For an instant it was like being submerged in warm water. When she came out the other side Lydia was howling,

> *Eye of newt and toe of hog,*
>
> *Wool of bat and London Fog,*
>
> *Lizard's leg and knightly shields,*
>
> *Crusader swords and Mrs. Fields,*
>
> *Bourbon, wine and Mountain Dew,*
>
> *Dragon's teeth and Motley Crue,*
>
> *An evil spell I now demand,*
>
> *By hatred, spite and coward's hand,*
>
> *A sight to blast a wizard's eyes,*
>
> *I command thee, Demon, to arise!*

"Bloody hell." Val walked up, cold-cocked Sarah and hoisted her over his shoulder.

Hawke gaped at the wizard. He started to laugh.

"Don't just lie there on your keister." Val grabbed Liz with his free hand. "We've got to get them to the other women."

Chapter Thirty-Four

Like a geyser from hell Lydia's demon spewed from the hillside. It wasn't so much the demon stood as tall as a six story building or wolfed down people like cocktail wieners. In a weird way, Thea rather expected that, even though this was her first real-time demon experience. No, it was the way pieces of animals, human limbs and features appeared, disappeared, then reappeared elsewhere on the demon's amorphous body. Thea shuddered. The demon writhed and morphed like a high speed CGI program. Only there weren't any computers in Domain.

"We have to link now, or we're going to die," Liz said.

Thea couldn't argue with her. All their choices flushed down the tubes the minute Megeara set her monster loose on the battlefield. Val cursed Megeara for not binding the demon to her or anyone else's command. But it was like cursing the sun for setting. You still had to deal with the dark. Only in this case, it was the biggest, blackest, scariest dark of Thea's life. Thea was grateful for the protective wall of magic power that kept the nine Daughters of Reyah and Ember relatively safe.

Outside the sparkling barrier, Alfred, a pitiful handful of soldiers and four of Reyah's Chosen knights formed a ragged line between the barrier containing the women and a larger blue dome created to shield the soldiers from the direct effects of Megeara's magic. The goddess Reyah's sons—Conlan, Hawke, Theron, Roarke and Jagger—and the Keep's Chosen wizard, Vallenius—ranged outside the second magical perimeter. Jagger, the most powerful mage among them, couldn't promise how much longer they could protect the women, even if they gave their immortal lives to the cause.

"You explained to them how the link works—and the dangers?" Liz asked Thea.

Seven women nodded in agreement to Thea's "Yes."

"It's not bad at all," Marisol assured them. "Liz and I linked to disperse the smoke. It was like sharing a hot tub with a friend."

"Marisol's right," Thea said. Actually, a true link went deeper, but why complicate things now? Thea extended her hands to Kait and Free. "Let's do it."

"Um, Liz, hey." Sarah backed away from the group. The former lawyer's shoulders pressed against the magical barrier surrounding them. "We never did anything like this in our fan fiction, and you can't make me do it now."

Liz said, "Sarah, this is nothing like our fanfic. The link won't hurt you, and we've got to stop Megeara's demon. It's a walking nuclear bomb getting ready to explode."

"Let the Vanyr handle it. I'm not letting you in my head! You don't have any right!"

Jagger, please, get Ember out of here. Now.

Liz's mental call rang in Thea's mind even as Liz's physical voice tried to persuade Sarah to see reason. But Liz didn't expect reason to work. Liz's memories of Sarah's battlefield rampage flowed through Thea's mind. A deep regret threaded Liz's visions as she clasped hands with Marisol. Liz gathered her power around her.

Thea had her own problems. Kait had taken her hand but not Free.

"No! I don't want to die!" Free screamed. "Send me back to the Keep!"

Kait's mouth thinned. She grabbed Free. "Do you want me to hit you again?"

Free shook her head.

"Take Thea's hand," Kait said. "No one can send you back to the Keep. They're all trying to stop the demon."

Free sobbed but allowed Thea to take her hand. *We're ready,* Thea told Liz, mentally crossing her fingers.

Ember vanished from the circle. The now familiar glow of magic streamed from Liz's eyes and hands, and whipped around her slender form. Brigid and Liz reached for Sarah, but Sarah struck their hands aside.

"Get away from me!" Sarah screamed. "You can't get in my head, you can't, you can't!"

The icy blue light of Liz's magic spun around the broken circle, growing faster, harder, stronger. Thea felt the weight of it press against her, almost too much for eyes and skin to bear.

Marisol cried, "Yes!" Liz poured through the open circuit afforded by the tall Hispanic woman. Liz's energy sluiced through Kait and Thea as if their material forms offered no more resistance than a curtain of gauze.

"Oh my God," Free whimpered when the magic leapt from Thea's hand to hers. Pandora, Anna and Brigid shrieked with delight.

"This is great!" Pandora yelled. "I love it!"

"Liz, stop this right now!" Sarah shouted. The intangible storm swept over her on its way back to Liz.

"We won't hurt you, Sarah." Liz's voice seemed to emanate from everywhere at once.

"Go to hell!" Sarah tried to claw through her enchanted prison. "I've heard that shit before!"

Sarah jerked to a stop, one hand lifted as if she was trying to protect herself. Brigid and Liz took Sarah's unresisting hands.

Jagger, Liz called across the mental connection she shared with Thea. *Get ready to open the dome.*

At your word, Lady.

A laser beam of blue white light shot from Marisol to Liz, pouring Marisol's essence into Liz's whirlwind. Marisol's nature bloomed in Thea's vision at the same time. Marisol was the sunlight chasing storm clouds out to sea. Wind danced over the waves, gathering strength in heat and motion until the currents soared up the hills and mountains of Domain, lifting the wings of the white hawk that was Liz.

Lizmarisol's power arced into Sarah. The lawyer moaned. Her contorted face smoothed.

Thea's inner vision perceived Sarah's essence as the tang of steel, the necessary balance to Marisol's sunlit warmth and the ice-edged clarity of Liz's power. But Thea sensed something else drifting beneath the scent of steel, something sickly sweet and…rotten? Before Thea could trace the sense to its origin, it was submerged in the sun and sea and wind of Liz and her pod. The blue-white hurricane of their combined force surged and trembled like an explosion in the making.

Now, Jagger.

Done. Luck be with you, my lady.

Thea dimly registered Donatien's alarmed shout as the top of the dome disappeared. The power of Liz's pod roared upward on a column of blue white light, while the pod's fused consciousness swarmed over Thea.

Laughter. Sorrow. Pain. Desire. Joy. AngerLongingDeterminationNeed. Lizmarisolsarah flooded Thea's eyes, mouth and nose. They sliced into the skin between Thea's fingers and bled into her pores. *Gather your powers*, they whispered. With a cry, part hawk and part berserker yell, Lizmarisolsarah leapt to the stars.

Thea reached out. Kait accepted the touch of Thea's mind easily. Free had to be tugged, but a moment later, she joined in.

My God, this is wonderful! Kait shouted in Thea's head. *I can feel you!*

Thea, I'm scared, Free cried. *Will this hurt?*

No, Free, Thea soothed. *Now hang on, because I'm going to join our consciousness.*

Taking a deep mental breath, Thea grasped the essences of her pod mates and drew them within. *Thea, please, I'm scared...you'll be fine, Free...oh, Thea, this so cool...I know, Kait, now let me show you what we need to do...yes...yes...we are...*

"What's it like? What's it like?" Pandora demanded inside and out.

Together, Theafreekait exulted. Lizmarisolsarah surged through Thea again. And again. And again.

Way cool, the part of Thea that was Kait marveled at the interlocking strands of Lizmarisolsarah's power. *Like a reverse double helix with a ribbon running through it!* The three greening spirits of Theafreekait flew upward, weaving in and out and around each other. Thea could feel the power vibrating through her bones, roaring in her ears, nearly blinding her with its brightness.

Now, Thea, Lizmarisolsarah called. *Now!*

Bright turquoise vines shot up the helix. It bound the magical energy tighter, closer, stronger. Blue green energies closed over blue white light. Lizmarisolsarah's light pressed against Theafreekait's restraints, shifting and swelling like a growing bud—or mace.

Crush that sucker, Kait chortled.

Hurry and kill it so we can go home, Free urged.

It was like guiding an avalanche with your bare hands. Thea struggled to control the magical energies making up the weapon even as she hurled its power at the demon. The "mace" smashed into the demon, splattering it to pieces.

Yes! Kait and Free cried in Thea's head.

Oh no, Thea groaned. The demon erupted from the ground and reformed, bigger than ever. Desperately Thea swung the mace again at the demon. Again their magic smashed the demon into the ground. Again it rose and reformed into another monstrosity.

Dear God. I can't kill it, Thea wailed. *Now what do I do?*

ᔥᲿ

Through the hammering pulse in his neck Roarke felt Liz calling to Sarah and Marisol, the sisters of her pod. The swelling harmonic of Liz's power reopened his link with Liz and Thea. He felt Jagger's magic too, but in a different way than he had ever experienced it before. The magic of release, of Liz's power, breathed in his mind as Jagger's power crackled like sparks of static across the mud. The magic spread under Roarke and over him, webbing him in protective energy like a fly in amber.

The demon shambled forward, a third leg gouging the mud like a multi-pronged tail. A mercenary too wounded to run slashed at the nearest clawed foot. The steel cut deep into tendon and claw. The demon yowled and brought its heel down hard on the offending mortal. Again and again the demon stamped. When the mortal stopped moving, the demon looked around for other mortals to punish.

Out of the corner of his eye, Roarke saw a large group of brigands run straight toward the demon. They kept looking over their shoulders, as if the demon was behind them instead of in front. Roarke remembered Jagger called it a "perception switch." It was the most basic of Jagger's illusions—a trick of last resort.

That was not good. If Jagger's magic failed, they might as well give up. Theron wasn't nearly as powerful as Theron liked the world to think he was. The embattled Vallenius showed more poise and power than any of them—Alfred included—had any right to expect. But Roarke wondered how much longer the boy could hold up. The young Chosen swayed as he raised his arms toward the demon.

Kalin's balls! Did the red-haired fool think his will was shield enough? Any instant now the demon would begin to feel the full corrosive effect of outer world air on the magical membrane giving it form. The pain, heightened by contact with edged steel, would soon become excruciating. The curious, hungry, intemperate, infant demon would become an unstoppable ravening force incapable of sustaining any shape long enough for it to be destroyed.

That was why magicians bound demons in shape, substance and intent. Inside his head, Roarke swore by everything he reviled. Megeara knew the magical laws that governed calling demons. Why had she done this? What had Deryk done to her mind when he revived her?

The first of Kaltar's lost men slammed into the demon's feet. The demon screamed again and stamped at them. Its left leg collapsed and oozed into its right. It stomped again and shrieked. More crazed men ran into the demon's substance. A second fanged maw opened across its belly. The new mouth's serpentine tongue lashed out and shoveled a running man inside. The man's clothes began burning before the demon's maw closed around him.

So many mouths screamed Roarke couldn't tell the sounds apart. The demon grabbed another of Kaltar's men and jammed the man's head and shoulders into its upper mouth. The demon convulsed before it released its hold on the brigand's leg. The spasm ripped the leg from its socket as easily as a glutton rending a roasted chicken. The demon hurled the still jerking leg from its hand.

Val's lips stretched wide to release what might have been a spell. The leg careened in mid-air, spinning over the dome toward Megeara.

Bright boy! Roarke crowed. *Take her down, and we might stand a chance.*

The still twitching leg struck Megeara full in the chest. She fell but wobbled to her feet. Green mage bolts flew wild from her smoking hands. She soared into the air like an arrow aimed straight for what might have been the demon's heart.

"You lousy crock of shit!" Megeara screamed. "I called you from Hell, and I can send you back!"

The demon raised a scaled arm as big as a kelan tree and batted Megeara farther and faster over the mountains than Roarke's link-augmented senses could follow.

Thea's pod roared to life. Roarke felt the power surge through his veins, swamping muscle and bone until he almost drowned in it. He gasped for air and found himself drinking all the green perfumes of spring. The blinding, overpowering strength of creation flooded the broken vessel of his magic and almost made it whole.

Almost. Only "almost". Not now or ever complete. Groaning from the weight of his loss, Roarke turned to the source and release of his pain. Blue-green columns braced the silvery jet of mind magic. Blue-green lace sheathed a blue-white bud straining to bloom. Half flower, half mace, the Daughters' weapon crashed down upon Megeara's demon.

The demon collapsed, but jetted up from under the blow like a splash of acid. Ground and bodies ignited under the splatter. Screaming, the substance of hell reassembled itself. The Daughters' mace reared back to strike again.

NO! Roarke's mind roared. *You have to surround it—bag it! Net it like a shoal of fish!* He threw every image of restraint he could think of at Thea and Liz to no avail. His mind couldn't breach their power. But he wasn't the only tactician on the field.

"Wait!" Brigid shouted. "That won't work! The demon's got no shape! Make a net!"

"Make a net! Make a net!" Anna and Pandora chanted.

"Nooooo!" the three women cried as the mace jerked toward the demon. In a rush of what Roarke could've sworn was laughter, the head of the mace erupted into a thousand spidery petals unfurling themselves like the blossom of a Paelinorian chrysanthemum. The bloom surrounded the amorphous poison of Megeara's creation and drew the demon inside itself like water up a straw.

The demon yammered. It shrieked and bellowed until Roarke felt something tear inside his head, and warm fluid trickled from the cavities of his ears. The demon's substance gathered at the base of the flower, punching and struggling against the magic imprisoning it.

The brutal cold of mountain air and the tang of fresh rosemary almost choked Roarke. The form of the flower began sparking and winking. Like the demon, the magic of the six sisters was power without material form. They needed their binders to contain it.

Roarke tried to signal Brigid, but she seemed as entranced by the magical struggle as Anna and Pandora...and Theron. Shit!

Roarke turned to Jagger, but the mind mage's arms were splayed and his feet braced like he was holding back some tremendous force. A weak chill shivered through Roarke. Restraining a tremendous force was exactly what Jagger was doing. Jagger's magic was all that kept the fighters nearest the dome from being atomized by the Daughters' power. And by himself, Jagger couldn't contain the women's magic much longer.

Val—if he still lived. Roarke waded through Jagger's magic to the last place he remembered seeing the Keep's young wizard. A muddy lump Roarke would've sworn was a corpse reared and fell upon Roarke's sword arm. Before he could react, the "corpse" yanked Roarke's arm toward Brigid. Fire hotter than the core of a volcano jetted through Roarke's arm, burned through the ends of his fingers and shot up the length of his sword straight toward Brigid.

Purple and blue fire shot from Brigid to Anna and Pandora linking them without warning or will. Waves of power rippled the earth under Roarke's feet, resonating in every bone of his body.

331

"Sorry. It won't hurt much longer," the boy promised before collapsing again.

No, the Chosen didn't quite collapse. Val pressed his body against the heaving ground as if he could keep it from quaking. Through the excruciating pain of his arm, Roarke wondered if perhaps that's exactly what the wizard was doing.

The triangle of purple light linking Anna, Brigid and Pandora reactivated the geometries of Thea's and Liz's pods. Power flowed from one triangle to another like water along a chain. Frieda's breastplate pulsed like the demon in the women's trap.

Something inside Frieda's armor needs to get out, Roarke thought dazedly. *But what?* Frieda's magic was linked to Thea. He had linked with Thea. Despite the agony of reconstructing immortal flesh, he couldn't resist trying a little magic.

The right shoulder of Frieda's cuirass unbuckled itself. A crystal the size of a hen's egg popped out. The egg spun over the linked pods, dazzling the eye with every color in the spectrum. *The demon's cage,* Roarke realized. *Now all they have to do is put it in there.*

Cold trickled down Roarke's spine. *Not now, Jagger, damn it. I was beginning to feel…*

Stupid, Roarke finished. The demon hadn't managed to kill all of Deryk's outlaws or Kaltar's bandits. The women hadn't given it enough time. Dropping his buckler and grabbing the blade of his sword with his left hand, Roarke forced magic down his right. His eardrums healed in the hurricane roar of the binders' magic.

An all-too-human war cry cut through the deep notes of Anna's binding spell. A brigand charged the prone Vallenius.

Roarke pivoted, turning the force of his entire body into the backhanded blow. His body seemed to take forever to unwind. The brigands gathering around the swordmaster moved slower still, raising their weapons too late to prevent his blade from shearing off the crown of the would-be killer's head.

Blood and brains splashed the right side of Roarke's face in double-time. The renewed din of battle spun faster, louder in his ears as Roarke recovered his balance. A wide-eyed, open-mouthed brigand with blood streaming over the stumps of his front teeth scrambled forward. He stumbled over Val. Roarke shouldered the outlaw into another brigand's knife. The move left Roarke open to a slash to his cuirass.

The new bruise was nothing. The pain of injury, the agony of healing flesh vibrated through Roarke's limbs as he raised his arms to strike and parry, butcher and maim.

Time departed for the Shadowlands, but the killing continued. Two brigands seemed to spring from the blood of each one Roarke killed. He fought on. He was not one of Reyah's killing machines, he swore bitterly to himself. Yet here he was, saving his Mother's ass and maybe—maybe if they were all very lucky, the lives of the women Reyah had tossed across the demon's—and Deryk's—path.

Not much longer, Roarke promised himself. *It couldn't be much longer.* Vallenius linked the binders. Roarke himself had handed them the perfect container for Megeara's demon. In the heat of the battle's madness, Roarke invoked the comforting memory of Anna's cantrips, the force of her oddly shaped spells.

Fine. Perfect. Why the hell isn't something happening?

Roarke plunged his sword in his next attacker's heart. The outlaw grabbed the blade as he sank to his knees and refused to let go. Using the outlaw for balance, Roarke kicked the next brigand in the gut. He smashed the man's nose into his brain when the brigand doubled-over. Roarke's blade grated against the first outlaw's sternum as Roarke yanked it free. Half of the dead man's fingers fell in the mud an instant before he did.

Panting, Roarke squinted through the sweat dripping into his eyes. The drying gore on his face pulled against his skin. He risked a deeper breath. No brigands. At least for the few yards he could see. No shouting, no screams. No sound except the hurricane wail of power at his back.

The faintest chill, the weakest echo of Roarke's own question splashed over the swordmaster's consciousness. What did Jagger want now? Roarke stole a glance over his shoulder.

Frieda's diamond egg whirled in mid-air. Its facets created coruscating rainbows like the crystal walls of the Voice's cave. Roarke narrowed his eyes against the burning color.

No! The colors were too dark for the rainbow. The howling grew louder, lashing his ears with its force. Roarke searched for Thea in the living geometry of the women's link. Like her sisters she stood with her arms stretched to the sky, her mouth frozen open as if she couldn't stop screaming.

Thea's blank eyes glowed. Kait, Frieda, Brigid, Sarah, Marisol, Pandora, even Liz screamed with her, their eyes likewise glazed and glowing.

But Anna's mouth was closed, curved in a tight little smile. Her head cocked this way and that as she contemplated the blended power of magic and demon. Anna's hands fluttered at waist level, fingering her chatelaine. Anna was supposed to close the spell. But she was as lost in the link as her sisters.

Binder! They needed a spellcaster to bind the link before it exploded! Roarke's university-trained mind had memorized the chants of the college's wizards, but his exhausted wits couldn't shape the words.

There was only one person left who could help. Theron's power resided in his binding spells. Roarke needed to find Theron. Where had he gone?

Theron stood a few feet from the circle of power. The glow from the runes on his staff formed a white-hot haze extending a hand's breadth from the polished wood. He stared at the egg. The tip of his tongue darted out and lapped the colored air.

Roarke raced over. He grabbed Theron by his doublet. Theron roared and gestured with his staff. Roarke ducked the fireball. With the sword still clenched in his hand, he punched Theron in the jaw.

Theron staggered and nearly fell. Eyes blazing purple blue, he bellowed, "You bastard! What are you doing?"

"Stop the magic!" Roarke shouted, hitting Theron again. "Break the link!"

The magic faded a little from Theron's eyes. "I can't."

Roarke hit him again. "If a Chosen wizard can break it, so can you! Break it now!"

"I can't. It is Anna's task to break it."

"She can't. She's lost in the link."

"Obviously. The women have proven unsuitable to be the Daughters of Reyah. Whether they live or die is the will of Reyah."

Roarke hit Theron again. "Break it, you son-of-a-bitch!"

"It's Reyah's will!"

Roarke pressed the tip of his sword into the skin beneath Theron's chin. "*This* is Reyah's will! Do it, or I swear I'll rend you into bloody bits of nothing."

Theron gargled. The sharp point chiseled deeper into his throat.

"Now," Roarke said.

Theron uttered a cantrip. The world stopped. The cyclone color hung suspended in space, then winked out. The women crumpled where they stood. The egg fell slowly to the ground, darkness drifting over it.

Roarke's breath, pulse and vision returned an instant later. Jagger lurched toward the egg. Roarke suspected Jagger reached it only because there was nothing and no one left in his way. Theron Ported himself to Frieda's side.

Roarke searched for Thea. Like her sisters, she lay still as death. Then her chest rose in a great shuddering gasp. *Breathing!* A fading echo of Liz's inner voice tickled Roarke's mind. Through the tatters of their link he felt Sarah begin to rouse herself. Kait he saw.

But over Kait's shoulder Roarke saw something else. Two troops of horsemen following the red banner of the Snake swept into Elsee Gap. Deryk rode at their head. The bastard must've Ported while they were fighting the demon. A trumpet sounded, and the trotting horses broke into a canter.

"Shit," Roarke said.

Chapter Thirty-Five

Somewhere in the confused, flashing darkness of mind that followed the demon's imprisonment, Liz heard Thea growl, hurting and angry. Liz clawed her way toward the sound. Dirt and splinters of grass forced their way under her fingernails and scraped the palms of her hands. She realized she'd lost her helmet. The stubble of the plain ground into her face as she inched in the direction of her friend.

So much for holding something back.

Rhythmic thuds drew Liz's attention to the Gap. Her link-extended senses registered that two troops of cavalry rode toward them.

Not more. Not now. We beat the demon. How much more can we take? Liz raised her head. Brigid and Sarah pawed the ground around them for weapons, forcing their sore and weary bodies to the ready once more.

Not far away, Thea rolled to her knees and shuddered. The effort it took her to transform herself into a saber-toothed tiger pulled at Liz's weary muscles and left Liz trembling. Tiny blue sparks sizzled over the cat's tawny fur. A memory not hers warned Thea's magic was on the brink of collapse.

Roarke stumbled past. He positioned himself at Thea's side. Liz opened her mouth to ask him to help her stand. But before she could speak, a reticulated black boot attached to a black-armored leg planted itself in front of her.

"Where do you think you're going?" Jagger asked.

"Out of my way," Liz forced the shreds of her magic outward in a desperate effort to push him aside.

Even dampened by exhaustion, Jagger's power was enough to defeat her kitten-weak attack. Liz wanted to weep, but she wouldn't give up. She'd find a way to her friends yet.

"If you're determined to die with your boots on—" Jagger hauled Liz to her feet. "—at least you can do it standing."

It was like dying. Life poured out in a blue stream, its strength building outside of her. Outside of them—Liz's and Jagger's bodies leaned against each other while their thin magic flowed through the veins of the earth toward Reyah's children, new and old, and the handful of soldiers standing between them and the enemy horses.

Deryk had an ace up his sleeve. I thought he was Porting to safety. I was wrong. He Ported to his reserves outside the Gap.

There's not enough of us, Liz thought as Deryk's cavalry hammered the spongy ground of the plain. She felt Jagger reach inside them both.

If we can turn one horse, just one. Spook it, make it shy.

Liz married her will to Jagger's, re-envisioning the plain for the standard bearer's horse. She thought she felt the pounding ache of a hairline fracture in the animal's left foreleg. *There!* She and Jagger pressed.

The brazen clamor of trumpets rocked the plain. Jagger and Liz staggered. Their link to the standard bearer's horse was swamped by the repeated, double-time bleats. But instead of despair, joy kissed Liz's straining nerves.

A legion of mounted soldiers following the purple and gold standard of Seshmeel leapt like show jumpers through a rip in the sky. Lines of iron-shod hooves struck the plain, galloping without a break in stride toward Deryk's forces. The steady measures of the unseen trumpeters whipped the riders on.

Deryk Ported. His red snake banner fell as the standard bearer's horse's collapsed over its left foreleg. The horse whinnied in agony, but the sound was lost in the impact of armored horses and riders crashing into the beast and over it. Riders to the left and right of the fallen animals shouted and tried to yank their mounts around before the cream of Seshmeel's cavalry mowed them down.

As the last line of Isabeau's troops cleared the edge of the giant Portal, the trumpets blared a fanfare. A few heartbeats later a final line of horses bounded out, their advance much more ragged than the others'.

An Amazon wearing a steel helmet encircled by a golden crown and an ornate gold-chased breastplate surged from the center of the line. One gloved hand clutched her horse's reins, the other flapped a large ceremonial sword in the direction of Deryk's diminishing forces. Her massive, barrel-chested gelding placidly flicked its ears away from her flailing blade while maintaining a steady, relentless pace.

337

To the would-be Valkyrie's right, out of the range of her sword, rode a tall, armored man. He carried a long, slightly curved sword like he knew how to use it. Liz tasted the knight's essence with Jagger's skill. A Chosen, Liz realized. The knight's name followed an instant later—Atlee.

Good Lord! Liz's gaze jerked back to the charging Amazon. *That's Isabeau?*

"Isabeau wants to be a battle queen. Atlee doesn't think she's serious about becoming a warrior. Yet." Jagger rubbed his sweaty cheek against Liz's equally slick forehead. His bare hands pressed her closer to the warm wall of his body.

"Copping a feel?"

"Mmmmm."

"What happened to your helmet and mask?"

"What happened to yours?"

Liz shook her head slowly. She didn't want to bang anything bony into Jagger's jaw. *Yet.* She'd save that maneuver for when he tried to kiss her.

Ah, damn, the blasted man could laugh without ever opening his mouth. Why did Jagger have to have a sense of humor? Glamour Liz could wither. Force she could withstand. But how much longer could she resist Jagger's enveloping contentment or the rose petal drifts of his amusement? Liz remembered how much she'd laughed with her husband, and grief ambushed her, raking through her heart like a serrated blade. Her breath grew ragged.

As if out of respect for her privacy, Jagger took a mental step back. He brushed his chin against the back of her head in a discreet gesture of comfort. Damn, damn, damn. He had her number now. Resisting him was going to be harder than Liz ever imagined.

೮ාඥ

The incessant trumpet blasts pounded Thea out cat form. The earth seemed to tip over on its side. Thea grabbed the nearest solid object for support. Which happened to be Roarke's leg. Roarke snorted or chuckled. He wasn't sure which. To her surprise, Thea realized she was still linked to his thoughts—and Liz's and Jagger's. Roarke sheathed his sword.

"About time Sejanus and Gwyn got here." Roarke tilted his chin toward the couple wearing chain mail shirts over long robes decorated with suns, stars and crescent moons. "And they brought healers. They might save some of the mortals yet."

Isabeau's horse circled the detritus of battle like an Olympic runner taking a victory lap. Sejanus and Gwyn walked their horses alongside the last of Free's thorn bushes and dismounted, tossing the reins into the brambles. As the wizards pulled a blood-stained Val to his feet, a second Portal opened near Theron and Free. The Lady Edytha stepped onto the plain, followed by a small army toting stretchers, bandages, splints and kettles of steaming water.

Liz called, "Hey, Edy! You wouldn't happen to have a little cold water to splash on Anna—the one in black leather over there? We wouldn't want her to miss this."

Liz canted her head toward a swaying leather-clad apparition to Thea's right. Anna's unconscious form slumped over one of the Keep's Blue Guards. At least, Thea assumed it was a guardsman. Tatters of dark blue fluttered over the gleaves and gauntlets splayed across Anna's back. Anna's head dipped, and Thea caught sight of a short thatch of dark brown hair and scar-split eyebrow. The soldier's light green eyes studied the woman cradled in his arms.

"Al?" Thea whispered as Liz's and Jagger's mental laughter tickled her mind.

"She did it!" Liz crowed aloud.

"She did." Reyah's voice belled inside Thea's head and across the plain. "And in binding Megeara's demon into its crystal prison, Anna—and all of you—fulfilled the promise of your creation."

Thea shared the reluctance with which Liz turned her head. *That's not what I...* Liz stopped in mid-thought. Very carefully, Liz trained her attention on Pandora and Marisol. Anna and the elementals stirred. They raised their flower-bright faces to Reyah's sun.

The elder goddess smiled. "Against villains and demon you fought as one, and thereby proved yourselves worthy to be My daughters in deed as well as name." Anna, Pandora, Marisol, Free, even Sarah glowed in the warmth of Reyah's approval.

But threaded through Reyah's voice was something Thea couldn't quite place. The quality sounded very close to smugness. Thea glanced at Liz. Liz's gaze was fixed on Reyah. Liz's face was still and pale as marble. She breathed in deliberate measures as if it took all her concentration to keep still.

Brigid bent over her staff, her face in shadow. Thea couldn't see Kait at all. Thea wanted to scream, "What's happening?" But she didn't. She couldn't. Liz was inside her, holding Thea's soul and body as tight as she once held Marisol's cuirass.

"Your wishes brought you to my Domain, but I could not have allowed you to remain if you proved yourselves undeserving of my gifts. As I planned, my son Deryk provided the means for your test: a Demon Witch." Reyah beamed at her Daughters. Thea saw Pandora, Free, Marisol, Anna and Sarah arch their necks like cats relishing a proper scratch. Thea winced as Liz angled her head in deliberate imitation of the rest.

"He chose well," Reyah continued, "and you may be sure I will reward him in the fullness of time.

"Even as I reward you now. You are truly my Daughters and true children of Domain. Henceforth, your place will be here. You will walk beside my sons, mating your strengths to theirs. Your beauty will delight their eyes. Your youth will invigorate their lives. You will teach them the virtue of unity in a sacred marriage of minds, hearts and spirits."

Brigid sank to her knees. Free's small hands grabbed Theron's robes. Her head tilted back, and she panted like a woman in the throes of orgasm. Anna's arm tightened around Al's neck as she joined Marisol, Pandora and Sarah in a wordless song of praise.

Reyah nodded, as if she found their adoration entirely appropriate. Reyah lifted her arms, intensifying the varied colors of the lights emanating from her silver-gowned form. The women's song rang louder until Thea thought the sound would tear her apart.

Tears started from Thea's eyes. She wanted to cover her ears with her hands, but Liz wouldn't let the movement give Thea's true feelings away.

Reyah vanished in a blast of rapture.

That complacent, condescending, murdering hag! Liz's mental voice tore into the silence of Reyah's wake. *How many people died here today?* Liz's mental vision swirled over the plain, over the upturned earth and mangled bodies, over men and horses whimpering and crying as death clawed its way into their hearts and brains. Thea gagged on the rotten stench of excrement and urine, blood and sulfur.

Alfred alone lost eighteen men—eighteen mortal men. Six of the rest are dying from their wounds, and all of the survivors on both sides are deaf from the demon's howls, including Ember. Unless Isabeau's wizards or Jagger can help them, Reyah's mind voice will be the last thing they ever hear, God help them. And Reyah—a goddamned goddess, God damn it—let all this death, all this devastation happen just to make sure she picked the right little wives for her precious sons.

But we're not. The ghost of Liz's bitter laugh chilled Thea to the bone. *She's not wiving the Vanyr; she's bribing them. With us. Remember what she said in Al's office. Her bastard sons have grown complacent, and all they do is fight. We're the prizes they get for playing nice. Well, I'm not some damned consolation prize, and I sure as hell don't play nice. My mind, my heart, my life belong to me. Reyah and her sons be damned!*

I'll never be anyone's pawn ever again, Thea stormed in reply. *Goddess, Vanyr—I don't care. I've been down that road, and I don't care if I have to fight her and her whole stinking planet, she can't make me go down that way again.*

Roarke started, but the movement led nowhere. Thea was shocked to find that her arms were still locked around his leg. Thea released them, and Roarke staggered. *Oh God.* She was still linked to Roarke and Jagger, as well as Liz. Roarke and Jagger knew what they were thinking.

Liz's spine straightened. Jagger dropped his arms and backed away. Roarke opened his mouth as if he wanted to say something, decided against it and retreated too.

From a great distance Thea heard Isabeau congratulate Alfred on a battle well fought. Edytha's army of healers bustled to and fro at Sejanus's command. Theron and Val offered to help with the wounded. Dozens of people went about their various tasks. Their clothing sometimes brushed Thea in passing.

Thea looked at Liz. Liz returned her gaze. Neither of them had ever felt more alone.

Chapter Thirty-Six

The Royal Palace, Salentia

The grandest staircase of Isabeau's palace in Salentia led from the Old Hall to the Great Chamber directly above it. Broad flights of kelan wood, worn and polished to a satin finish turned around square newels surmounted by gilded sculptures of the hawk and frog of Isabeau's family crest.

A gust of laughter and clinking crystal erupted from the open doors of the Great Chamber as Liz rounded the lowest turn of the staircase. She paused and angled her head over the balustrade.

An instant later, Marisol rushed down the stairs in a clatter of high-heeled shoes and the swishing whisper of silk.

"Finally! Where have you been?" Marisol demanded. "Everyone else took their places ages ago."

Liz smiled. "Not everyone. Isabeau, Edy and Atlee are still arguing damages with the Tambaran ambassador somewhere behind the throne room. It's not treason to be late until the queen sits down."

"How do you…" Marisol grimaced. "Never mind. It's your mental thing, isn't it? You weren't snooping on them, I hope."

"Not at all. I was doing research in Isabeau's library."

"Again! What's so interesting about the library when everybody we ever wanted to meet in Domain is here and dying to meet us? I bet you didn't even do anything special to get ready for the party."

Liz's grin widened. "What's special to do? I took a bath, I brushed my teeth, and I put on the clothes Yeves sent, Mommy. What more do you want?"

"I still don't understand why you keep spending your time in the library."

"Because there's so much I want to know about Domain."

"Why don't you just ask someone?"

"That would be too simple," Liz said with a laugh.

Marisol's brow furrowed. "You're lying. You and Thea are up to something, and you're not going to tell me what. Fine. Be that way."

"Now you sound even more like somebody's mommy."

"And you're acting like somebody's bratty sister—somebody's bratty older sister." Marisol cast a speculative glance in Liz's direction. "Is it a guy?"

Liz said nothing.

"Is it Jagger?"

Liz started. "No! Whatever gave you that idea?"

"Something about the way you were hanging all over each other after the battle. Or maybe it was the look he gave Hawke after the two of you got back with Sarah."

"No. Absolutely not. There's nothing between Jagger and me. What you saw at the battle was simply the after-effects of dealing with Megeara and her demon."

"Yeah, sure, and you're absolutely, positively not interested in the strongest, most gorgeous hottie in all Domain?"

"Hottie?" Liz choked on the word. "Jagger? He's not my type at all."

"You're joking, right?"

"No."

"You're serious. Wow. Oh wow, oh wow."

"I take it you think he's your type."

Marisol made a sustained clicking noise in the back of her throat and gave her silk-sheathed bottom a shimmy. Her skirts danced like waves over sand. "Oh man, you have no idea! You should've stayed in the pool with us. It's never been like that before. Thinking about it turns me into a puddle of goo. Our bodies fit together perfectly. It was like—"

"You were made for each other," Liz finished. Her smile didn't quite reach the rest of her face. "Yeah. And therein lies the problem, sweetie. One size does not fit all. But if he fits you, go for it. You'll make a smashing couple."

"And I bet Jagger can teach me how to use my magic, too!"

"Oh yeah," Liz drawled. "I bet he'll teach you all sorts of things."

Marisol giggled and joined Liz on the landing. "Let's go see what's on the menu," Liz said, putting her arm through Marisol's. "I'm starved."

Jagger emerged from the shadows of the Old Hall as Liz's and Marisol's footsteps melted into the thick Panshyur carpet leading into the Great Chamber. He gathered the lingering fragrance of their magics like so many ribbons and buried his face in the scent.

Marisol smelled of gardenias, inside and out—sensuous, sweet but somewhat cloying. The perfume reminded Jagger of sultry nights in Pleasure-by-the-Sea—limbs shackled by heat, senses surfeit, minds lulled to passivity and content to remain so.

Jagger smiled at the contrast between the faint muskiness of Liz's bath essence and the sharp, glacial trace of her magic—mountain air, redolent of pine and fresh snow. The rarified atmosphere of the traveler hawk Roarke compared her to.

How strange to taste the freedom he prayed for, after all these years, in the person of one of Reyah's captives. His bribe, no less. As might be expected, Reyah's handling sullied the presentation, but nothing could tarnish the fineness of the gift.

Willful, cunning, unbroken—a thoroughly fearsome little she-wolf was Elizabeth Anne MacMurray Devereaux. Jagger rolled the alien syllables across his tongue. Liz. She called herself Liz.

He was not about to abuse the shared secret of her outrage. He liked her—and her friend Thea Gardner—far too well. He would let Liz run free.

Jagger opened his hand. Liz's magic dissipated in a faint effervescence of clean smelling air.

For now.

Her liberty would serve him well. Her gratitude, even better.

Jagger grinned wolfishly in anticipation of his newly reconfigured future. But only for a moment. Only where no one could see him. By the time he Ported to his accustomed place as Isabeau's ranking guest, he would be Reyah's perfect Vanyr once more.

ಶೃ

"Will you please keep your voices down?" Thea pleaded. She latched the door to the small anteroom off the Great Chamber, muffling the sounds of the queen's inebriated guests. "This is supposed to be a celebration of our victory. Can't you let the battle go for tonight?"

"It was a tactical disaster!" Brigid moaned. "I've blocked better organized mob scenes."

"We won, didn't we?" Sarah huffed. "The only thing that went wrong was when your magic user failed to close the link. Anna could've gotten us all killed!"

"Where do you get off criticizing me after all those stunts you pulled on the battlefield?" Anna countered. "First you run off like some crazy woman. Then you try to kill Liz and Hawke when they tried to bring you back. And don't get me started on what it took to get you into the link!"

Thea wondered why she bothered trying to act as peacemaker. She should be helping Liz find a way to save their butts. Thea knew Roarke and Jagger were only waiting for the right moment to spill their guts to Reyah. She and Liz would be dead meat when they did.

This wasn't what Thea had wished for when she placed her finger on that damned crystal. She'd never said anything about being tied down to any man for eternity, and she'd definitely never wished to be stuck forever with a bunch of arguing, contentious women.

"Stop it!" The rumble in Thea's voice did more to grab the three women's attention than her words. *Great, now they're afraid of me too.* The thought made Thea's forehead throb. She could almost see the beginnings of a migraine aura.

Thea forced herself to sound reasonable. "Look, I know we need to talk about what happened on the Plain of Elsee. We did as well as we could, but we nearly got ourselves killed in the process. We've got to figure out what we did right and wrong."

"Like a post-trial wrap or briefing," Sarah said.

"Exactly." Thea sighed. "But not tonight, please. This is my first party in Domain, and I don't intend to think about the battle tonight. I'm not sure I'll want to think about it tomorrow either."

"Do you think you could bring yourself to consider it by the time we get back to the Keep?" Brigid asked.

"Maybe," Thea pretended to growl, "but don't bet on it."

Brigid chuckled. She clapped Sarah on the shoulder. "Thea's right about one thing. There's a party going on. I don't want to deprive all those lovely men out there of the opportunity to fall over their tongues when they see how fine I look in this outfit."

Sarah glanced down at the confection of brocade and lace Brigid wore. "Not bad. Of course, I look better."

"In your dreams," Brigid shot back.

Anna moved to a mirror and patted her hair. "You both look very nice," she told Brigid and Sarah. "Have either of you seen Pandora? I have this awful feeling that dingbat is wearing something totally unsuitable."

Brigid and Sarah looked at each other. They burst into laughter.

"Oh God!" Anna moaned. "How bad is it?"

Brigid and Sarah laughed harder. Anna rushed from the room.

"You coming, Thea?" Brigid asked before she followed Sarah out the door.

"In a minute."

Their departure brought blessed silence and equally blessed relief from Anna's heavy floral perfume. Thea leaned against a damask-covered wall and closed her eyes. She wished she had the nerve to send her regrets to Isabeau and go to bed. She felt like she could sleep for a week. But an invitation from royalty wasn't something you backed away from, at least, not according to Anna and Liz.

Am I really so tired, Thea asked herself, *or am I just trying to avoid the inevitable?*

Laughter erupted beyond the door to the Great Chamber. Thea knew she should return to her place at the high table, but it was peaceful in this little room. Cozy. There were enough wizard lights to read by, and nothing and no one to prevent her from curling up on a pillow-strewn sofa and taking a nap. All by herself. Without anyone popping in to check on her or seeing if she was all right or wanting a chaperone for a midnight kitchen foray. Thea found she missed the privacy of the cramped apartment she'd left behind.

A tremendous succession of crashes, squeals and outraged yells heralded the latest Pandora-borne catastrophe. "Oh Pandora!" Anna wailed. "How could you?"

"It wasn't my fault!" Pandora squealed.

Thea flinched in anticipation of Anna going postal on Pandora. But she never heard Anna say another word. A voice as pure and crisp as an icy stream sliced across Thea's thoughts.

"Don't ever do that again," Roarke said.

Thea's eyes flew open. Roarke stood before her, hands resting on his hips, the slight tension in his fingers belying his casual pose. The wizard lights of the antechamber rendered his patrician features inscrutable, dangerous and, because he was dangerous, perversely seductive. Thea's heart hammered against her ribs, but she couldn't tell whether it was from hormones or a basic animal need to run.

She guessed her all-too transparent face revealed her confusion and fear. The grim line of Roarke's mouth eased.

"Never ever shapeshift when you're as weak as you were after you defeated the demon," Roarke explained. "You'll die, no matter if Reyah or the Wishstone made you. It can kill a Vanyr. As far as I can tell, it's about the only thing that will kill us. That's how Reyah's firstborn son died—the one before Jagger."

"All right."

Roarke didn't move. He must've expected an argument.

Thea didn't have one. She waited for the other shoe to drop. She hadn't expected Roarke to confront her so soon about what happened after the battle. But she had to admit the setting offered the perfect opportunity for blackmail. How would he turn her complicity in Liz's treason to his advantage? Would he demand Thea share her power with him? It wasn't as if she could scream for help. The people in the Great Chamber would want an explanation neither she nor Liz could afford to give.

It wasn't fair, something small and insistent within Thea cried. A scoundrel and an opportunist shouldn't look as good as Roarke did. His hair shouldn't be so dark and so inviting to touch. He shouldn't have the long, perfectly muscled legs of a Greek god or be allowed to wear a dark gold velvet doublet that accentuated the green and copper prisms in his eyes. He shouldn't smell of fresh, starched linen, and the fine-milled soap and balsam scent Thea remembered all too well from their first, interrupted bath.

Roarke's dark lashes veiled his eyes. His mouth quirked in a humorless half-smile Thea suspected signaled some kind of decision. He turned toward the door.

"Is that all?" she asked.

Roarke blinked as if perplexed. "That's all I planned to say. Why? Is there something else you want to know?"

That was all there was to it. In his uncertainty, Roarke's soul blinked open too, as naked as it had been in the link and innocent of all thoughts of coercion. It was as if he never heard Liz's fury at Reyah or Thea's heartfelt agreement with her friend's assessment.

Laughter bubbled up from a deep, shuttered place inside Thea. Without thinking, she threw her arms around Roarke and kissed him. He kissed her back, capturing her face between his hands and her breath in his mouth. The ground spun under her feet, and something inside her shivered and splintered, fracturing wide.

Roarke broke the kiss. He stared at her, his breathing ragged.

Why had he pulled away? Didn't he want her anymore? Thea didn't want to know. Her brief insight into the enigmatic man standing in front of her was nowhere to be found.

"They're waiting for us at the table." Roarke's voice was only a little huskier than normal. He extended his hand.

Thea rested her fingers on his palm. "Yes. We don't want to be late."

"Personally, I don't want to miss Liz turning Bettyna into a ferret again."

"Roarke!"

"It could happen," Roarke said hopefully.

Thea laughed. "You know, I wouldn't mind seeing that again myself."

About the Authors

To learn more about Teri Smith and Jean Marie Ward, please visit www.wardsmith.com. Send an email to Jean Marie Ward at jeanmarie@samhainpublishing.com or check out the WardSmith blog at http://jmward14.livejournal.com.

GET IT NOW

MyBookStoreAndMore.com
GREAT EBOOKS, GREAT DEALS . . . AND MORE!

Don't wait to run to the bookstore down the street, or
waste time shopping online at one of the "big boys." Now,
all your favorite Samhain authors are all in one place—at
MyBookStoreAndMore.com. Stop by today and discover
great deals on Samhain—and a whole lot more!

Samhain Publishing ltd

WWW.SAMHAINPUBLISHING.COM

FLY AWAY

Discover the Talons Series

5 STEAMY NEW PARANORMAL ROMANCES
TO HOOK YOU IN

Kiss Me Deadly, by Shannon Stacey
King of Prey, by Mandy M. Roth
Firebird, by Jaycee Clark
Caged Desire, by Sydney Somers
Seize the Hunter, by Michelle M. Pillow

AVAILABLE IN EBOOK—COMING SOON IN PRINT!

SAMHAIN PUBLISHING LTD

WWW.SAMHAINPUBLISHING.COM

Printed in the United Kingdom
by Lightning Source UK Ltd.
120528UK00001B/224

9 781599 983608